Oswald Crawfurd

Portugal

Old and New

Oswald Crawfurd

Portugal
Old and New

ISBN/EAN: 9783337288129

Printed in Europe, USA, Canada, Australia, Japan

Cover: Foto ©Andreas Hilbeck / pixelio.de

More available books at **www.hansebooks.com**

PORTUGAL

OLD AND NEW

THE QUEEN'S STAIRS AT OPORTO.

PORTUGAL

OLD AND NEW

BY

OSWALD CRAWFURD

HER MAJESTY'S CONSUL AT OPORTO

AUTHOR OF 'LATOUCHE'S TRAVELS IN PORTUGAL'

With Maps and Illustrations

NEW YORK

G. P. PUTNAM'S SONS

1880

PREFACE.

THIS book is partly made up of contributions to the 'Fortnightly Review,' the 'New Quarterly Magazine,' and the 'Cornhill Magazine.' I have modified these papers greatly, interpolated much new matter, corrected where my knowledge has increased, and in many, I may say in most parts, I have altogether rewritten my first essays.

I have called my book 'Portugal: Old and New,' hoping thereby to make the title as descriptive as I could. I trust the name may not be thought pretentious, or the book altogether a nondescript, or the chapters of it disjointed.

I am afraid the title may to some critics seem to promise a great deal more than I have performed. *Portugal, Old and New,* may indeed be taken to mean an account of all that Portugal has been and all that she now is; but this of course would be an impossible expectation to fulfil with a work in one volume. I hope the reader expects nothing from me so exhaustive or so ponderous.

My book is so far nondescript that it is neither a book of history, nor of criticism, nor of pure description; nor an antiquarian work, nor a social nor a statistical one, nor a book of travel; but it is a medley of all these things, and yet, if I have only succeeded in carrying out my conception, it is not disjointed.

In the inns of the more uncivilized parts of this Peninsula it is common to offer to the traveller, not a dinner of separate courses, but one where they are mingled and compounded into a single dish. A large, deep pipkin is set before him, in which meat and game and fowl of all available kinds, vegetables of every variety, pot herbs and garnishing and spices, have been seethed all together. Into this pipkin, or *Olla*, the guest dips a spoon at a venture and, perhaps half famished with long fasting and eager for meat or game, he is disappointed at drawing forth nothing more satisfying than a piece of yellow gourd or a scarlet capsicum. On the other hand, the fastidious traveller, trifling with his *Olla* and diving for the lightest sustenance, may get a more substantial morsel of beef or bacon than he cares for

The reader of my book may, I fear, meet with ill luck of the same kind. There is reading in it that may seem over-heavy for some tastes, and reading that may seem too light for the tastes of others.

As a sample of solid ingredients there is the chapter on the great Warrior King of Portugal, and this perhaps is very heavy reading; but then, not to know about him is to be ignorant of all that concerns the rise of Portugal into the category of nations. Before Affonso Henriquez there was no Portugal at all. Since he lived and died, and because he lived, there has been in this corner of Europe an enduring kingdom which, in spite of its size, is in the true sense of the word a great kingdom.

Again, no account of Portugal can approach completeness which omits mention of the rise and progress of its literature, and tells nothing of its agriculture; for the nation is an essentially literary nation, and its agriculture has at all times been the source of its strength and its greatness. On both subjects I have only written after long and close study at first hand.

I suppose that when an educated foreigner comes to a country which is strange to him and with which he wishes to acquaint himself, he would first set to work by learning something of its early history, of its literature, of its chief industries, of the manners and habits of the people, of their government, of the physical aspects of the land and its antiquities; then, if he had the opportunity, he would travel a little over the country and see what he could with his own eyes. I have myself done something of all this, and in the following pages I have tried as well as I could to put before others the result of what I have learned.

OSWALD CRAWFURD.

OPORTO: *Christmas*, 1879.

CONTENTS.

LIST OF ILLUSTRATIONS.

PORTUGAL: OLD AND NEW.

CHAPTER I.

THE RISE OF PORTUGAL.

THERE is in human nature a craving for something beyond the mere chronicling of great deeds. In rude times, amid the selfish struggle of the more masterful passions of men, heroic or generous actions possess an impressiveness which strongly affects the sympathies of contemporaries; but such deeds do not always succeed in reaching down to the knowledge of succeeding generations, for it is unfortunate that a rare coincidence of poet and hero should be indispensable for any effectual tradition of renown, and that either without the other's help runs no small peril of oblivion. In primitive ages, the imagination of poets seems to be finite. There is no instance of a ballad-monger or early poet having evolved a hero. To most thoughtful men, Homer's poems are evidence enough that great deeds were done before Troy; and if we had no better voucher for the heroism of Ruy Dias, El Campeador, the hero of Spanish mediæval

B

romance, we might be content to find one in the great epic of ' The Cid.'

King Affonso Henriquez, who carved out with his sword a kingdom which his descendants still rule, was perhaps as great a hero as the Cid himself, but only a vague rumour of his exploits has come down to us. *Vate sacro caret*; he has lacked the meed of poet's song. The two warriors, the Cid and Affonso Henriquez, lived within a generation of each other ; both fought chiefly against the same powerful enemy, in the same age of chivalry ; but while Ruy Dias missed the purpose of his life, Affonso Henriquez attained the great end he had set to himself. While the mark made upon the age by the Spanish champion was obliterated even in his own lifetime, the achievements of the Portuguese conqueror have changed the whole course of Peninsular history, and established a dynasty which survives to this day ;— an impressive monument, among the shifting elements of Peninsular history, of the daring and wisdom of its founder. Yet what avails it to a man to have done great deeds, to live a great life, and to win a wide renown, if the chief part of his fame is to die with the death of the witnesses of his exploits, and only to find a short record in the stupid annals of monkish and Moorish chroniclers ? A noble life is rare enough in the world to make us regret that the story of one should be so nearly extinguished.

I shall endeavour in the following pages to revive so much of the life and doings of King Affonso Henriquez as can be extracted from the scanty annals of the chroniclers, Spanish, Portuguese, and Moorish, that have survived the seven hundred years which have elapsed since his death.

The two schools of modern history at present most in vogue might find a very promising battle-field in the life of this great Portuguese King and Conqueror. A writer of the one school might argue that King Affonso was forced by the tendencies of his age to the course he followed; while a historian of the opposite type might contend that the King's will and strong individuality had impressed themselves on the minds of his contemporaries, and had warped their wills to compliance with his own. Profounder inquirers will reject both theories as being thoroughly insufficient, and, discerning a clear expression of the great law of historical progression even in the scanty records of the early annalists, they will perceive that the changes in the community, both moral and political, were surely and irresistibly evolved from modifications of the opinions and habits and sentiments of the people. Nevertheless, had this warrior prince, the founder of an enduring nationality, been less of a true leader of men, Portugal would probably have shared the evanescent fate of the contemporary Peninsular kingdoms; and so also would King Affonso Henriquez have lost the labour of his life, had he not had to deal with a people singularly apt alike for the arts of war and peace, and had he not lived in an age when all the components of society were ready to be forced into fresh combinations by a strong will and a strong hand.

It is hardly necessary at this day to repeat at any length the history of the recovery of the Peninsula from the Moslem invaders. Nevertheless, to remind the reader of the state of the north-west part of the Peninsula during the eleventh century, and to give a slight sketch of the nature of the country itself, may serve to make what is to follow more clear and more interesting.

If we look at any fairly good map of Spain, we shall see that in the extreme north of the Peninsula the province of Asturias is almost wholly occupied, as well as the art of the map-maker can represent such features, by frequent, and lofty, and precipitous mountains. If the map be correctly drawn, the hills will appear with a gradual rise from the sea cliffs washed by the waters of the Bay of Biscay, till they tower, at the extreme south of the province, into a mountain range whose highest peaks are snow-capped for almost the whole year, and whose southern wall-like declivities face the modern province of Leon. If we look closer, we shall perceive—sure sign that these mountain ranges overtop those in the surrounding country—that the numerous streams and rivers taking their rise in the Asturian mountain system flow, some of them towards the west, some to the east, and some to the south; forming in each case great water arteries, which, both geographically and politically, have at all times exercised an extreme importance upon the history of Northern Spain and Portugal.

The Ebro, rising in or near the eastern spurs of

the Asturian ranges, flows south-eastward to the Mediterranean, and divided, in early times, the Navarrese mountaineers from those of the Asturias and from the people of the plain country to the south ; just as it has formed, more than once within the present century, a natural boundary between liberal Spain and absolutist Carlism.

The streams of the western Asturian watershed, meeting in the river Minho, flow due west to the Atlantic, separating modern Galicia from Portugal, and formed in mediaeval times the boundary line which sometimes restrained Saracen invasion of the northern region, and sometimes Galician aggression towards the south.

The waters that flow to the south from the Asturian mountains are more numerous, and the streams fuller, than those running east and west. They meet, in time, to form the great river Douro, whose tributaries, sweeping in broad semicircles through what was the ancient kingdom of Leon, wash the walls of many cities famous in Moorish and Spanish history

—of Leon and Zamora, of Carrion, Burgos, and Valladolid—and in time join their waters and enter Portuguese territory through the defiles and mountain valleys which lie along the frontier of Spain and Portugal. Flowing due west always, through a hilly and difficult country, the Douro is the chief water-way of northern Portugal—a deep and rapid river—and, entering the Atlantic, forms a harbour which possessed commercial importance before the invasion of the Romans, and which, during the long period before the Moors had retreated from the southern portion of the kingdom, was the principal seat of Christian trade, as well as the key of the Christian position It retained during these early times the designation *Portus*, first given to it by the Romans, which is preserved in its modern name of Oporto. The hill fort of Cale [1] stood on the southern bank of the river, within two miles of the sea, and Portus Cale, or Portugale, came to be the designation of the adjacent district, and, in process of time, of the whole kingdom.

The broad tract of mountainous country drained by these several rivers was the first battle-field of Christians and Mahometans, and here the great issue between the rival creeds and races was finally decided.

[1] Sir Charles Murray, recently our Minister at the Court of Lisbon, a gentleman intimately acquainted with the East, informs me that Cale is a pure Arabic relic, Calah signifying a 'castle' or 'fort,' the last vowel of the word being the guttural *a* unpronounceable by European organs of speech. I do not think that any writer has noticed that Portugal is a word in part of Latin and in part of Arabic origin.

The tide of Moslem invasion, which had swept over every other part of the Peninsula with a resist-lessness and a rapidity characteristic of Arabian con-quest, broke when it reached the precipitous ranges of the Asturian mountains; and a remnant of the Christian Visigoths, retreating among their recesses, preserved a perfect independence throughout the long Moslem domination over the rest of the Pen-insula.

Asturias became a kingdom in 718, only ten years after the Mahometan subjugation of the re-mainder of the Peninsula; and in the course of con-tention with the Saracens, the little kingdom enlarged its boundaries to the south and west, took in the richer territory of Leon on its southern frontier, and its monarch in time assumed the title of King of Leon.

A little later, other Christian kingdoms began to emerge, as the wave of Moorish dominion retreated from the unprofitable regions of northern Spain. On the southern slopes of the Pyrenees, a Christian nation was forming itself under circumstances some-what similar to those in Asturias. Confined at first to the difficult country north of the Ebro, the Kings of Navarre and Aragon in process of time won the land to the south of that river; and on the table-land of central Spain, Castile had also come into exist-ence as a kingdom.

These Christian kingdoms by no means contented themselves with fighting against the common enemy, and warfare against each other was as frequent and as fierce as with the Saracens. Into the vicissitudes of these petty wars it is not necessary to enter here. Suffice it to say that Sancho, King of Navarre, at his death in 1035, had, by the fortune of war, come to reign over the principal portion of free Christian Spain. His sway included what is now French and Spanish Navarre, a part of modern Aragon, the great corn-growing upland plain which now is more or less included in the province of Old Castile, and some portion of the kingdom of Leon.

This extensive realm was divided among three sons, the most notable of whom was Fernando, whose capacity for war and the kingly arts of intrigue and annexation elevates him somewhat conspicuously above the many warlike captains and rapacious sovereigns of that age and country, and has earned him the title of The Great. For Fernando the vice-royalty of Castile was, by the terms of his father's will, elevated into a kingdom ; and the new King almost immediately engaged in hostilities with the sovereign of Leon and Asturias, and won over him the bloodiest battle that had yet been fought in Christian Spain. The Leonese King fell, and Fernando forced himself upon the people of Leon, and assumed thereafter the title of King of Leon and Castile. Shortly afterwards, war broke out between Fernando and his brother the King of Navarre. Again was Fernando the victor. The King of Navarre died on the field, his troops and his Saracen allies were completely routed, and King Fernando's moderation, or his policy, was shown by his refusing the crown of

Navarre, thus easily within his grasp. He allowed his brother's son to succeed to the throne.

The rest of King Fernando's life was occupied with raids, more or less successful, into Saracen Portugal in the east, and as far to the west as Valencia; but these expeditions, depending for their success upon temporary dissensions among the Mahometans, were of no more lasting importance than the many other and similar marauding expeditions made by both Christian and Moslem in these ages into the heart of each other's possessions. With one exception: the Portuguese expedition yielded fruit in the conquest and occupation, in the year 1064,[1] of the city of Coimbra, in Portugal, an important stronghold set in the midst of the rich and beautiful valley of the Mondego. In the following year King Fernando died, and, like his own father, divided his dominions among his children.

I shall be forced to a somewhat fuller narrative of the events which followed upon this second partition of the country, for in the vicissitudes and in the fortunes of the rough soldier-kings who divided King Fernando's dominions among them, are to be found the more immediate causes of the rise of the Portuguese monarchy in the succeeding generation.

The King left three sons and two daughters. Sancho, the eldest son, became King of Castile; Alonso inherited the throne of Leon and of the Asturias; for Garcia the north-western province of

---

[1] The date of this, the earliest important event in the history of Portugal, is much disputed.

Galicia, which had hitherto been a viceroyalty, was made into a kingdom; and the two daughters became titular Queens—the eldest, Urraca, of Zamora, and Elvira, of Touro.

History is never so apt to the proverbial repetition of itself as in such rude times as these, where the passions of mankind are not complicated with the tastes and the repulsions, the convictions and the ideas, which a course of civilization and culture engenders. The new partition of the country led, as it had done before, to dissension and to war. A bloody battle shortly took place between Alonso of Leon and his brother of Castile, and the battle went against the King of Leon; but he retired to his capital unpursued by his brother. King Alonso, destined to high fortunes, was destined also to reach them through a series of strange reverses. A year or two afterwards hostilities again broke out; and this time Alonso, assisted by a great body of Galician troops, probably furnished by his brother Garcia, won the day, but again the advantage was not decisive.

It is on this occasion that the annalist corroborates the romantic legend of the poets. Ruy Dias, the Cid, was among the officers and counsellors of the defeated King Sancho. It is related that, after the battle, he advised his master to make a renewed attack by night upon the victorious Leonese. The stratagem was successful, and the Castilians in their turn gained the victory. King Alonso himself fell a prisoner, was carried in triumph to Burgos, the Castilian capital, and was subsequently thrust into the

Convent of Sahagun, and forced to assume the cowl. From this confinement the King of Leon escaped by the help of his sister Urraca, Queen of Zamora, and, flying to Toledo, he obtained the protection of the powerful Emir, Al-Mamon, the ancient ally of his father.

The immediate result to Urraca of her favouring of the weaker brother was the siege of her capital Zamora by the offended Sancho—a leaguer as famous in song as it was important in history; for while the ballads recount the romantic prowess of the Cid, the chroniclers join with them in recording an event which led to a complete revolution in the affairs of northern Spain. A Zamoran knight, watching the hostile lines from the battlements of the city, saw King Sancho passing incautiously near to the walls, mounted his horse, set his spear in rest, and charged furiously upon the Castilian King. Sancho received a mortal wound, and the Zamoran knight returned unhurt into the city. The death of their leader disconcerted the besiegers. The siege was raised, and Queen Urraca lost no time in communicating with her favourite brother, and advising him to claim the vacant throne. Alonso, hurrying from the Court of his Saracen host, received at Zamora the renewed allegiance of his former Leonese subjects.

Alonso thus became, by his elder brother's death, King of Leon, of Castile, and—by the seizure of Garcia's kingdom—of Galicia, including, as this latter kingdom did, a large portion of northern Portugal. Almost the whole of his long reign was occupied with

war against the Saracens. Dissensions among the
Moslem rulers of Spain, quite as much perhaps as
their own warlike capacity, befriended the Christian
soldiers and their chief. Toledo, the ancient seat of
Visigoth rule, and now a centre of Moslem learning
and government, fell into the King's hands, and
became the capital of Leon and Castile. But that
this ascendency of the Christians was not entirely
due to the superiority of their arms, is proved clearly
enough by the issue of the great battle of Zalaca, near
Badajos. Here Alonso found himself opposed by the
famous Almoravidian Emir Yusuf. Contemporary
chroniclers, Moorish and Christian, have, no doubt,
as usual, immensely exaggerated the numbers engaged
on each side, but it is certain that the whole fighting
power of the Peninsula, Christian and Moslem, met
on the field of Zalaca; and, what is significant of
the curious state of the country, and is evidence that
religion went for little in these early contests between
men of the rival faiths, it is related that while bands
of Christian knights had engaged themselves on the
Emir's side, no less than thirty thousand Moslem
troops fought under the banners of the Christian King.

The battle raged all day, and by nightfall the
Leonese and Castilian lines had been broken, the
rout became complete, and, by the admission even
of Christian chroniclers, the slaughter was enormous. Fortune, however, which had befriended
King Alonso before, did not wholly desert him now.
Tidings from his African home, requiring the immediate presence of Yusuf in Africa, reached the Almora-

vidian chief in the very hour of his victory. The prosecution of the campaign was left to a lieutenant, and the opportunity of curbing and perhaps of completely crushing the power of the Christians in Spain was for the time lost to the Saracens.

The latter part of King Alonso's reign and life was passed without any further great change of fortune. With the internal affairs of the Leonese monarchy we have now to concern ourselves.

During the long wars of the eleventh century, the Christian Courts and camps of Spain had been attracting all that was adventurous in the chivalry of Europe. At the Court of King Alonso two French knights of the princely house of Burgundy had made their appearance. Count Raymond and Count Henry were first cousins, and both princes quickly obtained the favour of the Leonese King. To Raymond, the eldest, he gave in marriage Urraca, his daughter by Queen Constance; on Count Henry he bestowed another and illegitimate daughter, Tareja, the child of Ximena Nunes, a Spanish lady of noble birth. To Count Raymond he confided the important government of Galicia and Portugal, but the hands of the young Burgundian Count were by no means strong enough to retain a firm grasp on this outlying dependency.

In the spring of 1095 Count Raymond marched southward towards the Saracen frontier, gathering to his standard a large army, the flower of the Galician and Portuguese chivalry. He reached the Tagus, and entrenched himself in the peninsula formed by

the Atlantic on one side and the broad estuary of the
Tagus on the other—a spot which has since become
memorable in military annals, as being that whereon
Wellington formed the famous defensive lines of
Torres Vedras.

The troops of Count Raymond, however, found no
protection in the triple lines of hills which cross the
neck of the peninsula. His troops were suddenly
surrounded, says the Compostellan chronicler, by
an immense multitude of Saracen fighting men, Raymond's army was overthrown, and slaughter and
captivity were the lot of the Christian warriors.

It was no doubt in consequence of this reverse
that Count Henry, the husband of the bastard Tareja,
was deemed fitter to hold the outlying province than
his cousin; and while Raymond's viceroyalty was,
shortly after his defeat, limited to the Galician
province, Henry was made governor of the whole of
Portugal between the Minho and the Tagus.

During the first years of Count Henry's reign the
storms of Saracen conflict were sweeping over
southern and eastern Spain; but the new ruler was
probably engaged, to judge from the scanty mention
of him by the chroniclers, rather in strengthening his
own government than in any offensive action against
the Moors.

Count Raymond died in 1107, and two years
afterwards King Alonso also died, leaving his
daughter Urraca, Raymond's widow, then about
nineteen years of age, the successor to the crown.
She had one son, Alonso Raimundes, a child of three,

and with the common testamentary fatuity of absolute
sovereigns, the succession to the crown was to
devolve upon this infant in case of the re-marriage
of Urraca. The young widow lost little time in
effecting this contingent reversion in her child's
favour, by contracting a marriage with the neighbouring sovereign, Alonso of Aragon, a young prince
whose activity in war had already obtained for him
the title of El Lidador—The Warrior. With the full
consent of the nobles, who expected to find in so warlike a prince a successful leader in their constant
warfare with the Moors, Alonso El Lidador at once
assumed the crown of Leon and Castile; but the
clergy opposed the marriage on the ground of consanguinity, and the distant province of Galicia,
whither Urraca had sent her child, broke into a
rebellion, instigated by the hidalgos who composed
the household of the infant prince. The revolt continued, notwithstanding the violence and cruelty of
the Aragonese King, who is related to have killed
with his hunting-spear a noble Galician while Urraca
was in the act of interceding for his life. Baffled in
his attempts to subdue the rebellion, the King retired
to his own dominions.

The period of five years that followed is occupied
by the dissensions and intrigues of the principal
characters of the age. The brutality of the Aragonese King lost him almost immediately the love and
the fidelity of Urraca, and the loyalty of his new subjects. Queen Urraca, possessing the inconstancy and
capriciousness of her sex and her age, possessed also

the ambition and disloyalty which were characteristic of most of the energetic sovereigns of the time. Her patent amours with a Castilian nobleman were probably the cause of the King's insulting her with a blow before the assembled Court, and imprisoning her at Castellar. The quarrel was appeased for the time by the nobles, but the Queen's treacherous nature, and her desire for further vengeance upon her husband, led her to send a message to the guardians of her child, still in Galicia, and to stir up a fresh revolt in that province.

Count Henry of Portugal had long before entered into a secret alliance with the King of Aragon against Urraca; but at the invitation of the infuriated Queen he readily abandoned the husband, to ally himself to the wife's interest, in the prospect of better furthering his own; but the shrewd and cautious Count of Portugal had forgotten to allow for the caprice and for the envy of a woman. The growing strength of Count Henry's position in Portugal began probably to alarm her ambition, and the chronicler tells us that Urraca's jealousy was aroused by hearing her sister Tareja, Henry's wife, spoken of by her own subjects as Queen.[1] She reconciled herself suddenly with her husband, to the discomfiture of her new ally; but by this time friends and foes had probably got to perceive the unstableness of her character. She was dangerous to plot with or against; and this is, no doubt, one cause of the uneventfulness of her

[1] 'La mujer del conde era ya llamada de las suyas reyna lo qual oyendo la reyna mal le sabia.'—*Chronicle of Sahagun.*

reign and the unfruitfulness of her long series of perfidies and intrigues.

These various plots and counterplots were interrupted by the death of Count Henry of Portugal in 1114. Tareja was left a widow with an infant and only son. This child was Affonso Henriquez, destined to become the first and most famous of a line of famous sovereigns and conquerors.

Tareja, the bastard daughter of the Castilian King, was probably at the time of her husband's death not much more than thirty years of age. The chroniclers, one and all, describe her as possessed of singular beauty and attractiveness, and as having a character marked by astuteness and energy. As a ruler she was ambitious but over-cautious, and, like her half-sister Urraca, more inclined to win her way by intrigue than by boldness; and she never, during her long reign, willingly committed her fortunes to the chances of war.

I pass over briefly the years occupied by the reign of Urraca, Queen or Regent of Leon and Castile. The King of Aragon was engaged during all this time with Saracenic warfare to the east and south, and only occasionally thought fit to invade his now divorced wife's kingdom. Tareja had promoted her lover, Fernando Peres, to a position in the state almost as high as that which had been occupied by her husband, the Count of Portugal. She slightly extended her possessions to the north, into Galicia, and thereby gave her sister and suzerain a pretext for invading her territory.

In the short campaign which ensued, in the circumstances which led to it, and the events which
followed, a new actor, Gelmires, Bishop of Santiago de
Compostella in Galicia, played a most important part.
This wily, ambitious, and turbulent churchman, the
prime mover in the affairs of Leon and Portugal
during several years, whose vanity seems to have been
as conspicuous as his other ill qualities, has left, in
the well-known ' Historia Compostellana,' drawn up
at his command and for his own glorification, almost
the only, and far the best, contemporary record of
this period which we possess. In this chronicle the
naïve immorality of the times is curiously evidenced
by the manner in which the unscrupulous disloyalty
and double-dealing of its hero are set down by the
annalist as proofs of his patron's dexterity and
policy.

Gelmires procured war - galleys from Genoa,
manned them with hardy Galician boatmen, and
harassed the Saracens of the south coast with a kind
of naval raid from which the Christians had themselves long been sufferers at the hands of the Moslems.
He made his influence strongly felt throughout the
whole north-west of Spain. The shrine of St. James
of Compostella, then, and perhaps still, the most
famous in Christendom, annually attracted crowds of
pilgrims of every degree, and was the source of a
large revenue to the Compostellan See. Their protection against Moorish attack led, fifty years afterwards,
to the institution of the famous Militant Order of
Compostellan Knights, and the service was at this

time performed by a body of armed men under the orders of the Bishop. Gelmires increased the number and improved the discipline of these troops till they attained to the numbers and organisation of an army. Many of the noblest Galician knights enrolled themselves under his banners; and when Urraca proposed to invade her sister's territories, she invoked, rather than commanded, the aid of this powerful prelate, her nominal subject.

The chronicle tells us that he was divided in his mind on the subject. He had already fomented civil war in Urraca's Galician provinces, favouring the now strong party which rallied round her son, the Infante Alonso Raimundes, and siding with Tareja. Urraca, however, was now in Galicia with an army. He feared to provoke her too far. Urraca had craftily encouraged the citizens of Compostella in their resistance to the Bishop; they had already formed themselves into a guild or *Hermandad*, one of those burghers' leagues which afterwards spread through Spain, and whose influence has lasted to this day. Gelmires was forced to side with Queen Urraca. He encouraged her to invade Portugal, not sorry probably to see the Leonese arms and the ambition of Urraca's adventurous barons diverted from Galicia and from his see.

Urraca invaded Portugal, and Gelmires—this ‘episcopal Mephistopheles,’ as he is angrily called by a sedate Portuguese historian—joined, with little pressing from the Queen, an expedition against his former ally. The armies of the rival sister Queens met on the banks of the Minho, near Tuy: Tareja was worsted; her troops were routed, and she herself, flying for her life, took refuge in the Castle of Lanhoso. Urraca besieged the castle, and took her sister prisoner; but this capricious, and—if we may judge her to be so from one or two incidental allusions by the chroniclers—this somewhat tender-hearted sovereign, did not choose to push her advantage as far as the scant humanity of the times might have allowed. Tareja and Urraca negotiated a treaty of peace, by which Tareja was left in little worse a position than before the campaign; and Urraca, thinking the moment propitious for an attempt to check the ambition of Gelmires, her secret enemy and professed ally, suddenly threw the Bishop into prison. But she had not calculated upon all the power of the ecclesiastic. Her own son, the Infante, had come strongly under the Bishop's influence, and he shrewdly guessed that his interests had more in common with those of Gelmires than with those of an ambitious Queen-mother. The Infante drew off his troops; the principal nobles joined him; and in less than a week Galicia was in revolt, and Urraca was compelled to release the prelate.

In the year 1126 died Queen Urraca, and the immediate consequence was that the whole of the powerful chivalry of Leon and Castile, divided till now in their allegiance between mother and son, went over in a body to the party of the young King. From this time forward he was the most powerful Christian monarch of Spain. In Portugal, affairs were unsettled. The Infanta Tareja had aroused the jealousy of the Portuguese by the favour shown to her lover, Fernando Peres,[1] and his Galician relations and friends. The country was ill governed, and the weakness of a ruler in statesmanship and war meant, in those times, danger of disastrous invasion from every powerful neighbour. Tareja was imprudent enough to refuse her allegiance to the new King of Leon. A destructive invasion of her territories was the immediate consequence, and she was compelled to admit his rightful suzerainty over the Province of Portugal. She had jealously kept her son apart from any share in the government, but the heir to the throne began to attract the attention of the dissatisfied nobles.

The time has now arrived to say something of Prince Affonso Henriquez. It is, unfortunately, the common way of early annalists and chroniclers to touch very lightly on the personal traits of the characters in their narrative, which to inquirers of a later age are of paramount interest and importance ; and the young Prince of Portugal fares little better

---

[1] Some Portuguese writers have contended warmly for the legitimacy of the connection between Fernando and Tareja. He was certainly, however, not her husband. There is no contemporary mention of a marriage. She indeed calls herself in one charter-grant, a Galician one, 'Comitis Henrici quondam uxor nunc vero comitis Fernandi,' but this proves nothing but her wish for good fame. In no contemporary Portuguese charter does she so designate herself. The *Historia Compostellana* distinctly says :—'Ego qui relicta sua legitima uxore cum matre ipsius infantis Regina Tarasia tunc adulterabatur.' This would seem to be quite conclusive.

than the many figures of sovereigns, **warriors, and
churchmen** which fill **their scanty historical can-
vases**; but Affonso Henriquez made too **deep a**
mark not to have left some trace **of** his individuality
even in the dry narratives of the chroniclers, and we
can gather a trait here and there wherewith **to make
up** a piecework portrait **which shall even now possess**
some lifelike features.

At the time of **his aunt Urraca's death,** the prince
was seventeen years old. **Even at this early** age he
had taken part in the annual border fighting with
Spaniards on the north and east, **and with Saracens** in
the south. **The** perilous state **of the** country, **and**
perhaps his own ambition, had led **to his receiving**
the order of knighthood **at** the unusually early **age
of fourteen.** Three years of incessant adventure
and peril had developed the character and shown the
high qualities **of the Infante.** He was already a
captain whom his men could **follow** into action with
enthusiasm, and in whose good judgment, and in the
very graces of his manner and person, they could
discern the rare qualities of a leader of men. Writing of him at this period, a nearly contemporary chronicler tells us that the prince was a skilful and valiant
knight, accomplished and persuasive **in** speech, most
politic **in** his enterprises, of a high genius, noble in
bodily proportions, and of a very comely presence.
At a somewhat later date, when **he** had already
redeemed **the** high promise **of** his youth, another
monkish writer of the period somewhat reproaches
him with his ardent temperament and love of adven-

ture. The youth, he tells us, though already well skilled in the art of ruling, is yet over-fond of fame, and is used to be carried away, like an over-light arrow, by every breath of heaven.[1] This mobile and ambitious temperament and this restless energy, little as they might recommend themselves in the eyes of a monk, were yet the very qualities to save a country in such a critical emergency as Portugal was now undergoing. Never till now had the province been so threatened with danger from without and within.

The differences between Tareja and the nobles under the Infante quickly resolved themselves into war, and a battle was fought on the field of San Mamede, near Guimaraens, the then capital of Portugal. Tareja and her lover were routed and expelled from the kingdom, and a single day's battle placed the rule in the hands of Affonso Henriquez. Two years after this, Tareja died in exile.

Affonso Henriquez owed an inherited allegiance to his cousin, the King of Leon, and it has been supposed to have been his desire to shake off this tie which induced him to invade his cousin's Galician provinces in the following spring; but it was probably nothing but the fire and imprudence of youth which led him to this rash enterprise. The King of Leon, elsewhere engaged in warfare, deputed to Archbishop Gelmires the opposing of the Portuguese raid, but the cautious churchman held back. He was,

---

[1] 'Qui juvenis etsi regendi imperii bene sciolus tamen amore laudis ardenter plenus ad quoscumque aurae flatus ut arundo fragilis ferebatur.' Ancient document quoted by Brandā.

or more probably he feigned to be, ill, and disobeyed the order; and Affonso Henriquez carried fire and sword through Galicia unresisted. In the following year he again invaded Galicia, was repulsed by his old enemy, Count Fernando Peres, on the frontier, renewed the attack, and defeated the Galicians. On this occasion Affonso Henriquez built a castle at Celmes, in that province, provisioned and garrisoned it. From this Galician raid, or from a similar and previous one, he was recalled into Portugal by the growing power of Bermudo, a brother of Count Fernando. This nobleman, rising to influence during his brother's ascendency, had fortified himself in the Castle of Seia, near the Spanish frontier, among the fastnesses of the great Estrella range of mountains, the wildest and most inaccessible in the whole western Peninsula. Here, surrounded by a race of hardy and warlike mountaineers, he thought it safe to defy the power of the Portuguese prince. Affonso Henriquez sought him out in the recesses of the mountains, besieged and took Seia by a *coup de main* and expelled Bermudo from Portugal. In the meantime the young prince had himself roused the apprehensions or the indignation of the King of Leon, who, with a numerous army, marched rapidly towards Galicia, and laid siege to Celmes in the absence of the Portuguese prince. In a few days, and after serious loss to its garrison, Celmes fell into the hands of the Leonese King.

It will be well to pause here for an instant, to consider the precarious position of the young prince

and of his people. At this time the Leonese and
Castilian nation was growing yearly in extent and
power. Under a warlike leader they had carried
their victories beyond the Ebro in the west, and the
supremacy of the King of Leon had been acknowledged by the Navarrese and by the Court of Barce-
lona, and even in the lands beyond the Pyrenees.
His great rival the King of Aragon, El Lidador, was
now dead; his successor had hastened to give in his
submission to King Alonso Raimundes, and with the
exception of the one small quasi-independent province
of Portugal, there was in all Christian Spain no one to
dispute the ascendency of the Leonese. Their King's
dominion was as wide as that of Fernando the Great,
and he now assumed without opposition the title of
Emperor.

With such powerful and aggressive neighbours
on the eastern and northern frontier of Portugal, an
enemy lay over the southern border, more terrible to
the Portuguese even than the Christian chivalry of
Spain, for they were more implacable, as being enemies
of their faith as well as of their race; more numerous,
for they had increased and multiplied exceedingly in
the great plain of southern Portugal, rich in corn-
lands and olive-groves; and they could draw to their
standards, on the emergency of battle, huge armies
of disciplined men from the adjacent Andalusian
provinces, and even from Morocco itself. Hemmed
in, between Spaniards on the one side and Saracens
on the other, the country ruled over by Affonso
Henriquez was in extent a mere province, a large

part of whose surface was occupied by heath and
wood and mountain. The Portugal of Affonso Henriquez comprised only the three northern provinces
out of the six into which modern Portugal is divided.
A broad frontier band of hill and forest, untenanted
by man and wasted by the annual passage of Moorish
and Christian raiding parties, separated the two races.
This desolated band of country occupied the northern
portion of what is now the province of Portuguese
Estremadura, and it stretched from the shores of the
Atlantic to where the impassable highlands of the
Estrella continued the border wilderness in a north-
easterly direction till it reached the Spanish mountain
ranges.

At Soure, in this desert, a few miles south of
Coimbra, the Knights Templars had adventurously
built themselves a fortress ; but this outpost of the
Christians was not enough to check the Saracen
invasions. A broad path lay open to them in the
easier plain country between Soure and the sea-
board ; and while the Christian border was thus ill
defended, the Saracens held fortified positions of
great strength on their side of the frontier desert.
One strong fortress lay secure from attack in
the steep granite range of Cintra, close to the sea.
Lisbon, already a populous city, and surrounded with
fortifications built with all the artifice of Moorish
architecture, was another defensive position : and
the city of Santarem, a few leagues to the north of
Lisbon, was a third stronghold, the nearest and most
threatening to Christian territory.

To guard the easy approach to his dominions, the Portuguese ruler chose as the site of a new fortress the tall hill of Leiria (due south of Soure), which rises from what is comparatively a plain country, lying between Soure and the sea. Here he built a castle, garrisoned it with a picked garrison, and left it in charge of the most renowned among his captains, Paio Gutteres.

While the Governor of Leiria was employed in harrying the unbelievers with raids from this fortress, the Prince himself had again invaded Galicia, and in the well-contested battle of Cerneja had utterly routed the troops of Leon; but in the very moment of victory he was recalled by the news of disaster on the southern frontier. The Saracens, harassed and irritated by the vexatious incursions of the governor of Leiria, had besieged that fortress; and the news that now reached the Portuguese ruler was that of the fall of Leiria and the slaughter of its garrison. Intelligence also came to him that the Emperor was advancing by forced marches from Zamora, in Leon, gathering together an overwhelmingly numerous army, and bent on revenging the defeat of his people at Cerneja.

It was a critical moment, and the course of affairs seemed to be inevitably hastening to a catastrophe fatal to the hopes of Portuguese independence; but this was not to be, and events in a distant and foreign country had long been preparing the way for a sudden and unlooked-for turn in the affairs of Portugal.

It is quite necessary to glance at these events. In

Mahometan Spain, the warlike sect of the Almoravides, invited into Spain some fifty years before to stem the tide of Christian conquest, had done so most effectually (as we have already seen) at the great battle of Zalaca, fatal to the chivalry of Leon. After this, the Almoravides, turning their arms against their own allies, had overcome the Moorish rulers of Spain one after another, and established their supremacy over the whole Moslem Peninsula; but now the state of affairs was again changed. Half a century of power had lessened the first austerity of the Almoravides, and weakened their influence, both in Morocco and in the Peninsular provinces. There was abundant room for social, and for political, and for religious reform; and such reform came about in the sudden and subversive manner which is characteristic of Oriental life.

The son of a servant in a mosque, a Berber of the Atlas mountains, travelling to Cordova and afterwards to Bagdad, had acquired at these famous seats of Arabian letters the consideration which was in those days always conceded to superior learning. Returning to Morocco, he denounced fiercely the prevalent religious laxity, and the vices of people and rulers. Flying from the persecution which he met with, to the mountains, he preached a reformed Unitarianism, attracted a huge following of armed men, became a political power, and the Almohades, or Unitarian soldiers, formidable with a puritan sternness of religious zeal, threatened the security of the Almoravidian power in Morocco.

An emergency so sudden forced the Moors of Spain to prompt action. A large army was drained from all the provinces of the Peninsula, even those touching on the unquiet frontiers of the Christians. Such an opportunity for the Christian powers had never before occurred. The impending campaign between Affonso Henriquez and his suzerain was suspended by mutual consent. A peace was hastily arranged at Tuy, in the year 1137, and both rulers prepared to betake themselves to the Saracen frontiers of their dominions. Thus was the storm which threatened to overwhelm Portugal for the time averted.

By the summer of the year 1139 the Prince of Portugal had begun his march southward, gathering to his standards, at every farm and homestead within reach of his line of march, the horse and foot soldiers whose tenure of crown land obliged them to render warlike service to their prince. Instead of passing through the frontier wilderness of Estremadura, the usual path of raiders from either side, the Prince, turning to the east, struck the Tagus in its upper waters, and found himself at once in a land where no Christian foot had stood for centuries[1]—the alluvial plain of Alemtejo, the richest land in Portugal—then the garden of the Moorish territories. The rough Portuguese spoiled the land and advanced

---

[1] Except, of course, the Mosarabes. Portuguese by race and Christian by religion, the Mosarabes conformed in dress, in manners, and in culture to the dominant race, lived among them, and contributed to the wealth and prosperity of the Moorish colonies of the Peninsula.

rapidly into the very heart of the Saracen territory.
On the plain of Ourique, to the north of the populous
city of Silves, a large Saracen army, drawn from all
parts, prepared to give battle to the invaders.

OLD HOUSE IN OPORTO.   PERIOD OF KING AFFONSO HENRIQUEZ.

CHAPTER II.

THE FIRST KING OF PORTUGAL.

THE warfare between Portuguese and Saracen had hitherto been a warfare of sieges, of forays, of surprises and ambuscades, of skirmishes at river-fords, or irregular fighting in the defiles of mountains or in the fastnesses of forests. The Christian Portuguese had never yet dared to meet their enemies in the open field. It must be remembered that the Christian remnant who had preserved their independence in the hills of the north were, in almost every respect, a people inferior to their enemies in all the arts of peace and war; inferior in numbers, inferior in organization, vastly inferior in civilization and social culture, and—what in such times was of chief importance to their very existence—in discipline, in strategy, and the mere practice of warfare. Against the Gothic pike and the short sword of the Christians, hardly improved from Roman times, the slender lance of the Saracens in the hands of their practised cavalry was what the rifle of the European soldier is when opposed to the assegai of the African savage or the rude matchlock of the Asiatic. Not till the Christian had borrowed the Arabian peaked saddle and the

powerful curb-bit used by his enemies, not till he
had learnt something of the skilful horsemanship of
the Saracen, could he acquire an efficient use of the
lance—that best of all cavalry weapons—and make
any stand at all in the open field against his Moslem
enemy.

In the long period before the faith feud between
the two races had turned to the religious enthusiasm
and animosity which made the Crusades a possibility,
many adventurous Christian knights took service, as
we have already seen, with the Saracens, and fought
without compunction against men of their own faith
and country. It was through such men that the arts
of war, and some social culture, and some of the refinements of military intercourse were borrowed by
the Christians from a high-couraged and a courteous
people, and grew at once into that spirit of Christian
chivalry, whose influence for good, if it has been
somewhat overrated, was certainly in no country and
at no time so conspicuous as in the Peninsula and in
this very generation.

Now, for the first time in the history of the great
racial struggle on Portuguese soil, the ascendency of
the two peoples was to be set on the issue of a
pitched battle on a field where, if tradition is to be
trusted for the exact site, neither side could derive
any material advantage from superiority of position.

Affonso Henriquez was completely victorious.
With this short sentence we have exhausted almost
all that the contemporary chroniclers have told us.
One curious circumstance, indeed, they relate;

namely, that a large number of women fought on the
side of the Almoravides, and though such a practice
was in accordance with the occasional usages of this
warlike sect, it testifies plainly enough to the fact that
the exodus of fighting men had been great enough to
cause them to resort to an expedient which can never
fail to be repugnant to human nature.[1]

A number of legends, some religious, some
patriotic, have clustered round the bare fact of the
victory of Ourique ; but the majority of these myths
can be traced to their origin in the fourteenth
century, a period in the middle ages the most fruitful of legend and pseudo-tradition. The least in-
credible of these legends, one to the effect that on
the victorious field of Ourique Affonso Henriquez
assumed for the first time the crown of Portugal, is
almost certainly mythical. It is not corroborated by
charters granted at a later date, and it is not alluded
to by any chronicler of the period.

Notwithstanding the importance attached by the
Portuguese themselves to the battle of Ourique, it
was not a decisive battle in the accepted sense of that
word, and it led to no immediate occupation of hostile
territory. It was nothing but one of the annual
raiding expeditions carried out on a larger scale, and

---

[1] 'Era M.CLXXVII. (that is, the so-called Spanish era = A.D.
1139). Julio mense die D. Jacobi apostoli fuit victoria Alfonsi
regis de Esmar rege Saracenorum et innumerabili prope exercitu
in loco qui dicitur Aulic tunc cor terræ Saracenorum quo per-
rexit rex Alfonsus. Fœminæ Saracenæ in hoc prælio amazoneo ritu
ac modo pugnarunt et occisæ tales deprehensæ.'—*Brevis Hist.
Gothorum.*

brought, by a combination of fortune, and of conduct and courage in its leader, to a larger and more successful issue than usual. It was, indeed, a victory important in this respect, that it immediately conferred a wide military prestige on the numerically very insignificant people who were now struggling for independence, and of this they were to reap the benefit before the year was ended.

In the same year Affonso Henriquez, for reasons which are not very clear, broke the peace of Tuy, and began a new Galician invasion. The campaign was in the beginning indecisive, and in a skirmish the prince himself was severely wounded, and for a time disabled, by a lance-thrust inflicted by a Galician foot soldier. The Emperor, though he was at the moment engaged in war with Navarre, hurried with a Leonese army to the defence of his Galician province, and came up with the invading Portuguese in the wild hill-country in the extreme north of Portugal; and here occurred one of those picturesque scenes characteristic of the age, and of the softening effect of the spirit of chivalry and the influence of the Church.

The two armies were encamped on acclivities rising on either side from the valley of the little river Vez. A preliminary skirmish had already taken place, and one of the Emperor's commanders, pushing forward from the main army, had been encountered and worsted by the Infante himself. The shock of a great battle was imminent, whose issue could not but have been decisive of events in Christian Spain. In relating what follows, it is fair to suppose, taking the accounts of Spanish and Portuguese chroniclers as our guide, that the Emperor hesitated before engaging in an encounter, whose results might be so serious, with an enemy numerically, certainly, greatly inferior, but of proved valour, fresh from the field of great exploits, and doubly strong in being commanded by so redoubtable a leader as the young Prince of Portugal. It is related that the Emperor of Leon, on the very eve of this battle, sent heralds into the camp of the enemy, and, through the intervention of the Portuguese Archbishop of Braga, obtained the consent of the Infante to an armistice. Thus again was an honourable termination put to what promised to be a most bloody campaign; but such a concourse of gallant knights could not part, according to the laws of chivalry, without the performance of some courteous and knightly feats of arms.

The long and narrow valley, known as Valdevez, which lay between the Portuguese and Spanish armies, broadens at one place into a level space, from which the surrounding hills, occupied by the rival armies, rise like the sides of an ancient amphitheatre. Into this natural arena, when peace was declared, rode the champion knights from either side, and fought for the honour of their native lands. The victory in this tournay, say the Portuguese chroniclers, was with their side, and several Leonese cavaliers were worsted and taken prisoners, in accordance with the usages of public duels, and one knight lost his life. The Spanish annalists state, on the other hand, that

prisoners were taken on both sides. The spot was
long afterwards known as *Jogo do Bufardio*, the place
of the tournament; and it is worth observing that the
almost bloodless tournay of Valdevez came in time to
be magnified into a great Portuguese victory, and the
very name of its site to be transformed, with curious
exaggeration, into *Veiga da Matança*, the field of
slaughter.[1]

So little really decisive had been the famous battle
of Ourique, that the Saracens, taking advantage of
the presence of the Portuguese army in the north,
entered the kingdom, and marched northward as far
as the important town of Trancoso, which lies within
a few leagues to the south of the Douro News of
the capture of Trancoso reached the Infante at
Valdevez, and he hastened to its rescue. In two
serious engagements the Saracens were overborne,
and retreated to the south.

The constant good fortune of the King in his
military enterprises had, by this time, attracted the
attention of Europe to the small country over which
he ruled. He was recognised at Rome as a valiant
and faithful soldier of the Church In the great
strife between Cross and Crescent, service as useful
to the cause of Christianity could be rendered in the
Peninsula as in the Holy Land or Iconium; and Spanish
and Portuguese knights were expressly dispensed from

[1] 'The scene of the engagement was the country between
Arcos and Santo André de Guilhadeges. The King of Leon was
defeated with great slaughter, and the place in consequence received the name of Veiga da Matança.'—*Murray's Handbook:
third edition, carefully revised*

any obligation of crossing the seas in order to seek for Moslem enemies. Affonso Henriquez now began to use his best efforts to free himself from any remaining allegiance to the Emperor. He perceived the importance of obtaining from the Pope some recognition of his independence, and he corresponded with the Holy See with this object. The Pope did not hesitate to contribute to the independence of so approved a champion of Christianity, and in the year 1144, Pope Lucius II. addressed him a letter in which his claims to sovereign powers are recognised, and even the title of King is almost actually conferred. From this period, and, to take the evidence of charters, shortly before it, Affonso Henriquez had assumed the title of an absolute sovereign, and we may, in future, style him King of Portugal.

Thus painfully, and by slow degrees, was this small semi-Gothic people—a mere handful of men among the surrounding hostile Christian and Moslem populations—educating itself to the knowledge of liberty and independence. In the veins of prince and people ran, with their half-northern blood, some germs of freedom, some conception of a solidarity between ruled and rulers, of respect for law and authority mingled with jealousy of encroachment upon public rights, something of antagonism to personal government and tyranny; and the germs of these noble ideas were now acquiring a goodly growth amid the successes of the nation under a great and congenial leader.

It is far more interesting to the student of a

people's progress to extract the story of the gradual emerging of the Portuguese into national life from the dry and scanty records of the time, than to read of the marvels of military prowess and the numerous instances of direct Divine intervention with which the patriotism and the piety of later historians have surrounded the rise of their country into the rank of nations. Nevertheless, even these exaggerations and foolish legends and allegations of the supernatural are interesting enough in themselves as an indirect testimony to the greatness of the work then done by prince and people.

In the meantime, the struggle between the Almoravides and the new sect of Almohades had extended to the Peninsula. Ibn Kasi, an Almoravidian renegade, an energetic, unscrupulous and ambitious man, had placed himself at the head of an Almohadian insurrection in the great Saracen province of Gharb; and he was appointed Almohadian Wali or governor of the important fortress of Mertola in that province. The contest between Almoravidians and Almohades in Gharb was long, bloody, and for a time indecisive, and Ibn Kasi bethought him of obtaining the alliance of the now formidable Affonso Henriquez. The Almoravides, the ancient enemies of the Portuguese ruler, issuing from their stronghold at Santarem, had recently again defeated the Portuguese Templars of Soure, and King Affonso Henriquez gladly availed himself of this opportunity to make reprisals.

He joined his forces to those of Ibn Kasi, but the Saracen and his Christian ally were ill mated. It is clear that Affonso Henriquez did not desire, and would not consent to lend his help to any operations likely to establish the permanent ascendency of either party among the enemies of his faith and country. He wanted warlike occupation for his troops, and the rich plunder of the populous territory of the Saracens. The astute Ibn Kasi found in the King a sagacity greater and a will far stronger than his own. In the presence of Affonso Henriquez, to use the picturesque phrase of an Arab chronicler, Ibn Kasi was like a slave before his lord, hardly daring to lift his eyes from the ground. With so intractable and so dangerous an ally, the Saracen hastened to make any terms, and Affonso Henriquez and his army in time took their way back into Portugal, laden with valuable spoil in slaves, in arms, in armour, and in war-horses of the Arab and African races.

The continued possession by his enemies of the great stronghold of Santarem, a *point d'appui* for yearly aggression, was, we are told, an unceasing vexation to the soul of the Portuguese king. This city and citadel lay, and still lie, on the north bank of the Tagus, in the centre of a rich plain, which extended wedge-like into the heart of the desert border-land of Estremadura. It therefore was the Saracen position which lay nearest and was most threatening to the Christians. Santarem was believed to be impregnable; an opinion justified to this day in the eyes of those who have traced out the ruins of

its Moorish citadel on an eminence overlooking the
Tagus, and surveyed the natural and artificial scarps
and counterscarps of the hill-sides along which it is
built.

Warfare in that age and country was, as we have
already seen, to a great extent, an affair of sieges;
and, in so far as it was so, the advantage was
altogether with the Saracens. In the art of building
strong places, of taking them, and of resisting capture, the Christian nations of Europe had inherited,
and had not improved upon, the clumsy artillery (if
we may use the word in its first sense) of the Romans;
and the Crusaders, in Asia Minor and Syria, found
themselves as much inferior to the Saracens in this
branch of the military art as did the Christians of
Spain and Portugal. The defenders of Santarem,
therefore, felt perfectly secure in a strong, watchful
garrison; in their lofty turrets, garnished with all the
artifice of Arabian war science; and securer still in
the proved ignorance of their enemies.

To take Santarem openly and in the light of day
was clearly impossible; but it was an age in which
stratagem made an essential and honourable branch
of the art of war, and in which branch of it the
keener and more subtle wits of the Orientals were
also greatly at an advantage.

In the spring of the year 1147, King Affonso
Henriquez lay at Coimbra, his capital, when he
schemed an attempt upon Santarem. He is said to
have obtained exact information of the height and
position of the walls and towers of Santarem, to have

prepared scaling-ladders, and to have sketched out a plan of assault. In three night marches, his small army had passed the fifty or sixty miles of wild and deserted country that lay between Coimbra and Santarem, successfully eluding the observation of the Saracen outposts and watchers by the way: on the third, some hours before daylight, he was under the walls of the city. The ladders were set, the walls scaled, and the troops, following their King with the war-cry of *Sanctiago e Rëi Affonso!* overpowered the garrison, and the redoubtable stronghold of Santarem was in the hands of the Christians.[1]

The capture of Santarem was of more importance to the Christian cause in Portugal than any event within the previous fifty years. It extended Christian territory to the Tagus, made Moorish aggression more difficult, and the Christian invasion of Gharb easier than before.

The King, however, now meditated an exploit far greater than this, and which, if accomplished, would carry the fame of the Portuguese nation to every Christian Court and camp in Europe. This was the capture of Lisbon itself. But although to take an

---

[1] The narrative in the text is probably very near the facts. The usually cautious Herculano tells the story in detail, closely following the account of this episode given in the Life of St. Theotomio, Prior of Santa Cruz, a contemporary and, according to the Cistercian monk, his biographer, an adviser of King Affonso Henriquez. The date of the Life is uncertain; its queer latinity, its half-romantic style, and the narration of many very improbable circumstances, do not appear to the present writer, after a very painful perusal of it, to be like the truth, or even like the pious fraud of a contemporary.

outpost like Santarem by a sudden and unexpected
assault had been proved to be possible, there were
circumstances connected with the defences of Lisbon
which rendered its capture, with the resources of the
King of Portugal, quite beyond the bounds of possibility.

Lisbon was at this time the richest and the most
populous city of the Peninsula. Moorish accounts
compute the number of its inhabitants at between
four and five hundred thousand. Its magnificent sea
approach had long made it the chief emporium of
trade between Europe and northern Africa. The city
lies on the northern bank of the Tagus, where the river
broadens into a lake-like estuary : from the edge of
the water rose the city, as it still rises, amphitheatre-
wise upon hilly ground. On the northern slopes of
these hills was situated the Kassba, or Moorish citadel,
with its round turrets, its ditches, and its battlemented
curtains. Strong lines of fortification extended from
either side of the fortress to the river, and enclosed the
whole city, except on the river side, where it was sufficiently protected by the Moorish fleets. The efforts of
the Portuguese against so formidable an enceinte would
certainly have proved futile, and it is not likely that
even the enterprising King Affonso Henriquez would
have made any attempt, but for a wholly unlooked-
for occurrence.

Two years before the capture of Santarem, the
first Crusade had ended in complete disaster to the
Christian arms in Asia Minor, and levies were already
gathering in France and in Germany for a fresh ex-

pedition to the East. A large force of Frenchmen
and Germans were at this time travelling overland to
Palestine, along the route which had already been
followed by a previous generation of Crusaders; but
the levies from England, North Germany, and the Low
Countries, not unaccustomed to the sea, preferred, to
the fatigues of a tedious journey afoot through
Hungary and modern European Turkey, the long and
dangerous voyage from the mouths of the Rhine, down
the British Channel, across the Bay of Biscay and
through the Pillars of Hercules into the Mediterranean.
News of these sea-travelling Crusaders had probably
reached the King of Portugal, through France, long
before its slow and timid navigation had brought the
fleet within sight of his shores; and it is almost certain that he had foreseen and planned the combination which he subsequently put into practice.

The German Crusaders under Arnulph of Areschot,
and the Flemings under Christian of Gistell, had put
in at Dartmouth, there to join the English contingent.
These latter were commanded by four Constables,
and the whole force assembled in the port of Dartmouth numbered about 13,000 fighting men, of whom
the greater number probably were Englishmen.[1]

It happened that among the English Crusaders
was a scholar, no doubt a churchman of inferior
rank, who subsequently drew up a lengthy account,
in the form of a letter, of the voyage and of its
various incidents, in a manner so graphic that it fur-

[1] 'Pars eorum maxima venerat ex Anglia.'—Henry of Hunt-
ingdon.

nishes us with by far the best and fullest description that has come down to the present time of the curious episode of the siege of Lisbon.[1]

The English portion of the fleet first made land on the coast of northern Spain, then, creeping round westward, they put in at Oporto to await the arrival of the Flemish and German contingent, from whom they had parted company in a gale.

At Oporto, the Crusaders were met by the Bishop of that city, who had the King's commands to receive them courteously, and to invite them to proceed to Lisbon and to join the Portuguese troops in an attack upon that stronghold. After some discussion, and upon the arrival of the rest of the Crusaders, it was agreed by them to join their forces to those of the King, in a work kindred to that for which they had left their own country. The fleet accordingly set sail for the Tagus, while the King's troops marched thither by land. Much of the letter is taken up with accounts of the dissensions between the members of the various nationalities which composed the crusading armies, and the mode in which peace was kept among these unruly warriors by the King of the Portuguese.

The powerful fleet of the Crusaders cut off the

[1] Under the title of *Cruce Signati anglici Epist. de expugnatione Ulisiponis*, this document is well known to students of history. It is mentioned by Cooper (vol. i. page 166) with the title *Expeditio francorum anglorum, etc., per Osbernum*. The MS. exists, I believe, in the library of Corpus, Cambridge. It was printed in 1861 in the *Monumenta Historica* of the Lisbon Academy, from which copy I quote.

communications of the Lisbon garrison by water, and
the troops, disembarking and joining with the Portuguese, were sufficient to encompass the whole city;
but the Moorish garrison was a strong one, and the
defences in good order. Continual sorties were made
from the city, and in the fighting which took place,
the advantage was as often on the side of the Saracens
as of the besiegers. Finally the English troops succeeded, after heavy loss, in penetrating the suburbs
of the city, which, though lying outside the city wall,
were tenanted by a large population. Here also
were the grain stores of the inhabitants, and from
this time the garrison suffered severely from famine.

In the various arts of siege warfare, the Saracens
had always the advantage. They were the more
ingenious, and the more watchful, and the more
active. A tower on wheels built by the English
Crusaders was burnt; another, constructed at great
expense of time and trouble by the Germans, met the
same fate; mining works, prepared by the Flemings
on a large scale, were countermined by the garrison
and destroyed. The war engines of the Saracens
were superior in size and power to those of the
Christians, and the besiegers were assailed by over-
powering showers of stones and darts whenever they
advanced to the assault.

Finally, however, a Pisan engineer devised a
wooden tower on wheels, of unexampled proportions.
Englishmen and Portuguese worked in company at
its construction, and fifty English and fifty Portuguese soldiers having manned this moving castle, and

each man of the hundred having been supplied with
a piece of the True Cross, it was rolled up to the city
walls amid the breathless expectation of the besieging
hosts.   The Saracens, seeing the imminence of their
danger, sallied forth in great numbers and attacked
the approaching tower.   The Pisan engineer, who
directed the operation, was wounded and disabled by
a stone hurled from a Moorish catapult.   The tide,
flowing unusually high, covered the sands on which
the tower was moving, and cut off support from the
besiegers ; but it came nearer and nearer, and finally
reached to within a yard of the parapets, whose
height it equalled.   Then a drawbridge was thrown
across, and the English and the Portuguese were preparing to enter the city, when the Saracens, seeing
further resistance to be useless, surrendered.[1]   The
city capitulated, and was mercilessly sacked.   The
King lost no time in devising for the captured city a
form of municipal government, which strongly testifies to his liberality, toleration, and wisdom, in an age
when the narrow bigotry and ferocity of kings and
rulers were usually as conspicuous as these qualities
in their subjects.   The Moslem population were
treated by the Portuguese in a manner which was in

---

[1] This is a slight modification of the account of the English
Crusader.   According to his statement, his countrymen had the
chief share in the capture of Lisbon.   A Flemish relation, on the
other hand, makes less of the English prowess, and takes credit for
a successful assault by Flemings and Lorrainers.   Herculano
shrewdly remarks that had a detailed Portuguese narrative of the
siege existed, his own countrymen would, no doubt, have received
their full share of credit.

singular contrast to the contemporary atrocities of
the Crusaders in the East, for the Moors of Lisbon
were neither put to the sword, nor compelled
to change their religion, nor enslaved, nor even
banished. They continued to reside in the city, and
they enjoyed, under a charter granted by the King,
considerable liberties and privileges. They retained
in their own hands the election of a judge, and the
taxation to which they were subjected does not appear
to have been excessive. The King's administration of
church affairs was equally liberal and judicious. He
appointed many foreign ecclesiastics to the newly-
created chief offices of the church; among whom
Gilbert, an Englishman, was the first Bishop of Lisbon.

The King likewise turned his attention to the
establishment of a navy, which his countrymen had
never yet possessed. He favoured naval enterprise
by conferring knightly rank and the privilege of
citizenship on native and on foreign sailors, and he
drew thereby Flemings, Englishmen, and North Germans into the new commercial marine of Portugal.
Thus encouraged by a wise protection and by impartial justice, soon after the capture of Lisbon and what
might have been its commercial ruin, its trade
acquired a sudden, and a great, and a permanent
development.

King Affonso, however, could give but little of
his time to the peaceful arts of government. The
Moors still occupied the country and the strong
places to the south of Lisbon. The trans-Tagan
province, most of which is now known as Alemtejo,

is a vast plain, containing only in its extreme east a
hilly region with valleys of great fertility. At the
two most commanding points of this eastern upland
district lay Iaborah, now Evora, and Bajah, now called
Beja, Moorish cities and strongholds, and both of them
important places at all periods of Portuguese history
At the western extremity of the province, towards
the Atlantic, the trans-Tagan district juts out into a
broad promontory, terminating in Cape Espichel,
and here again the country ceases to be a plain : the
land rises into hills, and each one is crowned, as the
Moorish custom was, with fortified places. Of these,
Palmella, which dominates the entrance of the river
Sado, had already surrendered to the Christians
during the siege ; and Almada, a stronghold on the
south bank of the Tagus, where sea and river meet,
fell almost immediately afterwards into the hands of
the King. Alcacer do Sal, a rich city, and an important place of arms, in the centre of this plain country,
resisted the sudden attack made by the King in person,
at the head of a handful of Christian knights, and the
King received a severe wound ; but within a year it
had again been attacked, and had fallen. There now
only remained Evora and Beja in the east, and when
these strongholds were captured by the Christians,
the whole trans-Tagan plain country was at the mercy
of King Affonso Henriquez.

In the meantime, he had been careful to apportion
out the conquered land among the more worthy of
his captains, and to endow the powerful Orders of
militant and other monks, who had at all times either

fought with him in the van of the Peninsular Crusade, or, in the case of the non-militant Orders, assisted in the colonisation of the land. One such endowment has survived almost to our own days—a monument of these rude times and the wisdom of the King's dispositions. The broad strip of deserted frontier which has already been described as lying between Christian and Moorish territory, was now available for occupation; but the tenure of Portuguese power was still insecure, as was presently to be proved, and the district which had so long been a waste was not readily to be repeopled. In its centre, not far from the great Christian stronghold of Leiria, the King now settled a monastery of Bernardine monks, at Alcobaça, which soon became the largest, and perhaps the richest and most important, of the many Cistercian monasteries which the zeal of St. Bernard was helping to spread over the face of western Europe; and the industry and the example of the brothers of this austere Order soon converted the wilderness of western Estremadura into a well-tilled district, whose exceptionally high cultivation, conspicuous to this day in agricultural Portugal, may, I think, be traced to the early lessons of the monks of St. Bernard.

Changes in Spanish and in Moorish affairs began, ten years after the capture of Lisbon, to threaten danger to Portugal. Alonso, the Emperor of Leon and Castile, dying in 1157, Leon passed into the hands of his son Fernando, and Castile into those of Sancho, the first-born, and the two brothers seem to have cast envious eyes upon the territories of King

Affonso Henriquez, and to have meditated some attempt upon Portugal; but Sancho of Castile died before these plans could be carried out. He was succeeded by an infant son. Fernando, the new King of Leon, lost little time in invading his nephew's territories, and civil war began to rage over northern Spain. It was then that King Fernando sought and obtained in marriage Urraca of Portugal, the eldest daughter of King Affonso Henriquez, by Mafalda, his queen. The King of Leon and the Infanta Urraca, then a girl of eleven, were married in 1165, but this alliance did not prevent subsequent rivalry and disunion between Leon and Portugal.

By this time a very powerful enemy was turning his attention in the direction of Portugal. The famous Moorish Emir, Abdu-l-mumen, successor to the founder of the reforming sect of the Almohades, had now conquered the whole of eastern Morocco, and prepared an expedition across the Straits of Gibraltar. The fame of Ibn Errik—the son of Henry —as the Saracens were accustomed to term their great Portuguese adversary, had reached his ears, and alarmed him for the future security of Saracen power in the Peninsula.

He landed, in 1161, with a large army of veteran soldiers, disciplined men, used to victory, full of religious zeal, and in every way of far superior war-like aptitude to any Moorish troops whom the Portuguese had yet encountered. The Emir des-patched 18,000 picked horsemen of this army to Gharb, under a leader who offered battle to the King.

The Portuguese were routed with a cruel loss to their armies, already reduced by a long series of campaigns. Thus was the long career of Portuguese victory checked in the moment of its culminating triumph : but the victory of the Moors, though complete, was by no means decisive. They retired with a rich booty, and the indefatigable King of the Portuguese recommenced his incursions into Moorish territory. He retook and permanently occupied Evora and Beja, the Moorish strongholds of eastern Alemtejo, which in a previous campaign had been taken and abandoned ; and probably it was at this time that he made his memorable expedition towards and across the river Guadiana—a river never yet forded by a Portuguese host—and captured Moura, Serpa, and Alconchel, hill forts on the natural frontier between modern Spain and Portugal, and penetrating into the very heart of the Moslem territory, took the important city of Truxillo by storm.

It was this never-ending activity in daring exploits, and this reiteration of success against great odds, that filled his subjects with admiration and his enemies with terror and respect. Of the King's personal prowess, and of his sagacity in those sudden emergencies where sagacity is most apt to disappear, we have an impartial testimony in the record of a Moorish chronicler.[1]

'This enemy of God,' says the exasperated annalist, 'would set about the taking of strong places in this fashion. Choosing a dark and stormy night, he

---

[1] *Ibn-Sahibi-s-salat:* quoted by Herculano.

would sally forth with only a handful of picked men.
Arrived before the castle he intended to attack, the
King it was in person who would be the first to scale
the walls. When he had reached the parapet, he
would throw himself upon the first sentinel, and
holding a dagger to his breast, compel him to answer
the usual challenge of his fellows without arousing
their suspicions. After this he would wait in the em-
brasure of the battlements till his men had followed;
then suddenly the King would raise his war-cry of
Sanctiago! and the whole party would fall furiously,
sword in hand, upon the garrison.'

It was about the year 1165 that dissension, from
some unrecorded cause, broke out between Affonso
Henriquez and his son-in-law, the King of Leon.
Without inquiring into the circumstances or the history of this quarrel, it is characteristic of the promp-
titude of the King of Portugal, that on the breaking
out of war he lost no time in sending an expedition
into Castile, where the Leonese King had already
provoked the hostility of the inhabitants, and he concentrated his attack upon Ciudad Rodrigo, the very
point which was looked upon by Wellington as the
key of western Spain, and of which King Affonso
clearly perceived the military importance.

On this occasion the King, occupied on the Moorish
borderland, did not accompany the army of the
north; and the Leonese troops, commanded by the
warlike Fernando in person—one of the most able of
the early Spanish princes—broke the Portuguese lines
and completely routed them. The bad news was

carried back, and Affonso Henriquez hastened from
his southern frontier with a small body of veteran
troops, rallied his people, and, with more than his accustomed audacity and success, carried the war into
the very midst of the territories of the victorious
Spaniards. Having forced a great part of the important province of Galicia to submit to him, he came
south, and laid siege to Badajos on the Guadjana—a
Moorish city, owing some undefined vassalage to the
King of Leon—desirous, no doubt, to add this strong
city to the line of frontier posts he had already won.

The Portuguese took the city, but the Moorish garrison escaped into the citadel, and before the King could
reduce it, he found himself besieged and hard pressed
by a large army of Leonese under King Fernando.
The garrison made a sally, while the Leonese forced
the walls, and the Portuguese were assailed in the
streets of Badajos by their Moorish and their Leonese
enemies. They were overborne. The streets of
Moorish cities are narrow and tortuous, and, as is
always the case in street fighting, the slaughter was
great. The Portuguese were outnumbered, and were
probably already beginning to give way, when the
King, in the mêlée, was dashed by his horse against
the jamb of a gateway. His thigh was broken, and he
fell senseless to the ground. His followers, losing
their leader, were wholly overmastered, and Affonso
Henriquez found himself a prisoner in the hands of
the Leonese King.

Those who find an interest in tracing the conca-
tenation of historical events from physical rather than

from moral causes, may entertain themselves with
conjectures as to the possible alteration of all Peninsular history had King Fernando chosen to exercise
to the full his rights of victor over his royal captive.
Fortunately, the King of Leon was a generous as well
as an enlightened prince—generous and enlightened,
according to contemporary record, beyond precedent
or example in those times.

It is not unlikely that in an age of chivalry the
young Spanish King may have been moved to some
sentiment of actual enthusiasm towards the man
whose heroic exploits were already the theme of the
wandering troubadour in every Christian Court in
western Europe. It is even more probable that he
feared also to hinder of his freedom the Christian
champion who was in himself the strongest bulwark
of the Church and of the independence of the Hispano-
Gothic races, and this, too, at a juncture the most
critical, when the Moslem power was day by day re-
newing its ancient strength in the Peninsula. Be the
reason what it may, King Fernando released his
prisoner, requiring of him only the restitution of his
recent Galician conquests.

A fresh cloud was now gathering on the
Portuguese horizon. Yusuf had succeeded to Abdu-
l-mumen as Emir of Morocco, and the new prince,
after consolidating his own government, sent an army
into the Peninsula to check the growing power of
Affonso Henriquez; but the general, on reaching the
Peninsula, learnt the news of the defeat of the greatest
enemy of his race at Badajos. He withdrew his

troops, contenting himself, for a time, with watching
the Portuguese frontier, and with a desultory warfare
of raids and forays. The reverse which King Affonso
Henriquez had met with at Badajos, his tedious recovery from his wound, his increasing age, and the
presence of strong and disciplined forces of African
Moors, were circumstances which were beginning to
diminish the terror he had hitherto inspired in the
eyes of the Moslems; and it was these reasons,
probably, which induced the Emir to order, and
perhaps to accompany, a fresh expedition into the
heart of Portugal. The danger was imminent, not to
Portugal only but to Christian Spain, and King
Fernando of Leon, unasked, marched his troops to the
defence of the common cause of Christianity. Yusuf
retreated from the combined Leonese and Portuguese
armies, and the peril for the time passed away.

The few following years passed more quietly.
The King, fatigued by the unceasing toils of a
soldier's life, his energy diminished by age, his body
enfeebled by many grievous wounds, felt himself to be
no longer fit for war. He deputed to his son Sancho,
who inherited no small portion of his father's warlike
aptitude, the task of carrying on the usual yearly war
of raids and forays across the Saracen frontier, while
he devoted himself to the task of reforming the wild
society which had grown up during a period of incessant warfare. He granted charters to cities and
to communes, rectified boundaries, dispensed justice,
and did all that a ruler can do to settle his country
and to strengthen the reign of law and order.

It was in 1179, in the sixty-ninth year of the
King's life, that the storm, which had long been
threatening, burst on the Christians of Portugal.
The power of the Almohades was now at its zenith,
under the great Emir Yusuf, and that prince determined to make an effort with the whole of his dis-
posable forces to restore the integrity of his Portuguese province, to retake the many castles fallen into
Christian hands, and more especially to reoccupy the
great frontier fortress of Santarem, and Lisbon, the
ancient centre of Moorish commerce and government.
Yacub, his son, was accordingly despatched to
Portugal, and war with the Christians was carried on
with varying success for three years.

In 1184, Yusuf himself invaded the Peninsula
with an army more numerous, probably, and
certainly better disciplined, than had crossed the
Straits of Gibraltar since his namesake, the famous
Almoravidian Emir, had brought over the troops
which had routed the Christians in the decisive battle
of Zalaca. Yusuf marched from Gibraltar, making
towards Santarem, and was joined on the way
through Andalusia by strong battalions of Almohadian soldiery. The Emir's troops crossed the
Tagus, and settling down in countless multitudes in
the rich plain which surrounds Santarem, encom-
passed and beleaguered that place.

Sancho, the Infante, commanded a powerful
garrison within the enceinte of Santarem, and fought
with at first some success against his numerous
enemies; but he was overwhelmed by numbers, and

the disciplined Almohadian troops left none of the
arts of siege untried to hasten the surrender of the
fortress. The besieged already counted the duration
of their further resistance by hours.

The newly acquired independence of the Portuguese nation seemed to be at last hanging in the
very balance, when, from the towers of Santarem,
the hard-pressed garrison perceived a numerous
troop of rapidly approaching cavalry. Presently
they distinguished the pennons and banners of
Christian knights, and as the troop came nearer,
they recognised the well-known form of the old King
himself, riding at the head of his knights. He had
come by forced marches to the succour of his son
from the extreme north of Portugal. The gates of
the city were thrown open, the garrison sallied forth,
and joining the King's men, they fell together upon
the vast host of the Saracens. The besiegers, panic-
struck at the sudden apparition of the terrible King
of Portugal, the triumphant shouting of the garrison,
and the sudden combined assault, were put to flight ;
the Emir himself was slain, and his armies driven
over the Tagus, and forced to a disastrous rout
across the Moorish frontier ; and thus, by what
seemed a real miracle in contemporary eyes, was
Portugal freed in a day from the greatest peril
with which it had ever been threatened.[1]

[1] Herculano, with, as it seems to me, an excess of his habitual
caution, inclines to follow the scanty Arabic Chronicles in his
account of the King's victory at Santarem. It is perhaps hardly
necessary to mention a fact which forces itself painfully upon the
attention of all students of these early periods of Peninsular

This was the last and crowning victory of Affonso Henriquez. In the same year he died, worn out by age, and his death perhaps hastened by this last great exploit. 'This prince,' says the Chronicle of the Goths, ' was a great lover of his people and a devout Christian; he defended all Portugal with his sword , he acquired a kingdom, and he extended the confines of Christendom from the river Mondego on one side as far as to the Guadalquivir, which flows by the walls of Seville, and on the other side to the Mediterranean Sea and the shores of the great ocean.'

These are the words, rising to a pitch of unaccustomed enthusiasm, of an almost contemporary annalist ; but we, of a later age, who know the long vicissitudes of Portuguese history, can perceive that

history: namely, the frequent difficulty of reconciling the statements of Christian and of Moslem chroniclers. That the Emir Yusuf invaded Portugal in 1184, that he laid siege to Santarem, that the siege was raised by the Portuguese, that the Moors were driven across the Tagus and the Emir was killed, are all incontestable facts. The Arab chroniclers speak of the previous despatch of a portion of the invading host southward, of a surprise and a panic in the Moorish camp. It appears to me that their account of these events is an attempt to make as little as possible of the great Christian triumph at Santarem. I give the narrative in my text with as much assurance as a man can feel who draws from the scanty and contradictory records of such distant times, and I consider that my version has sufficient voucher, for reasons which I have not space to enter into. I take this opportunity of saying that although I have consulted all accessible original authorities, and written no descriptive line of city, battlefield, river, or mountain-range, but after actual presence on the spot, I owe no light obligation to Senhor Herculano, whose enlightened and learned labours, and whose fine sequacious narrative of the reigns of the early Portuguese monarchs, place him in the very first rank of modern historians.

he accomplished for his country far more than this. He did what it is better to do for a people than to bestow upon them any extension of territory. He taught them the strength of the coherent loyalty of a whole nation; he showed them how their independence was possible, in despite of the smallness of their numbers, of their poverty, and of their ignorance of the arts of war. He showed them the value of constitutional freedom; he taught them how the hardest of all political problems may be solved, how independence can be preserved, and freedom not compromised; and he kindled a fire of patriotism and of loyalty in the nation which has never been extinguished through long periods of national reverses and depression.

These lessons have not been wasted on the Portuguese. If the nation lost its liberties during one short period, it has never lost the sense of what those liberties were worth; and Portugal presents at this day the unique spectacle of a nation of Southern race which can safely be trusted with a political liberty, free from the tyranny of rulers on the one hand, and from the dictation of the populace on the other.

The King died at Coimbra, which, once on the Moorish frontier, had become by his conquests the central city of the kingdom. They carried his body for burial to the conventual church of Santa Cruz, in that city. More than three centuries afterwards, the prosperous and peaceful King Emmanuel thought to honour his remains by building a gorgeous church in the flamboyant style of architecture on the site of the ancient building.

The body of the great founder of the Portuguese monarchy was disinterred, clad in the crimson mantle of the Military Order of Aviz, which he had instituted. The corpse was enthroned, crowned, and done homage to as a living sovereign and saint by King Emmanuel and all his nobility. Then was he re-interred under a splendid mausoleum in the newly finished building. The body of Affonso Henriquez lies there to this day. Other tombs of kings, prelates, and nobles, adorn the chapels and chancels of this magnificent church. It is a desecration. No tawdry architecture should surround the grave, and no meaner dust should mingle with that of this mighty Warrior King.

CHAPEL NEAR GUIMARAENS, WHERE AFFONSO HENRIQUEZ IS SAID TO HAVE BEEN CHRISTENED.

CHAPTER III.

THE POETRY OF THE PORTUGUESE RENAISSANCE.

THE Portuguese subjects of King Affonso Henriquez spoke a language which may be termed pure Portuguese in the same sense that the language into which our King Ælfred translated the works of Bæda and of Orosius is sometimes called pure English. The Portuguese written in the reign of King Affonso Henriquez is nevertheless hardly more intelligible to a modern Portuguese than the king's English of Ælfred's time is to Englishmen of the present day.

As our own language is the direct outcome of the historical events which made us Englishmen, so also the Portuguese kingdom and language both had their birth in the same era. In other words, the dialect of the Portuguese portion of the Peninsula began to detach itself more entirely from the other Teutono-Latin forms of speech around it, at the period when, as I have already mentioned, the King of Leon and Castile conferred upon Count Henry of Burgundy the governorship of Northern Portugal. The language spoken in the dominions of Count Henry was, it is nearly certain, identical with, or at least similar to,

that spoken in Galicia.   Whether the Galician tongue
crossed the Minho with the invading arms of Count
Henry's suzerain, or whether it already prevailed in
the district south of that river, is not now very easy
to determine.   Certain it is that, at this period, the
Galician was, of all the dialects which the corrupted
forms of the Latin was assuming in the Peninsula,
the most cultivated and the most perfect.   As the
Portuguese nation became more isolated from its
neighbours, the language would acquire a character
of its own in its progress towards full development ;
and the influence of a Burgundian ruler and his
Burgundian courtiers, soldiers, and adherents, would,
no doubt, add certain elements of refinement and
variety to the language of his subjects.   The province
of the Minho, the most northern of Portugal, was, at
the outset of the kingdom, at once the seat of government and the cradle of the language; and we may
presume that, as the districts to the south were
successively wrested from the Moors, the original
Galician or quasi-Galician dialect of the Minhotes,
would advance southwards with the arms of the
Christians, and finally become the language of the
whole of Portugal.

At this stage of Portuguese history men's minds
would seem to have been too much engrossed with
the great continuous war which the nation was
waging with the Moors, and with the Leonese and
Castilians, to be able to give much attention to any
sort of poetry, except short lyrical pieces touching
upon war or love.   Hardly any others have come

down to us. There is no great early Portuguese
epic, like the 'Cid';[1] though the struggle with the
infidels was as fierce, and the triumph of the Christians as great, in Portugal as in Spain. In all pro-
bability the poetry of the country was in the hands
of the wandering troubadours from Provence, and
the native bards would not have cared to be heard
in the presence of such masters of song as these. It
is noticeable that the earlier remains we have of
native verse are mostly sacred poetry—precisely
such a class of effusion as the professional minstrels
would be the least apt to produce. It is quite certain,
however, that neither poets nor poetry were despised
at this early period, either in Portugal or the neighbouring kingdom ; and if no other record of their
good repute existed, proof might be found in the fact
that, of all the Portuguese poets whose name or fame
has come down to us, in the thirteenth and fourteenth
centuries all were courtiers, knights of high birth,
princes of the blood, or kings.

Among a warlike people like the Portuguese,
called upon at this period continually to maintain
their existence by arms, we may imagine that the
Court and the camp were the centres of such literary

---

[1] Some fragments of a rhymed chronicle relating to the Moorish wars have indeed come down to us. It is doubtfully ascribed
to the earliest period of Portuguese history. It has no poetical
merit whatever, nor any claim to notice beyond its antiquity. The
Portuguese fragment—we have only a few stanzas left—is certainly
of much earlier date than the Cid ballads, as to which magnificent
epic nothing is more certain than that it is the work of a writer
who lived long after the events he celebrates.

activity as existed. The earliest remains we have of
the language are fragments of the poets Herminguez
and Egaz Moniz, who are generally held to have
written in the reign of King Affonso Henriquez.
These verses are, it is true, scarcely recognisable as
Portuguese: they are uncouth and rugged to a most
singular degree, and yet they are ascribed to two
courtiers, who presumably wrote and spoke the language in its fullest purity.

During the generations which intervene between
this period and the birth of Sá de Miranda, the great
poet who takes the place that Chaucer holds with us,
all such Portuguese poetry as existed was thoroughly
imbued with the spirit of Provençal verse. The troubadours and the jongleurs, the composers and the
singers of Provençal song, found, as we know, congenial audiences at the northern Courts of the
Peninsula. The Catalan, the Castilian, and the
Galician, or Portuguese, were so like their own
tongue that these minstrels would be understood
almost as well where these languages were current as
at Avignon or Toulouse. As the Portuguese gradually
extended their kingdom, and thus isolated themselves
more and more from their neighbours, as the nation
grew in strength and importance, and, perhaps, as the
native taste began to rise superior to the monotonous
frivolity of Provençal minstrelsy, so the language
began to assume the characteristics of modern Portuguese. Cristovão Falcão, and the more famous
Bernardim Ribeyro, are the first native poets who
attained any kind of lasting celebrity in Portugal.

Both poets wrote in the generation preceding that in which the Sá de Miranda lived and flourished. The language was now true modern Portuguese ; but while their eclogues and lyrics have some national characteristics of earnestness and truth of feeling, the verses of these writers are still redolent of the tedious conceits and affectations of Provençal poetry, and yet have little of the flow, melody, and artistic finish of the best troubadour lyrics.

In noting the changes which; throughout the Peninsula, were transforming the narrow spirit of Provençal verse into the higher and better poetry which prevailed during the sixteenth century, the unquestionably great influence of the Moors must not be overlooked. It has been over hastily concluded by some native chroniclers and historians that the relations between the conquered and the conquerors —who were, during so many centuries, masters of nearly the whole Peninsula—were entirely hostile and antagonistic. The rule of the Saracens was, however, as is now well established, on the whole tolerant ; and an immense Christian population, the Mozarabs, came strongly under their influence, and adopted not only the Arab dress, the Arab language, the domestic habits, the arts and intellectual culture of their masters, but in some cases carried imitation so far as to practise the most characteristic rite of the Moslems.

It was impossible but that the high literary culture of the Saracens, so intimately brought to bear on a less cultivated people, should have a strong influence on their poetry. It most certainly did have

F

its effect; but, on the other hand, it must be recol-
lected that the ultimate deliverers of Peninsular soil
from Moorish occupation were men who, in the
retreats and fastnesses of the northern parts of their
country—from whence they issued for its re-conquest
—had been, least of any of their countrymen, subject to
Saracenic influences ; and that it was chiefly, as I have
already shown, among the camps and in the various
Courts of the Portuguese and Spanish conquerors that
the national poetry was produced and fostered.

The Castilians had, in the fifteenth century,
while preserving much of the Provençal spirit in
their poetry, incorporated with it a certain national
strength and gravity ; and their compositions are far in
advance of those of their Portuguese contemporaries.
Though Portugal began her literary career earlier
than Castile, and her poets undoubtedly wrote much
more. I have found absolutely nothing in the poetry
of the smaller kingdom during the whole of this century to compare with the beautiful *coplas* of José
Manrique, or even the verses of Juan de Mena or
the Marquis de Santillana.

In the change that came over Peninsular literature in the early part of the sixteenth century, Portugal took as great a part as even Castile. The final
expulsion of the Moors in the reign of Ferdinand and
Isabella gave leisure for the cultivation of new forms
of poetry ; and the subsequent accession of a German
prince to the throne, and the greater intercourse,
during the reign of Charles V., between the Peninsula
and the various nations of Europe, led, among other

reforms and innovations, to the introduction of the
more artistic taste and handling of the Italians in
literature. Boscan and Garcilaso de la Vega, the
chief originators and assertors of the new style,
wrote sonnets in the manner of Petrarch and eclogues
in that of Sannazaro, in which Italian elegance and
Castilian vigour are blended with a success which has
never been surpassed. These men were the contemporaries of the Portuguese Sá de Miranda ; and
this great genius, besides being the father of all that
was good in the poetry of his native land, influenced
and reformed the literature of the Spaniards hardly
less than the two Castilian poets I have just named.

It is generally the first few steps from the rude
popular ballad or doggrel satire towards the refinements of cultivated or, so to say, literary poetry, that
decide the poetic future of a young nation. Then
only is the language thoroughly plastic, and it is well
for that nation if it be moulded by the hand of a man
of genius. Poets later on may have greater skill
with the instrument, but it is the first great poet alone
who has made it what it is and shaped the very stops
which he touches. I think I am right in saying that
the transition from barbarism to refinement is always
more or less sudden and more or less complete. It
was remarkably so in the case of Portugal.

The poet Miranda seems to have been born at an
hour propitious to Portuguese literature. Towards
the end of the fifteenth century the Portuguese
language had grown into some degree of maturity
and copiousness. The fame, power, and wealth of

the nation were at their zenith, and men's desire had
been awakened for something beyond the rhymed
chronicles and the simple lyrics of their fathers. Sá
de Miranda was, by training and native power, the
very man to stamp his own genius on the poetry of
his country. The son of a country gentleman of
good family, he became a student and professor of
jurisprudence, and attained to high legal learning.
He visited most of the Courts and cities of southern
Europe, and, returning to his native country, became
a courtier: but after some trial of this existence he
retired into the country, where he passed the re-
mainder of his life.

Almost all that is known of the history of Miranda
is contained in an anonymous memoir, prefixed to an
edition of his works published in 1614, and which
there is reason to believe was written, thirty or forty
years after the poet's death, by a nobleman who
married Miranda's granddaughter. This quaintly
written memoir gives interesting particulars of
Miranda's habits and way of life, and affords a curious
insight into the life of an educated Portuguese
country gentleman of the sixteenth century.

'Francisco de Sá de Miranda,' says the memoir,
which I translate freely and slightly abridge, 'was
born in Coimbra, in the year of our Lord 1495, the
year in which the King, Don Manuel' (that is,
Emmanuel, the Fortunate, of Portugal), 'took his seat
on the throne. After his first study of the human-
ities, in which he acquired distinction, he applied
himself to the law, less from inclination than to

please King John III., who had then re-established the
University; and at his father's wish he continued this
study, and arrived at great learning, took the degree
of Doctor of Law, and more than once filled the
Professor's chair. Nevertheless, because he knew
the danger that the use of this study may occasion
to the judgment, no sooner was his father dead than
he abandoned the schools and refused the office of
Desembargador (Judge of Appeal), remaining only in
the University that he might apply himself to the
study of philosophy, chiefly that of the Stoics, to
which his character inclined; and because this study
caused him to despise the things of this life, he
desired to travel through the world, in order that
the repose to which he resolved to betake himself
thereafter should never be broken in upon by the
hearing of new things of which he had had no
experience. He therefore went to Italy, after first
seeing all the principal cities of Spain, and after
visiting at his leisure Rome, Venice, Naples, Milan,
and Florence, and the best part of Sicily, he returned
to Portugal, and spent some time in the Court of
King John III., and there, solely by his personal
qualities and by his parts, without any such
advantages as some men—often unworthy ones—
possess, he made himself such a standing that he
became one of the foremost courtiers if not the very
first of the day; and this estimation he was held in by
the King as well as by his own companions, and what
is more to the purpose, by those worthy men who
choose their friends among such as are " more easily

broken than bent " (to quote the poet's own verse), and who despise the esteem of ordinary men, holding it a direct hurt to them only if they are blamed and set at nought by those who detest vice in general.

' However, this good standing of Miranda at Court did not last long. If it had, our poet might in some sort be said to be greater than envy itself, as Quintus Curtius said of Alexander; but envy could not pardon him, which stirred up to his injury a person very powerful at that period, who chose to apply to himself the character of Alexis in Miranda's eclogue; and the poet, not caring to suffer the effects of this wrath, accepted the office of Master or Bailiff of a Commandery of Knights of the Order of Christ, established near Ponte de Lima, retired to a country house in the neighbourhood belonging to him, named Tapada, abandoning the Court and the society of his friends and all his hopes of advancement, and here he remained, enjoying in peace the fruit of his studies and travel. Here also he married Donna Brialonja d'Azevedo, daughter of Francisco Machado, Lord of Lousãa de Crasto d'Arega and of the lands lying between the rivers Homem and Cavado; with which lady he lived many years in great conformity, she nevertheless being of little beauty (exterior beauty) and of so advanced an age, that when he asked her in marriage of her brothers (for her father was dead) they put him off until, they said, he should first have a good sight of the bride; and when she was brought in by her brothers, he said to her,—"Reproach me, dear lady, for this, that I have been so long of asking for you."

'It would appear that as Sá de Miranda lived in a way so abstracted from the world he was quite equal to his scheme of life in this matter, and be sure he did not lack the example of some ancient philosopher to guide him. He esteemed above everything the qualities of this lady, which indeed were incomparable, according to the testimony of men of that place, who even to this day speak of her zeal in the honour of God, in the ease of her husband, in the training up of her children, and in the good and profitable ordering of her household. Insomuch that her husband loved her so dearly that when she died he lost all joy of his life, and shortly afterwards died too, in grief of mind, which if not worthy of a man who professed the Stoic philosophy, yet testifies how greatly he esteemed and loved her whom he had lost.

'Sá de Miranda,' says the biographer, ' was a man of middle height, thick-set in make, of a pale but not sallow complexion, with remarkably white hands; his eyes rather large, of a greyish-blue and with a kindly expression in them, the nose long and aquiline. He was grave in character, of a melancholic humour, but easy and affable in conversation: *a man more sparing of laughter than of speech.* He was fond of wolf hunting, and likewise of using the knightly exercises of the tilting-yard. He played upon the violin, and though not over rich he had in his service several professors of music.'

Such was the man who, at a time when the general corruption which pervaded Portuguese society was pre-

paring the country for the great national catastrophe
which was soon to overtake it, was at once a patriot
and a poet. He used his great gifts for the noblest
purposes, to warn and to teach. He warned his
countrymen against the bigotry of priests, the grasping dishonesty of statesmen, and their own heedless-
ness of the future. His denunciations were too
eloquent to be unheard, but they were unheeded.
Miranda laid the foundations of a noble national
literature—but for him Camoens could not have
written his great epic; yet his greatest praise is that
he preserved his good faith among the faithless, and
that he had the courage to speak the truth when not
to be silent was a danger.

In applying, as I have done, the term 'renaissance' to the revolution which Sá de Miranda was
chiefly instrumental in bringing about in Portuguese
literature, I wish to guard against the acceptance of
that somewhat abused word in any narrow sense.
The renaissance which took place was not a simple
revival of the purer classic forms of antiquity, but a
strengthening and enlarging of the whole scope and
purposes of poetry. It was a moral as well as a
poetical *Aufklärung*, or enlightenment. Under the
new influences, the aims of poetry grew higher, its
sympathies wider, its morality purer; but the actual
form in which poetic thought was cast was by no
means, at least for the time, improved. Indeed, the
verse of the earlier reformers of it will bear no comparison in fluency and sweetness with the poetry
which it displaced. The renaissance was a reaction

against the narrowness of the models which had prevailed since the beginning of Provençal song, an out-
growth of its bonds rather than a continuation of the
same modes of thought recast into better form.

Miranda wrote much in the Castilian tongue. Of
his eight eclogues, six, and those the best, are in that
language. The Castilian was an instrument ready to
his hand, far more polished than the Portuguese; and
Miranda, a man of refined tastes, a scholar, a traveller,
and a courtier, may, in spite of his love of country,
have a little despised his native tongue as a vehicle
for poetic thought. The eclogues, sonnets, and
quintilhas, which he wrote in the language of Castile,
are ranked as highly by Spaniards as any similar
works of Spanish poets. Yet it may almost be
doubted if Miranda did well to neglect the Portuguese
language, which in some respects is admirably fitted
for lyrical expression. In comparison with Spanish,
it may be said of Portuguese that, while it lacks some
of the sonorous vigour of that magnificent language,
it has greatly the advantage over it in modulation,
smoothness, and fluency, from the absence of the
guttural sounds of the Castilian. Compared with
Italian—which neither Portuguese nor any other
language can approach in grace and delicacy—the
Portuguese is certainly less effeminate in sound, and
is also entirely free from those most unpleasing combinations of two or three consonants which it would
seem to be the constant task of Italian poets to weed
from their poems.

Before I proceed to give some specimens of

Miranda's Portuguese poetry, I would premise that, in so far as style and expression are concerned, they are, with some exceptions, signally inferior to his Spanish writings, upon which his fame chiefly rests. Miranda's Portuguese and his Spanish poetry might, indeed, easily be ascribed to two different writers; so clear, fluent, and melodious is the one, and so austere, inharmonious, and often obscure is the other.

Now, it may perhaps be asserted that the qualities of lucidity and harmony are, beyond all others, the very soul of great poetry—that other qualities are subordinate to these—that those subtle, untranslatable harmonies of utterance constitute, when they clothe great ideas, poetry of the highest class; and if it should fail of attaining a high degree of such harmony, by so much does it stop short of being the highest kind of poetry. The best poetry is, it must be admitted, untranslatable in any true sense, and it may perhaps some day come to be asked how far the valuable time and labour of so many of the ablest men among us are profitably expended upon the great and growing number of rhymed translations of the poets of antiquity. I am inclined to think that something far short of perfect acquaintance with a foreign or dead language will enable a reader to appreciate many of the beauties of its literature. There is even, as I believe, in these word-harmonies of which I have spoken, much which forms a language common to all those persons, foreigners or not, who are capable of their perception, just as a symphony of Beethoven is as intelligible to an Englishman as to a German.

These views have led me to give literal and un-rhymed translations of the specimens of Portuguese poetry which I am about to lay before the reader—preserving only such an approximation to the rhythm and metre as could be got without much deviation from literalness, and leaving to the reader the task of gathering, with this slight assistance, the form and spirit of the original from the original itself.

Miranda's Portuguese writings consist of epistles, sonnets, eclogues, and two comedies. Of these, the epistles are perhaps the most important works. They are addressed, some to the King, some to different friends, and one to the poet Ferreira. These epistles are quite original in style and handling, and are, I think, what the Portuguese themselves chiefly admire in the poet's works. Composed in short-versed stanzas of three, four, or five lines each, their form suits and excuses their direct style and their frequent and abrupt transitions. The epistle addressed to the King is the most characteristic, if not the most elegant. It con-sists of eighty-one stanzas of five lines each; and is, therefore, longer than I can afford space to quote in its entirety. Written in easy, flowing verse, the rhyming of so many lines within so short a stanza gives a considerable swing and vigour to the measure used by the poet. The stanza employed is the *quintilha* of five short lines, of which as a rule the first, third, and last rhyme, as also do the second and fourth. The versification is generally metrical, but here and there it has to be read by accent or cadence, without regard to the number of feet.

The epistle begins by a somewhat obsequious address to the King, which contrasts with the exceeding plain speaking of the remainder. Addressing him as King of many Kings, in allusion to the extended conquests of the Portuguese of that time, he hardly dares to ask for the royal attention, since it must be occupied with affairs of state.

> Que em outras partes da Esphera.
> Em outros ceos differentes,
> Que Deus tégora escondera,
> Cada huma de tantas gentes
> Vossos despachos espera.

> Since in so many different regions,
> Under so many other skies,
> Hidden till now by Providence,
> Such a multitude of nations
> Your high commands are waiting for.

To administer justice, if necessary in the most summary manner, is, says the poet, the first duty of a king. Then follows a long argument in favour of monarchy. The poet is careful to exclude tyrants and usurpers, and confines himself to *reys ungidos* —anointed kings—who are to redress the people's grievances, succour the poor, and forcibly put down the wrong. He goes on to say :—

> As vossas vellas que vão
> Dando quasi ao mundo volta
> Raramente encontrarão
> Gente de alguma rey solta.
> Sem cabeça, o corpo he vão.

> The royal ships which sail around
> Almost the circuit of the globe,
> Will seldom anywhere encounter
> Society without a king.
> Without a head, a nation dies.

Having established the necessity of some sort of mild paternal despotism, by a series of arguments and illustrations drawn from nature and from history, and of a sort which bear a striking resemblance to the reasoning in Lord Brookes' poetical 'Treatise of Monarchie,' written some fifty years afterwards, he proceeds to the chief object of his epistle—to warn the King and his countrymen against the intrigues of courtiers. The experience of a former courtier is obvious in the force and bitterness with which he inveighs on this topic.

> Velem-se com tudo os reys
> Dos rostos falsos, e manhas,
> Com que lhes fazem das leys
> Fracas teas das aranhas.

> Let kings be ever on their guard
> Of false men and of their false wiles,
> With which their wont is our just laws
> To sweep aside, like spiders' webs.

Such men, he says, only value virtue or justice by what it will fetch in the market.

> Quem graça ante el rey alcança
> E hi falla o que não deve
> (Mal grande de má privança)
> Peçonha na fonte lança,
> De que toda a terra bebe.

> The men who win the royal favour
> By flattery and unworthy arts
> (Ill consequence of friendship base)
> Throw poison in the fountain head,
> Envenom what the people drink.

Then comes a stanza which has been quoted perhaps as often as any passage in Portuguese poetry :—

> Homem d'um só parecer,
> D'um só rosto, d'uma só fé,
> D'antes quebrar que torcer,
> Elle tudo pode ser,
> Mas de Corte homem **não he.**

> **The man** of single countenance,
> Of frank address and simple faith,
> Readier to be broke than bended,
> May be anything he chooses,
> **But the Court he should eschew.**

These lines and those in the succeeding stanza have been **applied, and** probably with **reason, to the** character of Miranda himself :—

> **Gracejar ouço** de **cá**
> De quem vae inteiro, e são,
> **Nem se** contrafaz mais lá,
> ' **Como** este vem aldeão,
> Que cortezão tornará ! '

> Estas publicas santidades,
> Estes rostos transportados,
> Não em ermos, mas cidades,
> **Para Deos são** vaydades,
> **Para nós** vão rebuçados.

> I seem to hear the sneering speech
> At one who will not counterfeit,
> But shows himself as God has made,
> ' Here is a rustic speech and manner,
> See what a courtier **he** will make ! '

> This sanctity assumed in public,
> This sadness of feigned piety,
> Is found in Courts, not hermitages.
> God can assess such counterfeits ;
> We must respect the pious mask.

He wishes to put the King on his guard against these intriguers, their cunning, and their greed.

> Por minas trazem suas azes,
> Encubertos seus assanhos,
> Falsas guerras, falsas pazes,
> De fora são mansos anhos,
> De dentro, lobos robazes.

> Covered ways hide their attacks,
> Hid is their malice and their rage.
> False enemies and falser friends,
> Lambs are they in outward bearing,
> Ravening wolves they are within.

He shows how difficult the duplicity of such villains makes it to trace malicious actions to their actual perpetrators.

He cites the law of trial by battle, prevailing among the Lombards, as a wholesome resource; and recounts the history of the struggle between the great King Denis of Portugal and his rebellious son, in proof of the necessity of strong measures in such times as those in which he was writing, which he describes as—

> N'este tempo, quem mal cae
> Mal jaz, e dizem que á luz
> Por tempo a verdade sae !
> Entretanto poem na cruz
> O justo ; o ladrão se vae.

> A time when, if a man once falls,
> He falls for good ; and yet they say
> That truth in time shall see the light !
> But in our day they crucify
> The good man, while the thief escapes.

A patriotic Portuguese of those times (indeed, of any times) must ever have had before his eyes the peril to his country of ambitious designs on the part of Spain The bloody wars with that country, of the earlier years of the monarchy, had ended long enough before to incline the Portuguese to forget the danger of neighbourhood to so powerful a kingdom. The growing conformity in manners, and the identity of religion between the two peoples, might further serve to lull any latent suspicion of aggressive designs on the part of Spain. At this time Spanish nobles frequented the Court of Portugal, and probably shared more of the royal favour than was generally thought desirable. The bold denunciation of Spain by the poet must have come with peculiar force from a man who had travelled much, and who had enjoyed opportunities of closely observing the workings of his own, as well as of foreign governments. The following is sufficiently outspoken of a nation then ruled over by so warlike and aggressive a prince as Charles V. : —

Geralmente he presumptuosa
Espanha, e d'isso se preza,
Gente ousada e bellicosa
Culpãona de cubiçosa.
Tudo sabe vossa Alteza.

Spain is the land of arrogance,
Whose sons are proud, and vaunt their pride.
A daring nation, prone to war,
And blamed for their cupidity.
Your Majesty best knows their fame.

He accuses them of a grasping covetousness which

leads them to live at the expense of weaker men, and *dos suores alheos*, by others' toil.

> Que eu vejo nos povoados
> Muitos dos salteadores,
> Com nome, e rosto d'honrados.
> Vão quentes, vão forrados
> De pelles de lavradores!

> How many in our towns I see
> Of these brigands bear about
> The name and look of honest men.
> Brigands! who go warmly clad
> In the skins of simple men!

After some stanzas directed against profligate and mercenary priests, the poet bids the King remember the vital necessity of perfect impartiality in one who, like himself, is, but for the adjustments of the constitution, almost a despot; and the more so, that he rests his power on the love and the loyalty of his subjects, unlike the King of France, who has his Scotch body-guard, or the Pope, who trusts to Swiss defenders.

> Aqui nam vemos soldados,
> Aqui nam soa atambor.
> Outros reys os seus estados
> Guardão de armas rodeados,
> Vós rodeado de amor.

> Here we have no mercenaries,
> No loyalty by sound of drum.
> Other kings may guard their kingdoms,
> With sword and spear surround the throne;
> *Your* sole defence, your people's love.

He brings the epistle to a conclusion by reminding the King of his great ancestor, who expressed his ideas of government by the noble motto, *Polla ley e polla grey*—' By law and by my people's will.'

Such compositions as this, in spite of their wonderful vigour of expression and general eloquence, may seem dull enough to us of a modern age; and it is, indeed, difficult to bring ourselves, at the present day, to appreciate their importance and their influence on the bygone generations for whom they were written. Popular interest in, and sympathy with, current political movements, have with ourselves for so long a time found such early and constant expression in journals, in reviews, and in the multiplied reports of all kinds of public speeches and debates, that we do not at present require such isolated utterances as this. But when there was no newspaper to relate, to report, or to criticise; when news came tardily and scantily; when the most eloquent address must have died in the memory of its few hearers almost as soon as the speaker's voice was silent, the effect of such written eloquence as this of Miranda's must have been extraordinarily great.

To Miranda's sonnets I am inclined to attach considerable importance. True it is that they are formed on the model left by Petrarch, that they signally lack many of the merits of the Italian sonneteer, and that they too frequently reflect the fine-drawn, scholastic subtlety with which it was then the fashion for a poet to address his friend, his mistress, or his patron. Yet, notwithstanding this, and obscure and tortuous as is the style of most of them, they bear upon them that peculiar exquisiteness of thought and expression for which we have no exact name, but which the Greeks would have called *irony*. The melancholy of unrequited love is the theme of the greater number of Miranda's sonnets; yet the cruelty of the ladies of those days is, perhaps, hardly established by the fact that they were not won by pleadings which have in them a great deal more of the pedantic affectation of a schoolman than the genuine ardour of a lover.

I select for quotation the following two from among Miranda's Portuguese sonnets, as much from their comparative simplicity as their excellence, and from the difficulty of rendering into intelligible English the subtle turns of thought in the more characteristic sonnets. I do not profess to translate literally.

> O sol he grande, caem com a calma as aves,
> Do tempo em tal sazão que soe ser fria:
> Esta agua que d'alto cae accordarmehia
> Do sono não mas de cuidados graves.
> O cousas todas vãs, todas mudaveis,
> Qual he o coração que em vós confia?
> Passando hum dia vae, passa outro dia,
> Incertos todos mais que ao vento as naves.
> Eu vi já por aqui sombras e flores,
> Vi aguas e vi fontes, vi verdura,
> As aves vi cantar todas d'amores:
> Mudo e seco he já tudo e de mistura
> Tambem fazendomi eu fuy d'outras cores
> E tudo o mais renova, isto he sem cura.

> The sun beats fiercely, and the panting birds,
> Exhausted with unwonted heat, fall down;
> Rain from the parchéd skies above would break
> Not on my sleep, but on my heavy cares.
> O vanity of earthly things which change,
> Where is the soul who dares to trust to you?
> One day the thing we love is here, the next
> 'Tis gone, like wind leaving the idle sail.

Here, in this spot, lately was pleasant shade,
Flowers springing through green turf, the cooling gush
Of waters and the cheerful song of birds:
Now all is changed, withered and dry and bare.
Most changed of all am I, for while all this
Renewal has, I must endure, thus changed.

A morte de sua mulher.

Aquelle espirito já tambem pagado
Como elle merecia, claro e puro
Deixou de boa vontade o valle escuro
De tudo o que cá vio como anojado.
Aquelle sprito que do mar irado
D'esta vida mortal posto em seguro
Da gloria que lá tem de herdade e juro,
Cá nos deixou o caminho abalisado,
Alma aqui vinda nesta nossa idade
De ferro, que tornaste a antiga d'ouro.
Em quanto cá regeste e humanidade
Em chegando ajuntaste tal thesouro
Que para sempre dura, ah vaydade!
Ricas areas d'este Tejo e Douro.

The death of his wife.

Her spirit now has found its true reward,
That spirit bright and pure, impatient
To leave the shadowy vale and reach its home—
Its home congenial in the realms above,

     .   .   .   .   .   .

.   .   .   .

And now, at last arrived in harbour safe,
Passing the restless, stormy sea of life,
Has marked the course on which we, too, should sail.
Departed soul! Thy sweetest influence
Did change this age of ours—an age of iron—
To one of gold, and in our memories leave
A treasure to all time. Alas! how drear,
Tagus! thy sands, and golden Douro's banks.

The Portuguese eclogues of Miranda are but two

in number, while of his Spanish pastorals there are
four, every one of which is incomparably superior in
all the characteristic excellences of this kind of poetry
to those written in Portuguese.

Of all the writings of Miranda, his eclogues will,
probably, seem the least interesting to a modern
reader. The interest which such poems once aroused
must have been, to a great extent, owing to their
more or less successful reproduction of classical
models. It seems, indeed, extraordinary enough that
such artificial productions could have afforded
pleasure even in the lack of other literature. They
have neither incident, nor dramatic dialogue, nor
plot. The interminable conversations between shepherds and shepherdesses have little of the true flavour
of pastoral life about them, and either fatigue us by
their platitude or offend us by their affectation. The
allusions to the Court life and intrigues of the day
are, no doubt, more frequent than we can now
detect, and this source of interest is, therefore, wanting for modern readers. The model followed by
Portuguese bucolic writers is rather the artificial
and courtly pastoral of Virgil than the more natural
one of Theocritus; but so far as a foreigner may
presume to judge, the renaissance eclogue, whether
it be Portuguese, Spanish, or Italian, is signally wanting in the Virgilian ease and beauty of versification.
The bucolic verse of Miranda, however, if its general
tenor do not rise much above the level of the pastoral
writing of his age, possesses a vast superiority to it in
the poet's descriptions and love of natural scenes and

rustic life. The mountains, the streams, the fields,
and, above all, the animals, are introduced with a
singular naturalness and obvious knowledge of
country ways which are very delightful; and it is in
this chiefly, I suspect, that reside such vitality and
value as eclogue writing possesses; not in the tedious
commonplaces about peace and virtue put in the
mouths of impossible shepherds, nor in frigid second-
hand classicisms, but in the pleasant associations
which such poems call up of the fresh forest breeze,
the cool fountains, green turf and leafage, and the
peaceful country teams and flocks.

To an ordinary educated Englishman, whose
literature is less rich in, and whose taste is less
inclined to the artificial pastoral poem of the
classical types than those of almost any other European nation, the eclogue may well seem to be the
most dreary of all forms of human composition.
Whether it be owing to the early bent of the Portuguese towards this form of literature, or that it is
congenial to the national taste, it has happened that
Portuguese poetry has developed itself strongly in the
direction of the pastoral idyl. Far as the Spaniards
have carried excellence in this species of writing,
they are inferior to the Portuguese, who deserve to
rank with the Italians. Many circumstances probably
have concurred to foster this love of pastoral poetry
in Portugal, and chief among them the extreme
beauty of its country scenery, the serenity of its climate, the temperament of its people, the national
love of home and homely scenes, and, perhaps as

much as anything, the variety and richness of the language and its great resemblance to the classic tongue in which some of the best models of bucolic poetry are to be found. The farm life of Portugal is also infinitely more susceptible of poetic treatment than that of northern countries, whose soil and climate are less kindly, and whose agriculture is more advanced.

The world has come to regard, and not altogether without reason, the pastoral existence as depicted by Virgil and Theocritus as the most ideal form of rustic life; and this life is, in truth, not very different from that followed by husbandmen in Portugal at the present day. It is, indeed, almost inconceivable that fourteen centuries should have done so little to modify, among an ingenious people, the lessons taught them by their first masters in agriculture. The farm husbandry practised in Portugal to this day is virtually that which the Roman colonists left in the country, and such as is described in the rules and precepts of Columella. The Portuguese ploughman still works his fields with a plough which is identical in shape with the instrument of which Virgil has left a precise description in his eclogues. The farmer carries his produce in exactly such an ox-cart as we find drawn on Roman bas-reliefs and vases. The Portuguese shepherd in the mountains still lives among his flock by day, and lies down to sleep in their midst at night. The pastoral pipe of antiquity has been replaced by the guitar, but the shepherds still challenge each other to compete in alternate extempore verse *ao desafio*, in rivalry one with the other.

A native of Portugal enjoys, in consequence of his familiarity with the actual practice of the old classic husbandry, a signal advantage over natives of northern countries, in reading the pastorals of the ancient authors. Many allusions and illustrations will seem clear and natural to the one, which to the other are strained and obscure. The amœbœan song of shepherds and ploughboys—the very groundwork of the bucolic poem—and which a Portuguese hears daily on every hill-side, is to a foreigner at first sound an almost absurd stretch of conventionality. To give a particular instance of such necessary familiarity, many an English schoolboy has no doubt been puzzled to render the full meaning of Virgil's line, ' *Aspice, aratra jugo referunt suspensa juvenci*;' which the dullest Portuguese lad can translate at once, in the secondary or poetical sense, to mean that it was nightfall, when the ploughmen sling the plough between the oxen and carry it home. Such instances could easily be multiplied.

I have not space to quote at any length from Miranda's eclogues, and short extracts would neither serve to illustrate my opinions nor enable the reader to form any of his own.

Miranda's remaining works are his two comedies. Of these it may at once be said that, while they are excellent imitations of, or rather adaptations from, the Roman comic drama, they show clearly enough that Miranda was not eminently possessed of a strong,

original dramatic genius. Yet, short of this praise,
they are admirable productions. The range of the
poet's powers was so great that it easily compre-
hended what was not exactly in the direct line of his
genius. His plays were probably tasks, rather than
labours of love ; but, as literary efforts, they are full of
evidences of an accomplished, many-sided mind, and
show as wide an acquaintance with men as with
books.

The dialogue of both comedies is spirited, concise, not devoid of *finesse*, and, above all, natural and
racy of common colloquial sayings and proverbs ;
seldom witty, never overwrought in the direction of
farce, but often charged with a fine, extravagant
humour, which has more resemblance to the learned
pleasantry of Jonson than anything to be found in
the works of other Peninsular dramatists, though
Miranda falls far short of the dignity and erudition of
the English playwright.

In the comedies of Miranda the curtain is raised
upon a purely conventional life. It is a stage whereon appear nearly all the established characters of the
old Roman comic drama : the boastful soldier, the
edacious parasite, the scheming and faithful servant,
the tyrannical father, and the windy and purposeless
lover. The plot, the incidents, and the action, all
run along the ancient classical groove. It is the
drama of ancient Rome revived with wonderful skill,
but with as little as possible of the modern spirit. It
is a renaissance drama, entirely lacking the infusion
of the deeper purpose and imaginative wealth of

modern times, which have given force and vitality to
the so-called renaissance movement in painting and
the sister arts. Such a form of drama, capable of
affording mere amusement as it was in its own day,
was obviously neither earnest enough, nor varied
enough, nor true enough, to reach the sympathies of
audiences of a later age, with enlarged interests, a
more trained morality, and a stricter social and civil
polity. This resuscitation of the purely classic
comic drama in modern times was destined to last
but a short time. Men were born, even in Miranda's
lifetime, who were to create the splendid Spanish
comic drama of the seventeenth century, the truest
expression of the social life of the age and country of
its birth ; and when that drama arose, the old classic
style disappeared at once and for ever.

Quotations from either of the poet's plays would
serve little useful purpose. The comedies themselves
are, it must be admitted, rather dull reading ; and
any true perception of their excellences is only to be
got by a comparison with similar imitations of the
comedies of Plautus and Terence, and by clothing the
bare ideas of the author with the speech and gesture
of the actor. Such ' reading between the lines ' is
especially necessary in the conventionally framed
plays of Miranda, abounding as they do in passages
which only the manner and skill of a good actor could
make endurable, and, above all, in soliloquies of a
length which might seem intolerable to the mere
reader, if he did not remember that such monologues
afford extraordinary scope for either tragic or comic

power, and that some of the best acting French and Spanish plays extant are full of them.

The influence of Miranda over his contemporaries was not confined to his writings. A man of easy and accessible conversation, who had seen much of the world as an observer, rather than as an actor in it; a professor at a university which was the centre of the intellectual activity of the kingdom; the most famous author in Portugal, and amongst the foremost poets of the neighbouring nation; he became the leader, and, indeed, the oracle of his contemporaries. He had rescued the national literature almost from barbarism. He had discerned, or, rather, created wealth and beauty of expression in a language the most neglected and despised of all the romance tongues of southern and eastern Europe. He was reverenced and he was imitated by a host of men, some of whom rose at once into prominence.

Of his immediate contemporaries, far the most eminent was Antonio Ferreira, a poet who, himself the friend and imitator of Miranda, has left his mark on the poetic literature of his country almost as plainly as his master.

Ferreira's style is more classical, more correct, more polished, and, to a foreigner, infinitely more easy and intelligible than that of Miranda. Though Ferreira was but a generation the younger, more than a century separates their styles: that of the one, crabbed and antiquated; that of the other, as near to modern Portuguese as the English of Queen Anne's reign is to the English written by Wordsworth or Tennyson.

Of Ferreira's life we know little but that it was
respectable and uneventful.   Born in 1528, he was
thirty-three years younger than Miranda, and, like
him, he studied law, and became a professor in the
University of Coimbra.   Before he had attained his
twenty-ninth year he had written eclogues, sonnets,
epistles, and a comedy.   From Coimbra he migrated
to the Court of King John III., where he was well
received.   He obtained a high judicial appointment
at Lisbon, and shortly afterwards he died of the plague
at the untimely age of forty-one, in the midst of fame
and growing honours.

The great distinction between the two poets resides in this, that while Miranda was half-hearted
in the use of his native language, and wrote better
and more freely in a more cultivated foreign tongue,
Ferreira—*vestigia Graeca ausus deserere*—resolved
from the first to write no single line except in Portuguese.

He did not court any fame that was not won in
the Portuguese field of literature, or that was bestowed
by other than Portuguese voices.   Prefixed to the first
collection of his works is a sonnet in which he says
that all the renown he desires is that of being thought
a patriotic Portuguese, who loved his native land and
his own people :—

> En desta gloria só fico contente,
> Que a minha terra amei, e a minha gente.

This emphatic and amiable patriotism has particularly endeared the memory, and probably not a little

enhanced the influence, of Ferreira with his fellow-countrymen, among whom love of country has always possessed the intensity of a passion.

Ferreira, like Miranda, wrote epistles, but their elegant classicism has nothing in common with the forcible manner of Miranda. They are grave and didactic in their style, the utterances of a scholar who had always shunned the business of the world, rather than of a man who, like Miranda, had lived in it and knew it; of a man more taken up with the elegances of literature than interested in the schemes and passions of his fellow-men. The epistles and the odes of Ferreira are greatly praised and appreciated by his countrymen, and have, I believe, more than all his other writings, earned for him the title of the Portuguese Horace. Both in his odes and in his epistles he is a palpable and avowed imitator of Horace, and it is precisely this departure from originality which makes these productions of comparatively little interest to a foreign student of the language; but their influence, on this very account, upon the literature of his country was great. Ferreira's example has unquestionably contributed to the correction in Portuguese poetic diction of a certain bombastic fullness and Oriental exaggeration, which were characteristics of Peninsular national literature in his own day, and have not even yet entirely disappeared. Assuming that our Northern taste is correct in the matter, he must, by an Englishman, a German, or a Frenchman, be held to have been the greatest reformer and improver of the taste of his countrymen.

It may of course be asked, Is our taste in such matters supremely good? and is it not perhaps as much what it is from the poverty of our imagination as from the soundness of our judgment? Whether it be good or bad, literary taste in Portugal ranges itself on the French and English side in the controversy, and not with the Spaniards. The Portuguese began to be 'regular' and 'correct,' before even the French did, and since Ferreira wrote there has never been such a thing possible as a Portuguese Calderon, Rojas, or Lope da Vega, and a Portuguese Cervantes has never been possible either before or since the time of Ferreira. If Shakespeare had written in Portuguese, many of his lines would have shocked Portuguese audiences, and Marlowe's 'mighty line' and 'fine madness' would have been an utter abomination to any Portuguese of taste.

I wish to make a special point of this distinction between the two literatures. That extravagance and wild incongruity of poetic diction which our Elizabethans caught from the Spaniards, and in which contemporary Englishmen delighted, that quality in literature, which gave pleasure to such critics as Lamb and Hazlitt, has never been countenanced by the Portuguese: it has never ceased to find favour in Spain. This it is which differentiates the two peoples as well as their literatures.

> Climas passé, mudé constellaciones
> Golfos innavegables navegando.

This not very remarkable couplet—the first that comes to my memory as likely to serve—will illustrate

as well as any other passage a certain vital difference
between the Spanish and Portuguese notions of poetry.
The lines come from the 'Araucana' of the Spanish
poet Alonzo de Ercila y Zuniga, an epic of great
length, in which Voltaire, who, I would undertake to
say, never read it, saw an Iliad, and Sismondi, who
probably did get through the poem, not at all more
wisely, a newspaper in rhyme.

Plenty of verses such as these may be found in
the 'Araucana,' and many more as good or better are
dispersed through Spanish poetry. I will defy any
one to match them in Portuguese. There is plenty
of sound reasonableness in Spain, and in the poetry
of Spain, but Spaniards like sometimes to get out of
the groove of reasonableness and sound logic, and
they have often the art of doing it without any sort
of foolishness. The Portuguese have too much of
that moderation of judgment which common-place
people like to ascribe to themselves and to call common sense, to do anything of the kind. To be sure
they like sometimes to 'write fine,' but when they do,
it is in the penny journal style—stilted stuff. There is
none of the fine Spanish flavour in the performance.
The Spaniard is bombastic enough sometimes, but
there is often a magnificence in his very bombast, a
splendid extravagance of humour or of rhetoric.

Even in this rather poor couplet which I have
quoted, and quoted because it has no unusual force,
there is a certain largeness of conception of a kind
which no Portuguese would rise to. *Climas passé*—
I not only changed climates in my voyagings, I passed

them on my road as a wayfarer might milestones. *Mudé con-tellaciones.* What a grand astronomical climax! Nothing but downright hyperbole can take after that, and we get it in *golfos innavegables navegando!* Logic toils after such a poet in vain. The seas were not navigable, you say—then pray, how came you to sail over them? Of course in the answer to be given to such a query lies the whole gist, point, savour, and excellence of much Spanish writing, with the pomp and prodigality of which let no critic too sternly quarrel until he have learned how the members of this syllogism are to be reconciled.

Ferreira's eclogues do not conspicuously rise above the standard of the pastoral writing of his day. They lack the stamp of reality which Miranda has left impressed on his pastoral writings, but in elegance and grace of diction Ferreira attains a high degree of excellence. Many passages of exquisite beauty may be found throughout these productions, but it must be admitted that as literary compositions they are seldom anything but tedious. The amazingly rapid progress of the language in the direction of grace and smoothness may be instanced in the following passage from the first eclogue :—

> Esta fonte ouvio hoje aqui meu pranto :
> E como se o sentisse, parecia
> Qu'ajudava entoar tam triste canto.
> Hora fazia pausa, hora corria
> Com murmurio hora grave, e hora agudo,
> Disseras qu'algum sprito ali avia.

> This fountain heard me, in my verse, complain,
> And, as if sentient too, in unison

Joined with its harmonies in my refrain ;
Now it did pause, and now again run on
With murmurs hoarse at times, now shriller grown,
As if some spirit there did make its moan.

Passing over, from lack of space to quote them, the numerous sonnets of Ferreira—many of them masterpieces of this refined and difficult kind of composition—and the comedies of *Bristo* and *O Cioso*, in which the poet would seem to have feared to move beyond the narrow classic groove in which his predecessor had written his comic dramas, I propose to devote the space at my command to an examination of Ferreira's tragedy of *Castro*—the best and indeed almost the only high-class tragedy in the Portuguese language, and, in my opinion, by far the greatest work of its author.

The wonderful history of Inez de Castro, the Spanish mistress, and perhaps, ultimately, the wedded wife of Prince Pedro, son of Affonso IV. of Portugal, is too deeply engraved on the memory of all Portuguese to permit of a dramatist's adding to or modifying the story.

The jealousy excited among the courtiers by the growing influence of Inez and her friends with the heir to the throne, had induced them to procure the King's consent to her assassination; and King Affonso, counting upon a compliant temper, and a long habit of obedience in the Prince, his son, ordered her death. She was foully murdered in the Convent of Santa Clara, at Coimbra, in the absence of her lover.

The Prince at once took up arms against his

father : he ravaged the rich province of the Minho ;
he laid siege to Oporto, the second city of the empire.
Upon his father's death, two years afterwards, he
revenged himself upon those who had compassed the
murder of the Lady Inez : he is said to have looked
on while the hearts of the actual murderers were
torn from their living bodies. His vengeance
procured him the title of ' The Cruel.' He declared
himself to have been formally married to Inez de
Castro. He caused her body to be disinterred, to
be clad in royal robes, a crown to be placed upon
her head, and homage to be done to her as to a
queen. Her bier was carried at night to the mausoleum which he had prepared for her among the
kings and queens of Portugal, in the great Cistercian
Abbey of Alcobaça. The funeral train travelled
along a road thronged with spectators, each of whom
held aloft a torch ; so that, in the words of an old
chronicler, the body of Inez passed along an avenue
' lined as with all the stars of heaven.'

Such is the impressive story with which the poet
had to deal. He might have made his drama more
picturesque by introducing the whole of the episodes,
but he chose to regard the dramatic unities so far as
to end the action with the death of Inez, and its effect
upon the Infante. The civil war, the solemn declaration of Inez's title, and the strange scene of her royal
and midnight obsequies, are not employed by Ferreira.

The play opens with an address, by Inez de
Castro, to a chorus or band of Coimbra maidens.
She bids them rejoice with her in her good fortune ;

and then, in a dialogue with her attendant, she explains the circumstances of her happiness. The Greek form in which Ferreira chose to cast his tragedy is apparent at the outset. The concise, epigrammatic, sententious utterances of the speakers, in single verses, read almost like a translation from one of the tragedies of Euripides.

> *Ama.* Novos extremos vejo.
> Nas palavras prazer, agoa nos olhos.
> Quem te faz juntamente leda, e triste?
> *Inez.* Triste não póde estar, quem vês alegre.
> *Ama.* Mistura ás vezes a fortuna tudo.
> *Inez.* Riso, prazer, brandura n'alma tenho.
> *Ama.* Lagrimas sinaes são da má fortuna.
> *Inez.* Tambem da boa fortuna companheiras.
> *Ama.* A dor são naturaes.
> *Inez.* E ao prazer doces.
> *Ama.* Que força de prazer t'as traz aos olhos?
> *Inez.* Vejo meu bem seguro, que receava.

> *Attendant.* Two opposites in thee I see,
> Joy in thy speech, and in thine eyes are tears.
> What makes thee thus at once both sad and gay?
> *Inez.* Sad I am not—you see that I am glad.
> *Att.* Fortune, alas! can dash our cup of joy.
> *Inez.* Yet in my soul is nought but gaiety.
> *Att.* Of evil fortune tears give surest sign.
> *Inez.* Companions too, sometimes, of happiness.
> *Att.* To grief more kin.
> *Inez.* And yet in gladness sweet.
> *Att.* What great delight is it that makes thee weep?
> *Inez.* Good fortune safe, which I had feared unsafe.

Inez then proceeds to recount how Prince Pedro had fallen in love with her; how, for state reasons, he had been compelled to marry Constanza, the daughter of the Spanish Duke of Villena; how the Princess had brought over Inez in her train; how, upon the death of his wife, the Prince had now secretly married Inez herself.

There is usually no part of a play more trying to the attention, either of audience or reader, than that which contains such information as is necessary to the understanding of the plot, and which, by a dramatic device, clumsy at the best, one of the characters has to impart to another, who may well enough be supposed to know it all before. Ferreira has, with much art, relieved the tediousness and awkwardness of such a narration by making Inez represent dramatically, in a passage of the greatest beauty, the conversation which had passed between herself and the Prince, when she had foreseen the perils which his alliance with her would bring upon them both. 'My Lord,' says Inez, thus recalling her words :—

> Soam me as crueis vozes d'este povo,
> Vejo del rey a força, e imperio grave
> Armado contra mim, contra a constancia,
> Que em meu amor tégora tens mostrado.
> Não receo, senhor, que a fé tam firme
> Queiras quebrar a quem tua alma deste ;
> Mas receo a fortuna, que mais possa
> Com seu furor, que tu com teu amor brando.

> The cruel voices of the nation
> Sound in my ears. I see your father's power
> Armed against me—against the constant faith
> With which you hold to my true love for you.
> It is not that I fear that you should break
> Your plighted troth to her who has your heart ;
> But fate I fear—fate which can compass more,
> Through wrath and hate, than you with love prevent.

And yet, she goes on to say, if the fates should prove too powerful, she would count it kinder of him

to kill her with his own hand, than to force her to
root out her love from her heart. He assures her
that nothing will change his resolve to marry her.
Still narrating, Inez thus reproduces his words:—

> Não poderá fortuna, não os homens
> Não estrellas, não fados, não planetas
> Apartar-me de ti por arte, ou força.
> Nesta tua mão te ponho firme, e fixa
> Minh'alma ; por Iffante te nomeo,
> Do meu amor senhora, e do alto estado,
> Que me espera, e teu nome me faz doce!

> For neither fortune, nor the power of men,
> The starry influence, nor the fates, shall serve
> By art or force, to tear thee from my arms.
> Here in thy hand I place my heart, and I
> Do name thee wife, princess, queen of my love—
> Queen of the high estate which waits me, which
> Only thy love makes sweet!

I think that no one will deny that these passages
have the true dramatic ring. Ferreira seems to me
to be speaking, in *Castro*, with the natural voice of
human passion. There is none of the over-elabora-
tion, the over-thoughtfulness, and the over-subtlety
with which so many good poets have spoilt their
dramas for the stage. Such a play as *Castro* can
require nothing but good actors to stir an audience,
and one is not surprised to learn that it has achieved
great stage success in its own language and in several
literal foreign versions.

Throughout the tragedy, the Chorus plays a considerable part, but has no influence upon the action
of the piece. I know not whether it was intended
by Ferreira that the chorus songs should be sung,

as in Greece, or that they should simply be recited. The one beginning 'Quando amor nasceu' is a pretty lyric, and well adapted for choric singing ; so is the one 'Antes cego tyranno ;' both recounting, in short rhymed verses, the triumphs of love over gods and kings, with, however, rather commonplace instances and reflections, which would hardly bear serious recitation. On the other hand, the grave choric piece, cast into the Sapphic metre, in which the dangers and troubles of a high estate are contrasted with the ease and safety of a middle condition of life, must have been intended for recitation alone. The fine swing and cadence of these noble stanzas show the fitness of the Portuguese language for the highest forms of poetry.

Reys poderosos, principes, tyrannos !
Sobre nós pondes vossos pés, pisay-nos ;
Mas sobre vós está sempre a fortuna :
          Nós livres d'ella.

Nos altos muros soam mais os ventos :
As mais crescidas arvores derribam :
As mais inchadas vellas no mar rompem :
          Caem móres torres.

Pompas e ventos, titulos inchados
Não dão descanso, nem mais doce sono :
Antes mais cançam, antes em mais medo
          Poem, e perigo.

Como se volvem no grã mar as ondas,
Assi se volvem estes peitos cheios
E nunca fartos, nunca satisfeitos,
          Nunca seguros.

Princes and tyrants, absolute and potent !
Place on our subject necks your feet to crush us ;
Yet over you the fates have full dominion
          We can escape them.

The strength of the wind-blast tries the lofty palace ;
Tall forest trees are overthrown the soonest ;
Stateliest sails are soonest torn by tempest ;
    Loftiest towers fall.

The pomp and the empty vanity of titles
No ease afford, nor make our slumbers sweeter.
Rather, fatigue, disquietude, and danger
    Bring on their owner.

As the unceasing waves in midmost ocean
Turn and return, so do these restless spirits,
Full, but still hungry, never to be sated :
    Never in surety.

Like Shakespeare's Clarence, Inez de Castro is
visited, on the night preceding her assassination, by a
portentous and terrible vision. She dreams that, in
a dark wood, she encounters and is attacked by two
savage wolves, and is by them torn to pieces.

    E eu morria
  Com tanta saudade,[1] que ind'agora
  Parece que a cá tenho : e est'alma triste
  Se m'arrancava tam forçadamente,
  Como quem ante tempo assi deixava
  Sen lugar, e deixava para sempre
  (Que este na minha morte era o mór mal)
  A doce vista de quem me ama tanto.

    And I gave up my life
  With a despair that seems still present now,
  And thus my soul did flit, against my will,
  As if untimely snatched, in that I left
  (This in death's pain was still death's chiefest smart)
  The sweet aspéct of him who loved so well.

In the scene immediately succeeding, the Chorus

---

[1] The word *saudade*, the intense regret and longing for a
thing past and gone, has no equivalent that I know of in any
European language.

is again brought upon the stage, to declare to Inez
her approaching doom. Nothing can be more impressive, and certainly few situations in the less conventional drama of later days could surpass in stage
effect, the startling force and weight of the words in
which, in answer to Inez's questioning as to the
tidings they have to give her, the Chorus answers,
'Hé tua morte'—'It is thy death.' A long and
highly wrought dialogue occurs, where Inez pleads
her cause before the King himself, in the presence of
his councillors, and he, in spite of their advice to the
contrary, consents to let her live. In her absence,
however, he again yields a reluctant and wavering
assent to their solicitations. The perpetration of the
murder of Inez is announced on the stage, in a solemn
dirge, by the Chorus, who use the privilege of ancient
choric song to foresee and foretell the calamities
which Inez's death will produce. The fifth act is
obviously incomplete. It consists entirely of a dialogue between the Infante and a messenger who
brings him the news of his mistress's assassination.
With the expression of his great horror and grief, the
tragedy ends by his declaration of his resolve to
revenge his loss in the most complete and terrible
manner.

It will be seen, from the foregoing sketch and
quotations, that *Castro* is entirely a tragedy of unmixed and highly wrought passion. Minor incidents,
which might easily have been introduced, seem
purposely to have been rejected. The intensity of
Inez's agony and despair, of the Prince's grief and

rage, of the cruelty and selfishness of the courtiers,
are unrelieved by any elements of variety or contrast,
and modified by no subordinate emotion.

That human actions are ever guided by such
absolute singleness of motive as is imputed to the
dramatis personæ in tragedies of the classic type, is,
we know, not the case ; and for this reason we may
presume it was that the Greek playwrights made the
impelling influence of the Fates a principal circumstance in their tragedies—knowing that, otherwise,
the acute audiences of ancient Greece would fail to
recognise any resemblance whatever between the
actions of tragic characters and those of ordinary
human beings. Ferreira has not ventured upon any
such theory of Fatalism, and the consequence is that,
taken as a whole, his tragedy as a reading play utterly
fails in satisfying us that it is a true drama—that it is
a true representation of the motives and the passions,
the deeds and the talk, of actual men and women.
As a literary work, however, and for the purposes
of the theatre, his tragedy is excellent. Depending
upon a continued use of declamatory eloquence, his
language is never once exaggerated, and the sentiments of the various characters, if they are sustained
in a somewhat monotonous key, are never either
unnatural or ignoble ; but as a work of general human
interest for modern readers it fails entirely, from the
very nature of its scope and conception.

The two great poets whose works I have reviewed
begin a period which is the most glorious in Portuguese literature. This Augustan age culminated in

the Lusiads of Camoens, whose genius would almost
seem to have blinded foreign students of his country's
literature to the merits of his precursors and his contemporaries. Among these, Miranda and Ferreira—
the Chaucer and Dryden of Portugal—hold the
highest place; men of the most original genius,
whose great reputations are acknowledged, while
their lives and their works are all but forgotten, even
in the country of their birth :—

Ils meurent, et le monde n'en connait que les noms.

CLOISTERS OF BELEM CONVENT: RENAISSANCE PERIOD.

CHAPTER IV.

MODERN PORTUGAL: COUNTRY LIFE AND SPORT.

MOST travellers to Portugal land at Lisbon and dine at the *table d'hôte* of one of the three or four principal hotels of that sunny capital. I appeal to the majority of persons so landing and dining, if they have not heard at their very first dinner something equivalent to the following remark: 'Portugal is a country a hundred and fifty years behind the rest of the world.' I have myself heard and read this exact chronological comparison very often. I have heard it made when I was a new comer, and too ignorant to dispute it; and since then I have heard the proposition laid down again and again, when I was too sure of the ignorance of the speaker to pay any attention to him.

Of course it is a foolish and ignorant error, and deserves to be shown to be so. First, what is the rest of the world that Portugal has not caught up by a century and a half? It is Europe, presumably, for of course no nation in the Eastern world is in the race even now with the little Western kingdom; and again, we must leave out of comparison those sinks of political iniquity, the upstart republics of South and

Central America. The great and respectable *parvenu* of North America has no past, no real history apart from that of the mother country, and must therefore be excluded from comparison. Then, too, ' the rest of the world' must exclude the Turkey and Russia of to-day, for in Portugal at least there is free thought and free speech, equal justice, and neither the bastinado nor the whip, neither impalement, nor pachas, nor sentinel house porters, nor Siberia, nor the Sultan, nor the Czar. The comparison, too, must exclude even modern Italy, where, besides the foul Camorra plague and the religious feud, half the land is still cursed with brigandage; and Spain, which is to the full as bad with bigots and brigands; and Greece, which is more thief-ridden than either.

So the charge dwindles down to this, that the Portuguese nation is only behindhand in civilisation to the few nations of Western Europe who, in respect of progress, and civilization, and humanization, are, and long have been, the very salt of the earth; say Germany, France, and Great Britain, the four small constitutional Governments of the North, and Switzerland, whose peculiar institutions and circumstances make comparison not possible.

Now, Portugal is seriously accused of being a hundred and fifty years behind these favoured nations in all that distinguishes a crowd of savages from a coherent nation of thinking men. Let us see how laughably unjust the statement is.

Let us take France, and even less than a hundred

and fifty years will bring us into the company of
Louis XV. and Madame de Pompadour, a demoralised
Court and a down-trodden people—poor and misery-
stricken, enslaved by superstition, ignorance, and the
tyranny of priest and noble. What is there in all
this to compare with modern Portugal? A century
and a half ago in Germany, to take no worse a part
of it than Prussia, we have that most unmitigated and
grotesque of all royal and domestic tyrants, the father
of the great Frederick, and a people not unwilling or
unworthy to be governed by such a wretch. England
at the beginning of the eighteenth century we know
all about; and if anyone will seriously contend that
a minister as corrupt as Walpole could govern in
modern Portugal for a day, he must know very little
of government in that country. If he supposes that
a country like our own under the First or Second
George, in which one great party was openly treason-
able to the Throne and the Constitution, in which
armed rebellion was ready to break out at a hint
from a neighbouring sovereign, and of which one
great division was enslaved and terrorised by political
and religious disabilities, and another division so law-
less that the writs of the King's Law Courts would not
run through it—if any man can draw a parallel
between such a country and the Portugal of to-day,
he is either too ignorant to be heard at all, or his
statement is, as polite psychologists who hesitate over
a stronger term, say—' an act of imperfect cerebra-
tion.'

The amiable poet who moralised to the effect that

but a small ingredient in the mass of human suffering was that part which

Laws or kings can cause or cure,

never perhaps went very deeply into the ethics of tyranny. Let tyrannical kings and laws, he argued, do their worst, they must at the last leave 'our reason, our faith, and our conscience' to us. I should be very sorry, for my own part, to try the experiment in Poland or in Turkey; but, be this as it may, Goldsmith overlooked, I think, the suffering caused by those meddlesome laws which the stupidity of our ancestors imposed, and which that of many contemporary governments still imposes, upon every transaction in the traffic of man with man.

These are the things that make life bitter to the common run of mortals. A man may easily, leading the middle course of life, escape 'Luke's iron crown,' as the poet puts it, or 'Damien's bed of steel,' but he cannot escape the legislation of stupid and tyrannous lawgivers. This is a mill designed to grind the weak rather than the strong, to take the darnel before the wheat, and it grinds, as everyone knows, exceedingly small.

Those who hold to this before-mentioned theory of the non-progress of Portugal, must expect to find the fruits of such legislation as common in the country as under our First George, when the great majority of citizens found nearly everything they could buy made dearer to them by the law, and all they had to sell made cheaper—daily life turned into one long struggle to the poor and unfriended man, that it might be sweeter and easier to the rich and the influential ; the full dreariness and injustice of the world brought home to a poor man at every turn. But this is not so, and these evils have passed away as completely in modern Portugal as they have in modern England.

In modern Portugal there are neither the cruel criminal laws which disgraced England a far shorter time ago than a hundred and fifty years, nor are there any irrational municipal laws to help Corporations to grow fat at their fellow-burghers' expense, nor any of those monstrously foolish ordinances about *regrating* and *forestalling* which our forefathers believed to be wise. No wages are fixed by law in Portugal, and now, except for fiscal reasons and fiscal purposes, no commodity of daily life, neither bread, nor oil, nor salt, nor meat, nor drink, is to be bought or sold at any other than its natural, that is, its cheapest price. Of all the many monopolies which once existed in Portugal to hinder trade and impoverish the people, only two are extant—the one in soap, the other in tobacco, and they are for fiscal purposes and may be defended. True, protection survives, that easiest borne of all tyrannies of the few over the many ; but then its fallacies are fallacies invisible not in Portugal only, but by a majority of the people and of the statesmen of every nation in the world except our own, and protection is perhaps fated to die sooner in Portugal than elsewhere. Even now, protection in Portugal is nothing to what it was in Great Britain fifty years ago.

As to many departments of municipal law, of

primary education, of police, as to the laws relating
to land and the transfer of land, and those which
affect the succession to property, some reformers
may think that modern Portugal is ahead of modern
England.

In regard to Poor Laws, a man need be neither a
reformer nor a philosopher to perceive that Portugal
has legislated with far more wisdom than we have.
The Portuguese system of relief for the poor may be
described briefly to be private charity organised and
centralised, and only occasionally helped by grants in
aid by the State. Relief is wisely and humanely
administered, agriculture is not hindered by heavy
poor rates, thrift and hard labour are not discouraged
among the workers on the land, nor is a cheerless
and desolate and melancholy old age prepared for the
infirm and the poor.

Apart from all these possible points of comparison
between Great Britain and Portugal, Portugal possesses the inestimable blessing of a codified criminal
and civil law.

Of all possible subjects of comparison in modern
free Portugal, soberly governed as it is, with civil
and religious peace and tolerance, trade and traffic as
free as elsewhere on the European continent, life and
liberty secure, and equality before good and intelligible laws, I can think of but one point in which England under the first two Georges is not immeasurably
distanced by Portugal under its present enlightened
and law-respecting sovereign That one point is
— conscription, the terrible blood-tax of every Con-

tinental country, to whose cruelty and burden no
custom nor length of habit can reconcile the people.
Often and often have I watched with pity and strong
indignation the workings of this most damnable system.
To be sure, conscription seems at present to be a necessity to nations of the European continental family.
Nevertheless, *Homo homini lupus* appears a true saying to an impartial outsider at such times.

The heart-sickness of deferred hope seems to be
greatly prolonged by a Portuguese conscription, and
the risk of a conscript's lot is run even after the fatal
number is drawn; for if the man who should answer
to it is not forthcoming, dies, or falls ill, or escapes,
or in any way evades his fate, then the drawer of the
next number is called upon, and failing him, the next
and the next again, so that hardly any strong and
active Portuguese boy past conscript's age can feel
comfortably safe. No cottage is secure from the
pain of separation. Parents have to meet another
evil besides their children's death or desertion of
them; lovers, the pang of another cross besides the
old and common one of inconstancy.

It is good to consider this matter in all its bearings, for we in England may not perhaps always be free
from the curse of a conscription: indeed, only a few
weeks ago we were told in a leading weekly paper that
we must come to it in time. The devil is, we know,
not coal-black, nor even conscription quite so abominable an institution but that something may be said for
it. To be sure, it decimates a country in a fashion,
robs industry of many strong arms, and causes infinite

social and domestic harm and heart-burning. Nevertheless, a large conscripted army, passed quickly through the ranks and returned to civil life before it has lost the taste for civilian hard work, is a school of manners. In the United States, manners were said to be noticeably better after the civil war than the very bad ones which prevailed before. Now, good manners and respect for authority are, within proper limits, undoubtedly sources of strength to a man and to a nation, and their existence in Portugal is, I think, partly traceable to military service.

Most conscriptions spare married men, and a young man consequently has a temptation to marry which never entered into the head of the narrow-minded Malthus. The patriotism, therefore, which, like Parson Primrose's, holds that ' the honest man who marries and brings up a large family does the State more service than he who continues single and only talks of population,' may find something to approve even in a conscription. A family is a good investment for a man who cannot afford to pay forty or fifty pounds for a substitute, and the man who dislikes drill, or hates cold steel and gunpowder, marries a wife to insure himself against what he considers a worse fate.

Perhaps statistics would not bear out the statement that these prudential marriages are frequent. I only know that it is a matter of common jest that they happen. I heard it first, I remember, some years ago from a man who was carrying my fishing-basket along a trout stream in the province of Beira.

We had passed a village where the annual drawing was taking place. As my companion told me of this mode of escape from the horrors of war, I thought of the cynical old Scotch proverb—'Next to nae wife a gude wife is best.' There are few people so quick to take in a joke as the Portuguese. I translated the proverb for his benefit. 'I know the country,' I said, 'where the people have this for a saying.' He laughed. 'Perhaps the proverb is a true enough one,' he said; 'but is there any balloting for soldiers in that country?'[1]

Now, the question may occur to the reader—it has often occurred to the writer—how is it that a country where good government has been so backward in coming (for it does not date further back than the establishment of liberal institutions in 1833) should yet be so advanced in all the arts of social and political life; should not only enjoy a good constitution—which is a small matter (for good constitutions are as common as thistles), but statesmen honest enough and dexterous enough to make good use of it—which is a great matter? How is it that a country too limited in population to have a periodical press of any power, and where, in point of fact, the press is not very powerful for good or evil, where the debates in Parliament, the speeches of politicians, and the proceedings of the law courts are seldom or never reported, where the higher culture, literary or scien-

---

[1] The conscription law in Portugal is at present administered very strictly. Marriage is now no 'set off,' and when the final lot is drawn no substitute is accepted.

tific, does not abound; where, in short, there seem
to be absolutely none of those levers which we at
home believe to be the only ones to make the intellect
of the masses stir—how is it that among the Portuguese, a sanguine Southern race, there is so keen an
appreciation of the benefits of wise and sober administration? There is floating in every class of this
country, from the highest to the lowest, a mass of
sound and tolerant doctrine, political, social, and
religious—sound and tolerant from the point of view
of any Frenchman, Englishman, or American of
liberal and moderate views. How is this? Whence
does this doctrine come, and how does it find admit-
tance with all entrance thus seemingly shut out?

I believe the answer to all this to be, first, that
the Portuguese race is a blend of nationalities which
time has welded almost into homogeneity. There is,
therefore, no clash of race with race, and there is no
faith feud, nor much opposition of interests between
class and class, for the country is still chiefly, and
should, perhaps, be entirely agricultural. Then there
is a free constitutional government; there is liberty of
meeting, of printing, and, above all, of talking; ideas
are as free in free Portugal as they necessarily are in
bondage and subjection in despotic Russia. This
being so, all the new doctrine and all the true
doctrine of the whole world percolates as quickly
through every stratum of Portuguese society as the
drops of rain from heaven sink down to the plant-
roots in a well tilled soil. There is, moreover, less
need of a great periodical press, such as ours or the

American, because the Portuguese are a talkative and a sociable race. Ideas come to them not so much on a printed page as by word of mouth.

Lastly, to explain the advancement of political intelligence in Portugal, it must not be forgotten who the Portuguese people are. They are, as I have said, a race with a lineage happily blended of the strength of the North and the more subtle genius of the South. A race possessing great and rare qualities, dormant for a time, indeed, and temporarily debased by the corruption which goes with tyranny, but whose quick revival under the kindly influences of freedom is one of the marvels of modern history. It is a race which has at all times been marked by a rare union of enthusiasm and sobriety, and whose restricted numbers only have stood in the way of its predominant power and influence among nations; which, in spite of its numerical insignificance, has conquered and settled continents, crossed unknown seas, and carried its faith and language far and wide over the more distant regions of the earth. What wonder is it that men loyal enough to each other, steadfast enough in their principles, and high enough and bold enough to achieve these great things, should, the chance given them, appreciate at once the wisdom and the benefits of free government, and fall into the way and practice of it forthwith?

Though, as I have said, agriculture is still the prevailing pursuit of the Portuguese, country life, as we in England understand it, is a thing little known in Portugal. The reason, of course, is to be found in the tenure of land, as I shall further on take occasion to explain. Were it chiefly sublet on leases, as with us, the Portuguese country gentleman would doubtless be dotted over the land, to collect and lower his rents, patronise his tenants, to hunt, shoot, fish, grow his geraniums, turnips, orchids, or coniferæ, as his taste might dictate, or to cultivate that precarious little crop of politics which is all that the ballot and extended suffrage have left to our country gentleman in this domain. The Portuguese squire, if he existed, would no doubt, like his English representative, play at whist with his parson and at justice with his neighbouring squires, do the equivalent of reading his 'Times' and his 'Punch,' of subscribing to Mudie's, and, in short, he would aspire to that cultivated ease and dignity which distinguish the country squire from the country ploughman.

In Portugal there is either yeoman tenure, where the farmer is his own landlord, or communal, where the lordship is impersonal ; in districts where there are large estates and leased farms, the estates are of huge size, and lie for the most part in districts where the land is poor and mountainous, or in malarious plain country, with no temptation to the owner to settle. The landlord's work is therefore deputed to an agent, and the former lives in one of the great cities. The Portuguese never play at country life as our people are fond of doing—that is, they do not betake themselves to the country and lead a continuous existence there, without having real duties or interests in the land. I think they are in **the right**, and that to be secluded in a dull country neighbourhood, as **English** families seem to like **to** doom themselves **to be**, without ties or any contact with their fellow-beings, with no occupations but the visits from, or the calls upon, distant neighbours, is the surest of all methods of dulling the social faculties, and of slipping back in the race towards culture and the higher education.

The Portuguese, as **a** rule, care not a straw **for** culture and the higher education, but they hate seclusion of this kind. There is absolutely no such thing as the dull continuous vegetation of English country life—bad even for **the inertness of** advancing age: but for young people and **for girls** especially, who **cannot** escape to school or college like their brothers, simply stupid and abominable. **In** Portugal there are no ' Marianas ' in moated granges.

For all this, there are plenty of country houses, and very good and pleasant ones, only they are not much lived in. A certain well known family in Portugal—one with an infinite number of cousins, uncles, and collateral relatives of all degrees—boasts that a member of it can pass on horseback from the extreme north to the extreme south **of** the kingdom, and sleep every night of his journey **in a** kinsman's house. I questioned one of **the** family on this point, and he corroborated the statement, showing **me** even on a map how one **of** his parentage might (' though **with** some small parenthesis between ') travel through the country in this pleasant fashion, and without, as it

were, once leaving the family circle. I think I
recollect that the chain of these convenient lodgings
terminated at the frontiers of Algarve, the most
southerly province; but then Algarve is, in some
sort, a kingdom of itself, over which the Portuguese
monarch rules with some separation of jurisdiction—
'Rex Port. et Algarb.' is the legend on coins—so that
the boast that Portugal can be traversed by a man
who should never sleep but under a kinsman's roof is
still justified.

Now, the Portuguese gentleman's ideal of a country
house is the old Roman one of a *villa*, and his residence
in it a *villeggiatura*, after the modern Italian fashion
—a brief holiday time in the hot season, a voluntary
rustication by people whose love of country life is
shown by the fact of their literature containing more
good pastoral poetry than that of any European
nation. But as no sane and active-minded man can
read more than a very limited amount of pastoral
poetry, so no Portuguese cares to play at living a
more than very brief pastoral existence. He and his
family leave town for a month or two in August, or
September, or October, the worst and dullest season
in cities, the busiest and most cheerful in the country;
for then is the time of vintage and maize harvest,
and most of the fruits of trees are being garnered,
and then is the best season to shoot quail and hare
and the red-legged partridge.

There is, of course, every variety of size and pre-
tentiousness in the houses used for the *villeggiatura*
in Portugal; but almost invariably for grounds the

dwelling has round it the vineyards, orange and olive groves, and the cornfields of a farm. Generally the farm with its farmstead is an appanage of the villa; the farmer, its owner's tenant or his bailiff. When the landlord and employer runs down, he and his wife and children have plenty to occupy and amuse themselves with. The landlord has his live stock and buildings, his walls and his vine trellises to examine, his orchards to inspect, and, above all, the condition of the water-works to see to, that first necessity in Southern farm economy. Mostly it is the *Nora*, the old fashioned water-wheel, worked by oxen turning in a circular space overshadowed by vines. The power is conveyed to an endless chain, set a foot apart with buckets, which dip into the well and fetch up the water from the depths, spilling half of it by the way, it is true, but still making up a plentiful rill, pleasant to listen to and to see flowing off to the thirsty land. On the threshing floor are already the huge piles of golden red maize cobs, lying ready for the master's eye to assess, and the lesser heaps of more precious kidney beans, white, brown, or mottled. The great gourds and water melons are still in the fields where they have grown, getting their last mellowing touches of colour from the autumnal sun-rays.

It is a delightful time for all the family too. The children play at water-works, and swim oranges in the runlets of water flowing from the *Nora*, look out the sweetest bunches of grapes, or play at hide-and-seek in the rank growth of vegetation which the summer sun has raised. The girls saunter in the

flower garden, with its old fashioned box edged paths
and beds well shaded by camellias and Tangerine
orange trees, and filled full with flowering plants of
the older fashion, the asters, the balsam, heliotrope,
and scented verbena, cock's-combs, geraniums, blue
and scarlet salvias, dahlias and fuchsias of the more
primitive kinds, chrysanthemums, and great bushes of
the yellow-flowered sedum ;—all deplorable enough
in the eyes of any modern gardener, but gay and
bright and charming from sheer force of unchecked
luxuriance.

The house is a very plain one: a square building,
generally white-washed inside and out, with broad
overhanging eaves painted with vermilion underneath. Many of these houses have one large central
room with a number of little cells for bedrooms, opening out on three sides. This central room, uncarpeted
and furnished with a dozen or two of rickety chairs
and a large deal table, is hung with monstrously bad
framed prints—the Battle of the Nile, the 'Saucy
Arethusa,' a series showing the life and death of Pope
Pius VII., the Heroism of Egaz Moniz, the Loves of
Inez de Castro, or the legendary Vision of King
Affonso Henriquez. Here the family meet and take
their meals. An ox-cart or two full of extra furniture
is sent from the town house, and serves well enough
to make the family as comfortable as they care to be
on their two months' picnic.

Such is the *villeggiatura* of the middle classes not
over-burdened with this world's goods. Among the
country houses of wealthier people, who have been

fortunate enough to buy or inherit villas of the more luxurious kind, are some magnificent and singularly hideous modern dwellings, with huge earthenware greyhounds, or wild boars, keeping guard over pretentious gateways, painted glass in the windows, and enormous balls of silvered tin perched on portentous cupolas on the house top, buildings inviting the wrath of Heaven by every enormity of bad taste—a style of architecture defying all recognised canons of art, and gardens which would be as unpleasant as the houses but that in this kindly climate Nature takes these matters into her own hands, 'invading the quincunx' with the luxuriance of her plant growth, violating the 'trim parterre' most satisfactorily, and making an agreeable tangle and wilderness of the most correct design.

There are, however, in Portugal, villa dwellings and gardens of the richer and more luxurious sort, of an older and better fashion than this. One such is in my memory as I write. A stately house of plain, solid architecture, with a walled courtyard in front, wherein old orange trees overshadow the rippling surface of a stone-formed tank, into which descends a plentiful waterfall from a carved dolphin's head.

Inside, the wood-carved wreaths and trophies on the stairs and the doorways point to the period which connoisseurs know as ' *Louis Seize*,' and in spite of the great secular trees about the grounds, the house, I know, is no older than the reign of that monarch. This house is always maintained in good residential condition, fully furnished, and with a small staff of

servants in occupation the whole year round. There
are corridors hung with passably good oil pictures;
great china cupboards, crammed full of ware
purchased seemingly at all periods within the last
hundred years, chiefly the handsome but comparatively worthless Oriental ware of seventy or eighty
years ago; and, curious to note, next in abundance
to this are the wares of our own *fabriques*—Crown
Derby in great quantity and richness, Wedgwood,
Worcester, Leeds, and even Bow and Chelsea.[1]

There is a handsome private chapel on the ground
floor, dedicated to St. Anthony, large enough to hold
the whole parish on the Saint's holiday, and here
mass is said every Sunday and Saint's day throughout the year. In this chapel, as in almost every
private chapel I ever saw in Spain or Portugal, is
that curious arrangement by which the ladies of the
house can join in the service without mingling with
the crowd of worshippers on the floor. A grated
window, like the Ladies' Gallery in the House of
Lords, about half way up the wall, opens into one of
the rooms of the house, and the ladies and children
sitting there can open their windows and see and
take part in, themselves unseen, all that goes on in
the chapel. It is church-going made very easy. I
do not know whether the practice is a remnant of
old Moorish notions of women's seclusion, or comes

---

[1] The long existing commercial relations between Portugal
and Great Britain growing out of the port wine trade are the
cause why more last-century English porcelain and earthenware is
to be found in Portugal than elsewhere in Europe.

merely from fineness and a liking to be exclusive. One may suppose it had its origin in the old notions, and is kept up from habit and from convenience.

As in the case of the smaller villas, the house is connected with a farm, and the grounds and garden mingle in the same pleasant fashion with the appurtenances of the farmstead. A long, straight, over-arching avenue of camellia and Seville orange trees terminates in a broad, paved threshing-floor. In a little dell below the house, under a dense shadow of fig and loquat trees, is the huge water-wheel, worked by six oxen, and raising a little river from the depths below. The terraced fields, the orange and olive groves and the orchards, are all surrounded by broad walks overshadowed by a heavy pleached trellis supporting vines, and here in the hottest summer's day is cool walking in the grey half-shadow of the greenery overhead. Runlets of water course along in stone channels by the side of every path and roadway, and the murmur of running water—a sound of which the ear never tires in the South—is heard everywhere and always.

The well-shaded garden is laid out in the stately Italian fashion; with carved stone-work in its terraced and balustraded walks, its flights of broad steps, and its fountains and gold-fish ponds; and here, more than anywhere, the water-threads and jets and cascades fall and rise and splash with most refreshing murmuring. There is nothing the Portuguese so much delight in as this flow of ever-moving water, cooling the air, and associated with the very idea of

fertility and green luxuriance.   Camoens, in his great
epic, describing the enchanted Venus Island, mentions
how there flows on in it for ever, among the hollow
stones of the flower-enamelled hillside,

A sonorosa lympha fugitiva,

and I rather doubt if the expressive beauty of this
line would fully come home to anyone but a dweller
under some such summer sky as that of Portugal.
Camoens' description of the miraculous island, fine as
it is, is little more than an accurate picture of many
a bit of cultivated pastoral scenery in this country,
and I am in truth strongly reminded of the whole
passage in recalling the surroundings of the very
house I am speaking of.   Here, behind the house, are
the green, turf-clothed hills, with the water welling
everywhere, and keeping the vegetation lush and
green.   Here, too, is the wealth of fruit trees :—

Mil arvores estão ao ceu subindo
Com pomos odoriferos e bellos :
A larangeira tem no fruto lindo
A cor que tinha Daphne nos cabellos :
Encosta-se no chão ; que está cahindo,
A cidreira co' os pezos amarellos :
Os formosos limões alli cheirando.

Trees manifold here lift their branches tall,
Fruit-laden, fragrant, exquisite and rare
The orange tree with bright-hued golden ball,
Passing the golden hues of Daphne's hair,
Citrons with weight of yellow-coated fruit
And lemons odorous .   .   .   .   .

It is a far more concrete piece of description than
the Italian poet gives us of Armida's magic garden,
but not the less impressive ; the nymphs are very

real personages indeed in the Portuguese epic, and all the sights and sounds of nature have a most bodily presentment: the very scent of the flowers and savour of the fruit are exactly set forth.

Camoens, however, in truth, had not on his palette all the colours which, had he written in this age, he would have used in making his picture of a Portuguese landscape full and complete. In the three hundred years which have elapsed since the 'Lusiads' were written, and partly in consequence of the great deeds of prowess on which the poem is founded, Portugal has become the emporium of a wealth of plant form, chiefly in fruit and forest trees, from every quarter of the globe. Camellias from Japan have long been the chief ornament of every garden, growing to the size of apple trees in England. The loquat from China surpasses as a giver of shade the fig itself— the old-world type of shade-giving trees; in November it fills the air with the sweet scent of its blossoms, and ripens its refreshing yellow fruit in early summer. The gum trees of Australia, and especially the blue gum (*Eucalyptus globulus*, the fever tree), have positively altered the aspect of the more inhabited parts of the country within the last twenty years; so that a modern painter, to make a characteristic landscape, must now needs introduce into his picture this species of gum tree, with its slender, polished trunk, its upright branch-growth against the sky line, and its long drooping leaves, rich in winter time with a mellow splendour of russet red, and yellow.

Again, there is the Bella Sombra, a huge forest

tree from Brazil, which has taken most kindly to
Portuguese soil and climate; but finest of the imported trees is the great-flowered magnolia from
Carolina and Central America—a forest giant in its
native lands, and, where it finds a damp and congenial
soil, nothing less in size in this country. The age of
the very oldest magnolia in Portugal cannot exceed a
hundred and twenty years, and yet already some of
them tower to a height exceeding that of the tallest
English oak tree, rearing aloft huge clouds of shin-
ing, laurel-like leafage, starred here and there in
spring and summer time with their great white and
scented blossoms.

All these trees, together with many conifers from
the highlands of Brazil and the slopes of the
Himalayas, and countless shrubs, are going far to
make of Portugal a marvel for variety of rapid and
luxuriant growth in the eyes of arboriculturists from
our own country, who count the years' growth of their
exotic conifers by inches and fractions of inches.

Now, for all these arboreal varieties of foreign ex-
traction—these imported Circassian brides—which are
embellishing the native stock of trees, and reforming
the Portuguese pleasure woods and orchards, to my
thinking they are but material beauties at the best;
and the associations connected with some of the older
denizens of the garden and orchard, hallowed by time
and ancient culture, have in them some deeper and
more subtle beauty than the merely sensuous one of
stately growth and form, size, fine massing of light
and shade, and so forth. To say nothing of the

orange tree and its associations—as to which, indeed, travellers have not too greatly foreborne their rhetoric —there is the olive tree, which travellers have certainly not over-praised, or, for the matter of that, praised at all. In truth, I do not remember ever hearing, from tourist or traveller, a good word for the olive tree, with its stunted growth, its insignificant leaves and flowers and fruit, its ashy, or, rather, lead-coloured foliage. Yet how is it that the old poets of Greece have sung its praises with raptures exceeding, I think, what they have bestowed upon any other gift of nature?

I am reminded, as I write, of the famous chorus in the play of Sophocles, in which the poet, recounting in glowing words all the beauties and advantages of the Attic land—its fruits, its flowers, its sacred groves, its full and flowing streams; and again, its breed of horses and its seas, but, above all, the noble race of inhabitants apt and able to tame the one and cross the other—culminates his enthusiasm in his praise (which I imagine has often seemed a most ridiculous anti-climax to northern Europeans) of that gift of the protecting Deity, the 'grey-green olive tree.' Is it that with a surer æsthetic perception than we moderns possess, these old poets overlooked the homely aspect of the actual tree, and idealized it? That they saw in it the oil-producer, the giver of that which—to dwellers in a country like Attica, who drew most of their suste-nance from the orchard and from the forest, and from the waters of the neighbouring seas—was a boon of in-estimable value, a gift with a clear divinity about it?

Doubtless there is something of gratitude in the poets' songs of praise ; but they misapprehend greatly who suppose that this tree of great price is not also one of great and peculiar loveliness. To know its true beauty we must see it, not as it is looked upon by winter-sojourning travellers, such as most Englishmen are who have seen and probably despised the olive—not in the chill and heavy atmosphere of the winter season, or even under the light-blue skies of an Italian or Peninsular late autumn or early spring, but in the full glory of summer tide, when the air is clear and bright as a diamond, the sharply defined shadow of hill and rock rosy in its depth, and the sea and sky purple in the intensity of their blue. Then is the olive tree transformed, illuminated, by the blaze of sun-rays, till it looks to be an ethereal kind of growth, as of something in an enchanted land ; the dull leaden leaves glow now all the day long with a rare silvery hue, and the sunset lights up a golden haze upon them. Then one at last begins to understand the enthusiasm of the old poets ; for an Athenian, at such times as these, looking on a grove of olive trees, might swear by the great Pallas Athené, the giver of them, that nothing more rare and exquisite in beauty grew in all the Southern land.

Though I trust that no one who knows me at all well, either in private or in public and literary life, will think so ill of me as to imagine that I could venture to put upon paper a full and particular account of so everyday an occurrence as a sunset, yet

I must take leave to say, in justice to the country and to those aspects of it which are chiefly the subject of this chapter, that a Portuguese sunset is a remarkably grand thing.

I was lately reading an interesting travel-book upon Norway, and was disturbed to find that the very capable author recurs again and again to the beauty of the Norwegian sunsets. This, as cautious moralists say, ' is not as it should be ; ' every sunset everywhere, if there be but a single cloud on the western horizon, is a beautiful spectacle, but the spectacle in Norway is a prolonged, a monotonous, and a not very brilliant affair. We have much better sunsets at home in England ; and, as we travel south, the setting of the lamp of day is attended by more and more of glorious circumstance, till we come too near the equator, when the sun dives so quickly beneath the usually cloudless horizon that there is no time for a serious sunset, and the ' sudden glory ' of it is come and gone before the æsthetic observer has time to collect his admiration into focus. Humboldt, if I recollect rightly, makes the limits of the grandest sunsets in the Northern Hemisphere to extend from lat. 30° to 42°. Portugal is well included in this zone.

Other conditions, meteorological ones chiefly, besides latitude go to the making of good sunsets ; a mountainous region, a variable climate, and probably some electric conditions at which we can only guess. One might imagine that the level plains of ocean would supply all the necessary conditions of fine sun-

sets ; but it is not so,—sea sunsets as a rule lack
variety. All travellers by sea will agree with me.
Only once do I remember an ocean sunset that was
so immeasurably grander than any other I ever saw
that it is impossible to lose the memory of it; but
even here, land had as much as water to do with it,
and it was nearly within the limits of Humboldt's
zone.

We happened to be sailing at evening time in the
month of October unusually near the cliffs of the
Spanish Finisterre, and a great vivid cloud-picture was
suddenly spread all around us—the clouds all purple
and saffron in the far east, on a background of pale
citron, brightening towards the west through every
degree of the prismatic scale, and turning at last to a
fiery effulgence as they neared the sun's throne in the
western sky. The whole body of clouds moved slowly
through the great airy amphitheatre, and all the
broad welkin was reflected again on the glassy surface
of sea fluctuating in slow and swelling masses ; while
away coastward were upreared the tall cliffs of Finisterre, rosy red in the dying light of day : a spectacle
to awe a materialist. It is mortifying to think how
difficult it is to maintain one's æsthetic enthusiasm
at a high pitch for any time ; for while we looked
there came to our ears on the calm evening air the
sound of soft music, the instrument a banjo in the
forecastle played by our negro cook, the air a ' break-
down.' Presently came the steward respectfully to
remind us that tea was ready in the saloon. How
faithful a servant is memory at times ! I remember

that, seeing us a little loth to leave the deck, he sought to tempt us down with the observation that there were potted lobster and pickled salmon on the table, and we went below, leaving the glorious firmament of heaven to itself, while the air upon the banjo changed to ' Way down upon the Suwannee River.'

No one will accuse Portuguese country gentlemen of an over-sentimental admiration of sunsets; their sentimentality, where it exists, seldom runs in an æsthetic direction; and for plain, practical men who can fill their heads and hands with thoughts and work of other kinds, they perhaps do well to leave the less concrete aspects of nature alone. They certainly do not come down into the country to dazzle their eyes with the rising and setting sun. Art, literature, science, in Portugal are for the very few alone, and the high culture which undoubtedly pervades almost every class in the community is purely social culture, the not too easy or too common art of maintaining pleasant relations with superiors, with inferiors, and with equals.

So when the Portuguese gentleman comes for his annual holiday to the country, he looks to his garden, his cellar, his granaries, the warrens, and the woods wherewith to fill his mind. As a rule he brings no new books to beguile his leisure or widen his mental horizon, he never buys pictures, he seldom collects rare prints or art objects; old china, French enamels, Italian majolica, or German ivories are mysteries to him, and their accumulation a childish extravagance.

He will keep them, if he has inherited them, as convenient house furniture, and he may buy now and
then an old Indian or Japanese cabinet for the same
useful purpose ; but he would greatly prefer a modern
one of buhl or ormolu fresh from a Paris workshop,
and bright with all the hideous crudity of its newness.
Plate he likes to acquire, and the fine old Portuguese
silver *repoussé* work of two hundred years ago finds
a ready sale in the country ; but he would like it
infinitely better if it bore the hall mark of George
IV.'s reign, and was of the gorgeous style and massive
construction peculiar to the period of that gorgeous
and massive sovereign.

He loves the chase, but never owned an expensive
central-fire gun by a good London or Paris maker.
Not many years ago, he used nothing better than a
long, single-barrelled gun of great antiquity ; making,
however, most excellent practice with it upon red-
legged partridges and quail. Now he shoots quite as
straight with a cheap Belgian double-barrelled piece,
which an Englishman would not put into the hands
of his under-keeper.   His pointers are untrained, from
an English sportsman's point of view, but hunting,
pointing, and ' down-charging ' are hereditary in them.
They are of the heavy Peninsular breed, the progenitors of the race of pointers all the world over ; portentously double-nosed, thick-muzzled dogs, endowed
with the keenest scent, and very staunch.   They
potter along, ten or twenty yards in front of the
shooter, and never dream of ' ranging ' or ' quartering,' but have as a rule been taught to retrieve.

COUNTRY LIFE AND SPORT. 135

To shoot over pointers, however, is not what the Portuguese sportsman most cares for. It is not sociable enough. His motto, if he have one, is ' *the greatest amusement of the greatest number (of men and dogs)* ; ' and as the whole country, with the exception of walled enclosures of a certain height, is free to shoot over to any one responsible enough to be entrusted with a ten-shilling gun-licence, there is a paucity of game, and so to the sportsman's motto must be added —' *with the least possible expenditure of game.'*

If I describe a Portuguese shooting party, a *caçada*—I shall be accused by some grave and intolerant readers at home of wishing to make fun of a mode of sport which differs so entirely from our own ways of conducting these matters ; but this is not so at all. Some thoughtful persons who love to go deeply into the philosophy of things, may even think that the ethics of the chase are better apprehended in Portugal than at home. In England, to obtain three days of *battue* shooting in the year, we spend a little fortune in the wages of keepers and watchers, in preserving coverts, and in rearing birds. We go some way to corrupt the morals of a parish, and perhaps turn half a dozen idlers into felons ; we make tenants discontented, moderate people dissatisfied at seeing wealth and labour so ill and unprofitably spent, the humanitarian world is shocked at an unnecessary slaughter, and the non-sporting world of thinkers are mortified to see their countrymen engaged in one other form of indefensible folly. We make, in short, a small local revolution, financial and social, to get

three days of what is by general consent the very
dullest, most monotonous, and most unsatisfactory
form of sport in the world.

Nothing of this kind happens in Portugal. There
has been no preparation whatever for the sport, there
is no expense, and there can be no temptation to poaching where there is no artificial abundance of game.
There is absolutely no seriousness about the matter
at all, it is amusement and relaxation pure and
simple that is sought for ; there is no heart-burning
between rival shots, no bribing of keepers, no
favouritism, no ill-will possible anywhere or anyhow ;
and lastly, no unpleasantly heavy bag to carry home
after a long day's walking.

A dozen gentlemen agree to bring their dogs
together, and a pack numbering thirty or forty of all
degrees—lurchers, terriers, greyhounds, and even
pointers—is collected. Another dozen friends and
acquaintances join the party. Among the whole of
the gentlemen six or eight only carry guns ; the rest,
sticks, the cow-sticks or quarter-staves, which are so
much the badge of agriculturists of all classes, that
even amateur rustics, gentlemen-farmers on their
holiday, seldom go afield without one. Then does
the chase begin. Many such a one have I engaged
in, and of many heard the incidents narrated in the
fullest detail

In a long and vociferous line we range through
the great pine forests, or the chestnut woods, poking
our sticks into the matted gorse and cistus, banging
the tree trunks with resounding blows that echo

among the hollow forest aisles. The dogs hunt a little, wrangle, bark, and fight a good deal, and would do so still more, but for the occasional flight, into their midst, of a well directed cow-stick. Nothing in the shape of game is seen ; a brown wood owl, indeed, flitting from an ivied oak tree, is immediately christened a woodcock by some imaginative person, and is brought down, amidst shouts of laughter, by a short-sighted gentleman, who holds up his eye-glass in explanation of his mistake. Another enthusiastic sportsman walking by my side stops me suddenly, pressing my arm with so much emphasis that I look to see some very large game indeed afoot. He points to a holly tree.

' What is it ? ' I ask.

' Hush ; ' with his fingers across his lips, and he whispers in my ear, ' a blackbird ! '

My acquaintance is proceeding to a scientific ' stalk ; ' but though the blackbird is legitimate game in Portugal, the party is too large, the dignity of the occasion too great, for the pursuit of such small deer. Responding to the loud remonstrances of everyone present, my companion retires from the pursuit, while the blackbird takes wing and disappears, with a shrill, crowing call.

In the meantime, a great commotion is taking place in the centre of our line; every man shouts out ' *Coelho* ! ' Rabbit ! every dog gives tongue, every stick is waved in the air, thumped on the ground, or thrown with random aim into the tall undergrowth. Several guns are fired off. Nothing is hit, not even a dog. I observe that the older and more sagacious of the pack, when the first frenzy of excitement is over, retire a yard or two from the coverts, and watch for what may come out, as a terrier watches at a rat-hole. We all run to and fro madly, we charge and jostle each other, we scratch our faces in the bushes, we entangle our feet in the briars and fall head over heels, we scream with excitement, we shout with laughter.

As yet I have seen nothing: but presently I make out a little animal which I should take for a very large rat if experience did not tell me that it was a full-grown Portuguese rabbit, cantering in a leisurely manner towards two gentlemen with guns stationed on a neighbouring knoll, the only members of our party not in motion. These sportsmen cock their pieces, and, aiming apparently at the points of their own boots, fire simultaneously. We run up and look to where the ground is still smoking for the body of the rabbit. We find nothing but the hole of the burrow over which these gentlemen were mounting guard, and into which the rabbit has safely escaped.

We all stop for ten minutes to argue, to recount, and laugh over the misadventure, then set off again through the unending forest glades.

After this episode, a boy working at a saw-pit offers to show us a hare half a mile away; we close with his offer, and eventually we shoot both hare and boy. The hare we *bagged* in a most literal sense, but the boy we only wounded very slightly—so slightly, indeed, that he recovered almost by magic from the fearful contortions of face and body which he was making, when he was presented with a silver crown, and, on being questioned, volunteered to be shot in the same way at the same price once a day for the rest of his lifetime. At first, I was seriously alarmed by his howls, and some of the eight gentlemen with guns who had fired sixteen barrels, more or less, in his direction turned pale as possible murderers. The poor boy was an outsider, and his interested howls were no test of his courage. I am convinced that no one of our party would have made any fuss at all for a pellet or two; indeed, under the excitement of the rare appearance of game, the fusillade at these hunts is so hot and so irregular that no man who cannot trust his nerves under fire should ever join a Portuguese *caçada*. Still it is use and temperament that make men cool; and, well as the Portuguese have shown that they can stand fire in more serious fields than those of sport, I do not quite think they could come up to the equanimity which I have myself seen displayed by an English gamekeeper.

It is within my knowledge how, in a famous shooting county, an under-keeper was placed in the centre of a large wood to stop the birds. An Eton boy was among the shooters, and getting, as boys will, out of the regular line, and coming near to where the keeper was posted, he saw, glancing through the thick underwood, that person's brown-gaitered legs. The boy, taking them for a hare, fired; but observing that the beast, as he thought, hopped away a short distance unhurt, he loaded his single-barrelled gun and fired again, so continuing to load and fire in hot haste—the faithful servant dodging about a good deal among the bushes, but never actually deserting his post. At last the line of shooters and beaters came up :—

'Well, gentlemen!' said the keeper, 'I'm glad you've come at last; the little gentleman have been a-pouring of it into me, terrible!'

As to the hare of which I said that we bagged her in a very literal sense. it happened in this way : we found her on her form, and she had not, I am sure, left it two yards before she was coursed and caught by the greyhounds, attacked by the lurchers, and shot by everyone who had a gun; consequently she was killed before she had given any sport whatever. She made amends, however, afterwards. Among the pack was an ill-looking lurcher, whose bad character had caused remonstrances to be addressed to the owner by the other sportsmen. '*Coitado!* Poor dog!' said his possessor, 'let him come. He will be miserable if we leave him, and howl so that my wife will wish herself dead!'

He came, and stuck to his master's heels the whole morning in the most exemplary manner. When the hare was killed it was his master who carried her, holding her by the hind legs, and the dog, seeing his opportunity come, suddenly gripped the animal in his teeth, and held on with such force, as his master tried to pull it away, that presently the dog was left with the head and the master with the body. Others of the pack attracted by the noise, seized that part of the hare still held by the gentleman, and got it from him, while another detachment of dogs pursued the lurcher with the head in his mouth. Then began a novel kind of chase, with more shouting and flying about of quarter-staves, and laughing and tumbling down. Some of us tried to recover the body, some chased the head. We were very much out of breath before we again got together the two portions of the hare.

'Bring the needle and thread!' was called out.— *the* needle and thread! necessities in this kind of sport where the game is set upon by such packs.

They were brought. The decapitated quarry was cleverly sewn together, the fur smoothed down, and then *gravely insinuated into a narrow linen bag*, also brought for the occasion.

Then we pushed on again, and presently a volley from the whole force brought down a red-legged partridge; a little further on and the dogs started a fox in a thick piece of gorse. We shot him. Another volley at close quarters proved fatal to a woodcock, whose long bill was nearly all that remained to prove his identity and the straight shooting of the eight gentlemen who had fired. Then came luncheon, and we fought all our battles over again, killing the slain many more times than thrice. Then we degenerated into politics—local chiefly, and election matters, just as we should have done at home.

Now, I have noticed that Portuguese gentlemen

of all shades of opinion, when they get together
among friends, like to talk about and strongly to
declaim against the realization of a certain wild project which is well known to European politicians as
the *Iberian Idea*—the project, that is, of bringing
Spain and Portugal together under a single crown.
Oddly enough, this question is shirked in the Press of
the country, though Liberals and Conservatives alike
are against it, and, indeed, easily worked into a state
of patriotic and very natural indignation at a mere
suggestion of the possibility of such a thing. Even
the Miguelites, who are still not uncommon through
the country, though their cause is growing more and
more a chimera with every year of peace and good
government, and though their Miguelism now usually
sits as lightly upon them as did his Jacobitism upon
Dr. Johnson—even these, professedly unsatisfied men,
protest against Iberianism as a thing running counter
to all the interests, and the aspirations, and instincts,
and grand traditions of the country.

The truth about the Iberian idea is, I believe,
simply this—that the possibility of its realization is
not perhaps quite so remote as patriots and outsiders
suppose. A large party has always desired it in
Spain, and, curiously enough, a small one even in
Portugal. The country itself, however, unlike some
others, is too small for the unpatriotic, even when
swelled by the fools, to make a large party. Among
Continental politicians, the Absolutists, the Ultramon-
tanes, and the Reds would each for their own and
obvious reasons like to see the Iberianism of the

Peninsula an accomplished fact. In England, where
we know by experience something of racial antipa-
thies, no one, I suppose, would desire to bring about
any such union, or even a federation of Spain and
Portugal, always excepting the numerically insignificant and incurable party among our own countrymen
who tried to help on Carlism at the expense of
toleration and free institutions, and who seemed at
one time to expect in their unwisdom that Iberianism
would advance their views.

The only section of the British public who would
actually benefit by a realisation of the Iberian idea
would be the holders of Spanish Stocks. Spanish
Three per Cents. would certainly go up, and Portuguese as certainly go down.

After lunch we had better sport and even better
amusement than before. A brace of woodcocks
were brought down and cleverly snatched from the
dogs. A second hare got away from the guns, and
was run into after a good course. Its exceedingly
mangled remains were repaired as before, and fitted
into another little bag. But the several rabbits we
came upon gave more occupation and amusement
than anything, doubling backwards and forwards
among dogs and men to the most excitingly imminent peril of both. One gentleman, laying about him
with his quarter-staff in the direction of a passing
rabbit, struck his best friend so heavy a blow on the
ankle that he dropped to it, and had to be 'restored'
before he could limp on with the party.

I do not know whether it is that the air of a Portuguese autumn day in these great sandy forests of pine or chestnut, with their gay undergrowth of aromatic shrubs, is more exhilarating than other air, and peculiarly conducive to a flow of good spirits, or whether the good humour and enjoyment come from the incidents and circumstances of a Portuguese shooting party; certain it is that the thing is most enjoyable. In describing this particular one, I am not telling of what happened on any particular day, or to any particular set of people: I could not venture upon such an impertinence to my friends to please any reader. It is a general account of a typical *caçada*; and those who know what such a thing is will agree that it is not unfaithful. In many a one have I joined, and, coming home again, I have sometimes compared the day's sport with one spent in English coverts. In Portugal, a pleasant day's ramble in the forest, with not much game indeed in hand at the end of it, but the lasting memory of many very surprising and unlooked-for adventures and misadventures. In England, a return homeward often wet through and chilled to the bone, having stood for hours in the sleety wind, over the ankles in mud and water, my right shoulder stiff and sore from long and monotonous shooting, perhaps my host looking black at me for having missed the solitary woodcock of the day, or for having killed more than my allowance of hen pheasants.

When French people wish to say that a party of pleasure has been successful, they sum up with the phrase, '*Nous avons beaucoup ri.*' I could always have made the same remark after a shooting expedition into the woods of Portugal.

It is the poet Thomson, I think, who has said that 'a serene melancholy is the most noble and most agreeable situation of the human mind;' but admitting all the nobility and serene delight of melancholy, that mental attitude would be a most difficult one to maintain among an enthusiastic and good-humoured party of Portuguese sportsmen out for a *caçada*.

COUNTRY HOUSE IN PORTUGAL.

CHAPTER V.

FARMING AND FARM PEOPLE.

He who comes to Portugal in autumn in search of the picturesque must not, as a rule, expect to find it quite after the pattern to which he has become accustomed in Northern Europe. Here there is none of the calm and stately beauty of an English autumn, the leafage slowly bronzing with the early touches of frost, the russet bracken standing up in finer contrast than ever with the greenery around, and the fallen beech leaves spread like golden patines on the smooth sheep-cropped turf. This is very delightful,—and pleasant it is in the keen October air of our own country to walk out and see the slow and gradual death of the year; a summer mellowed and tempered with the coming breath of frost and snow,—a winter still warm with the sun of the waning summer.

After a different fashion does autumn come upon us here in Portugal. The meeting of summer and winter is not a gradual transition, but a sudden contest. To walk out upon an autumn day is not to assist at a euthanasia, but to see the victims of a great elemental strife: the fields are fields on which a battle has been fought.

The hot Lusitanian sun has stimulated an extraordinary wealth of branch and leaf growth, and suddenly the downpour of equinoctial rain has come upon it, and the strong winds have brayed and broken everything, and covered the fields with leaves sodden and decaying already in the warm and steamy air. In the most cultivated districts the waste and desolation are greatest, for the maize straw is mostly lying in the fields in discoloured stooks,—the most unsightly of harvests,—and the vines are no longer picturesque, but their long sprays straggling where the wind has left them, and their leaves either falling or hanging down half withered and unshapely, have lost all the rich sun-tints of summer.

The damp atmosphere which hangs over the land at this time of the year is to some susceptible constitutions a little ague-laden, and I warn the tourist against a visit to Portugal till the heat of early autumn be overpast, till the last week in October, when bright, clear weather is the rule for all the rest of the year. When St. Martin's summer begins—on or about the 11th of November—there have disappeared the very last of the mosquitoes; and though they are little troublesome in Portugal, attacking one only at night, their bite grows more and more envenomed as the summer gets older, till in September they are at their fiercest.

A far worse plague than mosquitoes is also past, —the plague of flies. The present writer may claim to have done his full share of the travelling which

modern society requires of its members.   He has
cheerfully set out on, and often more cheerfully returned from, rambles in most European countries. He
has come to the conclusion that among the greatest
evils of foreign travel in the South are the flies ; more
troublesome than beggars in Spain or donkey-boys in
Egypt, worse than the inn-keepers of Germany or
the brigands of Italy, greater pests even than vulgar Englishmen in Switzerland.

It is so much the fashion for modern philosophers
to deal with the infinitesimal, and triumphantly to
trace great effects to small and unsuspected causes,
that one may well wonder that science has so completely overlooked the influence of flies upon the
destinies of the human race.   The savant whose
guiding principle often is *de minimis curat scientia*,
might build up a very pretty theory upon the relations of *Musca domestica* and *Homo sapiens*, and a
difference of manners, of habits, of temperament, and
even of dress, might be traced between the people of
countries where the house-fly is numerous and active,
and countries like England where it can almost be
left out of account altogether.   The swarms of flies
are in the South no trivial matter in the economy of
life, but, though an every-day incident, one important enough to be had in serious consideration,—
to be made, for instance, the subject of grave simile
and comparison.   When Homer is describing the
heroic rally of the Trojan warriors round the dead
body of Sarpedon, he does not think it beneath the
dignity of the occasion to compare their numbers

and their obstinacy, and the noise of their arms in
fight to the clouds of flies which

> At spring time in the cattle-sheds
> Around the milk-pail swarm with buzzing wings.

To take but one point :—the habit of taking a
siesta, a habit in itself modifying the whole home-life
and character of a people, and one which we North-
erners consider so thoroughly effeminate, is certainly
due not to the heat of the South, but to its flies.
None but those who have suffered it can have any
notion of the exasperation which is caused to a man
who is the victim of a cloud of buzzing flies throughout a long summer day. Mental labour becomes
quite impossible when things get to their worst, at
three or four o'clock, when the afternoon is hottest
and drowsiest and the flies at their busiest. At such
a moment the human intellect is almost incapable of
exertion ; no brain could work out a long division sum,
no one could write a leading article or even a sermon.
A man is driven to a dark room where the flies will
not follow him ; he goes not for coolness only but for
peace, and being at rest and in the dark, he necessarily
sleeps. This is the rationale of the siesta of the South.

It is only inside the house that the flies are wholly
intolerable ; out of doors they are as numerous but
not aggressive. In Malta I once saw a regiment
seemingly of clergymen marching along the high road,
—a fearful spectacle ! A closer inspection showed
that this alarming infantry was nothing more formidable than a body of our own honest soldiers, with

their scarlet uniforms blackened and quite concealed
by myriads of flies. But flies in the open air are
stationary and on their good behaviour; indoors the
Southern fly is ever on the move, *quærens quem* and
quid devoret. It is the home-keeping women who
suffer, not the men who have gone afield; and therefore it is the women who always cover their heads
with hoods or handkerchiefs, the men only when they
live indoor lives,—hence monks are hooded, women
veiled. One step more and we have the *Yashmak* of
the Turk, the *Zenana*, a general invasion of women's
rights and liberties, and I know not what beside,—and
all to be traced, if philosophers would but see it, to
so seemingly trivial a cause as the common house-fly!

So far as weather is concerned, I do not know
that after all I do well to warn my compatriots
against the steamy air of a Portuguese autumn. We
all, Englishmen, Irishmen, Scotchmen, Welshmen, and
Cockneys, have a weakness for dull weather. We
have eaten and slept and walked and talked in fog
and rain; it has come to be a second nature to us.
In truth the Briton admires but does not always in
his heart love the climate of what he is pleased to call
'the sunny south.' Its brightness to him is glare, its
constancy monotonous. 'These blue skies are charming in theory,' I once heard a candid Englishman say,
'but the long droughts are too much for me, they
burn me up, the sunlight oppresses me,—I want
moisture, I want rain,—I want,' he said with a loving
emphasis on the words, '*nice, warm, muggy rain!*'

If the traveller is not to be deterred by dull skies and rain, and will come to Portuguese soil during the autumnal equinox, he will find the country, in so far as its agriculture is concerned, at its most critical and most interesting stage.

The social, financial, political, and even religious aspects of Portugal are almost wholly identical with its aspects as a country of farmers, of vine-dressers, of shepherds, and of graziers. Except for a small population of miners, of fishermen on the rivers and estuaries, and of sailors, the whole population should be, if political economy had proper sway in the country, purely an agricultural one. Unfortunately, very fallacious principles prevail among the governing classes, and several branches of manu-factures are encouraged to languish, and the people are heavily taxed by a high and omnivorous tariff. Portugal, however, is a country which, since its liberal awakening fifty years ago, has shown such progressive wisdom in all the arts of government, that I firmly believe that all these false protective theories wait but ' the inevitable hour ' to be swept away, and that when the country awakes to common sense in such matters it will become, more thoroughly than it is even at present, a country of farmers. Even now the intelligent observer of foreign social problems looks to find their solution in the condition of agricul-ture. I have met with more than one such observer on their travels, and their honest expression of opinions, even when they have little time or opportunity or perhaps ability to form them soundly, are always

interesting and often instructive, though not always
in a way they themselves might suppose or desire.

A stout, intelligent, and highly conversational
German was holding forth fluently at the *table d'hôte*
of an hotel in a certain important city of Portugal
as I not long ago took my seat at that board, and I
listened with patience to his opinions. The Germans,
as everyone knows, have lately, and only lately,
become a highly practical people. Delighting no
longer to hold aloof from the ways of ordinary men
and to keep to the cloudland of ideology and transcen-
dentalism, they have descended to *terra firma*, and are
willing to instruct the whole world in the business of
its daily life. Does a financier think he understands
the exchanges and the fluctuations in the bullion
market? Let him talk for five minutes to a German
and learn his ignorance. Do we Englishmen and
Americans think we know something by experience of
representative government? The first Berliner shall
show us our mistake. The schoolmaster who is now
abroad in the world is the German Professor, and he is
no longer either abstruse, or impracticable, or philo-
sophically contemptuous of Philistinism. Perhaps
we want to know how to fight or to farm, to garden
or to cook, to write books or to paint pictures? The
Professor will instruct us, and if we do not want to
be instructed, he will instruct us all the same—or all
the more.

'After all, these Portuguese are fools,' the German
was saying,—he qualified the word by an epithet
which need not be recorded—'they are fools, gentle-

men, as farmers: they fatten cattle without cake
or roots; they don't know how to make their hay;
instead of reaping their corn with a machine, they
cut it with a thing like a gardener's knife; and when
they might use improved ploughs by good makers,
they employ a crooked branch with a tenpenny nail
tied to the end of it!'

The wit rather than the wisdom of the speaker
(who delivered himself in an English which though
fluent I have ventured to transpose into a more
vernacular key) caused a laugh among those of us
who understood him.

I gathered from some further remarks which fell
from this gentleman, that he was one of the class who
travel in the interests of their friends at home, and
generally carry assortments of the staples of these
friends' business in bags or other receptacles. From
the cynical tone noticeable in his conversation I
concluded that he had found some difficulty in
' placing' these goods among the Portuguese. No
men are so full of information and opinions as
' travellers' of this class, or so anxious to impart
them, and I was willing enough to be instructed.

' I must admit,' I replied, ' that the Portuguese
farmers are little better than barbarians from your
point of view, but what I should like to gather from
you is, how it would better their condition to use all
these new-fangled improvements.'

My new acquaintance smiled a serene smile.

' You have perhaps, sir, not read the works of the
great English writer Smith?' he asked.

'I have read Adam Smith in the original,' I
answered.

'You will then perfectly understand how the
wealth of nations can be increased by division of
labour, and by economy of labour, and by perfection
of labour.   Now, it is clear that when a farmer cuts
a clumsy plough from the nearest wood, hammers out
his own ploughshare, and ploughs his own land with
this miserable implement, there is neither division of
labour, nor economy of labour, nor perfection of
labour.'

'You could not,' I said, 'put it more neatly.'

My stout acquaintance smiled again.

'It is the same all through the farm system.   The
farmer might use cake to feed his cattle and enrich
his fields.'

'I admit the cake.'

'And surely, sir, you must admit that he could
grow roots with advantage, reap his corn crop with a
patent reaper, and his grass with a patent mower.
He might cut his chaff by steam, pulp his roots by
machinery, steam them in one of our patent steamers ;
to say nothing of employing our improved elevators,
and rollers, and crushers, and scarifiers, of all of
which, poor man, he is as ignorant as the child un-
born.'

I took advantage of a slight pause, during which
the German took out an illustrated catalogue of a
well-known English firm of agricultural implement-
makers, to say—

'But, assuming that he could employ all these

improvements, and reform his ways with all these novelties, how would he be the better?'

'Sir, he would be the richer.'

'Would he be the happier?'

Herr Sacculator smiled for the third time. 'Really,' he said, 'I think we may assume that wealth is the first step towards happiness.'

'I believe,' I said, 'that we know as little of the first as of any subsequent step on that road.'

Irony was never well bestowed on a German, and he went on : 'The mere possession of good wages is certainly in itself a most excellent thing. It gives a man opportunities for dealing with the political machinery of his country, and leisure for self-culture and the various graces of life.'

'In some parts of the county of Hertfordshire in England,' I remarked, 'the women and children work at straw-plaiting, and each family makes a good deal of money. Yet the people do not care a rush for politics, and are so removed from self-culture and the graces of life that a more idle, poaching, ill-mannered, immoral set of sots are not to be found in broad England.'

Facts are as nothing when compared with general principles, and the German gentleman proceeded undisturbed.

'You will surely,' he said, 'not put forward such a paradox as that poverty conduces to a people's happiness more than wealth?'

'Sir,' I said, 'if I put forward, or seem to put forward, any paradox whatever. it is less to defend it than to give you the opportunity of refuting it. If you can show me that wealth and welfare are the same things, you are very welcome to do so.'

'If I can in any way conduce to the making of the Portuguese a wealthy people, it is clear that I make them also a happy people.'

'Then it is obvious,' I said, 'that the more chaff-cutters and patent rollers and scarifiers and elevators the Portuguese can be got to take, the happier they will become.'

'Certainly ; the more contented.'

'I know nothing of that,' I said. 'It may be less what he gains than what he looks to gain that makes a peasant contented. Peasants are only human after all.'

'Those are refinements,' said the German shrewdly, 'that I would rather not enter into. Wealth, I say, and contentment are correlative terms.'

Then we argued, or rather the German argued, and he declaimed, and he convinced himself, and convinced himself that he had convinced me, and finally at parting he shook hands with me, and expressed his pleasure at having encountered so entirely reasonable a person as myself.

I trust that I am at least not stupid enough to try to confute a man against his will ; I am sure that I have enough sense not to think I can convince any man against his interest. The German gentleman may possibly have been right in his conclusions, but he had arrived at them in considerable ignorance of the facts ; and there is certainly this one advantage in seeing much of the world, and coming into contact

with the great variety of unpleasing facts and people
therein contained, that a man gets at last almost to
lose the disagreeable habit of generalizing and any
undue sense of the value of general principles—most
fertile sources of disputation and argument.   A rolling
stone gathers no moss; a Professor vegetating in a little
German University—the educated German is ever of
the Professorial type—gathers a great deal, and
evolves in the unwholesome atmosphere about him so
much of prejudice and preconception, as that hardly
any collision with the hard edges of stubborn facts
shall ever afterwards rid him of.   Still my German
chance acquaintance was so intelligent a person that
he might have hesitated to suggest a violent reform of
the whole system of Portuguese agriculture, had he
known only as much of its conditions as it is my intention to communicate to the reader forthwith.   His
judgment was indeed becoming visibly affected by so
much of the true doctrine as I was able to instil into
him between the courses of the *table d'hôte* dinner.

Farming in Portugal is, as I must admit, at a
standstill, and it has moved very little for some fourteen hundred years.   There is consequently immense
room for improvement.   For every hundred bushels
of corn that are now produced another fifty could, I
have little doubt, be grown, with improved husbandry ; and two hundred beasts could probably be
fattened for every hundred that the farmers now sell.
The nation would therefore, if this be so, become a
richer nation ; but this could only be the case after a

profound modification of the existing condition of
things. Though the political economist might welcome a nation with a doubled power of consuming
cotton goods and hardware, and though the statistician
might like to write down on his tables so many more
millions of Portuguese souls, horned cattle, sheep,
pigs, and bushels of corn, it does not at all follow that
the sum of human well-being would be one jot the
greater, that the star of happiness would be one
degree higher in the Portuguese heavens, or that
some very disagreeable problems would not present
themselves for solution which now no Portuguese
statesman is ever called upon to solve.

If I did not think there were some lessons to be
learned from the conduct of a Portuguese farm, I
should not venture to say so much as I am going to
say about Portuguese farming.

Though we are so backward in all the arts of
agriculture, we yet in Portugal can do what if all
British farmers could do the wealth of Great Britain
would be trebled, and the tide turned against agricultural distress for a century.

We can grow corn in Portugal on the same land
year after year. I say ' we,' for I am myself a practical farmer, and have farmed in Portugal for more
than ten years. The reader shall presently see how
we solve this great problem of continuous corn-crop-
ing, and, if he be a farmer, he shall judge how far the
system can be made applicable at home.

I think our five bad English harvests have brought
home to us more feelingly than ever how great an

interest the farming is, how much more important than any other, almost than all others. An excellent authority has just been laying down almost as a new discovery what certainly should have forced itself on our convictions long enough ago as little better than a platitude. 'The success,' says this eminent economist, ' with which agriculture is practised in a country is the measure of that part of the population which is set free for other employment, or may subsist at leisure.' He could not have said a truer thing, though, perhaps, he might have put his truth more fully and more clearly.

Now, if we look back at the agricultural history of any country, which is not by some exceptional degree of fertility or vastness in its territory elevated above and beyond the reach and wish of competition from other countries ; if we look at the farm history of our own country, for instance, we shall see that its agricultural industry has thriven, not progressively, but by fits and starts : now a time of depression, now a revival, and after it, for a time, prosperity again. In countries like America and Russia, of great natural fertility and suitable climate, breadcorn, the staple of farming everywhere, may go on for ever being produced on their vast productive prairies and steppes, with the minimum of interference from man's intelligence ; but we know but too well how little that is the case at home. Here, if we are to thrive, it is our own wits that must beat the elements, and win the day for us against competition from the outside.

If we look back at the records of British farming

we may read plainly how its periods of prosperity,
local or general, have ever followed some capital device
of man's ingenuity, some invention, some new process,
or the novel application of some established principle.
Now the good times followed the introduction of the
new turnip-growing system ; now they followed the
system of artificial grasses ; now of the imported and
manufactured chemical manures, or of the artificial
foods for sheep and oxen.   Or again, it was the use
of farm machinery which filled the farmers' pockets,
or the improved breeds of cattle which fattened early,
and gave him beef where his fathers got bone ; and
always, as competition pressed on, the impulse lost its
force, and dying away left all farming better, all England the richer, but no one farmer better off than his
neighbour.

    Of these various devices and inventions many came
from abroad, as every farmer knows, and chiefly from
the north-western parts of Europe, where men's wits
are keenest, the population thickest, and the struggle
with nature most active.   I am not aware that any
one idea has ever come in recent years from the south
of Europe.   From Portugal certainly we have never
imported a single agricultural idea with the splendid
cattle and the many pipes of port wine which that
country annually sends us ; and yet it is in this backward country that the thing is done which, if England
could do, England's wealth would be trebled and quad-
rupled.   Nothing so astonished me, when I first saw a
luxuriant Portuguese maize field, as to be told that it
had produced such a crop summer after summer for a

century, and would continue to do as much for as long again. It was some little time before the solution of this problem became manifest to me. The reader shall have the means of judging whether it is in Portugal only that this profitable feat is to be performed, or whether our English farmers may not do as much.

The land in Portugal throughout the length and breadth of the country is held under five principal kinds of tenure—the allodial, the emphyteutic, the leasehold, the communal, and a tenure termed *Parceria rural*, which differs but little from the Metayer system of Bavaria, France, and Italy. Here, as in those countries, the landlord finds the land and sometimes the seed, and receives for rent a proportion of the produce.

The Allodial is the tenure which prevails chiefly in the wide and naturally fertile plains of Central and Southern Portugal. The holder of the fee simple of the land either tills his own broad acres with the minimum of capital, energy, and knowledge, or, if the estate is too large, lets it on short and uncertain leases to tenants who take his place and farm it, almost to as little purpose as himself. The Communal tenure is to be found chiefly in the wilder and more mountainous regions; the communist holders are, for the most part, the lineal descendants of the original communal grantees of the land at a time when the country had just been recovered from its Saracen occupants. Such holdings were, no doubt, frequent in parts of the country where now the original communists have been, in the course of successive ages, bought out, or forced or cheated out of their lands by neighbouring nobles or churchmen. Wherever remoteness or the poverty of the soil offered no temptation to such powerful encroachers and swindlers, the communes have endured, though often greatly mutilated of their original rights and privileges. On the mountain frontier between Leon and Portugal, I have found cases where they had dwindled to the common possession of a range of pasturage or a grove of chestnuts, a couple of rams or a single bull.

The metayer system is commoner in the South and Centre than in the North. It seems in Portugal, as elsewhere, to have grown out of the want of capital in landlords and in tenants, and, as elsewhere, it is probably the best possible system where such impecuniosity prevails. In Scotland, as is well known, much valuable land has been brought into cultivation through the working of this system, and every political economist remembers the discussion raised by Sismondi upon the metayer system, and knows all about its various advantages and disadvantages. In Scotland, payment of rent in kind has given place to money payments; in Portugal, neither enough agricultural nor enough financial advance has been achieved to make this possible, and for the metayer system this only can be said that, while agriculture under it is unprogressive, the condition of the people who engage in it is infinitely superior to where the lord of large estates cultivates the land himself, or

deputes it to tenants who can afford to the labourer
only the barest means of subsistence, and who are by
necessity alien to him in degree and in interest. The
metayer, on the other hand, is a man of small means,
but he is, as it were, insured against absolute ruin, for
he divides his losses as he divides his gains with his landlord ; he has the strongest motive for hard work and
good work, for his welfare depends upon both, and—
chief advantage of all—he himself being hardly higher
in rank than the peasant whom he has hired to work
with him, there can be some social sympathy between
employer and employed. The Portuguese metayer
need not be a capitalist, in even the most limited
sense, and every labourer may aspire to become a
metayer himself. The peasant, therefore, has that
without which labour is but another name for
serfdom : he knows that the lottery of life may hold
a prize for him, and it sweetens his toil to feel that
his own diligence and honesty can help him to the
winning of it.

There is in Portugal another tenure of land, the
Emphyteutic, in some of its incidents so singular, and
in its origin and development so unlike anything to
be found elsewhere, and in all these respects so instructive, that I make no apology for dwelling upon
it at some little length.

Portugal, as everyone must remember from his
first geography lessons, is a narrow strip of country,
extremely mountainous where it marches with Spain,
hilly in its three northern provinces, and having
broad and fertile plains in its centre, through which

plains the River Tagus flows to the sea. The most
southerly of its six provinces, Algarve, is in its
climate, in the aridity of its soil, and even its
palmetto-covered plains and hill slopes, like a bit cut
off from Africa. Here the communal tenure is still
to be found, but the land is also held allodially and
by leasehold. It is in the rich central provinces of
Estremadura and Alemtejo that the allodial tenures
chiefly prevail. In the remote frontier province of
Traz os Montes, lying beyond the important hill range
of the Marão, in the north-easterly corner of the
kingdom, the communal system of tenures is to be
found; and in the populous province of the Minho,
the most northerly of all, the estates are small and
numerous, and held, as a rule, emphyteutically.
This is the most prosperous district in Portugal, and
probably in the whole Iberian peninsula. The Minho
has been compared to Lombardy, and the Minhotes,
from their gentler manners, gayer character, and
better looks, have been called the Italians of Portugal. Yet this superiority is certainly not due to soil,
for the province is by no means the most naturally
fertile of Portugal; nor to difference of race, for the
population of the kingdom, from the Tagus, northward at least, are probably homogeneous, or nearly
so. Its prosperity is, I believe, chiefly due to the
existence of a tenure by which the length and
breadth of the province is parcelled out among small
yeomen landlords—a tenure with many of the incidents of our English copyholds—and partly again is
this prosperity owing to the vicissitudes in the history

of its peasantry, which have ended in the achieve-
ment by them of this excellent tenure.

I must ask for the reader's patience while I tell
him how it was that time and a somewhat fortunate
coincidence of events, and, not least, their own pru-
dence and determination, have won for the yeomen
of the Minho the happy condition in which they now
find themselves.

Portugal differs from most of the countries of
Europe in this, that no permanent and general settlement of the land was made or was possible until a
comparatively late period. The laws, the customs,
and the institutions left by the Roman colonists in
Portugal were more or less effaced by the incursions
of northern nations; and before these barbarians had
time to settle into the fairly decent feudal Christians
of mediæval Europe, their backwood laws, and their
customs, and their institutions were all but effaced by
the Saracenic invasions and occupations, and the subsequent conflicts of the eighth and following four
centuries. The advance of Saracenic conquest had
destroyed or swept into captivity the inhabitants of
vast tracts of the country; and though these regions
were gradually resettled and repeopled by the Portuguese, the final ascendency of the Christians was an
issue of such slow growth and such gradual consum-
mation, that when at last the Moors had been driven
from the land, no claimants were forthcoming for
much of the reconquered territory. A large share of
this unowned land was apportioned among the military leaders and the nobles; a larger share became

Church or convent property; and the largest share of all fell to the lot of the great Military Order which had waged a holy war on the soil of Portugal, and had mainly helped in its recovery.

If the land had come chiefly into the hands of the nobles, as in some other countries, the eventual formation of emphyteutic estates would probably have become impossible; but it resulted from the generosity towards the Church both of kings and private donors, and from the comparative parsimony of royal land grants to individuals, that the Church became the chief possessor of real property throughout the country; and the prelates and heads of monastic orders occupied the place and possessed the influence of the great landholding nobility of our own and of other countries of Northern Europe.

The contests between the barons and the kings of England were anticipated in Portugal by contests between the landholding prelates and their sovereigns. The history of Portugal in the two hundred years which followed the expulsion of the Saracens is the narrative of this strife, in which the churchmen never failed to lose ground, and the sovereign ever sought to lessen their influence. No better means of doing so presented itself than to diminish their paramount influence as landholders; and with this object, and also, it may be inferred, to re-occupy the wasted country, the efforts of nearly every successive monarch, after the departure of the Moors, were directed to establish proprietors and cultivators of the soil other than monkish ones. Particular care was

taken that these newly-formed holdings should be
limited in size. King Sancho I., the successor of the
first great king and conqueror, Affonzo Henriquez,
was unwilling to bestow on an individual more land
than he could cultivate with his family, his slaves
and his servants. This example was followed by
King Sancho's successors.

The waning power of the Church would no doubt
indirectly tend to bring about the same end—namely,
a multiplication of small proprietary or semi-proprie-
tary holdings; for the small convent farmers, origi-
nally tenants at will or for definite periods, as soon as
they perceived their monastic landlords to be losing
power, clamoured for and obtained fixity of tenure and
fixity of rent. The holding thus granted, or not disputed, was termed *aforamento*, or a holding by payment
of a *foro* or fixed rent ; and this good old Portuguese
word would have been the designation of the tenure
to this day, only that later on, when letters revived,
in the fifteenth and sixteenth centuries, there revived
too the learning of the Roman jurists, and the
pedantry rather than the necessity of the Portuguese
antiquarian lawyers led them to christen the old
tenure by the Greek and Latin name *emphyteusis*.
The ancient emphyteutic tenure is almost close
enough in its resemblance to the vulgar *aforamento*
to justify the pedantry of the antiquaries; and
though the farmers themselves will not part with
the old word, the lawyers use no other than *emphyteusis* for a copyhold estate and *emphyteuta* for a
copyholder.

By the course of events which I have been en-
deavouring to describe, the *emphyteutas* obtained
some sort of a hold upon the land; but it was still a
precarious one, and their position for a long succession of generations was wretched in the extreme.

Many causes were constantly at work to impoverish their holdings, and to perpetuate and aug-
ment the allodial estates and the wealth of the larger
proprietors—churchmen and nobles—their lords and
their neighbours. The very stringent law of entail
and primogeniture existing in Portugal, directly
devised to consolidate the great estates, was not
relaxed till late in the eighteenth century, and the
ever-recurring diminution of the emphyteutic estate
by fines upon alienation and succession (fines and
heriots were from the first incidents of emphyteusis)
could not but keep these small proprietors in a state
of miserable penury and dependence.

In the middle of the fifteenth century their condition had become—in their own opinion at least—
abject. In a memorial addressed to King Affonzo V.,
they speak of themselves in pitiable terms, as having
to part with their very cattle to satisfy their lords, as
being ground down by exaction, and as being—as
they express it—shorn like flocks of sheep. In
picturesque language, they represent themselves as
being driven into the towns by hunger and by oppression, and that the very beasts of the field, the
birds and the insects, had conspired to rob them of
the few grains of corn which they still possessed.

The patriotism of the kings of Portugal, or their

anxiety to countervail and impair the power of the
Church and the nobles, did not suffer them to leave
such petitions unanswered; but relief to the Portuguese yeomen reached them slowly. It is by no
means unlikely that their estates would have fallen,
in time, into the possession of the great landholders,
but for the action of two causes, both singular in this
respect, that one of them did not and the second
could not happen in any of the countries of Northern
Europe. The first of these causes was the sudden
growth throughout Portugal of a thirst for foreign
and distant discovery and conquest, fostered by the
Infante Dom Enrique at the beginning of the
fifteenth century.

This spirit of adventure continued for two centuries
to be almost universal among the upper and the upper
middle classes of Portugal. The natural desire of
these classes to acquire influence by acquiring land
was directed to this novel and speedier mode of gain-
ing money, influence, and fame. Wealth flowed into
the country, but it was spent luxuriously in the cities,
and country life has never since those days been
popular with the richer classes in the same way that
it is popular in France, in Germany or in England,
and the possession of landed property never such an
object of ambition.

The second cause of the consolidation and prosperity of the emphyteutic estates will appear even
more singular to an English agriculturist. This was
the introduction from America of the cultivation of
maize in the middle of the sixteenth century. Much

more than root crops and rye grass have done for
the Low Countries or the potato for Ireland has been
done by maize in Spain and Portugal. This productive grain has been a boon to Portuguese farmers,
and above all other farmers to the emphyteutic
farmer. It is obvious that, granting fixity of tenure
under unalterable conditions of rent, services and
obligations,—however burdensome they may origin-
ally have been,—the contract having been made in
unsettled times, and in a half-peopled country, these
conditions must necessarily grow less burdensome
with the increase of population, with the development of communications, with the growth of security
to life and property and with the general rise in
agricultural prices which always accompanies these
conditions. This has happened ; and no single cause
has contributed so much as the possession by the
farmer of the new cereal, which enabled him to more
than double the yield of his corn-fields.

As years went on, the grievances of the yeoman proprietors, as set forth in the memorial I
have quoted above, righted themselves ; the rack
rents became quit rents, and the recurring fines
and the exactions of the superior lords became
trifling in comparison with the increased value of
the land.

When the first great statutory reform of the emphyteutic system was made in 1832, upon the
ascendency of the Liberal cause and the establishment
of Liberal principles in Portugal, the emphyteutic
tenures were burdensome rather from the compli-

cated and uncertain state of the law relating to them,
than from any actual hardship to the holders.[1]

The operations of farming throughout non-pastoral
Portugal do not materially differ from those in other

[1] The law relating to Emphyteusis is now finally defined and
settled by the Civil Code promulgated in August, 1867. The
rent is to be fixed by mutual agreement, not by any custom; fines
on alienation and succession are abolished; the emphyteutic
estate, though hereditary, is not to be parcelled among the heirs,
except with the consent of the lord; the value of the estate is to
be discovered by assessment, and distributed among the heirs
according to law. (By Portuguese law, only one-third of the
testator's possessions can, in the majority of cases, be disposed of
by will; two-thirds are divided among the heirs.) If they cannot
agree upon a valuation, the value is to be decided judicially. The
heirs are to determine among themselves upon which of them the
estate is to devolve, with reference to a court of law in case of
their non-agreement; if none of them desire to hold it, the estate
is to be sold, and the price to be divided equally among them. In
case of non-payment of rent, the lord may proceed to recover it as
an ordinary debt, with interest, but has no right of re-entry even
though such a right be expressly stipulated for. An action for
the recovery of arrears does not extend further back than five
years. If the holder waste the estate, so that it fall below the
value of a sum equivalent to the rent capitalized, with one-fifth
added, the lord may re-enter into possession without making any
compensation to the holder; the holder may mortgage the estate
without the consent of the lord, provided the sum so raised do not
exceed the capitalized rent, with one fifth added. The holder may
alienate, after due notice to his lord, who has a right of pre-
emption. The lord may also alienate his part of the estate (his
seignorial rights), likewise giving notice to the holder, and in such
a case a corresponding right of pre-emption resides with the
latter. These provisions apply to emphyteutic estates created
after the publication of the Codes (except those provisions relating
to succession, which take effect retrospectively), and it will be
observed that, excepting the lord's right of entry in case of waste,
they are all in favour of the holder.

The emphyteutic lord has by this legislation come to be hardly

parts of Southern Europe, where wheat, rye, and
maize are the corn crops, where oxen and mules are
the beasts of draught, and where the cattle are stall-
fed. This is the farm system of the alluvial valleys
and great plains of Portugal: in the mountainous
regions, where there is continuous pasture, the people
are shepherds or herdsmen; in the extreme South,
orchards of the carob tree and the fig form no
small proportion of the farmer's wealth: in the
marshy, sea-bordering land, rice is grown. Olives
afford him good return everywhere but in the North,
and chestnut trees give him a precarious food crop—
and the best timber in Europe—everywhere but in
the extreme South. In almost every corner of the
kingdom the vineyard is an essential part of the farm.

The passing traveller through many broad tracts
of Central and Southern Portugal, if he be acquainted
with farms and farming in some of the countries

troublesome at all to the virtual owner of the estate, and to dis-
charge something of the functions of a useful police in the interests
of the community generally, as against wasteful and detrimental
farmers.

Existing tenures are otherwise only affected by the Code in insignificant details, with this important exception, that whereas the
tenure by emphyteusis might formerly be limited to one or more
lives, the choice of a successor either residing in the holder or
restricted by some clause in the original deed, or else the right of
presentment to the holding of the estate being in the lord's gift
(in which case the tenure constituted a simple tenancy for lives),
by the present law both lord and tenant are deprived of any such
right of nomination, and the estate becomes a purely hereditary
one, subject to the succession above described. By this reform
many ancient estates of most complicated tenure have been brought
into the category of simple emphyteutic estates, to the great advantage of the country and of individuals.

of Southern Europe, where over-taxation and ill-government have crushed the spirit of the toilers on the land, will find much in these portions of Portugal to remind him of such thriftless and unprofitable cultivation. It is not till he crosses the Tagus on his way northward that he will find some signs of at least more energetic farming in the western corner of the province of Estremadura. As he passes the boundary line of the Beira province, cultivation sensibly improves; but it is not till he finds himself on the north of the River Douro that he will see a land of small farms tilled like well-kept gardens, luxuriant crops in summer and winter, and a gaily dressed, thriving and contented peasantry. Yet it is a land where there is no Poor Law, no large estates, no squire justices, no high farming, no agricultural machinery, no resident landlords, and not even an occasional rich and educated parson to take the squire's place in a parish. Notwithstanding all these serious disadvantages, this small province is so thickly peopled, and its people so prosperous, that if ever our own rural districts should come to rear so dense a population of the same sort the production of our looms and iron works would have to be doubled and trebled to supply them, and we could any day put an army into the field to match the armed hordes of Continental Europe.

It is not probable that any other mode of holding the land would have resulted in the same agricultural activity and well-doing as now prevails in the provinces of the Minho, under the tenure by emphyteusis. The hilly nature of the ground and its necessary subdivision into small farms; the abundance of water of irrigation; the constant care which is required not only in its application to the land, but in the construction and reparation of tanks, waterwheels, and channels; the watchfulness necessary to uphold the farmers' rights and to prevent encroachments;—all these are circumstances under which the profitable tillage of the land can be accomplished only by small farmers, and by them only if their wits and industry be sharpened by actual ownership of the soil they till. The self-reliance, the perseverance, and the providence of these independent yeomen are qualities probably not resulting entirely from the nature of the tenure, but also from the long training of successive generations, during which they have slowly won their present rights and standing.

Emphyteusis is, as I have said, the largely predominating tenure of Northern Portugal. Being so, its influence very perceptibly extends beyond the parties interested in the emphyteutic tenure. It is the standard tenure of this portion of the country, and it has certainly modified the relations of landholder and landworker everywhere. When listening to the conversation of the tenantry of the Minho and the Beira, whether they be leaseholders or metayers, it is impossible not to be struck by the good sense and moderation of their opinions on matters connected with their relations to those above and below them. Without drawing any comparison with the not uncommon spirit of bitterness both of the landlord and

tenant classes, where the latter can never hope to
occupy his landlord's position, as is the case in some
of the southern provinces of Portugal, I may at least
express my opinion that the little distance which
separates the worker upon the land from the owner
of it is a powerful promoter of sympathy in either for
the difficulties and responsibilities of the other.

Farming in Northern Portugal is almost exclusively on a small scale, limited by the small size of
the estates; and the general reproach against small
farming—that it is unprogressive—applies truly to
this part of the country. Farms of fifty acres are
uncommon; those of from five to fifteen acres are
probably the average size in the Minho; and here a
a difficulty presents itself at the outset in writing
upon the farm system of Portugal, in this, that no
measure of the land itself is ever adopted, and
therefore no ready means exist of comparing its
powers of production with those of other countries.
The value of a farm is determined, not by its rent,
for from the nature of the common tenure, rent has
ceased to be a measure of value; nor by its acreage,
for land without water of irrigation bears no comparison in value with similar land possessing it; but
by the number of cartloads of Indian corn, or, in
mountainous districts, of rye, which the whole of it
can produce in average years.

The implements and tools in general use are
ploughs of two sorts, harrows, a broad, heavy hoe
(which takes the place of a spade), a smaller one for
weeding, and a small reaping-hook, which is used

indifferently to cut grass and to reap the various grain crops.

The ploughs differ very little from the old Roman type, and the description of the implement left by the Latin writers applies very nearly to the simpler and smaller of the two kinds now used by the Portuguese. This plough consists of a beam, body, share and sole, with, as a rule, only one stilt. There is neither coulter nor mould-board, but the share is carried far forward (as in the Kentish turn-wrest plough), is lance-shaped, and turned slightly downwards. The work of the mould-board is done by two upright pegs at the heel of the plough, which pegs press out the soil on either side. The whole plough can easily be carried afield on the shoulders of a labourer. It works only four or five inches deep, and stirs the soil in parallel, open furrows; and where the land is light and crumbling, as is generally the case, this slight working of it would seem to be sufficient. The other plough employed is a modification of the smaller and simpler one. It has two stilts, one or two wheels, a low double mould-board instead of the upright pegs, and occasionally (when it is required to turn over a furrow slice) a broad coulter is inserted in a hole in the beam, which works behind the point of the share, and serves to invert the slice, its inclination being changed at the end of each furrow; but the Portuguese ploughman has often no occasion to alter his turn-furrow, being given to the bad practice of driving a curved furrow from the boundary of the field, and continuing it circularly to the centre till the whole field is ploughed. This plough will work as deep as seven or eight inches. The fields are so small and so irregular in shape, and the ground as a rule so easily worked, and, again, the whole surface cultivated by each proprietor so limited, that it would be difficult to persuade a Minho farmer that a plough which only costs him twelve or fourteen shillings, which he can repair himself with very little expense, and whose use he perfectly understands, is less suited to him than a more perfect and complicated instrument of five or six times the cost.

The harrow is also of the rudest construction, having fifteen to twenty teeth of iron or wood set quincunx fashion into a strong, oblong-square, wooden framework with two cross-bars. Rollers are unknown, but as a substitute the harrow can be reversed and weighted with stones, and then drawn sledgewise over the land.

The hoe is indispensable in Portuguese field-husbandry. The larger kind is a flat piece of iron, shaped like and two-thirds as long as an English spade, fixed at a slightly acute angle upon a long handle. It is used in earthing up maize, in planting field-cabbages, in making and altering water-courses, and in supplementing imperfect ploughing. It is worked with a skill that no labourer used to the different movements required by a spade could probably attain to. Ground can be prepared by it for seeds or for planting more quickly than it can be

dug by a spade, although the soil is less completely
stirred and turned over.

The clumsiest of all Portuguese tools is the mowing
or reaping hook; which, as the cattle are mostly stall
fed, is in constant use. It is in shape a short segment
of a circle, of which the arc is about a foot in length;
the edge is serrated and very sharp, and the hook can
be used to cut grass not more than five inches high,
the tuft of grass being grasped in the left hand and
the edge of the reaping-hook being drawn against the
stems. The work of cutting grass is exceedingly slow,
and a man cannot cut more than half a rood in a day's
work.

The cart used throughout modern Portugal is, like
the plough, a modification of the old Roman type;
two low wheels of solid wood, without spokes and
with iron tires, are fixed immovably to an axle which
revolves with them. The body of the cart is composed of four or five boards laid flat and resting on
two supports, whose lower sides are grooved where
they rest on the axle. Straw or grass is retained on
the flat table formed by these boards by six or more
movable upright poles, fitting into iron-bound sockets
at the sides and corners of the table-like boards, the
centre board being prolonged forwards into a strong
pole, to which the oxen are harnessed. In carrying
stones, earth or grain, a thick, wattled, and flexible
hurdle about thirty inches high is fixed, in horse-shoe
shape, upon the table of the cart inside the uprights;
the opening behind is closed with a board. The
whole cart is enormously strong, and the separation

of the wheels and axle from the body allows it to stand the shocks and joltings of roads which are often little more than watercourses on the steep sides of hills.

The yoke is fixed to the necks of the oxen; in some parts of the country—the most hilly—to their horns, and when so fixed a leather cushion takes off the pressure from the foreheads of the animals.

The cattle are a small and beautiful variety of the dun-coloured breed found in most parts of the Peninsula. In this country they are bred for draught rather than for meat, and therefore their points are not such as an English grazier would approve. The oxen average fifty-two inches in height at the shoulder, and twelve hundredweight in live weight, when three-parts fat; but they reach sixteen and sometimes eighteen hundredweight. They are compact in shape, with deep and most powerful shoulders, sturdy legs, and carry straightish horns of great width. Their strength, hardiness, quickness, docility, and great beauty of shape and colour, are generally appreciated by observant persons accustomed to the working cattle of other countries. Both cows and oxen are used for draught purposes. The beef is close-grained and good.

The sheep of the Minho, and of the lowlands of Northern Portugal generally, are the worst in the kingdom; one or two sheep often live with and follow the farmer's small herd of cows and oxen, but flocks are hardly ever seen, except in the mountainous districts.

The breed of pigs is said to be improving; it has still, however, all the marks of a neglected race— length of leg, largeness of bone, and coarseness of bristle. They fatten very slowly, as a rule. Here and there a good breed has been produced by a cross with the Chinese race ; at Barroso, in the North, an excellent breed is to be found, and another is abundant on the plains of the Alemtejo.

The system of tillage in Portugal varies so greatly from the processes of agriculture adopted in Northern Europe, that a clearer perception of this variation will be given by a comparative calendar of farming operations in England and Portugal than by any long description of the divergences between the two systems.

ENGLAND.	PORTUGAL.
January.	
Hauling manure : ploughing of grass leas for wheat or oats : of stubbles for crops and beans.	In this month the maize fields reaped in autumn are either lying fallow, or, having been sown with artificial grasses, are mown throughout the winter for the cattle.
February.	
Wheat, bean, and pea sowing : preparation of ground for green crops.	Sowing of all corn crops, except rice, maize, and rye. The pruning and tying of vines should end this month.
March.	
Sowing corn crops, grass and clover seeds, vetches, peas, beans, and parsnips ; rolling of wheat.	Sowing of corn as in February ; and breaking up grass leas for maize sowing in following month ; planting potatoes.
April.	
Finishing the sowing as above ; sowing carrots, mangel wurzel, cabbage seeds in beds, flax, lucerne, etc. ; horse-hoeing wheat, etc. ; planting potatoes.	Sowing maize, kidney beans, gourds : planting Galician cabbages in maize fields. Haymaking on a very small scale.

ENGLAND.	PORTUGAL.

May.

| Preparing land for turnips; hoeing growing crops, etc. | Sowing of maize continued; hoeing of early-sown maize fields. |

June.

| Sowing first swedes and then turnips; transplanting cabbages; mowing clover and vetches. Early hay-making. | Harvest of barley, oats, rye, wheat, and broad beans; hoeing and thinning of maize; men engaged daily in the maize fields, putting on water of irrigation, etc.; cutting *serradella*, clover, and plaintain for stall-feeding. |

July.

| Turnip-sowing; hay-making; cutting beans and peas. | Continuation of harvest of all cereals, except maize, which requires constant attention wherever water is available; field onions gathered. The male flower of the maize is gathered. |

August.

| Corn harvest. | Work in maize fields as in July. |

September.

| Clearing of and ploughing up stubbles for winter wheat; sowing Italian rye grass, winter vetches, etc. | Harvest of early-sown maize; of rice; vintage. |

October.

| Winter wheat and bean sowing; ploughing land against spring sowing. | Harvest of maize, and vintage, continued; ploughing of stubble and sowing of winter barley, rye, and wheat; also sowing of rye-grass, with rye and barley, for winter forage; harvest of kidney beans; planting of kidney beans; planting of Galician and other cabbages. |

ENGLAND.	PORTUGAL.

November.

Root harvest ; ploughing up of stubbles and leas.	Sowing of broad beans, winter wheat, rye, etc. ; men busy on the threshing-floors and in the barns ; vine pruning, begun in end of October, throughout the month and next three ; olives gathered in this and following month.

December.

Hauling manure and threshing.	Sowing of rye, etc., as in November ; hauling manure out, and threshing.

The chief feature of the lowland tillage of the greater part of Portugal is the growth of maize, to which all other culture is made subservient. In deep, well-manured and irrigated land, maize will produce from twenty to fifty imperial bushels of a grain of a value averaging that of barley, about a ton of forage in early summer, and from half a ton to a ton of most nutritious and excellent straw food. The same acre of ground on which maize is grown likewise produces dwarf beans and gourds—about two to five bushels of the former, and from one to three tons weight of the latter to the acre. So productive a crop, which in land well-manured and with water of irrigation available would seem to be producible year after year without exhaustion of the soil, is a temptation to ignore any system of rotation whatever ; consequently, during the five hottest months of every year, the ground is occupied with this corn. I shall presently show how it is that this apparent flying in the face of all received agri-

cultural doctrine is chiefly the result of the consumption on the farm of all the straw it grows and the use
of gorse as litter.

Maize can be sown as early as March in this latitude, but it is profitable to put off the ploughing up
of grass leas—which are then in full production—
till as late as possible. The middle of April is the
average date for sowing, but seed-time may be deferred till the 15th or 20th of May, or even later. The
seed is sown broadcast, after one or more ploughings
with the larger kind of plough; if the land has been
manured for a previous autumn crop of artificial
grass, no manure (or but little) is put in at seed-time;
but if not, a very liberal allowance of well-fermented
cow-dung, sometimes as much as thirty tons to the
acre, is put upon the land.[1] The manure is spread upon
the unbroken lea, and covered in at once by a deep
ploughing. The land then undergoes some amount
of clearing and levelling with the hoe, which clears
away the surface weeds; in some cases it is harrowed
before sowing, but oftener not. The seed (from six
pecks to two bushels per acre) is then sown broadcast,
and harrowed in. With each bushel is mixed a
quart or so of some kind of dwarf kidney-bean, and
about half as much gourd or melon seed. The beans
and gourd plants appear before the maize. It is usual
to hoe the maize plant when the fourth leaf-spike
shows, and about twenty days afterwards the earth is
drawn round the plants; from this time forward they

[1] The manuring is repeated every year, but not every year to
this extent.

are thinned out for cattle feed. When the male flower has arrived at its full perfection it is broken off, within about eighteen inches of the top of the stem, and used as a food for cattle. Irrigation wherever available is freely employed, as soon as the plant has depth of root enough to stand the wash of the water, and until the whole plant begins to show yellow. The cobs are cut when the husks are quite dry and when the seed feels hard beneath it; and the less critical operation of cutting the straw is often delayed if the weather be wet. The operation of husking is often made the occasion of a feast—a kind of harvest-home, where wine and dried fish and bread are given by the farmer, and large parties of the peasantry assemble and work far into the night, to the music of guitars and violins.

The husked cobs are dried in the sun on the threshing-floor, and in a fortnight or less are ready for threshing out, which is the universal mode in this country of getting out the grain. The straw when cut is left in stooks in the fields till it is dry enough to carry home.

It is clear that this whole system is open to several grave objections; many of them, however, are incident to and inevitable in the nature of small properties. The mixture of several crops in one field has always been considered a fault in farming. In the case of the Portuguese farmer, it is the result of some amount of forethought; being too poor to risk his whole income on a single crop, he calculates that when he loses part of his corn in a dry year he gets

a larger return of beans, and that a year favourable
to neither may give him a good crop of gourds.
His sacrifice of some of his maize crop is therefore a
rough kind of insurance against a total loss of it.
The apparent waste of seed is required to allow of
enough young plants being thinned out for the early
summer food of his stock.   The great amount of
labour required in hoeing the land is a serious draw-
back to the system : but in a country of small proprietors, of small farms and capitals, and of small enclosures, it would be of far less advantage to replace
manual labour by drills and horse-hoes than in such
a country as the United States, and the cheapness of
labour in some degree compensates for the amount of
it required.

Imperfect preliminary cultivation of the soil is
perhaps the worst point of the Portuguese system,
and this also is, to some extent, excused by its friable
condition and its comparative cleanness.

With the last hoeing of the maize, rye-grass is
sometimes sown, from which a first cutting is taken
in October or November ; but it is more usual to
spread the maize fields, in September, with all the
manure which can be got, and to sow rye-grass,
mixed with either oats, barley, or rye,[1] or more
frequently these three corns together, on the manure
itself, and then to plough in with the smaller of the
two ploughs.   This very wasteful and slovenly
method of producing an artificial grass field, never-

---

[1] The classical scholar may care to be reminded that this is
identical with the *farrago* of the ancient Roman agriculturists.

theless, generally results in an abundance of green
food throughout the winter and spring. The rye
yields a first cutting in about five weeks, and a
second very abundant one is obtained from all the
plants jointly at Christmas time; but the uncertain
depth at which the seed is covered, some being left
bare and some buried too deep for germination, causes
much loss of ground and labour, if the weather be
either very dry or very wet at seed-time.

It is a constant practice in Portuguese husbandry
to plant cabbages in the maize fields. When this
corn is sown in spring-time, a labourer cuts a cleft in
the ground with a single downward stroke of a broad
hoe. He holds the hoe in the ground till an assistant
has placed two young cabbage-plants one at each
corner of the cleft; the hoe is then removed, and the
earth pressed down. The men walk in a straight line
across the field, planting two cabbages at every
second pace, and then trace similar parallel rows,
twelve or fifteen feet apart, till the whole field
is finished. In the heat of summer, and when
shaded by the growing maize, the cabbage plants
make little progress; but when the corn is reaped,
and the field manured and ploughed for its crop of
grass, the cabbages grow rapidly, and throughout the
winter afford a constant supply of leaves for house
use, and for feeding cows and pigs, and even sheep.
The cabbage used for this purpose is a large variety
of the cabbage known at home as the 'Jersey cabbage,'
and by the French as the *Chou Cavalier*. It grows
to the height of six feet or more, if allowed to attain

to its full size. The two lower leaves are picked off, week after week, till the whole plant is cut down in spring, to allow the soil to be again prepared for the maize crop. It is the presence of the rows of cabbage in the maize stubbles that makes it necessary to use the small plough, and to work the land so that the plants may not be disturbed. After the plough has done what work it can, the untouched ground in the line of the cabbages is turned over with the hoe.

Root crops are of little importance to the Portuguese farmer. The porous soil would suit the cultivation of turnips admirably, but not the heat and dryness. They are grown, but on principles and with results unknown to the British farmer. A common way of growing them is to sow them upon the maize stubble with rye grass ; the roots are never hoed, and, entangled and obstructed by the grass, seldom exceed a large apple in size. Again, they are sometimes sown after onions, as I shall presently show, and with fair success. Where, owing to bad seasons or bad cultivation, the roots do not swell, it is common to let the turnips run to flower, and a cutting is obtained of the leaves and flower-stems in January and February. Rape or mustard seed would probably be better suited for this purpose, but I have seen neither used.

Potatoes find but a small place in the simple system of Portuguese agriculture. Till lately they formed no part of the general food of the people, are not used for cattle feeding, and are seldom grown at all, except in gardens or near towns. The same applies to carrots, mangel wurzel and parsnips, the two latter of which I have never seen growing in a field in Portugal.

Wheat is the predominant cereal of the provinces to the south, where large fields and a stiff soil are commoner than in the north. Its cultivation in the north is adopted sometimes in rotation with maize, or on soils too dry for the latter and too stiff for rye, or when manure is not forthcoming for the maize crop. The small farm system does not, as may be supposed, favour the cultivation of wheat, and the crops are seldom good. To judge by their appearance on the ground, I should consider twenty imperial bushels to be an average crop of wheat in these provinces. Winter wheat is sown from November to the end of January; spring wheat from January to March; both kinds are reaped in June and July. I have noticed seven or eight varieties of wheat, mostly the bearded kinds. Hard wheat and soft are in about equal proportions. Red wheat is, so far as I have observed, unknown, probably owing to the absence of strong dark clays, to influence the colour of the skin of the grain.

Broad beans are rather a garden than a field crop, and the early sowing which the climate allows is very favourable to their growth. They are sown broadcast, and their cultivation is the same as in Great Britain. The sort used is, I believe, only a very large variety of the common horse-bean.

Much more important and extensive objects of cultivation are the different kinds of kidney beans (*Phaseolus vulgaris*), of which I have counted six chief

sorts of the dwarf variety, and four of the climbing
sort. Of the dwarf kidney beans, the small white,
the striped black and yellow, the brown, the dark
yellow, the mottled, the grey and the black beans, all
differ considerably, not only in flavour and productiveness, but in the soils they require and the greater or
less luxuriance of the plant ; thereby enabling the
farmer to grow the particular kind most suited to the
soil and exposure of each field. The climbing beans
are less used ; the large white, the common scarlet-
runner, a brown and red mottled kind, are all grown,
—sometimes on sticks, but oftener on the stems of
the taller kinds of maize. The climbing sorts all
require a richer soil than the dwarf beans.

The chick-pea (*Cicer arietinum*) is less cultivated
in the northern than in the southern provinces of the
kingdom, where it is an important part of human
food ; it is sown in autumn, and does well on light,
dry and sandy soils. I need hardly say that it is
identical with the *garbanzo* of Spain.

I have already described the cultivation of these
various plants in describing that of maize, and the
same remark applies to the gourd. Besides these
plants, the lentil, the lupine, and the grey field-pea
are all grown : the lupine very commonly for its seed
and likewise as a green manure ; the lentil less frequently ; and the field-pea very seldom.

The gourd and the tall cabbage together may be
said to take in Portuguese farming the important
place of root crops generally in the English farming
system. It is difficult to compute the yield of the

gourd by the acre, for the ground is never exclusively occupied by them; but it is probable that in a richly manured soil with water of irrigation, a weight of sixty or seventy tons might be raised to the acre,— about double the weight of a good crop of swedes. Three or four very well marked species are grown; the largest is the round, smooth kind (a variety of *Cucurbita pepo*), which I have seen grown in a field to the weight of two hundred pounds. The long, yellow, and striped sorts are, I believe, varieties of a different species (*C. citrullus*), and are those commonly employed.

The gourd is left on the ground for a fortnight or more after the maize is carried, and in that short time greatly increases in size with full exposure to sun and air.

For cattle and pigs, gourds are a most valuable winter food, and they also enter largely into the consumption of all classes of the people. They keep sound, in dry years, till the end of February, and are not injured by sun or rain if kept standing in a dry place; it is usual, therefore, to lift them to the roofs of low buildings, along the tops of walls, or to leave them standing on rocky ground, whence they are removed as they are required for use.

Melons and water-melons are objects of field cultivation in Portugal, chiefly the latter species. The kinds mostly grown are the cantalupes and the common green smooth-skinned sort, and more rarely the musk melon. The melon is not grown with other crops, but by itself, in land ridged up with shallow

furrows eight or ten feet apart. A rich soil, a dry
atmosphere, and water of irrigation in dry seasons,
produce very large crops. Water-melons are grown
on the same system, and give a less precarious and a
larger return than the sweet melon, and their abundance and cheapness allow of their very common use
by the peasantry.

Of the various artificial grasses and forage plants,
only a small choice offers itself to the farmer of the
Minho and of the maize-growing district generally;
of these, rye-grass is by far the most commonly used.
The object of the farmer being to leave the ground
in the occupation of such plants for as short a time
as possible, he sows oats, barley, and rye in autumn,
as I have already mentioned, solely for the sake of
the two or three cuttings to be got from them; the
rye-grass, coming later, gives at most two or three
more cuttings in the spring. In damp soils the
narrow-leafed plantain (*Plantago lanceolata*) is sown
early in spring or in autumn, and affords frequent
cuttings of a rich cattle food in early summer, the
time when herbage is scarcest with the Portuguese
farmer. It is sometimes left in the ground through
the winter in land subject to overflow or inundation,
and it is often grazed as well as cut.

The common meadow soft grass (*Holcus lanatus*)
is often grown in precisely the same way; it affords
a more abundant but not so good a herbage.

A leguminous plant of very frequent use is the
serradella (*Ornithopus perpusillus*), a plant which is, I
believe, untried in England, but which was introduced

into Germany about twenty years ago. The plant is annual, grows in sandy soil, but prefers a deep, sandy loam, where it will grow to nearly the height of a yard. It is sown in autumn, hardly shows above ground till Christmas, and affords one good cutting in May or June, in time, in favourable years, for the sowing of the maize crop. Red and Italian clover are grown very much in the same way.

Millet (*Panicum italicum*) is grown as a herbage plant. It is one of the few plants which can be sown with advantage at midsummer, and it is often made to follow rye or even wheat. It is usually cut before the seed has ripened, or, as often occurs when late sown in this climate, when the grain has formed, but ripened imperfectly. It is made into hay which has probably about the value of good meadow-hay—that is, three times that of wheat or barley straw.

It is to be observed of the climate of Portugal (as of most of the climates of Southern Europe) that winter and spring are the seasons when grass fields—natural and artificial—are at their best; and, whereas in Great Britain the farmer is most pinched for sheep and cattle feed in early spring, having consumed his roots, and his pastures being still bare, the farmer in Portugal is at this season better provided with forage than at any other time of the year.

I have now given some account of the various crops which make part of the regular system of tillage in the maize-growing portions of Portugal. Two other plants are extensively grown, but both are accessory to the general farming routine of the district—flax and onions : flax principally for home consumption, and onions for exportation to England and Brazil.

Wherever good, light, alluvial soil occurs along the banks of rivers and elsewhere, the flax plant is found growing, mostly in patches, but sometimes in great breadths. The farmers in the north of the province of the Minho—a chief centre of flax cultivation—speak commonly of two distinct species, the Galician and the Moorish ; the first of these being the plant cultivated in the country from time immemorial, the latter said to have been brought about sixty years ago from Northern Africa. The Moorish flax—perhaps *Linum perenne*—is a taller plant, with a stronger and coarser fibre ; the Galician is under the average size of flax grown in England, and not of fine quality. The Galician is the sort chiefly cultivated : it is sown in the last fortnight in April, and is pulled in July, having been from two to three months in the ground. The Moorish flax is sown before winter, and is taken up a month earlier —that is, in June—after remaining in the ground about seven months.

Great care is used in the preparation of the soil for both kinds. It is often ploughed three times ; all weeds, stones, etc., are picked out ; and for the spring (or Galician) flax the ground is lightly dunged with well rotted manure. This kind of flax is likewise irrigated ; but the Moorish flax is neither manured nor irrigated, and a richer and deeper description of soil is required for its production.

The Galician is steeped in river water for about eight days, the Moorish variety nearly double that time, according to the temperature of the air. The flax is in some cases steeped again for two or three days after it has been taken out and dried.

Some portion of the flax grown by the smaller farmer is broken and skutched by hand; but in most cases both these operations are done in a mill worked by mules or oxen, one of which mills is usually kept in every village in flax-growing districts. The final preparation, or heckling, is usually done by women in workshops in the larger villages and towns.

The flax produced in Northern Portugal is consumed in the country.

Oporto is the chief port of exportation for the large variety of onion which is known in trade as the Spanish or Portugal onion. Its cultivation is quite an agricultural operation, and is managed as follows. In the month of October the seed is sown in a sheltered spot in very well manured seed beds. In about ten days the plants appear, are watered in dry weather, weeded, and the surface occasionally stirred with a sharp pointed stick. The young plants, not subjected to any severe frost (for the thermometer very seldom falls below thirty-five degrees of Fahrenheit), enjoy an uninterrupted growth till springtime. In March they are taken up, being then some five to eight inches in height, and planted from nine to twelve inches apart, in furrows made by the hoe in well-ploughed and harrowed land. The furrows are filled to the depth of three

or four inches with well-rotted manure, with which
the roots of the young plants are placed in actual
contact. A very essential condition of the successful
cultivation of the onion is water. The abundant
and timely irrigation of the growing crop requires
great and constant care. After transplanting, the
crop has two or more hoeings and weedings. With
the last weeding are sown, either white turnips,
maize, or, more rarely, grass seeds. The onion crop
is off the ground in August, and sometimes in July.

The stolen crop of maize so obtained grows
rapidly in the enriched soil, and often produces as
large a crop as the spring-sown fields. The turnips
grown after onions are pulled in December and
January; and although the roots are left far too
near together, they are the only instances I have ever
seen in this country of fairly well grown turnips.

Although irrigation, as in most southern countries,
has so very important a share in the success of farm
operations in Portugal, yet the configuration of the
land, the absence of extensive plain country at a
lower level than an unfailing water supply in the
uplands (as is the case in Lombardy), the want of
long, fertile valleys connected with lakes, or accessible highland rivers (as in Southern Spain), have
stood in the way of any general system of canaliza-
tion for irrigating purposes in Northern Portugal.

The water of irrigation is obtained in four different ways:

1. By wells sunk into water-bearing strata,
whence the water is drawn either by a water-wheel,

worked by oxen and made to lift an endless chain of
buckets, or by some similar contrivance.

2. By wells worked by similar machinery and
sunk near the course of slow-flowing streams. The
water thus obtained is carried to the interior along
aqueducts.

3. By means of weirs, in rivers which have a good
fall in them, the water of which rivers works flour
mills in winter, and is carried in summer to irrigate
fields on a lower level.

4. By the water of springs, often got by carrying
adits far and deep into the hills.

This latter kind of irrigation is far the commonest,
it is increasing year by year. Water is prospected
for and mined for in Portugal as silver ore is in
Nevada. It is slow wealth, but it is sure: the metal-
liferous lode gives out, but the water flows on, *in omne
volubilis ævum*, and the miner who has struck water has
his profits in perpetuity. Some men have a curious
gift for water-finding, and scent it out by very faint
indications. To them a tuft of rushes in the forest,
the growth of the yellow iris on the mountain side, or
the purslane and water mints springing up away from
their accustomed haunts, are signs enough to betray
the secret underground. Of course many trial shafts
are sunk in vain, and if one wanders in the lonely pine
forest which covers so many leagues of Northern
Portugal, one is for ever coming upon these forgotten
shafts and air holes, dangerous pitfalls, bramble-
covered, into which men have been known to slip
unawares, and pass hours calling in vain to the

hawks and woodpeckers, till some chance charcoal-burner or woodcutter has come within hearing. In these subterranean channels the water is often conveyed for miles to the valley below, and the labour expended on these conduits represents a quite incalculable investment of profitable capital. The worst of the system is the ease with which a man can be undermined and defrauded of his dear-bought water. The law courts are filled with disputes as to water rights, and the proverb 'Stolen waters are sweet' seems to be one that should have originated in this country.

Irrigation in warm countries is generally understood in a different sense to the irrigation practised on grass lands in Great Britain, where the water flows on, over, and off the field. Here it is diffused over a larger surface, and the watering which maize, onions, and other plants get is equivalent to the watering of plants by hand in a garden. The water is brought to the roots and sinks in. The porous nature of the soil to a considerable depth, the great degree of evaporation, and the absence of any water-retaining strata near the surface, obviate any sourness in the land which might result from the presence of so much water upon it. I have never seen or heard of any description of land drainage in Portugal (except that by wide, open drains in marsh lands); and in the prevalent crumbling, decomposed granite soil of the North, where the earth only hardens into an impervious rock at some yards beneath the surface, and in the schisty soils which are as common and as pervious, no kind of drainage would seem to be required

In Portugal the straw of all cereals enters far more largely into the consumption of oxen, horses, and mules than in Great Britain. Hay is made in the mountainous pasture lands of Traz-os-Montes, and on the great hill range of the Estrella, but only to a very small extent elsewhere, and the expense of carriage is too great to allow of its use beyond the district of its production. Of the different straws, agricultural chemists assert that 300 pounds of wheat straw, an equal quantity of barley straw, 350 pounds of rye straw, 280 pounds of oat straw, and only 200 pounds of maize straw, are respectively equivalent in nutritive power to 100 pounds of good meadow hay. This calculation of the relative values of the different straws more or less corresponds with the experience of farmers here, who have incessant practical acquaintance with the subject. Rye straw is harder in this climate even than in England, and is called 'colmo,' or thatch, and the name indicates the use which is commonly made of it; but in the hilly districts it is often consumed from necessity in the feeding of cattle. Wheat straw is likewise hard and dry, and difficult of digestion, but is largely used. Barley straw is what is given, in preference to all others, to horses, the general prejudice against it in Great Britain being unknown here. Oat straw is produced only in limited quantities. The straw of maize, or rather the dried lily-like leaves of the maize plant, for the stem is mostly rejected by cattle, is supposed to be unsuitable for horses, and is not often used for feeding them. It is, with grass, the chief food of milch cows and of fattening and working oxen both in winter and summer, and, to judge by its obvious effects, and by the high estimation in which it is held by Portuguese farmers, it probably exceeds the value at which it is put by agricultural chemists.

Now I come to what I believe to be the solution of the problem of the continuous corn-cropping of the Portuguese farmer. The straw produced on the farm is almost exclusively—in most farms entirely—consumed as cattle food; and it is a peculiar and marked characteristic of the agriculture of this country, that the fodder used in the stabling of horned cattle, horses, and pigs is supplied by dried gorse, heather, and the various wild plants, such as bracken, cistus, rock-rose, bent grass, and wild vetches, which usually grow in their company. To secure a sufficient quantity of such litter, most farms have attached to them a portion of forest or wild land, from which these fodder-producing plants are regularly cut every three years, and which forest portion is often a mile or more away from the farm-yard. In other cases, the farmer enjoys a prescriptive right to cut as much of them as he chooses from the pine forest nearest to him. Of the plants so used, gorse is the predominating one, often to the exclusion of all others. It is the same species as is found in Great Britain; but the prevailing kind is, I believe, a variety of our native gorse, having the prickles rather less stronger and the stem less woody. The

decaying of manure made with this litter is slower
than with straw, but the porous wood of the gorse is
infinitely more absorbent both of gases and of
moisture, so that the atmosphere of a Portuguese
stable or cow-byre, is very noticeably purer and
sweeter than if straw were used, and the standing for
the beasts is also much drier. It is needless to point
to the economy of a system by which every particle
of straw is consumed as food. A second recommen-
dation is that, while the seeds of the various field
weeds are not returned to the ground with the straw
among which they were grown, those which are shed
by the forest plants, when removed from their native
soil, find no congenial seed-bed when they fall upon
cultivated land, and either fail to germinate or fail to
thrive. The gorse, heather, and other plants which
compose this litter are cut, or rather scraped up,
with the broad-bladed hoe, so that moss, creeping
plants, the decomposing needles of the pine trees,
dead leaves of trees and shrubs, and the crowns and
root stock of ferns and wild grasses, all find their way
together to the farmyard. I know no other country
where this practice is carried out in a systematic
manner as in Portugal. The amount of manure produced on a small Portuguese farm could not fail to
strike a Scotch or English farmer, and the disregard
by the Portuguese farmer of any system of rotation
of crops is, as I have said, principally due to the
abundance of valuable manure at his command.

The farm-buildings of the smaller proprietors are
simply but substantially built of squared granite, and

the whole lower floor of the house is often used
for the storing of grain and straw, and sometimes
even as a stable for cattle. A small yard, kept knee-
deep in gorse litter, is generally formed by the side
or two sides of the house, and the building which holds
the wine-press and cattle byres. High over this yard
are grown, almost invariably, vines on a heavy wooden
trellis, and the cattle in the heat of summer find coolness and shelter under their shade. Outside the
buildings, well exposed to sun and wind, is the *eira*,
or threshing-floor, of slate or granite slabs, to which
is usually attached a small barn.

The farmer in Portugal is almost without any
choice either of natural or artificial manure. Guano
is hardly known, though its concentrated form and its
known value in growing maize might seem to recommend it in a country of difficult communications.

Along the sea-shore various kinds of sea-weed
are regularly collected, allowed to ferment and decay,
and applied directly to the maize crop with good effect.
A still richer manure is furnished by a small species of
crab, caught for the purpose in nets in vast quantities.
At Aveiro and other places, where the coast is marshy
and intersected by estuaries, inlets, and slow-flowing
streams, boats are employed in dredging up the ground
weed, mixed with rich, decaying vegetable matter and
small shell-fish, from the bottom of these brackish waters,
to be used as a dressing to the fields in their neighbourhood. These various manures supply valuable phos-
phates and alkalies, and to some small extent take the
place of the artificial manures used in Great Britain.

The vine in the Minho district is grown on pollarded oak and chestnut trees, and on trellises. It is pruned when the supporting tree is cut back in winter, and gets no cultivation but what it shares with the crop growing beneath it. The vine strikes its roots so far into the soil that it probably does no harm beyond the slight injury caused by the shade of its dense foliage in summer. The vines give a harsh, dark-coloured grape, and the wine is of the kind known as *Vinho verde*, green wine, and rarely keeps sound a whole twelvemonth. It is a rough, harsh, acid wine, of powerful flavour, and exceedingly disagreeable to those who are not accustomed to its use

The inhabitants of Portugal, or at least of Northern Portugal, are, as I have said, probably homogeneous in race; but the character of the peasantry, their habits and their manners, vary considerably in the different provinces, with the difference of their condition, which again is generally traceable to their circumstances and surroundings.

The Minhotes are a well-fed, well-clothed, law-respecting, courteous people, of a cheerful and sociable disposition. They are good and intelligent labourers, and make excellent soldiers. On the other hand, the character of the inhabitants of some of the mountain parts of Beira, and of the more remote pasture lands of Traz-os-Montes, is of a more gloomy cast. Crimes of violence—agrarian and otherwise—were until late years not unfrequent in these districts, and often remained unpunished; and the gravity and reserve of the shepherds and herdsmen of these parts contrast strongly with the sociable manners of the lowland husbandmen.

I am disposed to think that the condition of the Northern Portuguese peasant generally—excluding the dwellers in some of the poorer and more unhealthy districts, whose penury and misery are often extreme—is, on the whole, superior to that of the great average of land-workers in Europe generally. A conclusion upon this point, drawn from the appearance of the people themselves, can hardly be deceptive; but such an opinion would be supported by a closer examination into the system of wages, the amount and kind of their food, and the social habits generally of the peasantry.

The mode of hiring labour differs in each province. In Estremadura and Alemtejo, and in other parts of Portugal where the tenure is allodial, hiring by the twelvemonth is common; and a labourer will earn from five to eight pounds a year, with food, housing, fuel for cooking, and a coarse woollen cloak given him every two years. The wages of labour are slowly rising in all Portugal.

In Beira, and generally throughout the northern provinces, hiring for parts of the year is the common practice. From three to four or five pounds are given for the five months from December to April; a general rehiring then takes place, and a wage of from four to seven pounds is earned for the rest of the year, to include the hard work of maize-hoeing and harvest work in the long days of summer. The contracts are

made at the different local fairs held in April and
December.

In the Minho, among the small emphyteutic
yeomen, a curious practice exists (with almost endless
modification), by which the yeoman proprietors take
upon their farms a labourer who is paid partly in
wages, partly in kind, and partly out of the profits of
the farm. The contract is by its nature so complicated and so liable to perversion, that without the
good sense, fairness, and moderation of the labourers
and peasant proprietors of this part of the kingdom,
the carrying out of it would be impossible. The
system seems to work perfectly, and possesses very
obvious advantages over any mode of simply buying
labour with money wages. The wages of a day
labourer, without food, vary from eight to fourteen
pence throughout the country.

The fare of the Portuguese peasant is coarse, but
it cannot be said of it that it is not comparatively
varied and abundant. The following scale was
furnished to me by a farmer in the Minho, and is
probably an average one :—

Food of three farm servants (two men and a woman) for a week.

Dried codfish	6 to 7 lbs.
Lard .	1 lb.
Olive-oil . .	1½ pint.
Rice . . .	1 lb.
Bacon	1 lb.
Bread (of rye and maize)	30 to 40 lbs.
Gourds or cabbages	. *ad libitum.*
Olives	. a quart in summer.
Wine .	. a pint to a quart in summer for each person.

The national mode of cooking food is in a stew, corresponding to the *pot-au-feu* of the French peasant, and of which gourds or cabbages, dried kidney beans, rice, beef and bacon, form the ingredients, according to means or circumstances.

Fish is much consumed by the peasantry, and dried cod is a favourite and universal food with all classes. It is considerably dearer than fresh beef, but having been deprived of its moisture and being in a concentrated form, it probably possesses superior food value. The sardine is another generally used food, both fresh and pickled. In the latter state it is consumed by the peasant in the remotest districts as far as the frontier lines of Spain.

The sardine is caught in immense quantities along the whole coast of Portugal. The sardine of these seas is a large variety, approaching in size and, most naturalists now affirm, identical in species, with the Cornish pilchard. The cod is imported partly from Norway, but chiefly from Newfoundland.

Potatoes are seldom eaten by field labourers, and the bread food is *brôa*, a strong, wholesome, and not unpalatable bread, composed of maize and rye. The universal use in Portugal of a double bread-food is to my knowledge a unique circumstance, and one well worth the attention of politicians and economists. The prejudices of mankind in regard to any change of the chief staple of their daily food are, it is known, all but insuperable, and it will be within most of my readers' recollection that during a recent famine in Bengal the Hindoos often preferred starvation to a change in the quality of their rice.   A food, therefore, composed of two different cereals has certain great and important advantages, for the proportions of maize and of rye can be altered almost *ad libitum* without much change in the quality or appearance of the loaf.

To the use of this bread-food I believe some part of the well-being of the Portuguese peasant may fairly be ascribed.   He is insured against periodical famine, with its many disastrous attendants and consequences, such as have followed rice famines in India, the great potato failure of Ireland, or even such as but for free trade would accompany a wheat scarcity in England.   An entire failure of the maize crop is almost impossible in Portugal.   The worst year is a very dry, hot one ; and such a season greatly stimulates and increases the productiveness of those low-lying lands which have an unfailing supply of water; while a very wet year promotes the growth of maize in the upland fields.   Again, the cold summer, unfavourable to maize, suits the rye crops, and a comparatively good harvest of this corn may be looked for whenever the maize crop is bad.

When maize is scarce and dear, less in proportion to the rye can be used in the loaf, and *rice versâ* ; and, in point of fact, this adjustment of the proportions of the two corns takes place nearly every year and in nearly every district.   In the maize-producing province of the Minho, and in the lowland districts generally, the usual proportions are eight parts of maize to one of rye, and in the rye lands among the mountains these proportions are almost reversed.

I like particularly to dwell upon the diet used by the Portuguese peasantry because I think it helps to make clearer some very important points in economics. The peasants are epicures in a way, with many multifarious tastes, as I, who have been a Portuguese farmer for several years past, very well know. They have souls far above the bread, beer and bacon of English ploughboys, and claim to have their stew cooked fresh three times a day. They are good judges of olives and dried cod-fish, and have a pretty taste (not our own exactly) in wine. It seems to me that this is a very desirable circumstance for them, for those they work for, and for the nation at large. Nothing astonishes me so much as the indignation of some honest and conventional people at home at the fact of English working men allowing themselves luxuries which their condition should, in these honest people's opinion, forbid their aspiring to. The colliers when wages were high ate *pâté de foie gras* and drank champagne. How deplorable ! Certainly it would have been desirable in the interests of the higher culture if they had spent their earnings in Rembrandt etchings, well bound books and blue china, but on the other hand it would have been infinitely less desirable if they had struck work altogether the moment they had enough to eat. Any taste is better than no taste, and surely it is better for a man to be knowing in dried codfish and 'green wine' than to know nothing at all. When the negroes of

Jamaica have gained a shilling by a **few hours' work**
they buy bananas and meal enough **to last a week,**
go to sleep in the sun, and laugh at the idea of another
stroke **of** work till the larder is bare again. The
champagne of our colliers was surely all in the interest
of morality, sobriety and hard work : it was an object
in life. Our farmers in England complain that with
the better wages of their labourers work is slacker
What wonder that it should be? Give them wider
tastes, and they will **do a** hard day's work to gratify
them. The Portuguese peasant likes dainty eating,
and aspires to wear a gold **stud in** his white linen shirt
and a good broadcloth cloak, and to give his sweetheart
a pair of massive gold earrings. Let no one accuse
him of effeminacy : he will work hard and cheerfully
for sixteen hours on a summer's day in the maize-field.
To be sure he has higher ambition than for good food
and fine clothes, **for he looks to** obtaining a slice of
the land ; and, with health, strong arms, long **life,**
a shrewd head and fair luck, the odds are that **a day**
labourer in Northern Portugal will live to be a landholder. It is that chiefly, **I** think, which sweetens
his sixteen hours' **toil** under the sun of Portugal.

The diet question, too, goes for something, and I
must come back to **it.** I have taken **an** opportunity
lately of saying in public that Portuguese olives are
pickled **when** they are fully ripe, **and** are therefore
more of a dish and less of a *hors d'œuvre* than the green
olives of France, Spain and **Italy. They are** necessarily more fit for human food, and in my opinion far
better to eat than any other kind of olives. I find

that most people who know them agree with me. A bad olive-harvest stints the population greatly ; butter being almost unknown. Though the olives are excellent, the oil is carelessly made and of generally inferior quality.

As for another chief item in the Portuguese peasant's bill of fare—*bacalhau*—it is really difficult for me (who am yet far from being an optimist) to approach this topic in its economic relations without seeming to be over enthusiastic.

Bacalhau is a word and a thing that philologers have wrangled about, politicians fought over, financiers rejoiced in, merchants contended for, fishermen fished for, economists been puzzled about, while the Portuguese people generally have quietly eaten it with oil and pepper.

It is still a question with the learned whether the word is taken from *baculum*, the stick with which the split and dried fish is kept open, or the Germanic word *bolch*, which means fish.[1]

---

[1] Sebastian Cabot, looking for the North-West passage towards North Lat. 67½°, in the year 1498, noted that 'in the seas thereabouts were such multitudes of great fishes, like tunnies, and which the natives call *Baccalaos*, that they sometimes stopped the way of the ships.' Dr. Kohl, however, says that the cod fishery had existed long before this on the Northern coasts of Europe, and the fish were called by the Germanic nations, *Cabliauwe* or *Backljau*. The word could not therefore have an Indian origin. The Portuguese changed it to *Bacalhau*. Brevoort, on the other hand, says, 'it is simply an old Mediterranean or Romance word, given to the preserved cod-fish, dried and kept open by the help of a small stick, *baculum*.' The Portuguese, I may observe, call both the fresh and dried cod-fish *Bacalhau*.

It is not enough to catch the fish, it must be brought to land and dried there, and a *locus standi* for the fishermen on the coasts of Newfoundland has before now been made an international question. In Portugal *bacalhau* is taxed about three farthings per pound, and the finances of the country are helped by its consumption to a very considerable extent. Political economists, however, ask whether it be right to tax a necessary of life, and social economists whether the people themselves do very wisely to eat, as an almost daily food, dried fish which costs more by the pound than ordinary beef. So much for the grave questions that have gathered round the subject of *bacalhau*: it is from the standpoint of its value as a food for the people that I wish to regard it.

If I could persuade my countrymen to use this most valuable food as the Spaniards and Portuguese do, it is my firm conviction that I should be doing more for their material advancement than most average patriotic statesmen accomplish in a lifetime. *Bacalhau* when cooked with oil, as it generally is, is probably, weight for weight, the richest food, in all the life-sustaining elements, of any known to mankind. In Portugal it is a luxury as well as a daily necessary I do not know what the poorer classes of this country would do if the great shoals of the Newfoundland Bank and Fjords of Norway should resolve to swim off to the North Pole; and richer people would be in as sad a plight. Nobody in Portugal thinks of existence as being possible without *bacalhau*. The working man carries a piece of it for his midday

dinner; the fishermen take it in their boats out to
sea—coals to Newcastle one might think; the rich
man eats it most religiously on Fridays and fast days,
and, if he is a gourmet, inconsistently orders it again
for his feast dinner on Sunday. Lent is shorn of half
its austerity for good Catholics in the Peninsula; and
bôlos de bacalhau—the fish minced, made into cakes
and fried—represents for the middle classes our turkey and roast beef of Christmas Day.

A rather serious objection to *bacalhau* as a food
is that it is not nice to eat—that is, at first—it is an
acquired taste, like coffee or caviare. The sooner a
traveller or resident in Portugal acquires it the better
for him. He might as well travel or live in England
and not like boiled potatoes, or in Scotland and hate
oatcakes and bagpipes.

Bacalhau is cooked in many ways: boiled, made
into a sort of Irish stew, grilled like Finnan haddocks,
or done into the *bôlos* aforesaid. There is always oil
with it and garlic. Our people might leave out the
garlic and use butter for oil.

The Portuguese also eat *bacalhau* quite raw. I
have seen them do it out shooting, taking a piece
from their game bags; and they seemed to like it.
The present writer might have expected to finish his
walk through life without having to eat raw fish, but
this was not to be. I have read that primitive man
ate his fish uncooked; the South Sea Islanders do the
same, and it has seemed to me a most uncivilized and
not a pleasant thing to do, but circumstances required
it of me once when I was travelling in a remote part

of Portugal, with a companion most properly particular, and curious, and learned in the preparation of
his daily food.

We were riding, and it was near nightfall ; we
were excessively hungry, and we had some leagues
between us and comfortable quarters.   We pulled up
our horses at a small solitary farmhouse, and we
begged for something to eat.   I asked the old woman
in charge of the house for anything she had ; but the
larder seemed to be all but empty.   'Had she white
bread ?' I asked.   She had none.   'Ham ? Bacon ?'
None.   'Meat or chickens ?'   Of course none.   'A
handful of olives ? or some eggs ?'   There was nothing
of all these things, but she had something, she hospitably informed us, better than anything I had inquired
for.   She went to get it, and returned triumphantly
with the half of a split cod-fish : an object more
resembling, in colour, size, shape and hardness, a short
piece of one-inch red deal board than any article of
human food I was ever before helped to.   She
was a most cheerful and kind and cordial old lady,
and, as we rode off, each of us with a piece of raw
bacalhau in our hand, she patted me amicably on the
arm, and said : 'It is very good for the head.'
Whether this was a subtle parting reflection on our
want of common sense about raw fish, for we had not
received it with any show of enthusiasm, or whether
our hostess only expressed the common belief there is
to that effect I know not.   It was certainly not in her
manner to be personal, and now that I think of it I
remember that physiologists and organic chemists at

home believe themselves to have discovered that · fish
nourishes the brain.' The savants at home are then,
so far, in accord with at least one old woman in
Portugal. It is not, however, on this account alone
that I should desire to promote the use of *bacalhau*
among all classes of my countrymen. It is in its more
serious aspects as a source of food supply that I wish
to recommend it. To the house purveyor it should
be invaluable : a raw material which admits of being
dressed, if necessary, at a minute's notice, and in so
many different ways, and which never taints, has
obvious advantages over every form of animal food.
Though *bacalhau* is apparently dearer than beef, it
is probably cheaper when compared with reference
to food value, and its price in Portugal is enhanced first
by the duty, and probably by the fact of the demand
being, in so small a country, more or less intermittent.
Distance, too, must lend something to freight-charge.
If there was a general demand for it in Great Britain
it would cheapen. If the Portuguese, who are rigid
economists, find their account in buying *bacalhau*
dear, we, if we got to like it, should certainly be no
losers by buying it cheap and consuming it freely.

As for the question of supply, it is practically inexhaustible ; the whole Northern ocean, by travellers,
accounts, teems with cod-fish wherever the water
shoals enough to get at them. The supply is, therefore, independent of seasons. The pasturage of
English and American fields determine the price of
beef and mutton, but the fields of ocean are never
bare : the cod shoals migrate from time to time, but

have never failed. The bringing them to England is only a question of capital and enterprise, in which our own colonists and countrymen are not likely to fail us.

All, however, depends upon whether we can ever get to like cod-fish dried, as we already like it fresh. *Ce n'est que le premier pas qui coûte*, as my friend and I found when we debated as to which of us should begin on his piece of raw *bacalhau*.

Both countrymen and countrywomen are warmly and comfortably clad, the women, perhaps, more conspicuously so than the men ; and while the latter have in many places adopted the dress of townsfolk (often possessing, in addition, a thick cloak of brown homespun cloth), the women still preserve the national dress, which varies a little in every district, and generally consists of a coarse white linen shirt, a dark bodice, a pleated serge or cloth petticoat, and a broad flat hat, with a black cloth cloak. The custom of wearing ornaments of very fine gold is universal, even among the poorer of the peasant women, and the value of these ornaments testifies to the present and long continued well-being of their wearers. Few peasant women have a less value in ornaments than one or two pounds ; and I am assured, and can believe, that many of them possess gold ornaments worth twenty or thirty pounds.

Women work habitually in the fields, and begin to do so as children : as quite young girls they accompany the ox carts, walking in front of the oxen with goads in their hands, while the men follow to load and unload the carts ; they drive the cattle afield, and mind them while they are grazing. As they grow older, they cut and carry home the grass, weed the maize and wheat, and do their share of all the work of the farm except ploughing and the harder work with the hoe.

The system of field gangs is utterly unknown in Portugal.

While this general employment of women nearly doubles the agricultural working-power of the nation, the women themselves are certainly neither demoralized nor physically deteriorated by their labours.

Such is the farm system in the naturally barren but artificially affluent province of the Minho, where, I have no hesitation in saying, the general social well-being of the tillers of the land is greater than in any part of the world I have yet seen.

When my German acquaintance at the *table d'hôte* —for whose benefit and at whose particular request I had condensed into a speech which took but a very few minutes in the utterance some small portion of the information which I have now (I fear with much greater prolixity) given to the reader,—when, I say, my German friend again spoke, he was somewhat less impressed than I should like my reader to be with my views.

' The torrent of human progress,' he said, ' (for it is a torrent in these days, and nothing less rapid) cannot be restrained by mere sentimental obstacles.'

I answered, ' In the meantime, and until the full

flood of utilitarianism is upon us. I venture to apprehend that you have found few customers for agricultural machinery in the northern provinces?'

'Very few,' he said : ' in fact, none at all.'

'And you will never find customers.'

'The people of these provinces are little better
than idiots,' he remarked, ' and do not understand
their own interests.'

'I should call them,' I said, ' a shrewd people, and
so far intelligent that it would be difficult to persuade
a farmer with twelve or twenty acres of land to give
as much as the whole yearly profits of his farm for a
machine that he could never find enough work for.'

'Humph!' said the German.

'You should go southwards; there, though the
labourers are thriftless and slothful, the land ill-tilled,
and the country poor, you will find at any rate estates
large enough for expensive machines to do sufficient
work to pay for the outlay upon them.'

'I shall go there and try,' said the German.

The German gentleman remained silent, and I
hoped he was impressed ; but he presently said,

'I admit that you have told me something that I
did not know before ; nevertheless I cannot but think
that there is a solution for the intellectual, social, and
moral obstruction which you describe, more in accordance with immutable general principles and the
doctrines of the great Smith than you perhaps
imagine.'

Here our conversation ceased, with the unspoken
reflection on my part that very intelligent persons are

sometimes singularly opposed to the reception of new opinions ; and when once they have taken in a full cargo of information and ideas, are very loth to do any further traffic in these commodities.

I am reminded of a similar limitation in the sagacity of the most sagacious of all animals after man —the elephant.

It is related of one of these thoughtful creatures that, his keeper failing to feed him sufficiently during the day, it was his habit every night to draw the heavy wooden post to which he was fastened by means of a stout chain, by main force out of the ground, and to make his way to a neighbouring rice-field, and there, after carefully fixing his post in a convenient part of the field—so great was the force of habit and association with him—he would proceed to feed upon all the rice within reach of his tether. In the morning he again drew his post up, and returning to his stable, refixed it in its accustomed place.

I could not but reflect that my German acquaintance possessed not a little of this rather narrow elephantine wisdom ; and he is, I fear, not singular. Many and many an intelligent traveller have I met, in, as it were, foreign rice fields, carrying his post with him, planting it firmly in the ground from time to time, and tethering himself thereto, to the very lamentable limitation of his outlook upon the world around him.

CHAPTER VI.

PORT WINE.[1]

If the secret history of many of the utterances on the subject of wine that have been made within the last thirty years could be made known to the world, the world would be singularly astonished at learning from whose hands it has been accepting the doctrine which it holds with a very firm faith indeed. A man writes a learned book, or a popular book, or a long review in an influential periodical, or a smart one in a newspaper; or he takes a scientific and seemingly impartial interest in the digestion of wine consumers and writes an essay, or he fires off a dozen

---

[1] I published some years ago in a leading periodical, under the transparent pseudonym of Matthew Freke Turner, a paper entitled, *Wine and Wine Merchants*. This paper I have now rewritten, with copious additions, into the present chapter. When it appeared, many worthy gentlemen, whose interests seemed to them to run counter to the facts and conclusions I put forth, were made very angry with me, and used strong language in print. Much as the original article has been altered to suit its present place as a chapter in a book on Portugal, I have been careful to take away from it nothing which could have the good effect of continuing to irritate and offend the aforesaid interested persons, being convinced that one of the most righteous and pleasing functions of literature is to tell the plain truth, and shame those who have any interest in suppressing it.

controversial pamphlets in succession; and in each one of these cases the good, easy public believes that the author has no object in view but its instruc‑ tion.

There are cases, no doubt, in which the writer has no other object before him; and there is, I am sure, no case in which he does not believe himself to be an impartial instructor of mankind; nevertheless, as human nature is at present constituted, it would be reassuring to be quite certain how the writers are circumstanced. It would, perhaps, be too much to expect that the author of pamphlet, article, essay, review, or book should begin by saying, 'I am a dealer in the ware I am about to describe,' or 'I am the brother, uncle, or intimate friend of some one who is, and I am interested in the good repute of cer‑ tain wares that I am about to praise, and in the ill repute of certain other wares that, as the reader shall presently observe, I shall run down;' but I can‑ not recollect a single instance in which such a pre‑ face has been written.

Now, I am not for a moment going to imply that a gentleman who lives by selling one kind of wine, say the fine vintages of our Australian Colonies, is anything but quite conscientious when he asserts in a printed book that Château Margaux is poor stuff, and Lafitte very much overrated. I only say that he is not a fit person to write a book to instruct the public. It is, no doubt, a very illiberal ordinance that a judge should not sit on the bench in his native county, but it recommends itself to the common sense of human nature.　As one of a simple-minded public, I protest against our having to accept our opinions about wine from gentlemen whom a customary rule would exclude from the wine committees of their London Clubs.

After saying so much, it is well that the present writer should observe that he is not himself pecuniarily interested, directly or indirectly, even in the remotest way, in wine.

The universal interest that is now taken in wine, and consequently the mass of literature dealing with the subject, dates from little more than about twenty or thirty years ago.　When port and sherry were the daily drink of English gentlemen, claret and champagne not very common ones, and the German wines hardly known, there was very little to make a book about.　The secrets of the trade were also better kept ; it was in fewer hands ; the duties were enormous, and the lighter wines which are now favoured by taxation were then so overburthened as only to reach a very few rich men.　There were few rivalries among wine merchants, seeing that wines of each variety were the staple of every merchant's trade, and therefore if a man sold claret he did not care to say a bad word for his neighbour who sold port, as it is to be feared he does now when wine-firms have multiplied and, as always happens with an increasing trade, businesses have been sub-divided.　It was then the golden age of wine-dealing, when an innocent and unsuspecting public drank over-brandied port, and

' plastered' sherry, and loaded claret, and paid their wine bills, and held their tongues.

Yet, even in those days of happy ignorance and guileless customers, some stir had been made, a panic created, and a dead set made against one of the truest, best, and *safest* (I shall explain this word presently) of imported wines. A fashionable doctor discovered that madeira contained acid in pernicious proportions. He was believed, and the Regent set the example of drinking sherry instead. Fear and fashion together did their work, and madeira has never regained the prestige which it then lost; while sherry, which had before been little used, not only took its place but has found greater favour, to judge from the evidence of the quantities imported, than any wine, even port, has ever had in these islands; and, be it observed, the sherry that superseded madeira was not the light white wine which grows on the hills round Xeres; it was not the wine which once was a famous drink in England—the 'Sherris sack' (*Xeres secco*) known in Shakespeare's time—a dry wine which had to be sugared as we sugar tea.[1] It was not this natural wine, but a fabricated liquor which took its place,—a wine coloured and sweetened with burnt sugar and boiled *must* to imitate the flavour of madeira, brandied to make it keep, and 'plastered' (doctored with plaster of Paris) to take away the over-acidity. This it was that captivated the simple-minded wine-drinker, the

---

[1] So commonly was this done that, as will be remembered, Poins addresses Falstaff as 'Sir John Sack and Sugar,' and that worthy remarks piteously, 'If sack and sugar be a fault, God help the wicked!'

absence of sourness. The natural acidity was
neutralized with an alkali, and became what chemists
call a ' salt: ' and as his doctors told him to beware
of acid, and he was satisfied that there was little of it
in sherry, he never stopped to inquire whether, in its
new form, it was possibly not as harmful as before.
It was enough that he did not taste the sourness ; he
was no chemist, his palate was his only laboratory.
Let it be observed that the sherry I thus disparage
is the sherry of years gone by, of what architects
would call the *transition* period—the transition between good modern sherry and madeira. Everyone
knows that good sherry now is a very pure and wholesome wine. It is, perhaps, hardly necessary to say
at the present day that this theory of acidity was
founded on a misconception.

The various acids in madeira, the free and fixed
acids, the tartaric, which mostly pre-exists in the
grape and is in moderation harmless, and the acetic
acid, which is another name for vinegar and usually
marks some degree of unsoundness—all these acids
are found in less proportion than in sound claret, and
yet claret is admitted, and rightly admitted, to be a
wholesome wine. In truth madeira was condemned
on false evidence. On dietetic grounds there is no
particular reason for its loss of favour, but it is too
late for a new trial or an appeal from a wrong verdict
whose justice has so long been acquiesced in. The
day of madeira has probably gone by, not to return.

It is to Mr. Gladstone, as everyone knows, that we

owe the change in the wine duties twenty years ago which has brought about quite a new state of things in the wine trade, and which shook to their foundations the thrones of the old established wine-firms.

From the year 1703, when Lord Methuen concluded his famous treaty with Portugal, which admitted Portuguese wines through our Custom-house on easier terms than the till then favourite wines of Gascony—from that time port wine began to be drunk in England, and the wines of France to be neglected. It was our subtle British policy to drink the wines of our ally, and to eschew those of our hereditary enemy. As time went on and anti-Galli-canism grew stronger during our wars with France of the middle of the century, it was in the wines of Portugal and of its colony Madeira that we drank success to our arms and confusion to our enemies. At the commencement of the present century the policy which favoured port wine, and imposed accu-mulated duties that came in time to be prohibitive on those of France, was more and more approved and seconded by the nation, which the abominations of the Revolution, and our long struggle with the power of Napoleon, had converted almost entirely to high Toryism ; so that a patriotic Englishman got to reckon it to be one of his privileges and blessings that the State had interfered to prevent him from drinking claret and to let him fill his glass with port and madeira, wines which by this time he had got to like beyond all others.

Moreover, nature herself seemed to conspire with the ruler of France to make the State-favoured wines more than ever acceptable to Englishmen.[1] From 1802 to 1815, inclusive, there was a succession of splendid vintages, both in Portugal and Madeira. Never before had such wines been made. Most of these fourteen vintages were abundant ; all were good ; one was the famous 'Comet Vintage,' of 1811 ; and the last was the magnificent vintage of 1815, which has never been excelled in Portugal. On the other hand, the wines made in other parts of the world during this period were of indifferent quality, and most of the vintages of the Médoc, always excepting the · Comet Vintage,' were bad. But even in this last year of its apparent complete triumph, a very keen observer of the times might have foreseen the eventual weakening of the long-continued bond between wine and the State, and that a great politician would arise in the future, one of whose titles to fame

[1] I say ' Englishmen' advisedly. Port was never greatly in favour in either Ireland or Scotland. It would be difficult to name a period in which good claret was not obtainable in Dublin. The Scotch retained, perhaps from their ancient connection with France, a strong liking for the wines of Médoc, and the poet did not speak the literal truth who rhymed as follows :

> ' Firm and erect the Caledonian stood,
> Old was his mutton, and his claret good.
> " Let him drink port ! " the English statesman cried
> He drank the poison, and his spirit died.'

There was more rhyme than reason in this doggrel; and as long as a smuggler chose to run a cargo of Gascon wine on Leith Sands, Scotchmen were found to drink it in spite of the English statesman and his tax. Edinburgh has never lost her old reputation for claret.

would be that he had enabled his countrymen to drink the wine of their hereditary foes (at fourteen shillings the dozen). For, in this very year 1815 the great battle was fought from and after which our antipathy to Frenchmen began to lessen, and our desire to drink their wines to increase. Then came the opening of the Continent, and Englishmen went abroad again and found, to their surprise, that there were wines fit for an Englishman to drink besides port and madeira. Then it so happened that the vintages in Portugal, and also in Madeira, for the next four years were detestable. Then came an event which, little as it might seem to be connected with any diminution of the veneration for port wine in English breasts, was in truth the ' beginning of the end.' I dwell upon this circumstance, because I am not aware that it has been so much as mentioned in any one of the many works treating of wine.

The year 1820 is memorable in the chronicles of wine as the most remarkable vintage of port wine ever known. The wine made in that year was not indeed so fine as that of 1815, but it was nearly as good, and it was such in other respects as had never been known before; for the wine made in 1820 was as sweet as syrup, and nearly as black as ink, it was full of naturally-formed alcohol, and of all the various con- stituents—most of them far beyond the analysis of the ablest chemist—which go to make of wine a liquor differing from all other liquors. It was this seemingly most favourable circumstance which, in time, injured the good repute of port wine ; for the public, having once tasted this dark, liqueur-like, highly flavoured wine of 1820, would accept of nothing less dark and less rich as genuine port. Then set in the adulteration of port wine, and all the various manœuvres by which wines lacking colour, flavour, and bouquet are endowed artificially with characteristics which nature has not bestowed upon them.

These tricks began before the grapes had left the winepress, into which were thrown bags containing dried elderberries, whose colouring matter was transferred to the grape-juice. When the *must* had gone some way towards fermentation—before, that is, the whole of its sweetness was converted into spirit—brandy in far greater proportion than had previously been employed was added to check the fermentation. Here, then, was a wine to which artificial means had imparted colour, sweetness, and spirit; but nothing could give it the full, natural vinous flavour, for this was hindered by the over-interrupted fermentation. Such tampering as this would ruin any wine but port, and the result would be a poor, undrinkable stuff; and with port it only did not entirely fail because the Lusitanian grape, ripened in the intense heat of its native hill-slopes, develops such powerful vinous qualities as even this hard treatment of it could not entirely suppress.

Things went on without much change for the first half of the present century. Sherry, as I have shown, took the place of madeira. Port, however, though much abused, still held its ground: but the

easy public was beginning to feel aggrieved; the
processes of port wine making began to leak out,
and the evils sometimes connected with those processes began to be greatly exaggerated: bad jokes
about blacking and logwood began to circulate.
'Your *old* port, mind,' said Douglas Jerrold, ordering
a fresh bottle at an inn, 'not your *elder* port;' and
the insinuation, as we have seen, was not unjustified.

In 1852 the grievances of wine drinkers had not
lessened, while their knowledge of wine had greatly
increased. Things were ripe for a change. In
this year occurred two events which mainly brought
it about. One was the session of a Committee of
the House of Commons during the summer of 1852.
The other was the vine disease—the *oïdium* [1]—

---

[1] The *Oïdium Tuckeri* appears in early summer as a white,
filmy mould or fungus on the leaves; later on, it shows on the
unripe fruit; and if allowed to run its course, it stunts the growth
of the grape, and in most cases causes it to dwindle, to split open,
and to rot. The panic produced in districts where the vine represents eighty or ninety per cent. of the farmer's produce, may easily
be imagined. The finest growths of wine suffered first, just as the
most highly-bred animals succumb soonest to an epidemic. A
large vineyard in Burgundy produced that year twenty-three
hogsheads (*pièces*), which the year before had yielded over two
hundred. The Médoc wine farmers suffered greatly, but somewhat less than those of other parts of France. In the port wine
district the year 1852 was disastrous. The farmers who grow the
vines that make port grow hardly any other crop. One of the
best vineyards, which had seldom given less than one hundred
and sixty pipes, made in the year 1852 but five; and the quality
was so poor that the labourers on the estate could hardly drink it.
In Madeira the destruction of vines was greater than elsewhere;
and for several years no wine at all was produced—none at least
that could rank as madeira. If science or empiricism had not

which, though observed seven years before, first appeared in great virulence in the same summer; and, for the time, almost ruined the vineyards of Europe.

The French were the first in the field with a remedy, which is found in sulphur. Blown on to the vine leaves and grape bunches, in the shape of an impalpable powder, from a pair of bellows, the cure is perfect. The fungus growth is arrested, and if the plant be well dredged over with sulphur periodically from early spring-time, it is seldom even attacked. The French vine growers, to whose quicker wits the value of the cure came home sooner than to those of the farmers of Spain, Portugal, Madeira, and Germany, got their vineyards into full production while the farmers of Southern Europe were still employing their priests with bell and book to exorcise the evil spirit that had invaded their vineyards. Thus did the Frenchmen push forward in the race; and would have come near to winning it, so far as Great Britain was concerned, had their competition not been hindered by the heavy import duties which, though now greatly reduced, still most unfairly handicapped them.

The other event, the evidence taken in Committee, caused a great deal of commotion in the world of wine consumers. What happened in most Parliamentary Committees happened in this one. A

devised an almost perfect remedy, there is good reason to believe that at the present day not a vineyard, vine, or wine-merchant would exist in Europe.

huge mass of evidence—some valuable, more worthless, and most of it *ex parte* and interested, and therefore worse than worthless—was laid before a party of not very competent judges, who possessed neither capacity, nor the necessary knowledge, nor even leisure, to sift it.

Among the witnesses the one whose evidence created by far the most interest was the late Baron Forrester. He was the only witness who could speak from personal experience of port wine making, being a merchant residing at Oporto, and he did not hesitate to speak out boldly what was in him to say. Certainly, *liberavit animam*, he made a clean breast of it. This gentleman, an energetic man, very assertive of opinions unpalatable to his fellow port wine merchants, but which were by no means wholly destitute of soundness, had arrived at the conclusion that port could be made without any adventitious spirit, or with but very little, and without the help of colouring matter.

These modest propositions were not enunciated without arousing a violent controversy, in which Mr. Forrester argued his point with much strong denunciation of his trade rivals. His evidence, however, produced, and deservedly produced, a great effect in this country.

I do not agree with a great deal that was advanced by Baron Forrester, but it is incontestable that this remarkable man left his mark on the history of the English wine trade, and that the effects of his writings have been on the whole salutary.

Mr. Forrester paid his theories the compliment of acting up to them. He proposed to himself to make wine as he had said it should be made, and he delivered lectures in various towns in England, explaining his views and his intentions—and these were to sell pure port wine. It was triumphantly asserted by his opponents that much of his port wine did not keep sound, and was returned to him by his customers. Even if this allegation had been true, which it probably was only to a limited extent, it proves nothing beyond Mr. Forrester's want of skill or luck, or his too vehement belief in a sound theory ; for that port will keep which is made without brandy added to check fermentation, is a quite demonstrable proposition. Whether the wine does not require a little brandy afterwards is another matter ; and it does not appear that Mr. Forrester denied this, or that he failed in most cases to make this subsequent addition of spirit.

The true point at issue has always seemed to me to be, not whether port can be made without the addition of distilled wine, but whether wine so made is worth making or worth drinking Such wine is an unmarketable product, and I think deservedly so. It is a strong, rough and comparatively flavourless liquor. If a man were to add six drops of ink to a glass of very common red burgundy he would get something exceedingly like unfortified port. Every Oporto wine merchant has tried the experiment of unfortified port wine It is a pity they cannot sell it for they would quickly make their fortunes; but the plain truth is that it is an abominable drink.

Public opinion was in this state when Mr. Gladstone turned his attention to the question of wine. It was clear enough that a reform was needed, and if the then Chancellor of the Exchequer had been an ordinary man, the reform would have been brought about in a very simple and straightforward manner, and—with due deference be it suggested—with a result possibly more satisfactory to the exchequer, to wine consumers, and to the majority of wine merchants, than that which has followed upon the revolution in the wine trade effected in 1860 and 1861. But Mr. Gladstone is not an ordinary man, nor could a great Budget speech be made out of so very simple a matter as a reduction of the wine duties by a reasonable amount, and the fixing of a maximum of spirituous strength beyond which wine should cease to be classed as wine, and be taxed as spirit.

There had already been enunciated theories about pure wines, unbrandied wines, and so forth, and these somewhat vague notions were fixed, crystallized, and made popular by Mr. Gladstone.

Nothing could be more elaborate, nothing more ingenious, and yet nothing more lucid and, to quite ignorant people, more convincing, than Mr. Gladstone's exposition of the grand principle that was brought home to the comprehension and convictions of the whole British nation the morning after the Chancellor's Budget speech. The argument was shortly this : wine is fermented grape juice, and this juice generates in the course of fermentation a certain percentage of spirit, say from eighteen to twenty-six per cent.,[1] more or less. Any addition of spirit over and above this naturally developed quantity is an unnecessary, an altogether abominable and reprehensible addition, and a thing to be discouraged and even punished. Moreover, it is a defrauding of the spirit revenue that a liquor should pay the lower duty on wine, and be all the time partly composed of that which is liable to the higher duty upon spirit. This was the argument, and the inference, and the corollary. The reasoning is just, but the premises are quite false.

Wine, to be sure, does not very often naturally generate more than thirty per cent. of spirit, though the Australians claim to make natural wine containing forty per cent., and the Spaniards have sometimes claimed as much or more, but the addition of some extraneous antiseptic substance, in greater or less quantity, is an incident in the preparation of every red wine of which it is intended to preserve the original soundness, that ever was made, or that ever will be made. The natural wines of Europe— those made to be consumed on the spot, and which are

---

[1] Of proof spirit, which is about one-half pure alcohol and one-half water. It has always been sturdily contended by the 'pure wine' doctrinaires that wine cannot naturally generate more than twenty-five per cent. of spirit. It is an error pure and simple, but it is an error enshrined in one of those models of truth and disinterestedness, an English Blue-book, and is, in consequence, brandished on all occasions by the 'pure wine' people as an unassailable fact.

probably in the proportion of something like a thousand to one of the wines prepared for exportation—are intended to be drunk in the summer after they are made. Very rarely will they keep two years. Great care in vinification will indeed go some way, but it cannot perform a miracle. Science has suggested many variations in wine making but it can do little but complicate what is a very simple matter. In order to show how simple and easy is the process of wine making, I proceed to describe it very shortly.

The ripe grapes are thrown into a vat, and trodden under foot; the skins, the stones, the juice, and some or all of the stalks are allowed to remain till the liquid ferments. When the heat of fermentation begins to abate, the wine, for it has already the chief attributes of wine, is run into casks, or tonels, which are casks of a large size, whereby the active fermentation is checked, but it is usually not quite arrested till the cold weather of early winter sets in. The wine then clears, the casks are filled up to the top, the bungs are driven in tight, and the wine is fit for consumption. This is how the peasants and farmers of France, Italy and Greece, of Spain, of Portugal, and of Hungary, make the wines that quench their thirst in the heat and burden of the southern summer's day; and this probably is how red wine has been made since first the juice of grapes was pressed out and fermented. The ingenuity of the most ingenious people in the world has added almost nothing to these time-honoured processes.

In some of the vineyards of Burgundy, indeed, a

machine is used to separate the stalks and the grapes, and the pressing of the grapes is done by machinery, but the great growths of the Médoc, the Château Margaux, and Château Lafitte are the result of processes nearly as simple as those employed by the peasant wine growers of Southern Europe, whose rough red wines are used as our labourers use beer or cider. The differences are differences in degree only; in the care with which the grapes are picked, and green and decayed ones rejected, and with which a due proportion of the stalks is removed; the attention with which the fermenting liquid is watched and drawn off at the right moment, the number of subsequent rackings, the scrupulous cleanliness of all the vessels used; but the process which I have described—and my descriptions are not taken from books but from personal observation in several of the wine-producing countries of Europe—are those which suffice only to make wine that is not wanted to keep more than a twelvemonth. There is in all red wine,—and none other quite deserves the name of wine, or contains its full constituents,[1]—there is in every red

---

[1] White wine is usually wine that is fermented without the skins and stalks; it does not, therefore, contain its full share of the various 'extractives' which are factors in the result which we call wine. Common experience tells us that these wines have not the flavour or the bouquet of red wines, and analogy would lead us as surely as experience does to conclude that they do not share their remedial and restorative virtues. White wines are rather grape ciders than true wines. It is a well-known fact that when the vines of Madeira were destroyed in 1852, a liquor was made from apples and pears, and even from the fruit of the loquat tree, and that such fermented liquor was near enough in character to

wine, with one or two exceptions which I will notice presently, some element of decay which, in a longer or a shorter time, brings about its destruction.

In ancient times, as soon as a wine had obtained any repute beyond the district of its production, some artificial mode of preserving it was devised. With every respect for the skill of wine makers and wine merchants of modern days, they must be pronounced to be mere children in comparison with the wine artificers of ancient Greece. The people of Cette and Hamburg profess to imitate any wine they are asked for, but then who that has tasted ' Hambro' Sherry,' or ' Cette Port,' can speak of the performances of these French and German rogues with common patience? Sticky, pungent, sickly, and altogether abominable compounds of potato spirit, treacle, and unknown chemical flavourings—often, it is asserted, without a drop of grape juice—these are what a German writer positively boasts of as triumphs of applied science. Very different were the practices of the Greeks. Their imitations of the best growths of Italy were, we are informed, preferred at Rome to the genuine wines themselves.

The wine doctors of the present day, in possessing alcohol, have one signal advantage over those of ancient Greece and Rome, who knew not the art of distilling spirit. Alcohol is the sheet anchor of the modern

the true wine of the island to sell in England as inferior madeira ; and champagne made of gooseberries and rhubarb, abominable as it is, is not so unlike the French wine as to fail in finding a ready sale.

wine maker. What, then—might a wine maker in
Cadiz, Bordeaux, Macon, or Oporto ask—were the
methods they employed by which, in the absence of
brandy, wine could be preserved for ten, twenty, and
even sixty years and upwards ? We have fortunately
several of the treatises upon wine making by ancient
authors, and we are able to follow step by step the
ingenious processes formed on discoveries which the
Romans and the Greeks, our masters in the art of
wine making, had arrived at ; not by means of
scientific deductions, but by the pure empirical
method of frequent failure and occasional success.

These forgotten processes have an important bearing upon the question of the preservation of wines
and their so-called adulteration. It is the question
which underlies the whole subject of wine for us in
this country, who can as a rule drink none but such
as is so prepared artificially as to enable it to travel
by sea and by land, and to keep sound a longer or
shorter time. It is, moreover, a question upon which,
for obvious reasons, those who are most capable of
enlightening the public are the most interested and
least impartial of teachers. Its importance then
being such, the present writer, who claims to have
enjoyed peculiar opportunities of watching the application of some of the processes of the ancients in the
very countries where their wines were grown, makes
no apology for dwelling for a moment on this subject
of ancient wine making.

In ancient times the preliminary treading out of
the grapes and the expressing of their juice were pre-

cisely such as I have already described, and the colour
of the wine and its astringency were, as they still are,
greater or less according as the *must* was allowed to
remain a longer or shorter time with the stalks and
skins. The *must* was in all cases eventually drawn into
dolia—large, wide-mouthed jars of porous earthenware, coated inside with pitch—and in these vessels the
liquid was allowed to ferment, and, on or about the
ninth day, had become wine. A lid was then fitted
closely to the top of the great jar, or *dolium*, and, it
is presumed, *luted*, to keep out the air. The lid was
removed once a month, the wine skimmed, and the
loss by evaporation made up from another jar. The
wine was now ready for consumption under the name
of ' *vinum doliare*,' which we may translate freely
' *vin ordinaire* in the wood.'

Red wine so made in the latitude of Rome or
Naples would exactly resemble the commoner country
wines with which every traveller in the South of
Europe is familiar, with this difference, that it would
have a flavour of pitch from the lining of the jar in
which it had been kept, and this taste every single
wine made in ancient times must have more or less
possessed. This is perhaps enough of itself to condemn
such ancient wines in the opinion of modern wine
drinkers, but if the reader will take the word of one
who has drunk wine so flavoured, the taste is by no
means disagreeable. The pitch used in the South of
Europe is not the coarse gum distilled from the pines
that grow in Northern Europe, but the much milder
and more aromatic pitch yielded by the pine of Italy,

the Stone Pine; and men soon acquire a taste for such flavours.

Before I begin to describe the methods whereby the ancients, who possessed neither spirit nor sugar (the two substances without which modern wine merchants and wine doctors could not move a single step), practised the art of wine curing, with a success now lost, I will state in a very few words what is the nature of the problem offered to them and to us by the preservation of wines.

The juice of grapes contains among many components, mostly in infinitesimal proportions, such as gelatine, gum, wax, potash, soda, lime, iron, and many others which need not at present be regarded, considerable percentages of acid, of sugar, of albumen, and of tannin.   It is with these four constituents only that we need for the moment occupy ourselves.   It is the presence of the albumen chiefly that makes grape juice a fermentable liquid when it is exposed to a temperature of between sixty and eighty degrees of Fahrenheit.   Sugar has, as is well known, no power of fermenting and of passing into decay—of which fermentation is one of the first stages—is by itself incapable of change, but the albuminous part of the must, the so-called ferment, causes the sugar to be decomposed, to break up and separate into spirit and into carbonic acid—in plain English, causes the must to ferment, and when most of the sugar is thus transformed into spirit, the wine making is complete; but the process does not end here, seeing that vinous fermentation is but one step towards complete decay.

If left to itself the liquid would next undergo the acetous fermentation, and thereafter the putrid. A natural wine, accordingly, with due deference to certain 'doctrinaires,' is a wine that, whatever may be its present soundness, is on the high road to decay. Wine making is therefore the art of stopping, for a longer or shorter time, and by artificial means, the progress of putrescence after the liquor has passed the first stage towards it. I have shown how with common wines this is done by drawing the wine from its lees, removing it, that is, from a part of the ferment-producing albumen, fibrin, and so forth, which, so soon as spirit begins to form, fall to the bottom. To do this, and to transfer the wine to a cool cellar, does not indeed quite stop fermentation, but it nearly arrests it. The process goes on slowly for a month or two, more and more of the sugar passing into carbonic acid gas and into spirit, and more and more albumen falling down as sediment, then the frosts of winter come and stop even this slower fermentation, and then, as I have shown, the wine clears.

The problem in wine making then is simply this— how, without imparting any ill savour or unwholesome quality to the wine, to get rid of this aptitude to decay The difficulty of course increases with the richness of the wine; with wine, that is, which possesses the largest share of those constituents which go to make what is called ' body ; ' in other words, with the wines that contain the least water, and that are, therefore, *cæteris paribus*, the most valuable ;— with the burgundies, the ports, and the various rich but commercially useless, because imperfectly made, red wines of Spain and Italy. It is precisely with rich wines of this character that the Greeks and Romans tried and solved the problem before us.

Sugar, spirit, and the tannin contained in the wine itself, are the three chief preservative agents in wine making, with the addition of one very important extraneous one—sulphur. We shall see how the ancients applied every one of these agents, always remembering that, having no sugar nor distilled spirit, they could not make direct use of those substances, and how they anticipated in their practice some of the so-called discoveries of modern days.

The wine which we have followed in its course as far as the 'dolium' was by the ancients racked again and again so soon as the fermentation had completely ended ; being received each time into a vessel charged with the fumes of burning sulphur,[1] each time acquiring a fresh impregnation from the various resinous and antiseptic substances with which the jar was lined, and each time losing more and more of its albumen, and therefore each time getting nearer and nearer to being an indestructible fluid. In the meanwhile, some of the first and sweetest runnings from the wine-press had been kept apart, and the fermentation of this liquor arrested while it was still full of

---

[1] The antiseptic properties of sulphurous acid gas are better known than understood. Sulphuring wines is a universal practice at the present day with the wine makers of all countries. The sulphur probably destroys the spores and germ growths which exist in most vinous liquids.

sugar.[1] To possess this sugar-charged liquid, whose sweetness was increasable by boiling, and whose albuminous portions were precipitated by the same means, was equivalent to and even better than the possession of sugar itself, whose use is so indispensable in the 'improvement' of such wines as burgundies and brown sherries. When the wine had made all the spirit it could, and parted with most of its sugar, its austerity would have been great; so great, indeed, that old wine of this sort made without sugar was drunk mixed with honey, in the proportion of four of wine and one of honey. It was therefore to restore the saccharine matter that the sweet *must* was added to the fermented wine, just as at the present day, in the great wine factory of Bercy, where the wines drunk in Paris undergo their final preparation for the metropolis, thousands of tons of sugar are mixed annually with the too austere wines of southern and central France. Here the advantage would clearly be with the ancients. To add unfermented grape juice, containing in itself all the elements of wine, is obviously better for the consumer than the simple addition of sugar.

The ancients, however, knew a great deal more than this of wine curing. A French savant, Monsieur Appert, has professedly *discovered* the preservative and ripening effects upon wine of a heat nearly equal

---

[1] The possibility of this feat without the employment of alcohol is a measure of the skill of these old wine makers, and of the strength of their antiseptic compounds, that will come home very readily to the comprehension of modern wine merchants.

to that of boiling water, and M. Pasteur has more recently fully explained the rationale of the process in
a learned volume.   By exposing wine in closed vessels for a few hours to a temperature of 185 degrees
of Fahr., these effects are, according to the French
savant, produced.   They were produced two thousand
years ago, but in a much more complete way, by the
application of artificial heat for weeks and months to
the jars of wine ; and this practice was so universal
that an ancient writer tells us that a heating-house,
an *apotheca* or *fumarium*, was an indispensable part
of every country house.   The constancy of this practice was, I make no doubt, one main cause of the
soundness and durability of the ancient wines.   The
red wines, such as the Falernian,[1] were, we are told,
hardly fit to drink under twenty years, and even the
commoner wines required from four to ten.   The
Appert-Pasteur process, though much talked of at
the time, has found but little favour with wine merchants, and is a proof how lamentably modern science,
for once at least, falls short of ancient empiricism.

[1] The learned have concluded, very much to their satisfaction,
that this most famous of the wines of antiquity was a white wine,
like madeira. It was certainly, however, a red wine, and the
'amber' colour ascribed to it (Pliny says that amber of a good
colour was called 'Falernian') would apply only to its tawny
appearance after long keeping. The frequent rackings and finings
to which it was subjected would in a few years deprive it of colour.
Red wine almost always loses its colour with keeping. Old burgundy is invariably tawny, and port wine thirty or forty years old
is of the very amber colour that distinguished the Falernian. A
wine that possessed in some cases the austerity, and in others the
sweetness ascribed to Falernian, could only have been a red
wine, made with the full and perfect constituents of the grape.

The mellowness which all wine acquires by age is supposed, and I believe rightly supposed, to be partly due to its slow, or rather, its gradual oxygenation, and the heating of it would certainly promote this oxygenation, besides destroying the germs of a fungus growth which has been proved to be the forerunner, and perhaps the cause, of the decay of the wine. All, then, that modern science professes to accomplish by the immersion of the wine, in bottles or other hermetically-closed vessels, in hot water for two hours, was accomplished in the *fumarium* ; and a good deal more was done, for the *fumarium*, as its name implies, was a smoke-house, and there is not the smallest doubt that the pyroligneous acid of wood-smoke penetrated the comparatively porous texture of the earthenware jar, and communicated its flavour and its preservative virtues to the wine inside. The smoky flavour, unless in excess, was no more objected to than the similar flavour in Westphalia hams or the peat reek in whisky at the present day.

I have reason to believe that a further effect was produced by long exposure in the *fumarium*. The well-known property of the vapour of water to pass through interstices of certain substances impermeable to the vapour of alcohol [1] was, I consider, taken advan-

[1] A property not so well known, perhaps, as it should be. The Australian wine-growers tested the wines they sent to the Vienna Exhibition, and were astonished to find them stronger in spirit when the voyage was ended. The evaporation of the watery vapour in the tropics had reduced the quantity of the wine, and increased its strength by several degrees. This phenomenon takes place, as every experienced wine merchant knows, more conspicuously with white than with red wine.

tage of, and if so, the wine, after long exposure in the smoke-houses, would have become less bulky but more spirituous. In other words, the brandying of wine would have been virtually effected by a people who had never learnt how to distil spirit.

Occasionally the reduction of bulk was carried much further. The wine was inspissated by heat—deprived, that is, of most of its water, and rendered therefore, bulk for bulk, much more valuable. Such inspissated wines were diluted with water when they were drunk, and the advantage of having wine in so portable a form is of course conspicuous enough in times when overland transit could only be effected by beasts of burden, and when traffic by sea was slow, difficult, dangerous, and costly.

Having thus seen how the Greeks and Romans 'cured' their wines, I am now going to tell how this object is attained with the principal varieties of wine drunk in Great Britain at the present day.

I have said, and I most emphatically repeat, that *all natural red wine is subject to decay, and that all wine whatsoever must be treated artificially before it will last more than one or two years.*

To begin with Claret. The finest growths of the Médoc district are peculiar in this respect, that they contain less fermentable matter than probably any known wine; and this they owe partly to admirable care in vinification, partly to a very complete fermentation, but principally to the fact that the grapes that make the wine are not so charged with the elements of vinosity as those ripened in warmer climates.

They require in consequence less artificial treatment than any other, and in the cases of the so-called 'first growths' of Châteaux Margaux, Larose, and Lafitte, when the season has been a good one, the 'curing' seldom goes further than repeated fumigation with sulphur ; and the adulteration of the wine, if the word must be employed, amounts only to its very slight impregnation with the sulphurous acid gas, which is immediately converted into sulphuric acid, or vitriol. This, however, need cause no alarm ; the percentage is infinitesimal, and vitriol, though it has an ugly name, is, as every doctor will tell us, one of the best of tonics.[1] The quantity of spirit added to the fine claret is so small as hardly to be worth considering at all. A few pints are thrown upon the grapes before the crushing begins, and a few more are added, ostensibly to rinse out the casks, whenever the wine is racked, and before it is shipped. In some cases perhaps clarets get no addition of spirit at all. The 'loading' of claret is adopted chiefly for those wines intended for the English market, and is effected by the addition of fuller bodied, more astringent, and more spirituous wines, such as those of Hermitage.

The above remarks apply to the half-dozen finer growths of the Médoc, wines which owe their potentiality of preservation to a happy coincidence of soil,

---

[1] This existence of vitriol in wines is, as might be supposed, a common ground of attack, but a very unfair one, seeing that the vitriol, or sulphuric acid, or the much greater proportion of it, would find substances that would immediately reduce it to the nearly inert condition of sulphates.

climate, quality of wine, and care in cultivation and
in vinification. The majority of these exquisite wines
require to be kept four years in the wood to gain
mellowness, and four in bottle to acquire 'bouquet.'
After this, except in rare cases, claret (if unbrandied)
slowly degenerates, loses colour, and acquires acidity
and a bitter taste, then gets thick, and is sooner or
later a ruined wine. Longevity in clarets not of the
first growths is rare, and though instances of it may be
quoted, they are chiefly found in wines that have
never travelled twenty miles from their native cellar.

The fact, then, that clarets can in rare instances be
made without antiseptic treatment with spirit, is
therefore an apparent but not a real exception to the
rule I have laid down as to the necessity of such
treatment in all red wines. The life of fine claret is
indeed often greatly prolonged, but it is not preserved
indefinitely.

So much for the fine clarets. In them the tannin,
or astringent quality, the great natural preservative
against decay, and the natural acid of the grape, are
both subordinated to its other constituents to make
them in their way perfect wines. Not so the inferior
growths of the Médoc, which we alone of the consumers of them have christened 'claret.' It is from
these latter wines, whose acidity and astringency are
as a rule in most disagreeable preponderance, that
are fabricated the wines known in the wine trade as
Château Margaux, Lafitte, and Larose.

When we remember that these three vineyards
together hardly cover five hundred acres, and never

in the most abundant years make so much as two
thousand hogsheads of wine, scarcely enough to
furnish the cellars of a score of wholesale wine
merchants, it is somewhat ludicrous to reflect that
any number of dozens of these expensive wines can
be ordered from any number of wine merchants in
any large city in Europe or America. From St.
Petersburg to Lisbon, from Glasgow to Constantinople,
from Montreal to New Orleans, and thence southwards
to Rio and Buenos Ayres, and round the world to
the great cities of Australia and India, a man
may walk into any wine merchant's and order a
dozen of Château Margaux or Lafitte, and be reason-
ably disappointed if he is refused.

The performance of this 'inexhaustible bottle
trick' over so wide a geographical area is only possible by treating the inferior growths (not of the Médoc
only, for the exports from Bordeaux of so-called
Médoc wines are said by French writers to be twelve
times greater than the whole production of that
district) in such a way as to give them a fictitious
resemblance to the first growths. To remove the
excess of acid an alkali is employed, and of course a
neutral salt is produced by their combination. Thinness and absence of flavour are remedied sometimes
by the addition of more generous wines, occasionally
by fruity syrups; bouquet is sold in bottles in the
chemists' shops of Bordeaux at '*two francs and upwards, according to quality.*' To get rid of excessive
tannin is more difficult, but it can be effected by
repeated fining, at some cost, however, to the flavour

of the wine. This process is troublesome and expensive, and the majority of cheap clarets, if they are not rough, have a flat taste which reveals the secret of their treatment to all wine makers; the majority of cheap clarets sold in this country, unless they be very poor and very watery indeed, are, when they contain all their native tannin, so rough that no one with any pretension to delicacy of palate cares to drink a glass undiluted with water. In France the commoner Bordeaux wines are used with water, and those that are drunk unmixed are prepared at Bercy for immediate consumption in the restaurants of Paris, by being watered and sweetened, flavoured and alcoholized. In this way the excess of tannin is not removed, but it is lessened by dilution or masked by sugar.

All this, to be sure, is adulteration, but it is almost certainly harmless. It is easy to frighten simple and ignorant wine drinkers by telling them they are drinking vitriol, and sulphate of potash, and grain spirit, but it is a question of degree. Light French wine by common consent and judged by common experience is a wholesome article of diet, let who will speak against it. Its fault is that it is expensive. A wine, according to a writer who is considered an authority upon the subject, may be called cheap that costs not more than half-a-crown a bottle. Now, if such a wine be of French growth, let it be considered how very little vinous quality there is in a half-crown bottle of claret—in other words, how much water there is in proportion to the wine;

not necessarily water of adulteration, but water that
has been the original constituent of grapes ripened in
a climate not hot enough to bestow upon them the
full richness and vinosity that are found in the wines
of the south, in port or burgundy, or even in sherry
or madeira. Claret at fourteen shillings the dozen
was to become the drink of the people, the drink of
working men, and the reign of sobriety was forthwith
to commence; but the working man is no fool:
before he spends fourteen shillings upon twelve
bottles, that is, two gallons of 'Gladstone Claret,' he
asks himself how many quarts of plain water he will
have to deduct, and he refrains from the bargain.
Light claret is not economical as a wine. It has
never reached lower down in the social scale than the
middle classes.

Of sherry adulteration the same can be said as of
claret. The finest wines of Xeres are soft, dry, and
somewhat spirituous wines, and but little artificial aid
is required to enable them to preserve their soundness to an age far exceeding that reached by claret.
Even with the majority of such wines as these, and
certainly with all the commoner sherries, the system
of so-called 'plastering' is followed, which consists in
throwing about thirty pounds of dry plaster of Paris
upon the quantity of untrodden grapes required to
make a butt of wine. The result is to precipitate the
natural wine acids, and to substitute for them sulphuric acid; this mineral acid coming into contact
with the potash in the *must*, converts it into sulphate
of potash, whereas had things taken their course,

bitartrate of potash (commonly called tartar) would have been present—a salt always to be found in young wines. This is the head and front of the offence known as 'plastering,' made so much of by those who desire to exhibit sherry in its worst colours. Tartar is well known to be a not over wholesome constituent of newly-made wine. Sulphate of potash is certainly no very deleterious substance, and to put it in the stead of tartar may, for any evidence the other way, be rather a benefit than not.

A heavier indictment against the sherry makers is their apparently too abundant use of spirit. A white wine can possess little or no tannin, and therefore requires a preservative ; but, on the other hand, if well made, such a wine should not be troubled with the fruitiness and fermentable matter of the more vinous red wines ; it should therefore not need such a dose of spirit as it too often gets. It is probable that the demands of consumers, rather than the necessities of wine makers, are the cause of the excess of spirit in sherry. The same taste also causes the dyeing of the wine with burnt sugar, and the sweetening and fortifying it with *dulce*, or half fermented grape-juice. These are quite harmless adulterations—if they deserve the name—as innocent, indeed, and as openly employed, as the putting of sugar and cream into our cups of tea. On the whole I am convinced that sound sherry is a wholesome wine, and one which we could very ill afford to do without.

Of champagne I need say little. Everyone knows

that it is an imperfectly fermented grape juice made
of grapes not thoroughly ripened, sweetened with
sugar-candy dissolved in brandy. The want of tannin is supplied by oak shavings or tannic acid. Rack-
ing and sulphuring are the chief methods of ' curing '
it. Experience, which is always immeasurably superior to the most positive utterances of theoretical
chemists, teaches us that, in spite of its being so artificial a wine, champagne is not only wholesome, but
a remedial agent of the very greatest value.

Hock and burgundy can hardly be regarded as
common wines in England. The common, rough
burgundies, indeed, find their way into consumption,
and an indiscriminating public classes them with
clarets; and not unwisely, seeing that the inferior
French red wines are artificially brought to something
of a common standard. The ' great wines ' of the
Burgundy district, the ' Clos Vougeot,' ' Richebourg,'
and ' Romanée Conti,' the most exquisite of wines,
true ' drink of the gods,' will probably never be known
in their full perfection beyond the region of their
production. They will hardly bear travel by land,
and transit by sea almost always injures them.
Unfortunately, in the case of the wine of modern
times, which is immeasurably superior to all others,
the skill of the modern wine curer utterly breaks
down.

Though port wine has the reputation of being the
most adulterated and the least natural of all wines, it
is, to the best of my knowledge and belief—and I
have had opportunities of watching all the processes

of making it during thirteen years—one of the very purest. I believe that a man who drinks a glass of port drinks as nearly natural and as concentrated a form of fermented grape juice as it is humanly possible to set before him.

There are no secrets and there is no reserve about the processes of port vinification. All the world may learn all about them, and the Wine Committee of the House of Commons of 1879, which has now ended its labours, has collected and sifted so much evidence on the subject, and examined and cross-examined so many impartial and partial witnesses, that no one has any longer an excuse for ignoring the facts.

Adulteration is in wine, as in everything else, mostly an affair of competition and of public taste. Formerly Englishmen liked port wine to be almost black in colour and very fruity and strong, whereupon dried elderberries were employed to help to stain it. If one merchant did it, his rivals had to follow suit. It was deplorable enough, but a little too much was made of it, for the wine was by no means seriously injured or made unwholesome. The light wine people, oblivious of their own misdeeds, were terribly hurt by the thought that anybody could dye a wine with elderberries. They did their utmost to publish the fact and to proclaim their own innocence. Doing this they perhaps did not mean to benefit the port wine trade, but they were Balaams unawares: meaning to bring a curse, they brought a blessing on the trade, for though the public were not made to leave off liking port wine, they left off liking it over dark and fruity; and straightway the elderberry staining ceased.

As for adulteration by logwood it always was a libellous fable. Any chemist knows that the peculiar *reaction* of logwood makes it absolutely inoperative as a dye in any sort of wine. As long as the public want port wine to have no more than its own true garnet-red colour, which turns with age to a dark amber, no merchant would be so extravagant as to put elderberry into it. If the wine is required to be made darker, there is a much cheaper dye and a far more beautiful one always at hand in Portugal: it is the natural colour of the darker varieties of the port wine grape. To say that grapes are cheaper in Portugal than elderberries in England seems an exaggeration, but to my certain knowledge they are much cheaper. About three years ago I was offered more for the produce of a few elderberry trees in Surrey than I could get for an equal weight of the produce of my vines at Oporto. I wish to make this point clear in support of my contention that port wine is pure, because there is nothing so cheap as port wine itself to adulterate it with. A curious fact is that the common rough clarety wines grown in the neighbourhood of Oporto and drunk by the peasantry are often dearer than the choice vintages of the port wine district. The apparent anomaly is to be accounted for by the fact that while the commoner wine is drinkable within six months of its leaving the wine vat, new port wine—the trade speak of it as *young* wine—has gone but one stage of its journey towards being drinkable port wine. It has to be kept, to be racked, to be fined, to be skilfully ' turned over,' to be carefully watched, to be fortified with distilled wine, and previous to all this to be carried a perilous voyage down the River Douro, to pay warehouse charges in Oporto and England, to pay a tax on export, a heavy import duty, merchants' profits, freight charges, insurance charges, and several others. Port wine had need then to start cheap, for else assuredly none but millionaires could ever drink it.

My friend Mr. Gallenga, the eminent correspondent of the ' Times,' in the course of his recent impartial investigations into the mysteries of the great wine question, informed me, in illustration of the cheapness of wines in the country of their production, that a pint of an honest red wine could be bought in Piedmont from the cask on a market day for 20 centimes ; I was able still further to extend the limit of Mr. Gallenga's illustration by informing him that I, a farmer in Portugal, would be glad to sell sound red wine, excellent of its kind, from my own vineyard at considerably less than three pence per quart. To be sure my wine, made on a granite soil, though sound and strong, would not recommend itself to a cultivated taste. It has the *gout du terrain,* which, if my recollection serves me, nearly all the wines of Northern Italy possess. Nevertheless wine is wine, and it can cost no more to make it on a good soil and with a good aspect than under the most unfavourable circumstances. Mr. Gallenga naturally asked, ' Then where do all the profits go ? ' So far as port wine is concerned I think I have already given an intelligible answer to this question.

Port wine is made in only one corner of Portugal. It is a district marked out by nature itself to be one huge vineyard; its soil is a peculiar brown, crumbling, slaty schist; it is cut off from the sea by one lofty range of mountains, it is shut in from the north and east by others. This district of the port wine vineyards is hilly and precipitous, and the vines grow on the barren-looking soil built up into multitudinous terraces often from top to bottom of the hills. This singular tract lies about sixty miles up the Douro and on its banks, and it occupies a strip of country about twenty-seven miles in length, and five or six in breadth. It is cold here in winter, but in summer the sun shines into the narrow valley, and is reverberated from the hill amphitheatres with a particular intensity. The whole region, cut off from the breezes, lies still and becalmed under the summer sun: the heat is tropical. Nowhere else in Europe can the vines get such a roasting, nowhere else are the juices of the grape elaborated into such a rich and potent liquor. One understands port wine at the first glance of the wine country. It would of course be easy to get a hotter summer in the tropics, but the vine is not a plant of the tropics, it wants the severe cold of winter to give it a seasonable rest. It gets this: the port wine district is one of the few parts of Portugal where I have seen ice that will bear a man.

The population of the wine country is scanty, and is of course composed chiefly of wine farmers.

Labourers are few, but when the vines require their annual hoeings and pruning, and at vintage time, men flock in from the neighbouring provinces and from as far off as the mountains of Galicia in northern Spain.

In the port wine district the vines are grown as bushes—something as currant trees are with us. They are closely pruned down early in the year and the summer shoots are supported by stakes. Elsewhere in the Peninsula (except where a specially good wine is wanted) the vine is trained over trellises or against pollarded trees. It is pretty and there are more grapes got in this way, but the wine is poor.

The vintage begins towards the end of September; it is conducted more or less in the manner I have already described. Much care and knowledge are required in the selection of the right proportions of the many varieties of grapes that grow in the district, some for colour, some for flavour, some for bouquet, some for strength; and scientific instruments (saccharometers) are used to determine the right moment for drawing off the must. It is drawn into tonels, huge casks often with a capacity of over thirty pipes. The drawing off and the slight addition of alcohol now made arrests or nearly arrests the fermentation.

When I say alcohol in connection with a high or fairly high class of port wine, I ought to say distilled wine. It is a spirit distilled from the wine itself and contains of course only that which is inherent in the wine it is derived from. This spirit thus added during the growth, as it were, of the wine, becomes chemically incorporated and combined with it. This fact came out clearly in the evidence before the last Parliamentary committee.

With the cold of autumn the wine deposits its lees; it is then racked off into the ordinary port wine pipes—a long and narrow cask containing 115 gallons. In the spring it is carried down the Douro to the warehouses of the merchants at Oporto.

It is the practice of the established English wine merchants at Oporto to buy the grape produce of the vineyards and to have the wine made by the farmers under their own superintendence, watched and warehoused by their own *employés*, and finally brought into their own keeping at Oporto. The wine firms hold enormous stocks of wine in their warehouses ripening for English consumption. This large stock is essential to the business, for the wines shipped are of two sorts: ' vintage ' wines, that is, wines of a particular year ; and ' brand ' wines, which are usually made up of the vintages of several years. When a shipper gets an order for, say, a hundred pipes (more or less) of wine of a particular character, he naturally requires a great variety of wines wherewith to make up the order. It is to be observed that a brand wine is not by any means an inferior wine: it may often indeed be superior to a vintage wine, and depends of course upon the quality of the wines of which it is made up. Except in remarkable years, where nature combines in one vintage all the various excellences which port wine can possess, I am inclined to think that port, like hermitage, is the better for being made up of the produce of different vineyards and even different years. The wine district, as I have shown, is one huge vineyard; beyond its limits little good wine is made, within them little that is not good. There is therefore no need for classification of wines by the names of their vineyards as in France. Some few port wine vineyards especially favoured in soil and aspect are known to fame. Vesuvio, Roëda, Roriz, Noval, and a very few others have reputations beyond Portugal.

It will be seen from my account of port wine growing, making, and selling that the trade is something of a monopoly—a monopoly of a legitimate kind enough, resulting from the skill and knowledge applied to it and the capital invested. The supply too is limited by the limits of the region which furnishes it. What with the ravages of the oïdium disease in the past and of the Phylloxera Vastatrix in the present and future, I do not think the port wine country will in future years ever send more than 40,000 pipes of wine to England.

When I speak of a monopoly, I do not mean that competition does not exist. It is active enough—witness the low price of port wine—but it is confined in the long run to the established firms. An outsider can only satisfactorily enter the trade by the slow process of establishing warehouses, getting together a skilled staff and purchasing a stock. To be sure there are occasional opportunities of buying wine in open market, and such wine may even bean honest wine, but it may also be nothing of the kind. There is a class of persons in the wine district who have got themselves the name of *Boticarios*—apothecaries—and who have the reputation of compounding their wines with queer ingredients. Their wine may seem fair enough, but wines, like men, must have fair antecedents as well as a fair seeming. A wise man will no more take such doubtful liquors into his cellar than he will take a servant into his service without a character. The one is apt to turn sour, and the other to steal his spoons. I do not think such wine as this often finds its way to England. I hope it does not. Fortunately for us there is a demand for wine not of the highest quality in Portugal itself, and for shipment to Brazil.

There is a method of adulterating port wine which I fear is not uncommon, but it can only be practised in Great Britain. It consists in mixing it with the red wine made in the neighbourhood of Tarragona in Spain. This Spanish wine is as nearly as possible half the price of the very cheapest port wine. It is made as port wine is made, and is quite a harmless, sound and honest wine, very like port wine *to look at*, but having little or none of those qualities of high flavour and *bouquet*, none of those essential etherous attributes which make port wine a wine apart. A mixture with 'Spanish red,' as this estimable liquid is called, only spoils port wine in the sense that it dilutes it. It may be well supposed that 'Spanish red' is sometimes a sore subject with port wine merchants. It may be argued, however, that the

demand for port in England is so much greater than
the supply, that it is just as well for producers and
consumers alike that it is adulterated with nothing
worse than red Tarragona wine. The adulteration
only applies to the cheapest kinds of wine—such as
is sold in public houses ; but working men are getting
to be connoisseurs, and many such establishments I
am told enjoy a reputation for selling only the pure
port wine of known firms. I do not suppose that
any really respectable English wine merchant would
mix his wine with anything. Nevertheless, whenever
port wine seems to the customers to lack flavour and
the price is not very low, a civil inquiry pointing to
the possible presence of ' Spanish red ' might be
judicious.

Some years ago, ' it came to my knowledge ' (as
policemen say) in my official capacity in this city that
a very curious error in geography was being perpe-
trated. Some eighteen casks of red wine had come
all the way to Oporto from the east coast of Spain
for transhipment at this port to England. It seemed
to me quite to come within the sphere of my official
duties to mention the fact of this circuitous voyage
in a telegram to the Customs authorities at home, and
when the ship reached its destination a custom house
officer was ready with a branding iron to mark the
eighteen impostors indelibly with the words ' Red
wine from Spain.' No one consequently was a loser
by this freak of navigation, and the spirited importer
was no gainer

It would not very well become me to go fully in

this place into the question of the wine duties, which there is some talk of modifying, nor do I think my readers would be greatly entertained with me if I did. Yet it is a great question with much of human interest about it : a subject for a three hours' Budget-speech, a question for bold financial generalization, full of interesting detail, bristling with facts and data ; with all sorts of conflicting interests to steer between, and the haven in sight of great commercial development and of great philanthropic results. It is a thing for only one great statesman and orator to meddle with.

I will therefore say no more than this—that our wine duties oppress no one very much. They are not a pressing grievance. They bring, in a very comfortable way, not very far short of two millions sterling. We can get along with them very plea-santly, but if France, Spain, and Portugal like to make it worth our while, we will reduce the duties in their interests, in our own, and in those of free trade. Instead of making France pay a shilling a gallon on her wine we might let her off with six-pence, and Spain and Portugal might obtain admission for their sherries and ports with a shilling payment on each gallon instead of half-a-crown, which is the present duty. If we lower our duties in this way and make no treaty bargains with these three countries it is free trade and good sense, but it is freer trade and better sense if we lower the duties and make good bargains too : always assuming that the achieve-ment of three commercial treaties abreast is a diplo-

matic possibility, which is extremely doubtful. Only
let the arrangements be for a long term, that there
may be no turning back towards the road to protection.

I have been often questioned, as a person who
ought to know, as to the dietetical properties of port
wine. Certainly if the general public are in no
better agreement on the point than the doctors there
is plenty of occasion for such questioning. We
have recently had an active controversy among the
faculty chiefly on this very point, and it struck me
when I read it that anyone with strong opinions on
either side might find the fullest medical authority
for his views. My own modest opinion about wine
entirely coincides with that which the world at large
has held for several thousand years past, and will
probably hold for as long a time to come. It is that
wine in moderation is the best and most harmless
restorative in health and sickness that the ingenuity of
man has ever invented. I think that the more a wine
is a wine the more restorative it is. Whatever may
be the theoretical views of some medical gentlemen, I
find there is a consensus of practice among the doctors
of all nations to give wine to the convalescent and to
the weakly, and to give them the most vinous wine
for choice. The consumption of port wine at the
London hospitals is, to my knowledge, enormous.

The pure wine theorists conceive that sound light
claret is more digestible than sherry and port. I
think there can be no doubt about it ; so also is claret
and water more digestible than pure claret, and rice

pudding lighter food than beef and bread ; but if a healthy man, in full work of brain or muscle, wants to maintain his health and his strength, or having been ill to get well again, he had better drink something more restorative than claret and water, and eat something more substantial than rice pudding.

Some few doctors in the controversy differed from their brother doctors to the extent of advising people to drink spirits and water rather than wine. This suggestion seems to me to be singularly opposed to common sense, and to be put forward on the assumption that it is the alcohol in the wine that is chiefly restorative and of value, which is altogether a mistake. It is not the alcohol, but the ethers and the other various and purely vinous ingredients, the cunning product of nature's own laboratory, which chiefly are restorative. It is not exactly a chemical question, for the best chemists can tell us little on these obscure points. It is a question settled by any one who drinks a glass of fine old burgundy, or of port, or of sweet tokay. *Solvitur bibendo.* I consider this suggestion of the doctors to be a particularly mischievous one, because raw spirits, with or without water, spirits not incorporated and combined with wine, are to most people stimulating, and certainly neither soothing nor restorative. They certainly also are injurious sooner or later. If a man takes a glass of wine when he requires it he is satisfied : he has taken a calmative and a tonic. If he drinks the equivalent alcohol in the shape of spirits and water he is not satisfied or made the better, the dose is too

small to calm his nerves, and large enough to do him
a hurt. He wants more and he goes on. I think
if we English drank wine and beer, eschewing spirits,
we should cease to be a nation of drunkards.[1] I
hardly see a drunken man about Oporto, where strong
port wine is to be got for a trifle in every public house.
The southern Spaniards are as sober as the Portuguese,

[1] But it must not be light wine. That the light wine of France
was to wean us from spirits, close the gin palaces, and make England sober and virtuous, was the pleasant vision raised for us in
1860, and too soon discovered to be a dream. It is found in practice that the general run of men who drink light wine qualify it
by drinking spirits neat. The *Assommoir* is set up in the Paris
wine shop, men want alcohol all the more for getting little of it
in their wine, and take a dram with nearly every glass of claret.
It almost sounds like an exaggeration to say as much as this, and
though I know very well it is true, I should hardly venture to
put it on paper but for the admissions of some of the French witnesses before the recent Parliamentary Wine Committee.

M. Lalande, President of the Chamber of Commerce of Bordeaux, says (No. 5268): ' In spite of the enormous increase in the
duties on our spirits since the war, the consumption has increased,
and also the consumption of wine has been increasing too. There
seems to be not much relation between the two.' That is, one
does not supplant the other. The evidence of M. Teissonnière,
Vice-President of the Chamber of Commerce of Paris, is stronger
still. He actually suggests the lowering of the duty on light
wines in this country, on the ground that more consumption of
them includes more consumption of spirits, and would secure a
larger spirit revenue! ' This drink,' he says (Answer No. 50),
meaning light wine, ' brought into general consumption would increase the consumption of your alcoholic liquors, and I will give
you examples in proof of that from France.' . . . 'The city of
Paris which consumes annually 4,000,000 hectolitres of wines
consumes also 1,173,000 of alcohol.'

This is on the whole the best argument I have yet met with
for lowering the duties on those strong full wines which certainly
do harmlessly supersede the use of alcoholic drink.

though strong wine is their drink too. I hope the small minority of doctors who recommend raw spirits to their patients will take all these points into their consideration and modify their opinions.

So much for the doctors, who, though they do not agree among themselves, and might therefore be left to answer each other, are yet practical men. As for the wine specialists, they are nothing of the kind, and no more to be implicitly trusted than other specialists in science. If I did not fear to seem malicious I could tell some queer anecdotes of certain conflicts of practice and theory on the part of these gentlemen. Their theories are gospel truths to them and to people who run after new doctrine, only until they are reversed by newer theories; and impartial observers see that this reversal happens in a cycle of about three years. Such theories as they favour us with would never get a footing among us at all if only we could afford time and patience and knowledge and preliminary scepticism for a close examination of them. In short,

'C'est notre crédulité qui fait leur science.'

In conclusion I will repeat in very plain terms what is after all the most important axiom in connection with wine. It is that such a red wine as port, grown in the centre of the geographical zone which is the *habitat* of the vine plant, and under favouring influences of soil and aspect, is so full of all the finest vinous attributes, and therefore, unfortunately, of all the elements of decay, that it requires a fuller antiseptic treatment than other and poorer wines. I have shown how the ancients, skilful œnologists, indirectly alcoholized their wines though they knew not the art of distillation. Falernian was, I am absolutely sure, as fully alcoholized as the strongest port wine. Modern port wine makers alcoholize their wine directly, and no impartial man can deny that the result is an excellent result. If it be alleged that they put too much spirit into their wine, they reply very convincingly that spirit is six times dearer than wine, and that it is clearly to their interest to use as little as will keep the wine sound.

Whether port contain much or little spirit—I am myself in favour of the least that is possible—it has one signal advantage over all other red wines of its high vinous quality : it is safe, it will travel, and it is long-lived. A man may invest in it with the confidence with which he buys into the three per cents. If a man buys a cask of fine burgundy in England and bottles it, the odds are, so far as my experience goes, considerably against the wine's remaining sound for two years. He may as well lay out his money in Turkish or Egyptian stock. If a man makes a similar investment in good claret, the odds are certainly greatly in favour of the wine's keeping and of its improving, at least up to a certain date ; but if a man invests in port wine, it is not a question of odds at all. Let him buy a pipe, or a hogshead, or a quarter cask of port wine at a fair price through a respectable wine merchant and the element of chance is eliminated. It is an absolute certainty that the wine will not only keep sound but will improve in value every year of its life. Not only is his capital safe but the wine will pay him interest.

If I am asked what is a fair price, I must answer that, not being a wine merchant, it does not become me to say.

CHAPTER VII.

A PORTUGUESE TROY.

NATURE, whose mastery of hand in decorating the scenes, flies, and slips of her own great airy theatre, has been the theme of scenery-loving travellers' admiration from all times, is, it must be confessed, not seldom a very poor landscape painter.

The tourist who passes over the river Tagus at Lisbon may, if he pleases, get a striking illustration of this fact. The ferry steamer from that city crosses in less than an hour the broad estuary of the Tagus, and lands its passengers at Barreiro, amid black and muddy beach waves whence the paddles of the boat churn up fearful exhalations. Barreiro is the terminus of the railway which runs eastward to Evora and Beja—famous cities in Roman and in Moorish times, and now still goodly resorts of men— and southward to Setubal.

As I was making this little voyage on my way to Setubal, and as the steamer neared the southern shores of the Tagus, I heard the words ' How fine ! ' break, as it were, involuntarily from the lips of an English traveller standing by my side among the crowd on board. I regarded first the view and then the very intelligent-looking person who had admired it.

'Pray,' I asked, 'do you mean this view here in front of us over the shore flats, with the green fields and white and red houses in the distance?'

'Not at all,' said the intelligent person; 'I mean the one to our right, where those beautifully coloured red and yellow hills rise from the river edge, and the stone pines, growing along the hill-crest, cut the blue sky; and see how the waves ripple and foam upon the sandy beach. Lovely! Lovely!'

I easily perceived that my intelligent-looking acquaintance had belied his expression, and was talking nonsense. There was indeed some little attempt at a picture, but the result was absolute failure. Nature indeed always draws correctly—so does photography—but of composition, harmony, effect, breadth, keeping, suggestiveness (the most important of all), there was not a trace. Offences there were against every canon of art, as we dwellers upon earth have come to lay them down. The red and yellow of the bare cliff-side were crude, and harmonized neither with sea nor sky; the sky looked more like a newly-painted blue wall than the transparent vault of heaven; the water between us and the cliff was deplorable as water, it seemed distinctly convex instead of flat, as I have too often seen the seas and lakes of young amateurs in water-colour art; the foam of the waves on the shore could have been represented by a line drawn in white chalk with a ruler. The puny stone-

pines—those charming accessories in my acquaintance's eyes—were in fact no more picturesque than,
and very like, a long row of dark-green cotton
umbrellas opened and planted in the ground.   It was
altogether as an art-work a pitiable failure.

As one secret of the art of being good company
is to know less and have worse taste than one's companion, of course I expressed nothing of my views to
the intelligent-looking person in question.   If these
pages should unfortunately fall under the eye of my
acquaintance, if he should remember his fellow-pas-
senger on the ferry-boat, who affably responded,
'Ah, to be sure!' to his eulogy of the southern shore
of the Tagus, he must bear him no malice, but reflect
that thought is free and tastes may differ.

I lost sight of my acquaintance at the station,
Barreiro: he may have gone east; I went south to
Setubal.   Had he been with me, I suspect that we
should have found ourselves in most perfect accord
in our opinion of the hideous and dreary wastes of
country over which the train passes.   Never, I think,
anywhere have I seen agriculture fighting at such
odds against the soil, and fighting successfully too, for
these thin, sandy dunes, with here and there a mud
creek, here and there a patch of rusty moorland, the
whole flat stretch of country treeless, dreary, barren,
inhospitable, produce the best-flavoured and most
famous wine of Southern Portugal—the Lavradio, so
called from the hamlet of that name, whence, too, a
name far better known to England than the wine,
that of H.E. the late Count of Lavradio, the most

popular of Portuguese ministers at the Court of St. James's.

Had Dante chosen to represent the future state of the wicked and impenitent farmer, he might have placed him in some such region as that which we are now passing through. Mr. Arch himself could wish our English tenant-farmers no worse an Inferno!

Soil, sun, and wind fight against the tiller of the land. The soil is no more consistent than the contents of an hour-glass, the rain sinks through it without benefit. The fervid sun generates indeed some rare œnanthic fragrance in the grape, but its fierceness withers and kills, as I can see, half the vine plants in the vineyards ; and these vineyards, what almost weird and dreary things they must seem to the first glance of eyes not used to vine growing ! Now in early spring there is hardly a green leaf showing, and no suggestion of the lush leafage of the graceful ' gadding vine,' as it shows itself on trellises in Italy and Northern Portugal. Hereabouts a vineyard is a rough field, unenclosed save by a low sand mound, stuck along its ridge here and there with a stunted aloe or prickly pear,—a poor pretence of a fence, passable everywhere. The weed-grown, sandy expanse within is the vineyard, and at every two yards there uprear themselves dark twisted stumps, like black snakes with their heads and half their bodies in the air, contorted in their struggles to free themselves from imprisonment in the earth beneath. These are the vines. pruned back. and as the spring

goes on they will put forth leaves and four or five
weakly, yard-long shoots.

The wheat-crops on the sandy soil are not more
promising; they are indeed almost ludicrous in their
scantiness. Each seed grain has sent up but a single
stem, quill-like in its thinness and untillered. What
farmer could set about seriously to reap and stack
and garner and thrash such a hollow mockery of a
crop? Why, one might hand-pick half an acre of
such poor stuff and carry it off like a nosegay! A
couple of active English gleaners might clear a field
of it in a day, and garner it in their cottage kitchens!
The wind draughts passing east and west along the
great Tagus estuary peculiarly torment this unsheltered
plain. Hardly a tree will stand against them anywhere, and the great reed cane, indispensable to make
stakes for the vine plant, three times a man's height
in more favoured localities, dwindles here to walking-
stick size. The very instruments of labour seem to
be such as might have been devised to add to the
husbandman's burden of toil. The hoe is but a cubit
long in the handle, and the worker with it must bend
to the very earth. The blade is constructed to suit
the soil he works in; it is broader and a good deal
longer than an English spade, and set on at a sharp
angle with its handle. One sees innumerable flashes
of these great hoes in the sun, for the toiling of
labourers seems to be incessant, and of the load of
dry, sandy soil lifted into the air, a third seems each
time to run off like water before it can be turned to
its new position.

Malaria hangs in the air here; the inhabitants are all ague smitten—there is no mistaking the signs of it on their pale and haggard faces. There is hardly a bird or a wild flower, though the farmer generally is no appreciator of either. Only, for wild flowers, is the little moss-like wild sorrel, whose blood-red blossom stains the ground in broad patches as if real blood has just been shed on it—fit adornment for our Inferno. The air is quite songless, and the only beat of wings is when the great marsh-harrier or the dark-feathered buzzard flits overhead, brooding, as a poetical fancy might have it, like the spirit of evil over this curse-stricken place, and also, as the farmer's fears no doubt more often suggest, on the look-out for his stray chickens near the farmstead.

Now, see what a cunning artist is Nature after all, and what force there is in contrast! When our senses have become quite impenetrated with this dreary scene, with the stagnant mud-creeks, the tawny sand, showing unseemly among the straggling wheat plants, with the want of greenery, of shade, of growing and moving things—for there is not a cloud even to drop its shadow on the level earth—then suddenly the train passes through a dividing ridge, and in an instant we are in a new and a marvellously beautiful land. League-long groves of orange and lemon trees fill the valley, their new-shot blossoms are already showing, the air is full everywhere of their scent, while still the fair ripe fruit is hanging on the branches, 'golden lamps in a green night' of leafage. The fields are dark green with the rank luxuriance of growing crops. Fruit trees of every kind, peach, almond, pear, and cherry, are in full blossom, and every corner of waste ground is radiant with the bloom of spring flowers.

Geology is what will best explain this sudden transformation. We have left the alluvial sand-flats of some ancient sea, and are now among the rocks, clays and schists, sandstones and limestones of the oolites. Few formations have such boldly contorted rock-peaks, such triumphs of Nature's masonry in mountain and cliff, such intensely red rock surfaces, such perfect harmonies of greys and purples.

On a great massive cliff in the valley is set the ancient Moorish stronghold of Palmella—still a strong place of arms—with the oblique rays of the morning sun slanting brightly on its square towers and tall battlements. Palmella commands all the six miles of fertile valley reaching to Setubal, which has its own hill fortress. Setubal lies close to the beach, and its white houses glitter in the sun, doubly white in their setting of dark green orange groves and of the clear, deep blue waters of the bay. Everywhere in this delightful landscape the earth-surface contrasts its pure, deep reds against the green of grass and leaf with surprising force of colour. Beyond everything, in the west, overtopping town and valley and tower and all lesser hills, stands the great range of the Arrabida, peak upon peak, till the Atlantic is reached: treeless mountains showing on their nearest ridge the red stone softened by distance to a tender purple: further off in the clefts of the mountain tops

are clear air-depths of exquisite ultramarine, and in
the furthest distance of all the early morning sunlight,
striking full upon the bare peaks and pinnacles,
shows them powdered with pearl and gold.

In all this scene, in its infinite variety of hill, dale,
wood and water, in its strength of colour and bright
airy perspectives, there is a resemblance to those
wonderful landscapes of the early Italian masters,
who make of such pictures a sort of epitome of
human life—of life under the sunny skies and in the
genial air of the golden south. We see in these
pictures of theirs the labours of men in field and
vineyard, wayfarers on foot and horseback along the
roads; the city with each dwelling in careful detail, the
church below, the feudal castle on the cliff above, the
flocks and herds feeding in the pastures, the winging
of birds through the air, the winding river, the frequent bridges; the blue, transparent waves of the sea,
with boats and ships on it; the fleecy clouds hanging
aloft—all drawn with exquisite fineness of clear outline and force of pure and subtle colouring; and in
the far distance just such peaks, pinnacles, and precipices as we have here in the Arrabida mountains.
Such an outlook upon nature and man's work with
nature as we get it through the art of these old painters
is not a landscape in our narrow modern sense, but a
panorama; and such as I am trying to describe it do
we get here amidst these orange-growing valleys,
these hills and distant mountains, and this Portuguese city by the clear waters of its bay. It is
nature in the south, with its warmth, its light, its

brightness and its gaiety epitomized into one great picture.

There are two or three inns at Setubal, and I happened to choose the one near the sea, a comfortable enough place of lodgment; and I will observe here that the wayfarer in this country need never much trouble himself to inquire as to the best inn. There is nothing very good and nothing very bad in a town of the size of Setubal. Competition equalizes the accommodation and equalizes prices. Everywhere one gets great civility and extraordinarily hard beds, abundant and not uneatable food, much dust, many flies, a passable wine, not very passable coffee, and most excellent green tea without milk, at five minutes' notice, day or night. One sometimes gets, to be sure, more—much more—than all this; but he is a poor traveller who regards these unfeeable attendants —*non ragionam di lor.*

My coming to Setubal this spring—I had passed through the town once before—was with the object of visiting the ruins of an ancient city, buried in the sand-hills of a low-lying promontory in the bay over against the town of Setubal. The site of the ruins has long been known, probably for five or six hundred years, as Troia, and I suspect that this curious name may date from Renaissance times, may have been bestowed by the learned, a prevailing party in those days, and may simply have been equivalent to 'a place of many ruins;' but its first name, or rather its very ancient name, was, it is almost

certain, Cetobriga, or some variation of that name.
Resende, the Camden of Portugal, and the predecessor
of our great English antiquary by a generation, is, to my
knowledge, the first writer who has noticed these ruins.
He describes the discovery at Troia of a statue, Roman
inscriptions in abundance, and the ruins of a temple
of Jupiter Ammon. Subsequent Portuguese archæologists—there was no lack of antiquarian industry
in the sixteenth and seventeenth centuries—discovered
more remains, and discoursed at still greater length
than Resende, the father of them all in Portugal.
Then came the abeyance of all intellectual movement
in this and some other countries. There came to be
a time when there were no antiquaries even, in Portugal. While some of us woke out of our sleep
through the eighteenth century, Portugal slept on,
and misgoverned herself, and was a perfect Gallio of a
country in every respect. She woke up, however, to
most excellent purpose with the first strokes of the new
century, to astonish the world with her capacity for
loyalty, for patriotism, and for hard fighting, but thereafter turned to sleep again for a while, and forgot, amid
more important matters, all about Troia and its ruins.

I do not know that anybody would have thought
again about them, but that it happened that, in the
autumn of the very year in which the last French
soldier had been driven from the Peninsula—in 1814,
that is—there came a most portentous storm of rain.
The rivers which feed the estuary which washes
Troia and Setubal were swollen beyond what had
ever been known, and the floods carried away great

lumps of the sand of the shore at Troia, and then
again the ruins were visible, and many curious things
were found—the skeleton of a man, a great leaden
casket containing objects of silver, a patera, a
candelabrum, all of silver; and these objects were
pronounced by the learned who saw them, and
theorized upon them (as is and ever will be the way
of the learned), to be Phœnician. It was not till
1850, however, that the archæologists bestirred themselves in the matter. Then, under the patronage of
the Duke of Palmella of that day—the Dukes of
Palmella are great people at Setubal, and have land and
a great palace in the neighbourhood—a society was
formed with a long name (so long, that I forget it) to
explore the ruins of Troia; and subscriptions were
raised, and the Duke headed the list; subscribing, no
doubt, more in energy and learning than in paltry
money, for I find that the whole funds of the Society
amounted to the very non-magnificent sum of 253l.

The society was considerably more successful
than the parsimony of its members deserved, for
they found a great deal. Probably the ruins lay
very thick. They began to dig on the 1st of May,
1850, stopped on the second day of June, on account
first of heat, then of rain, began again in the autumn
of the same year, and exhausted their funds and their
patience in the following March. They uncovered a
very perfect and very beautiful Roman house of considerable size; they found all that might be expected
to be found in Roman ruins—columns of coloured
marble, Saguntine vases, lachrymatories and cine-

rary urns of glass, bronze and earthenware lamps,
amphoræ, mosaic pavements, *styla* of bone, and so
forth—all pointing to a period of later Roman
domination. Of coins great numbers were found, none
Phœnician—had they existed, they would probably
have lain at a lower level; but Roman coins of bronze
to the number of about sixteen hundred. Trajan
and Antoninus Pius were represented by one or two
coins of each only, two only were found of Julian the
Apostate, seventeen of Constantius Gallus, or of Constantius, three hundred and forty-one of Gratian, who
died A.D. 383, a hundred and eighty-five of Maximus,
who overthrew and succeeded him, and was, five years
later, overthrown by Theodosius the Great. Of
Theodosius himself no fewer than four hundred and
eighteen coins were found in the few months of exploration; of coins of his two sons, Arcadius, first
Emperor of the East, and of the stupid Honorius,
Emperor of the West, who reigned twenty-eight
years and died in 423, the numbers dwindle, only
two hundred coins having been found of each of
them, and these are the last emperors whose coins
were found in Troia.

With all these facts before him, the antiquary—
indeed, a plainer man than an antiquary—may conclude with some agreeable degree of certainty that
Cetobriga as a Roman town flourished chiefly between
A.D. 300 and 400, and that its decadence began soon
after the appearance in the Peninsula of the Visi-
gothic invaders in about 411, under their King
Athaulf, brother-in-law to the Emperor Honorius.

Perhaps Cetobriga did not cease to be an inhabited place till the time of Euric, late in the same century, when nearly the whole of modern Spain and Portugal fell into the hands of the Visigoths. I have not heard of a single Gothic coin being found, and certainly these barbarians were not people to care for a luxurious *villeggiatura* in the soft air and amid the perfumed groves of this lovely Lusitanian Baiæ.

Arrived at Setubal, I bargained with two boatmen to take me across to Troia, intending to spend the day there. Returning to the inn, I found a well-dressed and courteous Portuguese gentleman reading, with the help of his eyeglass, the name on my portmanteau. Having acquainted himself with my name, he did me the honour of addressing me in the French tongue, and lost no time in giving me much useful information. Setubal was a fairly civilized place, he said; the streets were clean, and the authorities, on the whole, enlightened; the sea-bathing was not at all bad, the sands smooth and firm, and the water as salt nearly as the ocean itself. As for Troia, which I informed him I was about to visit, he did not think much of it. He smiled contemptuously as he told me the story of the French company who had—as is well known to archæologists—recently purchased the whole sandy promontory, for the sake of the *finds* to be made there. 'Much good might it do them,' was my acquaintance's ironical remark; 'a foolish set of fellows, spending good money on a barren sandbank.' He had never taken the trouble to cross the water

to see Troia; it was four miles away, and it was
quite a useless trouble, for the place was visible from
the inn windows. He would show it to me.

He did so, pointing out a break in the opposite
coast-line, which seemed to rise abruptly from the
sea to the height of from thirty to fifty feet. The
break or gap was where a little river ran in, and to
our left of that was a large roofless building. That

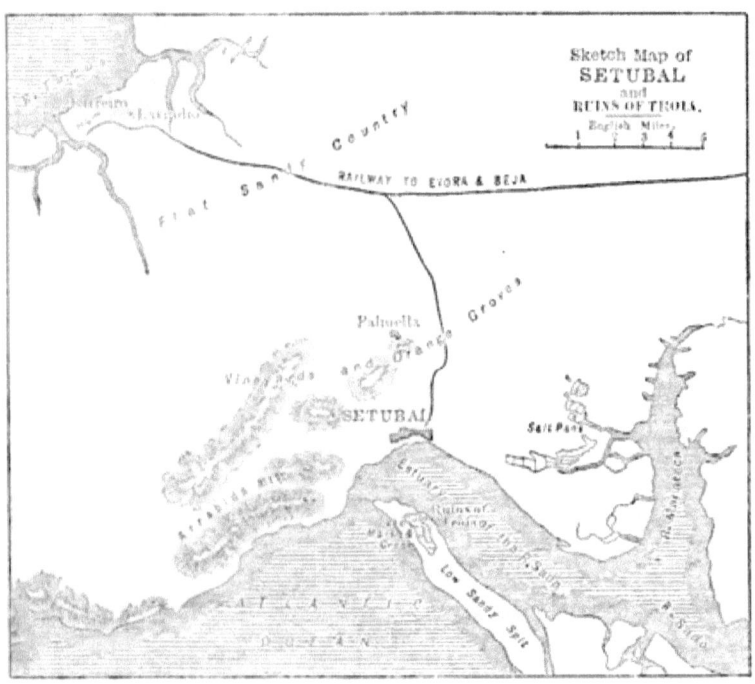

was the ruined shrine of Our Lady of Troia: beyond
it, a hundred yards to our left, close to the water, I
could make out the indistinct outlines of a building;
that was, he told me, a house excavated forty years
ago by the antiquaries; it was Roman—at least so
they persuaded themselves; he had never had any

curiosity to see more of it than he could see from
this side.

This philosophic contempt for the ancient Romans,
who are so bound up with the history of the town,
and the very moderate praise accorded by my new
acquaintance to Setubal itself, led me to apprehend
that he was not a native of the place. It turned
out that he was not, but had been living for some
six years, as he informed me, at the famous town
of X——.

Now, the Portuguese are fuller even than we ourselves of wholesome local patriotism, and nearly as
much so as the Americans. When the stage coach
on the American frontier of Canada passes through
the scene of those well-contested campaigns where
our troops and our enemies scored almost exactly
the same number of victories, it is the custom of the
Yankee driver to ease his horses, and even to pull up
altogether, as often as he comes to the scene of some
American victory.

'Here it was, gentlemen,' he cries to his passengers, 'that we whipped the Britishers in such a year.
Down that hill did they run, horse and foot, bag and
baggage, pursued by our brave fellows, bayonet in
hand.' But whenever the place of a British victory
is reached, the coachman holds his team well together,
cracks his whip, whistles to his horses, and gallops
past it at so fearful a pace that even if there be a
Britisher or two on the coach, or perchance an
American with an historical conscience, the jolting
and the holding on to their seats for bare life deprive

them of all power of speech and remonstrance against this one-sided mode of illustrating history.

I can imagine a Portuguese coachman capable of this amiable Chauvinism; but to speak the plain truth, he would very seldom have occasion to hurry his horses—many are the fields of battle, and very few the scenes of Portuguese defeat. The Portuguese love to dwell on the great victories of their forefathers, and certainly they do very well, to keep green the memory of those splendid achievements which have won them, against enormous odds, freedom and an enduring national existence; and they like (as we like) to be reminded now and then of these great feats. So it was that when my acquaintance at the inn informed me that he was connected with the town of X——, I alluded, almost as a matter of course, to its fame as the scene of a great Portuguese victory; it being, indeed, the best authenticated of all their early triumphs over the Moors.

I was wrong; my friend was a philosopher, and I should like to believe that his impartial philosophic standpoint, and that of many Continental freethinkers who resemble him, was based on any broad acquaintance with either the past or the present.

When I spoke of the connection of X—— with this famous historical event, he smiled, and was silent for a moment; then he spoke :—

'Il faut avouer, Monsieur, que les anciens ont dit beaucoup de sottises sur ces choses-là.'

'We must forgive them,' I suggested, ' in consideration of the paucity of their lights.'

'The report is,' he asked, cautiously feeling his
way, 'of some great victory at X—— over the
Romans. Is that not it?'

'The report I have heard is not quite to that
effect, but it comes, after all, to very nearly the same
thing in the end.'

We parted with protestations of mutual respect.

It took us over an hour to cross the bay with a
light wind from the north, and, at the boatmen's
desire, we landed to the west of the little stream
before described, to fill their jar with water, which
they maintain to be better than any in Setubal. I
followed the boatmen a quarter of a mile through
the strangest vegetation that I have ever seen in
Portugal. I found myself like a man new landed in
some unknown island. We passed through a grove
of a tall, broom-like, very graceful shrub some twelve
or fifteen feet in height, bearing racemes of a whitish
flower, not unlike laburnum in shape, and having a
delightful scent. All the trees of it were in full
blossom, and the air was heavy with a spring-like
perfume. Innumerable small butterflies of a pretty
brown and yellow kind fluttered in the air, the large
harmless ringed snake of Portugal glided among the
roots of these shrubs, and every smaller bush held
one or two large grey sand lizards. The ground
in places was almost covered with a dull brown
scarabaeus beetle, the size of a sixpence.

When we had reached the top of the bank of
hard sandy soil which commences to rise from the

water's edge, I found that I was looking down upon a little plain some half mile across, surrounded and protected on all sides by a similar bank or rim of shrub-covered sand hills. In its centre was a lagoon, tenanted by water and shore birds, and all round it meadows firm to the tread and brightly green, not with grass, but a thick growth of some compact, aromatic shrub. March and April are the months for wild-flowers in Portugal, and the ground was enamelled, like a rich *cloisonné*, with the blossoms of many familiar bulbous and other vernal plants, conspicuous among the latter the red and yellow tufts of the rock rose; but there were flowers here whose presence, till I learnt to account for it, was a complete puzzle to me. There were roods upon roods of ground, sloping to the south, thickly overgrown with a prickly shrub, bearing flower and fruit together— the large, star-like flower a dull blue, the fruit, of plum size, a gay orange in colour, and so abundant as to give a very distinct local colouring to the whole landscape. This shrub, unless I am mistaken, is the common mad-apple of the East Indies,[1] but the most striking plant was a free-flowering one of lowly

[1] 'The mad-apple of the East Indies,' *Solanum insanum*. It has become a sea-shore weed in most tropical and sub-tropical countries, east and west. The large brown lizard I saw was the *Amphisbæna cinerea*, whose European *habitat* is almost confined to Portugal. The snake at Troia was the common and harmless *Coluber natrix*. The butterfly I saw was one of the genus termed by entomologists *Skippers*, but I did not recognise the species. The bulbous and tuberous rooted plants of Portugal are so innumerable that I will not attempt to begin to name them. The scarabæus beetle I cannot give a name to.

growth, the flower a deep, pure blue—that colour so
rare in our gardens—and so free a bloomer that
every tuft of it glowed like a bit of southern sky.
The plant is of the family of the Boraginaceæ; more
than that I cannot say, for I never saw it before or
since, nor have I found anyone who has seen or
knows it, or can name it. Besides this blue flower I
found many other plants, in and out of bloom, which
were absolutely new to me.

The solution of the problem of the congregation
on this little headland of so much variety and such
luxuriance of plant growth is very simple. Setubal
is resorted to by vessels coming for cargoes of salt
from all parts of the world, for they make here the
best bay salt known anywhere. These vessels often
come in ballast, that ballast is generally sand or
gravel, and before loading with salt they have to dis-
charge it. Formerly they threw it into the sea near
their moorings, but this practice was gradually shoal-
ing the harbour, and by a recent order of the harbour
authorities, the ballast has to be carried across the
estuary in lighters, and discharged high and dry on
the beach at Troia. My boatmen told me this, and I
saw myself the heaps of sand ballast on the shore.
Containing as it must a variety of seeds and germs
and eggs of insects from all the corners of the habitable world, a most interesting experiment in acclima-
tization is thus being carried on. I have no doubt
that half the plants I saw at Troia were exotic. It
does not follow that they would thrive elsewhere in
Portugal than at Troia, for both soil and climate and

exposure favour them greatly. It lies nearly on the
38th parallel, but its climate is milder even than that
summery degree of latitude, for it is protected from
the north not only by the great Estrella range which
ends at Cintra, just north of Lisbon, and modifies the
whole climate of Southern Portugal, but it is absolutely cut off by the tall Arrabida hills from every
breath of northerly winds, and therefore must enjoy
a climate very far superior to that of Lisbon.

I lost a great deal of valuable time in wandering
about this interesting valley, and I could pleasantly
have spent days there. Every fresh step showed me
some new and strange plant growth : aromatic shrubs
in great variety ; here a curious grey lichen standing
up from the ground like turf, three or four inches
high, and so rigid in its substance and fibre as to
bear a man's weight without bending ; there a
creeping plant not yet in flower, with a pointed leaf
quite unknown to me in shape. I walked half round
the lagoon, watching the gobies and the bright-finned
gurnets darting to and fro in its clear, brackish water,
the dunlins and sandpipers in flocks by the shore,
the solitary heron angling in the farthest corner, the
little white-winged terns hovering over, and ever and
anon dipping with an audible splash into its smooth
surface ; then I turned back to the boat, and we set
sail, running up the shore to Cetobriga.

I took a piece of bread and began to eat, wishing
to lose no time, and my boatmen too got out their
provisions, and hospitably asked me to join in their
dinner of cold fried fish. I did, and found it very good.

'I see,' I said, 'that you gentlemen who follow the sea live very well; your bread is of the whitest flour, your wine is as good as a man need wish for, and as for your fried fish, one might look in vain for anything better all over Lisbon itself.'

'We are poor men, your Excellency,' said the more lively of the two boatmen, 'but we work hard; and it is true we gain money, but we spend it again as quickly. And your Excellency may think that my brother-in-law and I, being owners of this good boat, with sail and mast and rudder, might be proud and lazy, but that is not so at all, for as often as God sends us work to do and money to gain, so often do we set to, heart and soul, to gain it. It is not every day that we have a rich English or Russian Lord Captain who wants to run down in our boat to the Arrabida Convent, or up the Bay to the salt pans, nor can we use our nets and catch fish every week. Then we take a few days at unloading salt into the holds of the foreign ships, or we work at salt making till something better turns up.'

'You are certainly the best kind of men in the world,' I replied, not without conviction, 'and I heartily wish there were more like you.'

Compliments are never wasted on a Portuguese, and he started anew in his discourse.

'So it is that we eat well, drink well, and lodge well; but if your Excellency thinks that this wine has a good flavour, and this fish is good, what would you think of our way of living when some thirty or forty of us have come from the sea-fishing and stop our

boats yonder under the Arrabida hill, where we have
built ourselves a square, walled enclosure. Then we
take of the best and freshest of our catch, light our
fires, cook our fish, and eat it—not as this is, cold
and tasteless, but quite hot and steaming, and for
sauce we squeeze over it the juice of fresh lemons,
which this is without; and instead of this wine, which
is a fair enough liquor, and which comes from Alferva
near the town, then do we drink no wine but that
which grows on the Arrabida itself, which is a wine
of the mountains, and twice as good as this. Thus
do we feast and make merry when we come back
from the sea-fishing; and I can assure your Excellency that even the Duke of Palmella himself in his
great palace does not fare better than we do, nor
even the Lord Captain of the English brig there, now
loading in the harbour, even when he sits down in the
saloon of his ship to a table covered with white linen,
and has china plates and dishes, and sailors in gilt
buttons to wait upon him, and many crystal glasses
and bottles beside him, as I have seen these Lord
Captains do scores of times with my own eyes.'

Thus it was that I became acquainted with the
ways of polite society, native and foreign, at Setubal.

As my boatman was thus developing his views
with a fulness of diction which I am hardly attempting to reproduce, and with a wealth of appropriate
gesture which added greatly to the charm of his
conversation, I was drawing most interesting ethno-
logical conclusions from his manners, and from his

dress, and from the cast of his features. His dress
was simple, and one might fancy that but a very few
days' work with a salt shovel in the ship of a foreign
'Lord Captain' would purchase a whole suit of clothes.
A white linen shirt, a pair of loose blue cotton trousers
reaching to just below the knee, and a scarlet sash
wound three times round his waist, with a red Nea-
politan cap, made up this light and picturesque
costume. No doubt he had a hooded cloak of brown
Saragoça cloth at home, for winter wear and sea-
going, but the only extra clothing I observed, the
only great-coat (if I may venture on such a bull), was
a pair of cloth trousers thrown under the seat of the
boat, for use in case of wet or cold.

Every antiquary will allow the Oriental character
of this dress, and not even an antiquary could dispute
the perfectly Eastern cast of my head boatman's very
handsome face, with his thin, well-cut features, large
and piercing eyes, smooth skin, and dark, olive complexion. If there is any truth at all in hereditary
physiognomy, he was a Phœnician of pure lineage;
and the archaeologist who reads this will be glad to
have this confirmation of the hypothesis, which I
know he has already made, as to the Phœnician origin
of Cetobriga from the presence in that word of the
undeniably Phœnician 'ceto,' 'citho,' or 'sytho' (the
learned spell it in all three ways), together with the
mention of Phœnician colonization on this coast by
the early writers. My second boatman, on the other
hand, the companion and brother-in-law of my Phœnician acquaintance, was, on the evidence of his round

face, high cheek bones and blunt features, his easy temper and slower intelligence, a pure Visigoth.

I am sorry to perceive, in the interests of comparative ethnology, that the two races are beginning to commingle at Setubal. It is, however, satisfactory to observe that if in the old times the primitive Phœnician colonists, and even the Romans of Cetobriga themselves, had to submit to Euric and his Goths, the tables have at last been turned; the Phœnician was the better man of the two, and his ascendency over his Gothic companion was satisfactorily complete. It is clear, indeed, from all history that numbers only ever made my second boatman's progenitors formidable—overwhelming numbers and a servile habit of discipline—just as certain modern Goths in a recent great war in Western Europe owed their triumphs over better men to these very two circumstances.

While I was thus agreeably generalizing and playing at archæology, our boat presently reached this Portuguese Troy.

A Spanish proverb says :—

> 'La sciencia es locura,
> Si buen senso no la cura;'

which may very properly be translated, 'Most savants (especially antiquaries) are a little wrong in the head.' Notwithstanding which warning, it is incumbent on me to theorize a little before introducing the reader to these ruins of Cetobriga.

First, we want a hypothesis to account for the fact that any people should have made a settlement on this absolutely barren headland, when the good, fertile

shore of Setubal was apparently ready to receive
them. So far as the Phœnicians are concerned, if
they were the first colonists it is indeed quite intelligible that a handful of traders coming to make a
settlement should choose this narrow tongue of land,
surrounded by the element of which they had the
full command. To account for the presence of the
Romans here, we must theorize more boldly.

Now, I think we may safely guess first that the
high bank of sand which now rises, almost abruptly,
not quite from the water's edge, but from the narrow
beach a few yards in width, did not exist in Roman
times. It is an accumulation—geologists may settle
how formed—of quite recent date; and it was the accidental removal by a high flood of some of this accumulation which revealed, as I have told, the existence of
the ruins in 1814. Pompeii is covered about fifteen
feet in height by the sand and ashes from a volcano;
Cetobriga is similarly embedded in mounds of testa-
ceous sand, brought either by the winds or the waves.

When the Duke of Palmella's Society made their
excavations they simply removed this sand from the
top, and came in time to the roof, or the place where
it had been, then they laid bare the upper story, then
the ground floor. It is a plain well-built house of
rubble stone, with courses of thin brick. The mortar
is a strong cement, such as the Romans well knew
the secret of preparing; and it is noteworthy that an
excellent hydraulic cement, identical I believe with
that used in this house, is obtained to this day in the
Arrabida hills.

If the whole of the sand dune which lies along the water's edge at Troia could be removed, we should undoubtedly have revealed to us the ancient Roman town of Cetobriga, in probably a very fair state of preservation. The sand removed, there is reason to suppose that the peninsula on which the ruins stand was good fertile land, for I found the level ground on which the house was built to be a deep loamy soil, quite capable of growing plants and trees. Then again, unlike Pompeii, from which the sea has retreated a mile, at Cetobriga the sea has encroached upon and greatly narrowed the land. Through the clear and shallow waters of the bay, one sees the *débris* of walls, bricks, tiles and masses of concrete, for thirty or forty yards from the shore. The excavated house faces the bay, and its front door is not ten yards from the water's edge, and not half that height above it. There was probably in former times an intervening shingly beach fifty or sixty yards in width.

Having examined the house itself, which seemed to me larger and loftier than the ordinary houses in the Pompeii streets, I walked some three quarters of a mile along the shore, finding the same lofty sand dune rising everywhere from the beach, well covered with shrubs and flowering plants; and, in places where the sand had been washed away by the great floods of last autumn, there were visible portions of Roman wall, of archways and vaults, showing how rich would be the result of even a few days' hard work with pick and shovel. This walk along the beach was, I have no doubt, a sort of marine parade of the town. The best houses were 'sea-view residences,' as the Brighton lodging-house keepers say, and this part, no doubt, a gay enough place in old Roman times.

On the beach there lie innumerable remains of shallow reservoirs or receptacles, from ten to fifteen feet long and from five to ten broad, and about four or five feet in depth. They are built with good foundations in the ground, of concrete, and are finished off very smoothly with cement inside. Anyone who knows that the Romans were a luxurious people fond of sea-bathing, would come to the conclusion that these shallow cisterns were baths; he would even think the device a most happy one, where the bottom of the sea, as it is here, is shingly But the learned never arrive at an obvious conclusion, and the weighty Hübner [1] is of opinion that these receptacles were used for the curing of fish.

[1] 'The weighty Hübner.' I use this epithet advisedly. Herr Hübner's voluminous work, the 'Corpus Inscriptionum Latinarum,' is (so far as a traveller not unused to the powers of pack animals can judge) more than a load for the strongest mule. It is also much more than a load for the strongest reader. The learned German consents to the conclusion arrived at long before by Resende that the remains of Troia are the ancient Cetobriga, and that Cetobriga was a place of considerable importance. 'Signorum nonnullorum,' he says, 'reliquiæ, nummi literis indigenis inscripti, supellex ex auro argentove facta sæpius ibi reperta et ædificiorum cum aliorum tum officinarum salsamentariarum prope litus sitarum rudera oppidum olim fuisse non ignobile demonstrant, quod ipse testis oculatus affirmo.' I cannot, however, bring myself to believe that the dwellers in Cetobriga could have consented to have so disagreeable an operation as the salting of fish

Though so very little work of exploration has been done at Troia, we can thus, as will have been seen, make a very plausible guess as to what Cetobriga was and till when it lasted. As to its founders, its name, preserved with no great change in the modern Setubal, tells us something; *Ceto* is perhaps Phœnician, and *briga*, the termination, is almost certainly Celtic, or what generally passes for Celtic. The traveller may, if he lends himself thereto with proper anthropological enthusiasm, find in the lineaments of the people and in the dress of the fishing population, at least some confirmation of the Eastern derivation of its inhabitants. I hope no sceptic will attempt seriously to deny the Phœnician origin of Cetobriga, for we archæologists—the most generally reasonable and open to conviction of all men—are peculiarly tenacious when it comes to believing in the presence of the Phœnicians. In this case there is really more to go upon than the vague conclusions of philology or those, quite as vague perhaps, to be drawn from the features of the population.

Strabo, as all hard readers know, has told us of the traffic of the Phœnicians, those bold seafaring traders, along the Mediterranean and Atlantic coasts of Spain and Portugal. Avienus corroborates him.

---

carried on under the windows of their best houses, and on ground which must have been more valuable than any other in the headland. Moreover, the receptacles, in size, shape and position, are not in any way fitted to the curing of fish. I hold strongly to the bath theory, and if an alternative one is required, I would rather believe that these cisterns were small *vivaria*—aquaria, as we should now call them—for the preservation for a time of living sea-fish.

We learn that they established trading stations—
'factories,' or assemblages of factors or agents, such
as we ourselves used to have all over the world—in
Portugal as well as elsewhere.   Herein our Phœnician
hypothesis is very pleasantly supported by such facts
as we have on the authority of the old writers.[1]   The
Turduli, they say, inhabit the coasts of Portugal from
the Tagus northward to the Douro.   The Bastuli are
settled between the Tagus (which lies but fifteen miles
north of Troia) and the Guadiana—a stretch of rich
and beautiful coast ; the soil fruitful, rivers abundant,
harbours many, and the air soft and balmy.   The
question of course is, Who were the Bastuli ? and the
answer is, Almost certainly a Phœnician race.   They
probably came to Portugal from Carthage or its neighbourhood.   Ptolemy calls them Bastuli-peni.   What
more can an antiquarian want in the nature of corro-
boration ?   Strabo goes even further to help us to
identify the founders of Cetobriga, for he speaks
particularly of certain Bastuli who lived upon a
narrow strait of land near the sea.   Now, looking in
the map at the whole line of sea-coast between the
Tagus and the Guadiana, which the geographers give
to the Bastuli, I find but one such tongue of land as
Strabo describes: it is Troia itself.   In addition to all
this evidence, Phœnician coins have been dug up at
Cetobriga.   That good and diligent Portuguese antiquary, Gama Xaro, found one there which bears on
its obverse a head in profile which, if the coin is
Cetobrigan, gives us a poor idea of the looks and

[1] Pliny and Pomponius Mela.

amiability of its inhabitants; on its reverse are two
dolphins or perhaps porpoises. Porpoises might well
be made symbols of Cetobriga, for in its Bay they are
always to be seen playing and leaping through the
waves. The people call them *golfinos*.

I explored to the best of my ability at Troia;
passing over, as non-Roman, a house on the south-west
side of the headland facing the little river, said by my
boatmen to have been dug out by the French exploring company. It seemed to me to be a large barn-
like building, not more than three or four centuries
old. I found buried a few inches below the surface
on which its foundations are built, fragments of green
glazed pottery which cannot, according to our existing knowledge of the potter's art, be of an earlier
date than the twelfth or thirteenth century.

When I had done my day's work—a hard one
under the perpendicular rays of the Setubal sun—I
was induced to sail across the Bay to the Arrabida
mountains before nightfall, so tempting did the bright
waters of the Bay look, and the hills themselves
in the already slanting sun rays, with their colours
and their brightness so splendidly intensified, standing
up before me in the rich western light, like huge cliffs
and peaks of various translucent gems—opal and
amethyst, garnet and chrysolite.

We ran over the five or six miles very quickly
with a fresh breeze, and landed at the nearest point;
and I took directions from my boatmen as to how I
was to reach a particular lofty peak of rock :—' Your
Excellency will pass through the orange groves till

they end on the hill-side, and there is a vineyard, and
after that a clump of olive trees which you can see
from here; then you are on the bare hill-side, and
you walk straight up till you come to a ruined
hermitage; keep that to the right——' or to the left,
it may have been, for, like most other people, I
suppose, I invariably forget such directions one
minute after I have heard them.

I am inclined to think that on the southern slopes
of these Arrabida hills may be found a climate
warmer and more healthy—for there is no marsh-
land about—than any spot in the whole of Portugal.
Here the monks—a body of Grey Friars, an order
always judicious in their choice of sites—set up an
important monastery. There is a story, too, of a
young man, a native of Lisbon, who, having been sent
to Madeira for a chest complaint, returned from that
island not bettered in health. As a last resource, his
friends sent him to the Arrabida. There he bought
a goatherd's house, with his goats, living summer and
winter in the former, and mainly on the produce of
the latter. His health came back to him, and he
lives there still, offering, hermit-like, to chance
visitors to his mountain, shelter and a share of his
simple fare. This is the story as I heard it from
several people. I did not see him.

Another testimony to the geniality of this climate
is that Brotero, the Portuguese botanist, gives the
Arrabida range as the sole *habitat* of many Portuguese
plants which grow nowhere else in Europe. I did
not, indeed, in my very hurried walk, find any plants

that were new to me, though the ground was carpeted with spring flowers ; and I noticed that none of the strange plant growths of the Troia headland were to be found here.

It was nightfall when I reached the bottom of the hill, and nine o'clock before our boat got back to Setubal. I was very tired and hungry, and glad to remember that a conference had taken place that morning between the cook and myself, which had ended in that very affable person promising to have dinner ready for me at whatever hour of the evening or night I might return. He kept his word : and I hope no one at Senhor Escoven's inn may ever fare worse than I did that night.

A party of burgesses, worthy people, probably from the capital, were supping with some of their friends at the *table d'hôte* as I came in. A man is never so critical as in the ten minutes before his dinner, and my chance table-mates must set down my cynical contemplation of them to this circumstance.

An English master of the art of social well-doing has laid down the maxim that no man should ever monopolise the conversation for more than half a minute. (I myself think the time is too long.) The Portuguese do not adopt this rule, and in truth I have never sojourned among the people who do. Among the supper party at Setubal two gentlemen strove with each other as to which of them should break it most completely. When two well-known French orators, members of the Legislature, were contending

for the ear of that assembly, the one who had lost it for
the moment smiled pleasantly upon the audience during
the flowing rhetoric of his rival, conscious of his own
latent power of talk, contenting himself with remark-
ing behind his hand, '*S'il crache, il est perdu!*' I
noticed something of this polite self-confidence in that
one of the two Portuguese gentlemen who happened
for the moment to be silent. The rest of the party—
terrible conversationalists too, after their kind, I dare
say, some of them—were witnesses and seconds only
while this duel of talk was proceeding, merely smiling
or nodding, or being properly moved or indignant, as
was required of them.

The night was pleasant, yet several of the party
had woollen comforters on. Some of the women wore
worsted knitted hoods and were discordantly dressed;
men and women leant slouchingly over the table,
curving their elbows and hands and wrists half round
their plates (so do crabs and lobsters, I believe, at
their own ocean dinner-tables curve unwieldy claws
round their food); and these otherwise pleasant ladies
and gentlemen might well seem to the straight-backed
Briton, taught not to let his elbows stray at meal
times too far from his sides, to be departing not a
little from the proprieties to be observed at table.
How easy is intolerance in such matters, and how
poor and miserable the triumph of finding food for
frivolous laughter in such trifling differences as these!
How few of my countrymen would think of setting
against all this the fact that one bottle of port wine
had sufficed for the whole party of twelve, and that

it was but half emptied; or that every man of the
party showed his wish to be gracious by bowing, as
he rose from the table, to the stranger who had sat
at meat with him.

On the other hand, it would have been a truly
ridiculous thing for a newly-landed tourist, had one
been there, to see that as the two sections of the party
took leave of each other, they did so in a manner to
offend and even to excruciate all our insular suscep-
tibilities. The women kissed each other—and this indeed might pass—but the men likewise embraced;
and this really was too great an outrage on a critical
British traveller waiting for his dinner. The Portuguese
of the male sex, when they meet after absence and when
they part for any time, rush into each other's arms as
people in England do nowhere but on the transpon-
tine stage. They are a thickset population, and they
perform the ludicrous act not without a certain burly
dignity, and yet tenderly too; not, I must say for
them, kissing each other on their too often chubby
cheeks, as I have seen Italians and Southern Frenchmen do; but when they find themselves in each
other's arms they thump each other gently on the
back in token of amity; anon each draws back his
head and contemplates his friend's countenance,
pleasantly with smiles if meeting, mournfully and
tearfully if about to part.

It is easy to laugh at all this, but it is an old
custom in Portugal. There is nothing really
effeminate in the usage any more than in those who
practise it. Heroes have done it ere now. Not

otherwise, be sure, was the great Vasco da Gama
clasped in the arms of his friends when he came
back, having, after perils innumerable, doubled the
Cape and found the sea route to the Indies. In no
other fashion, I am certain, did the still greater
Prince Henry the Navigator embrace the famous sea
commanders who had carried his exploring ships
into unknown recesses of the mysterious ocean,
thumping their brave backs with friendly gratitude
and enthusiasm.

How we English shake our honest sides, seeing
for the first time this Portuguese *amplexus*, with all
its queer accompaniments; yet what a foolish and
insular thing it is to laugh—not so very insular
indeed, after all, for we used to do the very same
thing in this country. '*Come! Let my bosom touch
thee,*' says a chief character in one of our old comedies
to two other personages in no very affluent circumstances. How much would I—boasting myself to be
somewhat of a citizen of the world—like to see a
revival of this good, hearty, old-fashioned custom of
the *accolade!* How pleasant would it be to see
some padded, gouty old general running up in Pall
Mall to a half-pay subaltern, the friend and mess-
mate of his youth; or some goodly bishop, sleek with
episcopal honours, meeting an old college friend of
forty years' standing, still a curate. '*Come!*' would
his lordship exclaim, standing with extended arms in
Waterloo Place, '*Come! Let my bosom touch thee.*'

Except for the trifling circumstance that the bed-

rooms of Sr. Escoven's hotel were constructed with
such an economy of partition wall that they only
reached three parts of the way to the ceiling, nothing
could be more satisfactory to the most exacting
tourist than the arrangements of his hostelry. Even
this peculiarity of mural construction has some advantages. The bedded traveller is indeed only screened,
not walled off from Sr. Escoven's other guests; but
the Portuguese are essentially a sociable people, and
by this simple device the pleasures of conversation
may be enjoyed far on into the night. There is also
a pleasant flavour of mediævalism about it. Exactly in
this fashion, as I have read, were the guest chambers
disposed in those great semi-ecclesiastical *hospices*
which in the Middle Ages occupied the places now so
much more comfortably filled by the modern hotel.

I do not dwell on this detail of arrangement as
blameworthy; and, on the other hand, the way in
which at the Setubal inn the traveller's bill is delivered to him is, in regard to rapidity of presenta-
tion, simplicity of statement, and reasonableness of
amount, worthy of all praise. As civilisation goes
on, the *mauvais quart d'heure* of Rabelais has become
a more and more disagreeable interval of time. It is
not the exorbitance of the amount which irritates us,
for we are, I trust, my readers and I, fairly solvent
people—so much as the delays in getting our
accounts given to us (with a train just starting,
perhaps, or an appointment to keep), and their unnecessary complication when they are given. There
is also cause for great exasperation in the now too

common habit of English hotel-keepers of having a printed form on which the plain requirements of a simple traveller are lost amid a multitude of items which he might, could, and—as the bill and its author clearly suggest—*should* have ordered. So that when a guest pays his bill for a day's and night's lodging, he is positively almost ashamed at finding due registry of his having wanted neither liqueurs, nor stationery, nor warm baths, nor douche baths, nor shower baths, nor pots of jam, nor carriages and pairs, nor draught stout, nor imperial pints of pale ale, nor ginger beer, nor the hotel hairdresser, nor mulled wine at night, nor sherry bitters by day; and he reflects what a poor shuffling impostor of a guest he is to have had so few requirements.

What may be called the antipodes of this magnificent and pretentious kind of hotel account prevails at some of the remoter inns in Portugal. Here, when the traveller asks for his bill, the landlord pleasantly rubs his hands together and answers, 'Whatever your Excellency pleases to give.' This will not do at all, for the traveller is sure to offer too much or too little, and to be thought either a spendthrift or a niggard; so he has to make a speech, thank the landlord for his courteous confidence, and beg for a detailed statement.

Then the landlord, politely deprecating anything of the kind, is slowly persuaded to check off the various items upon the fingers of his hand, with a long argument before each successive finger is done with and doubled down.

'What does it come to?' asks the traveller, taking out his purse at last, when the hand and the account are finally closed.

'Diacho!' (which is polite for *Diabo*, which again is contracted from the Latin). 'Did his Excellency not add up?'

His Excellency having been incapable of this act of mental arithmetic, the addition is gone over again, from the little finger backwards, with a finger or two, perhaps, representing forgotten items, brought into account from the other hand; and the sum total is gladly paid, and host and guest part mutually content —the guest well knowing that he has not been over-charged more than perhaps a thumb and one or two fingers.

At Sr. Escoven's inn the bill is drawn up and presented in a manner which may be called a com-promise between these two opposite systems of ac-count, and is an improvement on each. As I am writing as a traveller and for travellers, I can do no better than give full particulars.

At six o'clock A.M., I asked the woman servant, who was bringing my breakfast, for my bill. In less than two minutes it was placed on the table before me, written on a piece of paper two inches square. It contained only the following figures:—

$$1.500$$
$$1.500$$
$$\overline{}$$
$$3.000$$

The waitress, placing her finger on the second

1.500, reminded me that this sum had been advanced
to me by the landlord the night before to pay my
boatmen. The rest, she said, was my inn account.
1.500 reis is a *milrei* and a half, and a *milrei* and a
half is about six shillings and eightpence, this sum
representing the whole charge for bread and wine to
take with me to Troia, dinner, bed, and breakfast
next morning. There was no charge for the conversation on both sides of me, which lasted half through
the night.

I have written this account of a thirty-six hours'
expedition from Lisbon, made hurriedly between two
engagements, because I have often heard it said that
little or nothing was to be done or seen from the
capital of Portugal. I hope I have shown that a
traveller following me in this little expedition need
expend neither much time or trouble to find himself
among very beautiful scenery and an interesting and
courteous people The Arrabida range, small as it
comparatively is, has peaks and recesses which would
well repay a visit of days. Setubal itself, of which I
have said hardly a word, is in population the third or
fourth city in the kingdom, and has antiquities of its
own. The estuaries of the Sado and the Marateca,
forming the Bay of Setubal, are a congregation of
waters more beautiful than any in Portugal, not excepting the estuary of the Tagus itself; and upon it,
within easy reach by boat, are towns famous in the
history of ancient Portugal.

CHAPTER VIII.

THE LOST CITY OF CITANIA.

TEN years ago, locomotion in Portugal was certainly neither easy nor pleasant. Within that period, however, railways have increased, and a multitude of good high-roads have opened up many new and interesting districts which were once only accessible on horseback. In almost all the larger towns excellent inns have taken the place of execrably bad ones. Moreover, a system of transit has been established by a public company, under the name of the *Companhia da Viaçao do Minho*, which affords great facilities to the traveller. In all the principal cities and towns of Northern Portugal, offices of this company are to be found where, at a moment's notice, any sort of carriage can be obtained, from a roomy covered *calêche* to a light phaeton: and the company having a well-organized system of correspondence between their various stations, the traveller can order a carriage to meet him at the most remote point of the Northern Province. with a reasonable expectation of not being disappointed.

It will be tolerably evident that I am describing what is, when combined with the lovely scenery of

Portugal and numerous points of interest of every kind, nothing less than a paradise of tourists. That it may seem still more one, the country still more accessible and still more civilized, the reader shall learn something about Portuguese railways.

As regards the railway system of the country, it is as yet very simple, consisting of one direct main line of communication between Lisbon in the South of the Kingdom, and Oporto in the North. From each of these termini, or rather centres, there diverge short branch lines, or feelers, which are still, except at two points in the South, unconnected with the railway system of the rest of the Peninsula, and which are for the most part in process of annual extension.

It is along one of these branch lines, and the newest of them all, the railway opened within the last few months northward to Braga and thence to the Spanish frontier, that I am about to conduct the reader. Though the distance from Lisbon to Oporto is very nearly that between Liverpool and London, the time employed for the journey in Portugal is considerably more than double; and as competition may be called the soul of brevity in railway matters, and there is quite certain to be no competition in Portugal for the next hundred years, Lisbon and Oporto may, for all intents and purposes, be considered to be, not two hundred, but four hundred miles apart.

I pass over this journey without comment, for my present purpose is to visit, first Braga, the archiepiscopal city, and afterwards Guimaraēns, famous in the history of mediæval Portugal, and to find, and when found, to explore and make notes of, a mysterious buried town, supposed to lie somewhere between these two cities, and of which a great deal more presently.

The Minho Province is, as everyone knows who has ever opened a book upon Portugal—even a guide-book (blind enough guides, too often)—is, I say, as everyone knows, the most lovely portion of Portugal. The traveller from Lisbon who crosses the Douro to arrive at Oporto, and, in doing so, gets his first sight of this Northern Province, might almost come to that conclusion then and there for himself, as he sees this fine river running between its lofty, precipitous, fern-clothed cliffs, with the city of Oporto rising amphitheatre-wise from the edge of the river, which here broadens suddenly into a lagoon, reflecting on its still surface the confused, picturesque, multi-coloured architecture steeply piled, terrace over terrace, to the granite hills beyond. Two miles from the river we reach the station of the Northern Railway, situated in the suburbs; and even as we drive to it, we get a glimpse of very characteristic Minho scenery, which makes us wish for more. In the foreground and middle distance pine-covered hills, rich in their endless harmonies of subdued greens of every shade, from the sunlit grey-greens of the common pine to the indigo-green shadows thrown by the solid-looking umbelled heads of the darker-foliaged stone pine. Then the eye travels into immense distances, filled in with great, bare, solid mountains, peak upon peak, rosy grey where the sunlight bathes them, purple where the cloud-shadows fall, and fading in the far-off airy perspective into what seems thinner and more unsubstantial than the thin vapour-wreaths of early dawn.

The thirty miles which separate Oporto from Braga are got over with such an absence of indecent haste, that fully two hours elapse before the journey is accomplished, which is a mistake on several accounts —first, because the traveller is sure to carry away a poor idea of Portuguese railway engineering when he has such leisure to note how wastefully the line has been constructed; not ballasted with that foresight in making cuttings and embankments and that happy economy of material, which, in an engineer's eyes, have an æsthetic beauty of their own, but with great heaps of earth and stone 'shot' here upon the way-side, and perhaps, but half a mile further on, a valuable bit of land dug bodily out for an embankment —all very deplorable in its way, and a very proper subject for disdain to the foreign traveller. Then, again, the traveller—apt as all we travellers are to generalization—might conclude from his experience of this journey that the dogs of Portugal, who may frequently be seen racing, and generally out-racing, the trains, were gifted with an abnormal speed. This conclusion can, as we have seen, be easily corrected by a reference to the time-table and a knowledge of the mileage.

The railway takes us through a picturesque country, but by no important towns till we reach

Braga. Here I get out. It is nearly nine, a dark, dimly-starlit night late in April; and I have a drive of four miles before I reach, not Braga, for I disdain its inn and crowded streets, but the great hostelry on the Hill of the Bom Jesus. This hill is one of the two most famous Holy Places in Portugal, and one of great religious resort from all parts of the kingdom, and even from Spain, during the summer months. Up four miles of stiff ascent we drive: for the great inn built here for the pilgrims is near the very top of the hill, and it cannot be less than a thousand feet above the elevated plain on which Braga is situated. As the carriage creeps slowly along the winding road to the summit, I know that the veil of soft night air is hiding from me a series of very lovely foreground landscapes. I know, too, for I have been here before, that at every upward turn of the road there is a grand panoramic extension of the great plain below, and that, but for the darkness, the distant hills should be seen to be rising tumultuously, one above the other, like sea waves or the airy mountains of cloudland. But for the present, all this is for the imagination only; I shall have to wait till the moon rises, or till to-morrow, for the landscape. Like the famous Spanish fleet, 'it is not yet in sight.'

Nevertheless, something of the charm of it comes to me through the dimness of the night. I know that we are passing at one time through woodlands; for now and again the road is overarched by great oak trees, whose half-expanded foliage I catch in outline against the sky: now I know that we are passing through fertile, well-tilled farm-lands ; for I hear the soft, continuous ' churr ' of the mole-crickets—a sound as much associated with the early hours of southern nights in spring time as the cicadas' cry with the hours of hot sunshine—and these dainty insects love to dwell in the rich soil of gardens and deep ploughed fields, and I know therefore that we are close to such land. And then again the fresh scent of new-shot vine buds comes to me, and the richer warm fragrance of rye-fields, with the bloom on the ears. And now we are passing by a farmer's cottage, for the heavy perfume of orange-blossom is wafted to me, or the fainter odours of a wall covered with the flowers of the Banksian rose, or the Wistaria. All this is very delightful after the dusty atmosphere of the railway carriage. Then, as we mount higher, we get away from cultivation alto-gether, and pass through successive oak groves, and the banks are overgrown with furze and cystus, and rock-rose and broom, all in flower, and all betraying themselves by the scents they give out on the dewy air of night.

A church rises against the sky near the hill-top—now the night is lightening a little with the rising moon—and opposite to the church stands a great dreary pile, two storeys high, like a barrack much more than an hotel, and yet one of the best country hotels in the kingdom. Till the middle of May it is but half occupied, fully crammed then and thereafter, not by guests alone.

Inns in Portugal are not much after the fashion of inns in England, France, or Germany—not such inns

as tourists are used to find on any of the roads they
haunt. Comfort, after the ideal of it which we have
come to form in England, is not to be found in these
inns—the comfort, that is, which consists in neatness,
warmth, bright hearths, plenty of carpets and arm-
chairs, soft beds, bustling waiters, attentive porters,
and smart chambermaids. Not a single one of those
qualifications is there which, in travelling bagman's
phrase, go to the making of a 'good house.' The
Portuguese inn is rather of the type of the Eastern
caravanserai. The house is large, airy, carpetless,
with whitewash instead of wall-papers; an arm-chair
is unknown; there is but one hearth, and that is in
the kitchen; the few waiters do not bustle, the rare
chambermaids are barefooted, and by no means smart.
In regard to the beds, an Englishman was once heard
by me trying, after his first experience of them, to
achieve a sorry jest about his host having succeeded
in combining 'bed and board.' The beds are, in fact,
straw palliasses; and the inexperienced traveller who
makes his first acquaintance with a Portuguese bed-
room thinks that, by some mistake, a hard bran-stuffed
pincushion has been taken from his dressing-table and
laid upon his bed. This, however, is an error. The
pincushion in question is the normal Portuguese
pillow, and some prudent travellers in this country,
having bruised their cheeks and ears against this
little instrument of torture, in their struggles to get a
night's rest, habitually carry real pillows in their portmanteau. An unworthy piece of Sybaritism! I set
my face against anything so unmanly. I feel as the

Highland laird did, who, when he and his clan (on a cattle-lifting expedition) were bivouacking in a snow-storm, found that his son had rolled a snowball under his head for a pillow. He kicked it away indignantly, swearing that no son of his should indulge in such effeminate luxury. So do I protest against the effe-minacy of carrying with one the pillow of civilization. It marks a degenerate age.

The Portuguese hostelry is, as I have said, some-what after the fashion of the Eastern caravanserai. The summer traveller in Portugal—and travellers do mostly travel in summer—is tried, not by any ele-mental rage in the way of wind and rain, hail or snow, but he is fatigued and oppressed by the heat and dust of the long summer day, and often his nerves are singularly over-excited by long exposure to the keen, dry air, and the unblinking glare of the Lusitanian sun. So he finds in the lofty rooms and cool atmo-sphere of the unfurnished inn great refreshment, and its semi-obscurity—for the sun has been kept out all day by thick shutters—is wonderfully soothing to his spirits. Also, he is never over-oppressed by offers of service. According to Charles Dickens the idea of an English inn is, that when a guest has passed its threshold, he should deliver himself over into the hands of the head waiter unreservedly and as if he were a new-born child, with a volition, indeed, but no power of realizing it except through his nurse—the head waiter. Nothing of the kind prevails in Portu-gal. 'Here,' says your Portuguese landlord, 'is shelter, shade, and security—a caravanserai in short

—and I have so far conformed to modern ideas as to employ a cook and a bedmaker.'

The beds we already know about; the dinner is at a *table d'hôte*. We conform so little to Gallican ideas, always unfashionable in Portugal, as to call it a *mesa redonda*—a round table—though dinner is invariably laid on a long and narrow one. Now, it is of the convenient nature of Portuguese cookery that the dishes are not appreciably the worse for being kept waiting; consequently, if one arrives at any hour of the day or night, and says—' *Quero jantar*,' I want dinner, the meal is brought in five minutes, and laid at a corner of the long table. The guest need not trouble himself about ordering it, and if he ordered twenty different bills of fare on twenty different days, he would always get the same dinner, or one with the same generic features.

As travellers are often as foolishly particular about their dinners as about their pillows, and as I have no wish to inveigle any of my countrymen to Portugal under false pretences, I think it well to let them know what, if they do come, they will have for dinner.

First, they will have soup, a thin *consommé* of beef, with rice, cabbages, and probably peas floating in it. This is followed by the piece of beef and the little piece of bacon which have made the soup, and as this soup is served up very hot, so is some degree of variety skilfully obtained by the *bouilli* always being half cold. Then follow several indescribable stews, very good to eat, but inscrutable as to their

ingredients. After this, when one has ceased to
expect it, comes fish broiled, almost always hake,
which in Portuguese waters feeds on sardines, and is
therefore a better fish than our British hake, which
fares less daintily ; then rice made savoury with gravy
and herbs ; after that come ' *beefés*,' a dish fashionable
in all parts of Portugal, and in whose name the Portuguese desire to do homage to our great nation and
one of our national dishes, the word being a corruption of ' beef-steaks.' and the thing itself quite as
unlike what it imitates as its name. Then follow, in
an order with which I cannot charge my memory,
sweet things, chiefly made of rice ; the dinner invariably ending with a preserve of quince.

It will be seen that the Portuguese *cuisine* is very
national in its character, and perhaps the day may
come when philosophers, having exhausted comparative mythology, grammar, and philology, may
think it worth their while to extract some of
the lost historic life of nations from comparative
cookery. The Portuguese *cuisine*, let us say, *Scientia
Coquinaria Portugallensis*, will certainly be one of
the most interesting chapters of this book of the
future.

The archæology of this subject is simply that the
Portuguese people, conservative in their tastes and
yet open to new ideas, have borrowed from every
nation with whom they have come into contact ; from
the Romans their kitchen stoves—I have seen in
Pompeii a range of fire-places, each with its blowhole
through which to fan the embers, absolutely identical

with the cooking hearths of modern Portuguese houses—from the Moors they have got their earthenware stew-pots and the way of using them. From Roman times they have preserved innumerable names of meals, dishes, and cooking vessels; from the Moors, again, the art of preserving fruits and making them into cakes and jellies, from them, too, come the names and recipes of many sweet dishes, among others the *rebanadas*, a dish as much eaten in Portugal between Christmas and the New Year as mincepies with us in England. The dish is purely one of Southern lands, of countries 'flowing with milk and honey,' and of pastoral peoples, being composed of thick slices of wheaten bread soaked in new milk, fried in pure olive oil and thickly spread with honey. It is a dish of the nomad tribes from Arabia to Morocco, and is made to this day by the Moors under the name of *rabanat* or *rabanadh*. Then again contact with ourselves has given the aforesaid *beefés* to the Portuguese *cuisine*, and also initiated the nation into the mysteries of plum and seed cakes, their Portuguese name being still *quéqué*. All this is surely very instructive and edifying, and I regret exceedingly to have to leave the subject for the present.

We have wandered a little from the subject of Portuguese inns. In them a traveller need never give orders to be called in the morning; the tone of voice in which the internal economy of the house is conducted answers all the purposes of an alarum. At an early hour in the morning I get up to, as old

Indians say, 'eat the morning air.' The balconies of
the inn look westward, and command a really magnificent view. I have somewhat discounted it over-
night, and therefore I need say the less about it now.
Some miles below is Braga in its plain, surrounded
by grey mountains, on which the mists of morning
are still hanging. An hour earlier I should have
seen their peaks sharply defined in the transparent
air of early dawn; now the thin mists are in
process of absorption by the sun, or tending sky-
wards to incorporate themselves into detached clouds
which, as the day grows older, shall throw their
shade-mantles on the land and make it ten times
more lovely than before. The sun glints obliquely
on the city of Braga at my feet, and makes a rich
colour harmony of the red and green and yellow
houses, showing me in clear outline the great square
turrets of the castle dominating the other buildings,
and bathing in its potent rays the mellow brown walls
and towers of the old cathedral.

At this early hour of the morning, and with the
sun thus slanting his light over the great vine-
covered plain country below, there is a strange thing
to be seen, which never elsewhere have I looked
upon; not in France, nor in Spain, nor in Greece,
nor even in Italy, though in all these countries there
are lands giving in the spring time much promise of
purple wine; for hereabouts the yield of wine
is famous even in Portugal, not of delicate wine that
strangers seek after, but of a generous liquor, cool,
wholesome, and fortifying after labour, and so

plentiful that no man is poor enough to go without it, and the very mouth of the resting horse that has carried the traveller through the day is stained with draughts of red wine. Now, in spring time, when the sun at its rising, or just as it sets, strikes the land slantingwise, this is the strange sight that I see here—that its rays gleam hotly upon and into innumerable upward-pointing young vine shoots, set with tender, transparent green leaves, and so brightly that veritably it would seem that from the earth were issuing not living foliage, sky pointing, but flames of pale greenish fire, as of burning sulphur, thrust out by some subterranean force—some 'cosmic energy divine'—and this sight so strikes the fancy that, in an age of faith, a traveller telling of this in other lands, it might easily grow out of his relation that in this favoured region the kindly earth marks this wonderful yield of her great bounty of wine by a mysterious shooting forth of flames of living fire.

To all which the sceptical and cynical reader will say, 'I don't believe it!' and I reply, 'Go to the Bom Jesus at the proper hour and season and see;' and if he retorts, 'Anyhow, I don't believe about the horses drinking wine,' I rejoin, 'Travel through the Minho Province, and you will see horses drinking wine and eating maize bread many times in a day.'

Reaching the top of the hill, we look down westward towards Braga, and eastward towards the city of Guimaraens. The mountain ridges which separate the two cities are those of the Falperra range, and as the eye travels over them it will rest on a white speck

on an outlying spur of the mountains, about six miles
off as the crow flies. This is a tiny chapel, dedicated
to San Romão, and on a certain day in the year a
goodly number of pilgrims flock thither. To us,
however, the interest of the chapel hill is that it is
the site of the buried city of Citania—of the so-called
Citania. Now, the city of Citania, if city it be, and
Citania it be, is still a puzzle to the antiquary. Till a
few years ago there was but a vague rumour of the existence of ruins on the hill of San Romão ; within that
period archæology owes it to Senhor Francisco Moraes
Sarmento, of the neighbouring city of Guimaraens,
that certain excavations have been made and explora-
tions set on foot ; but the exertions of one antiquary,
single-handed, against a mysterious buried city, however energetic and enlightened he be—and Senhor
Sarmento is both—can go but a small way to tell us
the story of these ruins, and they are still, therefore,
an unsolved mystery.

The hill of San Romão stands out boldly from the
range of which it is a spur, and from its summit a
view is commanded of a great level extent of country,
through which, amid rich corn-fields and vineyards,
wind slowly the full waters of the river Este. The
hill itself is treeless ; its summit is some eight hundred
feet above the plain, and the ascent is so steep that
it takes three-quarters of an hour to climb to the top.
Within a few hundred yards of the very highest
point the steepness increases ; here vegetation almost
ceases, and the surface of the ground is occupied by
a thickly lying crop of granite boulders of all sizes

and shapes. A very stiff climb of five minutes more
over and round these obstructions leads to the summit, and here we find ourselves on a comparatively
level bit of turfy ground, fairly clear of stones, two
or three hundred yards across. On this table-land,
and some little way down the incline, on each side,
are the ruins. There is very little indeed to see, and
until Senhor Sarmento's excavations were made, an
unobservant person might easily have walked up and
over the hill without guessing that it had ever been
the dwelling-place of man. The ruins have by time
or by human hands been all nearly levelled to the
ground, and all that was visible, till the digging began, was here and there a portion of circular wall,
solidly built of well quoined stone, projecting from
the ground.

The first thing that strikes one is that these wall
fragments form parts or segments of complete circles.
Wherever one of the bits of wall showed above the
surface. Senhor Sarmento has dug, and what he has
come upon is this:—At a depth of from two to six
feet down, both inside and outside the segment, he
reaches a rough pavement. That which is inside the
circle is clearly the stone flooring of a building; that
on the outside, the pavement of a street. When this
digging has taken place round the whole circle, and
the earth and stones are removed, there is left a perfectly round building about twenty-one feet in diame-
ter, of course unroofed, and with a single doorway.
The great majority of the remains are of this circular
character, but to every eight or nine of the round

Y

towers or houses there is a square building of rather
larger dimensions, and again there are a few detached
walls which seem in most instances to have been built
at the slope of the hill, simply to keep the earth and
stones from slipping down.

The first question one asks oneself is how the
upper portion of these round houses was finished off,
and how roofed in. The answer to both questions is
to be got from the rubbish dug out from inside the
houses. There is just material enough in the way of
quoined stones to carry up the building another three
or four feet high, and the fragments of a quantity of
earthenware tiles of a curious pattern answer the
question as to the roof. Few modern houses are
so well roofed as these ancient buildings must have
been, for the tiles used were broad and square, with
their two opposite edges upturned an inch or so ; and
being laid side by side on the roof, and a common
convex tile (of which there are fragments also) being
placed over the joint, a strong and perfectly water-
tight roof would have been formed. Senhor Sarmento
has gone to the pains of reconstructing one of the
houses, and even of having tiles moulded for its roof
of the very size and shape of the ancient ones. The
building is almost certainly exact in its resemblance ;
a tower about ten feet high to the eaves, and with a
conical roof, the inside forming a single chamber of
fair size—a beehive-looking structure, singularly unin-
viting as a dwelling. Senhor Sarmento, I notice, has
carried his tiles only half-way up to the roof apex ;
the rest he makes of thatch, and this, I think, is a

mistake, because if the place was a stronghold, as its
position leads one to suppose, a straw thatch would
certainly have invited attack by fire.

Now, a curious point connected with the ruins is
that, as a rule, the buildings are so crowded together
that in some cases only three or four inches of space
intervene between them—in one case a single finger
would fill the space between two buildings; and this
is odd, because one is puzzled to understand why,
when the builders had finished one wall, they did
not make it serve as a party-wall between two houses.

When the traveller has seen so much of the ruins,
he is no true traveller if he do not begin to form his
theories and make his guesses. Who built these
ruins? Who lived in them? And why and when
were they deserted?

It is obvious enough that the place was occupied as a stronghold. So much is quite certain, for
though there was water, no doubt, to be got by sink-
ing a well on the top—springs still gush out in three
or four places from among the rocks on the hillside
—yet there could have been no other necessary of
human life on the hill, neither corn for man, nor
pasture for cattle, nor possibility of garden produce.
Therefore, the dwellers here could have come but for
one necessary, and that perhaps in rude times the
most conducive of any to health and longevity—security. A handful of the most unwarlike possible
defenders of this hill top could have held it against an
army. The tall granite boulders on the crest stand
as thick as battlements on a castle wall, and would

afford full protection to a bowman, or a slinger, or
the hurler of a javelin; smaller stones stand ready to
hand, and even a child's or a woman's throw would
send them leaping down the precipice to carry destruction to an advancing host.   Then, looking to the
great agricultural plain beneath, one fancies how a
rural population, the dwellers on it, might have flocked
to the hill for safety at the first alarm of danger,
using it for occasional refuge only ; but this obvious
suggestion has to be abandoned, for the way-worn
pavements point to a long and continuous occupation,
so also do the many fragments of pottery.   It was
certainly therefore a dwelling for men, for women
and children, as well as a stronghold.   We can pick
up fragments of the pitcher for water, of the jar made
of a finer and less porous earthenware to hold oil ;
and, though the shapes of these vessels are not such
as the Romans used, it is all but certain that the men
who made them had learned their trade from the
Roman potters.   The present writer presumes to
speak with some little authority on this point, as
being himself not unacquainted practically with the
potter's art.

Then there are women's and children's personal
ornaments, baubles of blue and green glass; they
came, we know, in the stream of Phœnician traffic ;
and there were smiths at work on the hill, for we find
the clinkers of the forge here and there, and scraps
of rusted iron innumerable ; and the smiths seem to
have been men of peace rather than of war, for Senhor
Sarmento tells me he has obtained no single warlike

weapon of iron—neither spearhead, nor arrow, nor
sword ; and millers ground their corn on the hill, for
it is difficult to take two steps where the earth has
been disturbed, without seeing the fragments of mill-
stones ; and there were artists—or perhaps, as with
us at home, idlers only and amateurs in art—for there
are rough incised ornamentations on stones, and at
least one rude representation of a human group.

So, then, the problem is narrowing itself somewhat.
We are agreed that it was a stronghold and a place
of permanent abode ; but for whom, and when?   The
when is partly answered by the fact that no single
flint or stone implement or weapon has been discovered ; but of iron, as we have seen, very many.
The place then was occupied in the 'Iron Age,' as
antiquaries have it, and if I may frame a new eth-
nological term, it was in the later Pottery Age—an
age when unglazed pottery with close, smooth texture
was made—that is, after the Romans had come into
the country ; but almost certainly the dwellers here
were neither Romans nor a Romanized people.   Not
only is there not a single inscription, but the character
of the architecture is not at all of the kind used by
the Romans ; the stronghold being, indeed, of that
type which Roman writers called an *Oppidum*, and
describe as being used by the aboriginal tribes of
Northern and Western Europe.

Again, the incised ornamentations on the stone
slabs are most markedly non-Christian ; and this is
especially the case of one very conspicuous stone
which the traveller will find on the very summit of

the hill. A huge slab of granite, a foot or so in thickness, some seven feet in height and about nine in length, attracts the traveller's attention almost immediately. It is pierced near the bottom by a hole through which a boy could creep, and adorned with a complicated incised pattern of small circles and squares intertwined with much quaint artifice, and with straight and scroll-shaped lines. The work, though not strictly Runic, is more of that character than anything else ; it is certainly pre-Christian, and the stone, from its size and importance, must clearly have been the work not of one man, nor of several, but of many—probably of the whole tribe. It was, no doubt, connected with some religious rite.

It is obvious what a very important part this stone must play in the construction of any theory which the speculative tourist may form of the lost history of the ruins. I admit that it had its weight with me, and my two learned and ingenious companions, on the occasion of my first visit, were, I know, as much occupied as myself in fitting this singular stone into the edifices of their respective theories; more diligently, apparently, even than myself, for as we descended the hill in silence, revolving each man the pros and cons of his own hypothesis, they left to me the honour of discovering a rare Portuguese fern, *Cheiranthes fragrans*, growing among the boulders of the hill.

By the time we reached the bottom of the hill our respective theories were fully evolved and developed in all their bearings, and quite ready for publication. What then was our consternation, what was our be-

wilderment, what was the utter upsetting of everything in the shape of a theory when, arrived at a little
roadside inn in the village of San Estevão at the bottom of the hill, we learned from a farmer there
drinking a cup of wine, that the great stone was no
' native of the rock,' but had been carried thither by
the enthusiastic Senhor Sarmento!

'But,' we exclaimed, with the natural irritation
and obstinacy of disappointed antiquaries, 'the thing
is palpably impossible; a road must have been made
up the hillside on purpose!'

'A road *was* made,' said the farmer calmly.

'But,' I insisted, 'it would have taken fifty oxen
to draw that enormous stone up!'

'Not so,' said the farmer, 'it took only forty-
four.'

The farmer further informed us that it had
formerly stood in the porch of the parish church, and
that Senhor Sarmento in his apparently misplaced
archæological zeal, had insisted upon carrying up to
the site of his excavations this huge slab of granite,
which I believe must weigh fully ten or fifteen
tons!

Our feelings of blank dismay may be imagined:
fortunately there was no one to laugh at us but ourselves. Here was a story to match the similar misadventure of Sir Walter Scott's 'Antiquary,' and
scientific discomfiture quite as ludicrous as that which
befel Mr. Pickwick. When should we ever have the
heart to build up a theory again after the ground
had thus been so completely cut from beneath our

feet, and all the probabilities so stupendously violated ?

The reader may guess that had the matter rested here, he would, perhaps, never have heard this story ; but it turned out, fortunately for our archæological acumen, that the apparent blunder admitted of easy explanation. On my return from this expedition, I looked at Argote's well-known work upon Braga, published in the last century, and learnt therefrom not without a feeling of relief, that the stone was standing in his day on the hill itself. Senhor Sarmento, has subsequently told me that he knows or knows of the parish priest who brought it down hill for the adornment of his church, and it was Senhor Sarmento, as the farmer had informed us, who, to the lasting honour of all archæologists, had caused the stone, which the peasantry had long known under the name of *Pedra Formosa*, to be carried up to its original position.

Under these altered circumstances, I no longer hesitate to put forward my theory. Citania,—it is convenient to have a name for a place, though it is probable that the ruins have no true title to this one,[1]

---

[1] The Roman historian, Valerius Maximus, mentions the town of Citania, and some antiquaries have fixed its site on this hill of San Romão, near Braga ; the name Citania has consequently been given to the hill. It is not a popular name, therefore, but an antiquary's name. Valerius Maximus fixes Citania on a mountain in Lusitania, and praises the bravery of its inhabitants , but there are more mountains than one in Portugal, and there is contention over Citania, as over the birthplace of Homer. Some six Portuguese antiquaries have chosen six different mountain sites for

—was in my opinion a stronghold, built either by the Celtic or by the Celt-Iberian race. It was probably occupied during a long period, perhaps during many centuries, and until after the Romans were in possession of the country, through Roman times, and probably until and after the establishment of the Visigoths in Portugal. All this is proved, so far as proof is possible in such cases, first, by the different kinds of masonry shown in the walls, marking different periods of construction; that in the western portion of the ruins is of the kind known as Cyclopean, and here the stones are larger, the work coarser, the fittings and quoining less perfect than in the presumably more recent portions; secondly, by the immense quantity of potsherds, their character, the absence of flint implements; the presence of articles of bronze and iron, and lastly, the absence of Roman inscriptions and of Christian symbols. It was probably destroyed by the Visigoths, or we should have found some token of the presence of this Christian people; and that it was never occupied by the Moors is nearly certain, because there is no trace of their very characteristic handiwork. That it was not again occupied on the reappearance of the Christians in the country is certain, because if it had been we should have had some historical record of the fact.

Now to account for the circular character of the buildings, with their low, thin walls, large doorways, and absence of embrasures—all which would have

Citania, and a seventh—as good a man as any of them—confesses that he knows not where it was.

made them quite unfit for military defence—and for the curious fact of their being crowded together in such a way as makes it clear that no sane people would have ventured to stand an attack in them. I should account for all this by supposing that these well-roofed, circular towers were simply granaries for the corn produced in the fertile plain below; that the place was a depôt used by the inhabitants wherein to store their produce, which otherwise would have been at the mercy of every marauding band from the surrounding hills. The low, circular turrets, with their walls uncemented, and therefore affording good ventilation, with their waterproof roofs to keep off rain, and their stone pavements to keep out vermin, would have been ideal granaries. The necessity of ventilation for grain storing would also perfectly account for the small size of the turrets and their complete isolation, while yet so closely crowded together. The square houses or mills where the corn was hand-ground were probably the dwellings of the guardians of the depôt, who, no doubt, occupied their leisure in grinding the corn they guarded. None of the buildings, probably, were fortresses, for the hill, with its natural crenelations and battlements, is itself a stronghold; such as Moirosi and Secocoeni found in their boulder-covered mountains.

The apparent remains are not numerous enough to have been a large centre of population; but the spot where the chief wealth of the district was preserved would, no doubt, be the main place of public resort. Here all the bargaining of the neighbourhood

would have been done, all the buying and selling, all
the petty traffic of a rude period carried on ; here, in
the assurance of security, pedlars would have established their stores of foreign stuffs and toys ; here
artificers would have built their workshops, blacksmiths
set up their forges, the potter his wheel and his kiln
—it would become, in fact, the bazaar of the district.

If all these surmises be correct, a wider exploration
may be expected to reveal plentiful signs and tokens
of the resorting together of men and of women; ornaments for the women, weapons for the men, coins
—a few have already been found by Senhor Sarmento,
but I attach little weight to such discoveries, work-
men are always anxious to find coins for their em-
ployers, and in Portugal, spurious ones are only too
common. Those which have been found, however,
quite support my theory.[1]

So much for the buried city of Citania, one of the
most curious and interesting places of its kind in
Portugal ; the traveller who desires to reach it from
the Bom Jesus, may do so in a delightful two hours'
walk along the breezy ridges of the Falperra moun-

---

[1] One thing at Citania is puzzling—the great number of
conical, or rather frustral stones found in the ruins. These stone
pillars vary from a foot to three feet in height, and their proportions are about those of a common sugar-loaf. They are seen
whole or in pieces all over the hill. If such stones were found
near a temple in India or Thibet, one would know to what to
refer them. They may perhaps denote here too some species of
nature worship. The sculptured stone to which I have referred
seems to bear out this view. Perhaps after all they were nothing
but the upper stones in the querns which are so numerous on the
hill.

tains, part of his road lying beneath the shade of trees,
or else he may take a carriage to Braga and proceed
thence by road towards Guimaraens : a league will
bring him to the valley of the river Este, in which
are situated the sulphurous baths of Taipas.   Thence
he can travel two miles further by road to San
Estevão, the village at the foot of the hill of San
Romão.   However Citania be reached the journey is
pleasant, and if archæology do not tempt the tourist,
botany or entomology may.   He may botanize ad-
vantageously on the hill : two rare ferns, *Cheiranthes
fragrans*, already mentioned, and *Asplenium marinum*
grow, the first abundantly and close to Citania itself;
and the very site of the ruins is the haunt of a rare
and beautiful species of butterfly, *Parnassius Apollo*,
the only spot in all Portugal where I have seen it.

We return to the Caldas das Taipas, where the remains of Roman baths exist, and which are still
much frequented by the modern Portuguese, for
they inherit all the belief in the virtues of bathing
both in the sea water and the waters of warm sulphur
springs.   The granite hills get loftier and barer of
trees and more boulder-covered as we near Guimaraens,
but the geologist who is tempted by their appearance
to climb up their steep sides will find little to reward
him.   The boulders show no trace of having been
' erratic,' the *roches montonnées* bear no traces on their
surface of glacial action.   The loose boulders, the
' tors ' on the hill tops, and the rocking-stones piled
often one above the other in magnificent confusion,
are, in the case of the boulders, only the hard nuclei

from which the surrounding softer parts have
weathered off; the tors and cliffs are only points and
ledges which time cannot eat away.

Though architects do not condescend to class
granite as a stone, and point to the poor architecture
in districts where this formation is prevalent, they
must allow that for the building of castles or towers,
and turrets, where strength and simplicity are the
prevailing motives, there is no material like granite.
Its very surface, its rough granulation, its sombre
greyness, the massive proportions of its blocks—all
this gives it an air of grandeur, when worthily employed, which no other stone possesses.

In Guimaraens the traveller will have an excellent
opportunity of judging whether this be so. Guimaraens is the oldest city of purely Portuguese origin in
the kingdom. I have told in a previous chapter how,
when the Leonese monarch sent his Viceroy Count
Henry of Burgundy to rule in Portugal in the
eleventh century, it was at Guimaraens that the
Viceregal Court was held. Here the Count's son,
Affonso Henriquez, the true founder of the Portuguese
Monarchy, was born ; here he spent his early youth ;
and in the wild country round Guimaraens he first
learned the art of war, and in his very boyhood became a trusted leader of his troops in their yearly
forays against Moor and Spaniard.

Here, as was natural, the first great Christian fortress was built, and I think that a man might travel
from the Northern frontier river Minho to the mouth
of the Guadiana in the furthest south of Portugal,

and find nowhere a nobler monument of a people
destined from the very first to great fortunes, than this
grand, granite-built castle of their earliest king.

The castle is simple in its structure. A thick
curtain wall heavily battlemented, and set in each
of its angles with turrets, surrounds a level area from
whose centre a huge square keep rises straight as an
arrow from the living granite rock—the very earth-
crust itself—on which its foundations are built; and
so deft were the early masons, so tractable was the
rugged granite in their hands, so perfectly squared
and fitted in is each enormous block, that looking
down to-day from its giddy height the traveller won-
ders to think that eight centuries have not thrown
the ashlar stones an inch beyond the plumb line that
the first mason dropped. All that time has done is
to deepen the grey of the stone, and to redden its
surface here and there with a thin sheathing of lichen ;
each block is still in its place, every corner sharp,
every chisel mark, struck probably while our first
King Henry was yet on his throne, is as fresh nearly
as if it had touched the stone only yesterday. It is
still not a ruin, though it has withstood the siege of
human enemies as well as of time ; and it tells the
story of the strong spirit of the race of men who built
it, far more eloquently than I have read it in any
page of native chronicler or historian. The huge,
pointed granite blocks, each taller than a man, which
form the battlements, still stand erect and immovable,
giving evidence of such immense power and energy
in the very piling up to this height of these huge

stones, that the coldest imagination cannot, I should
suppose, fail to be affected by it, and to reach by a
sort of intuition at the true meaning and history of
this fortress.   It is not the story of rapine, of wrong,
of selfish isolation and oppression of the weak, so often
told by the ruined feudal strongholds of Northern
Europe, but that of a united and loyal people, free
and warlike, under congenial rulers, working out
by the strong hand their independence against the
oppressors of their liberty and their faith.

In evidence of what can be made of granite,
treated in a more purely art spirit, there is in
Guimaraens the belfry tower of Nossa Senhora
d'Oliveira.   This fine tower is one of a kind which
is not rare in Portugal, and which, as a rule, the very
Vandalism of the church-restorers of the last two
hundred years has respected.   Under the evil art-
influences which prevailed during this whole period,
everything Gothic was denounced and, where
possible, destroyed.   That which has saved so many
a fine building in Northern countries—the poverty
of the restorers—did not protect the fine art work
of older times in Portugal.   From about 1600 to
1750, or later, immense wealth was poured into the
country from India and from South America.   Much
of it was spent in iconoclasm, and now in the larger
and richer towns of the kingdom hardly a Gothic
building remains.   In Lisbon only one or two
churches of a good period are to be found ; in Oporto
but two, and those maimed of their beauties.   But
when the iconoclasts destroyed an old building, and

built up in its stead a monstrous erection, in the
later Renaissance style, or the Italian, or the pseudo-
classical, or, worse than all and commonest of all
in Portugal, in that mixture of the classical and the
rococo which I have christened the Jesuit style—
when they set about doing this, it fortunately either
happened that their funds ran short, or their destructive propensities a little failed them ; or, perhaps, the
love of the people for the old place wherein they
and their forefathers had worshipped found a tongue
in indignant remonstrance. Sometimes they would
let an old arched doorway, with its deep romanesque
mouldings, stand uninjured ; sometimes it seemed a
sacrilege even to them to destroy the elaborate tracery
of a fine *flamboyant* window. Often they left the
outside of some grand building, and only assailed
the more exquisite work of the interior—as the white
ants of tropical countries eat out the whole inside of
valuable articles, and leave a thin outer crust, a
mere hollow simulacrum of that which they have
consumed.

At Braga they have gone only so far with the
Cathedral, and left much fine exterior work ; at
Guimaraens it is the same ; while in both cases the
traveller's expectations are completely disappointed
when he enters the building to find the heavy,
tasteless, Italianized interior. In both these cases,
however, and in many others, the cloisters are
standing—though carefully whitewashed !—and at
Guimaraens the typical granite belfry tower is wholly
intact—a beautiful building, graceful and stately,

and well worth dwelling upon for an instant. It
is a square tower on the west of the church, so
admirably proportioned, and with ornamentation in
such true artistic subjection to its construction, that
the least architectural tourist in the world must stop
to admire it, and try to understand why it is so
beautiful. Its height is divided by three horizontal
string-courses, and on the summit are set pinnacled
crenelations. The upper string-course, running
along the second course of ashlar from the top, is
set with gargoyles; the other two are plain.
Between the two upper string-courses is the belfry,
containing a peal of eight bells, two showing through
the double-pointed arched window openings on each
side of the tower. Each corner of the tower is
carved in a twisted cable ornament, running per-
pendicularly, and giving a singular air of finish and
relief to the whole. This moulding is relieved by a
carved grotesque head between the two upper
string-courses, and a gargoyle half way between the
two lower ones. Later additions to the tower are
an outrageous little conical spire, now whitewashed,
and an ecclesiastical coat of arms between the two
lower string-courses, of a date not much later than
the tower, and contemporary probably with the
crenelated work on its summit.

Guimaraens is a delightful old town, full of
rarely picturesque ' bits ' for an artist—old ' *Azimel* '
windows, telling of Moorish influences ; narrow alleys,
with the eaves of opposite houses all but meeting
overhead ; colonnaded streets ; old doorways, with

queerly carved mouldings ; lights and shadows everywhere to delight a Rembrandt, and some of the
street vistas terminating in a grand view of the
mountain-side, white in places with the bloom of
fruit-trees, green with waving patches of rye and
clover among the grey boulders ; and here and there
the waters of rills and rivulets are seen tumbling in
foaming cascades down the steep hillside.

The tourist or traveller might do worse than
make Guimaraens his headquarters for a while.
There is now at Guimaraens an excellent hotel—
where there used to be only very bad ones—I forget its
name, but it is in a square nearly opposite the church
already described, and will be known to all drivers
and others as the *Hospedaria Nova*—the New Inn.
There are high roads from the city in all directions, all
leading through lovely scenery, mostly mountainous,
to interesting cities ; and these roads are so uniformly
good that there is not the slightest temptation to do
what a driver in Ireland of old days once proposed
to his fare when at last he had come to a tolerable
mile of road, ' Won't I drive your honour back over
this last bit again, just for the delight of it ? ' There
used to be, and for that matter still are, roads in
Portugal which make this story intelligible, but in
those about Guimaraens there is now a positive
monotony of excellence.

Go where he will in Portugal, the traveller should
be provided with Murray's Hand-Book. To be sure
there are great omissions in it, and some things to
which omissions would have been far preferable—

but as a guide book it is *facile princeps* among such *biblia abiblia*, whether English, French or German. It is comparatively far more useful and more trustworthy than the others. I lay claim to some generosity for saying this, for in an enlarged and amended edition Mr. Murray has called me some very unkind names, simply because I set him right in a most astounding blunder about Lucius Junius Brutus and the historian Livy. Mr. Murray, after correcting the blunder (without acknowledgment), adventured a dreadful insinuation to the effect that he did not believe I was myself very thoroughly conversant with the works of Livy. Although there was nothing in my text to ground this very grave charge upon, I am ashamed to say it is well founded. I am not well read in Livy.

CHURCH PLATE IN BRAGA CATHEDRAL.

CHAPTER IX.

THE ship that leaves the shores of Great Britain in
October or November, and steers due south, does not
leave fog and leaden skies, and cold winds, and
driving rain and sleet well behind her until she has
crossed the storm-vexed Bay of Biscay, and passed
Cape Finisterre, the Land's End of Spain. Then, as
a rule, the sky clears, the wind dies, and the sea, no
longer lashed into surge and foam, reflects the
serenity of the heavens in its own darker bosom.

Travelling on south through these summer seas for
nearly a thousand miles after leaving the Bay, we sight
the land of our destination, the Purple Islands, as the
ancients are fabled to have named them—Madeira
and the islets adjacent. The first to rise from the
sea is Porto Santo; then, some forty miles further
west, Madeira itself, and the Desertas Islands.

It has been disputed whether these islands were
indeed those anciently known as the Purple Islands,
and it has been further questioned whether the
epithet 'purple' is applicable to their appearance,
or to the fact that a purple dye can be obtained
from a lichen which still grows in great abundance

at Madeira, and is known in commerce as Orchilla Weed.

It requires no little exercise of faith to believe that the ancients ever had discovered these islands, and a good deal more to accept the theory of this anticipation by 2,000 years of our comparatively modern invention of the purple orchil dye.

If they knew the islands at all, and knew them as the Purple Islands, it is probable that they applied this name to Madeira on account of the dark and almost purple colour of the volcanic cliffs which border the sea shore, towering in places into peaks which mimic the turrets of a castle, in others rising sheer up for hundreds of feet from the water's edge like huge walls of masonry, or forming quaint jutting pinnacles and bosses of dark stone: so dark, indeed, that if, as the traveller comes near, a cloud happens to intercept the sun's rays, these sea-facing rocks look as if they had been washed with an inky rain. Only when the sun shines upon them do their true colours show—here a jasper-like red, there a green vivid with moss and weeds, there with the tones of burnished bronze, and again through infinite gradations of greys and violets, to where the line of white foam divides them from the blue sea.

The ship which steers for Madeira passes the last promontory, the Brazen Head, and enters the little Bay of Funchal, safe lying for ships in all winds except when it blows from the south, for the hills behind the town rise in an amphitheatre to a height

nearly as great as that of Snowdon, and keep off the
north, the east, and the west wind not from the town
alone, but from the whole bay. A curious sight is
often seen from the houses of the town—a tempest-
tossed vessel two or three miles out in the offing,
where the billows are raised by a strong north wind,
and the waters of the bay, meanwhile, placid as a
mill pool.

Landing in this sheltered spot—it is sheltered for
nine months out of the twelve—the traveller finds
himself in a balmy, delicious, soft and perfumed air,
full of the sweet scents of flowers, a perpetual spring,
an atmosphere not to be recommended perhaps for
those who want a bracing climate, not a country
where the late Charles Kingsley would have found
materials or inspiration for his Ode to the East Wind,
but a spot where the Laureate might have placed
his Lotus Eaters, a land ' in which it seemed always
afternoon.'

To one newly arrived from England, the town of
Funchal would, no doubt, present much attractive
novelty in its non-English aspect, but to the present
writer, not unacquainted with ' men and cities' in
the south of Europe, the chief attraction of the town
is its singular cleanness. There is, of course, no
building earlier than the end of the 15th century,
the island only having been discovered by the Portuguese in 1419; and regular streets, plain buildings,
and abundant whitewash, combined with the entire
absence of a respectable antiquity and of any his-

torical associations, make Funchal comparatively un-picturesque and uninteresting.

The most experienced traveller, however, if he is unprepared for it, is likely to be taken aback at the extraordinary mode in which he is landed. Calm as the waters of the bay appear to be, some amount of surf for ever breaks upon the stony beach, responsive to the never-ending surge of the great ocean outside ; and the boatmen, as they come near the shore, turn the boat's stern beachwards, and, watching for a strong wave, let themselves be carried in by it. As the boat gets into the broken water, and before the re-ceding wave can carry her out again, they jump into the water and make fast the boat to a chain attached to a yoke of oxen, who drag the boat and its occupants up the somewhat steep shore and several yards over the shingle. This singular mode of disembarkation is, of course, not accomplished without an immense amount of splashing of water, vociferation, and general wrangling of every islander within shouting distance.

A queer race of men are these natives of Madeira. Mainly of Portuguese origin, they clearly are a nation of half-castes, and the Negro cross is conspicuous in their good-natured, ugly faces, in their stature—they average two or three inches more than the Portuguese of the continent—in their shambling gait, and in their ill-knit frames. Their morality, too, is said somewhat to partake of Negro laxity. They are, however, by no means flagrant offenders, and practise only the lesser vices of pilfering and

story-telling, compounding, as it were, for their in-
dulgence in petty larceny and white lies by a rigid
economy in the greater crimes. Perhaps they
derive their standard of morality from the fact of
their living on a very small island—Madeira is only
forty miles long by about ten or twelve in breadth—
for it is a noticeable fact that the dwellers on small
islands are seldom given to marked enormity of
criminality: a man's Nemesis being, it is to be presumed, too certain to overtake him, in a confined
space, to make it convenient to perpetrate any very
great wickedness. So, it is related, the late Mr.
Smith, proprietor and virtual king of the Scilly
Islands, banished all the more serious offences from
among his tenants and subjects by the simple threat
of exiling those who should commit them, carrying
a Draconian code so far as to make the pulling of a
feather from his peacock's tail punishable with instant
banishment. A code as stringent would go some
way to depopulate the island of Madeira.

The native Madeirans have retained few of the
characteristics traits, either of dress or habits, which
are still prevalent in the mother country. They
speak a broken-down Portuguese, not immediately
intelligible, as I have myself had occasion to observe,
to a native of continental Portugal; they have few
of those traces of Moorish ways and customs, which
are so evident to one who has observed the habits of
the Portuguese peasantry; and, altogether, I am inclined to doubt what is generally asserted—that
there is a large admixture of Moorish blood in the

inhabitants of the island. I see, as I have said, no sign of it in the people's faces, and I can find no historical confirmation whatever of the fact.

Throughout the sixteenth century, the period when Madeira was peopled by Portuguese colonists, and when sugar began to be extensively cultivated, the tillage of the land was effected by Portuguese labourers brought over by the large proprietors, among whom the island had at once been parcelled out. These labourers were nominally free men, whose condition, however, was probably very little better than that of Indian or Chinese coolies on tropical sugar plantations ; and they were supplemented by negro slaves, whose numbers in the seventeenth century are asserted to have amounted to several thousands. The hardy, easy-going Negro would, no doubt, quickly assimilate in habits and religion to the superior race, and, in time, intermingle ; not so the Moors, if any of that nationality were, indeed, at that time in slavery on the island. Between Moor and Christian the faith feud in the Peninsula was at this time more bitter than at any other, and any commingling of the races was out of the question. If there ever were Moorish slaves in Madeira, and I see no evidence even of that, there would have been too much of mutual repulsion between them and the Portuguese to admit of the two races co-existing, except as lord and serf, far less of their mixing their blood.

The Madeirans, as a rule, wear no peculiar costume. The women, indeed, cover their heads with a handkerchief, but in other respects their dress

might pass without observation in an English village.
The men also dress like English peasants, showing
a tendency to white 'ducks,' in imitation, no doubt,
of sailors, and adopting the hideous 'wide-awake'
hat, a head covering which, originating among the
plantation slaves of the United States, promises in
time to spread over the whole civilised earth. Two
eccentricities of dress, however, the Madeirans indulge in. The men, when they do not wear 'wide-
awake' hats, use, perhaps, the most singular head
covering worn by any race of Christian men. In
shape and size it exactly resembles a common tea
saucer; it is made of black cloth, and fits on to the
very point of the back of the head, covering, of
course, only about a hand's breadth of its surface,
and being kept in place, as a resident tried to explain to me, simply by the force of suction. This
'*carapuça*,' or skull cap, is put on and taken off
by a handle made of rolled cloth, which projects
from its centre, and stands up from the wearer's
head; this handle is as thin and half as long as the
stem of a long clay pipe, and the general appearance
of the islander with one of these caps is indescribably
ludicrous. The Madeirans may boast of having
evolved this remarkable head-gear within the last
hundred years, for no notice is made of it by
travellers visiting the island until the year 1782.

Another peculiarity of dress is the universal
wearing of top-boots of yellow goat's leather by
persons of both sexes and all ages. The use of the
Moorish slipper by the peasantry of so many parts of

Spain and Portugal, is a marked vestige of Orientalism, and the abandonment by their descendants of a
chaussure in which a man can neither run on level
ground, nor walk up a steep hill, is, no doubt, due to
the mountainous nature of the island, and perhaps
to the extensive growth of the prickly pear, which
would make walking barefoot quite impossible. The
use of high boots is therefore sensible enough, but the
appearance of a little girl of ten or twelve in a pair
of top-boots is apt to strike the conventional stranger
as singular.

The chief interest of Madeira, however, lies
neither in its inhabitants nor in its history, but in
the extraordinary beauty of its scenery and the
delicious mildness of its climate.

In Madeira, as a health resort, I desire to express
my strong belief. True it is that for many years
past it has been denounced by certain medical
authors; every doctor who has wanted to write up a
new winter health resort begins by attempting to
write down Madeira, as likely to prove its most
formidable competitor. I venture to think that
few non-medical persons have read more about
European health resorts or read with stronger
interest in arriving at the strict truth in the matter
than myself. The result of my investigations was to
go to Madeira, and inquiries on the spot, among persons who can have had no object in misrepresentation,
strongly confirmed my choice. The chief charges
against Madeira, I found, as I expected, quite untenable.
These charges are three in number : first, the preva-

lence of the scorching Leste or Sirocco, the east wind which blows from Africa and comes to Madeira charged with the heat and dryness which reign over the Sahara desert; secondly, the damp of the climate; and thirdly, the frequency of rain. But it turns out that the Leste is never disagreeable and never frequent except in summer; in winter it blows but once or twice, and its effect at that season upon human beings is rather pleasant and exhilarating than otherwise. The dampness, so evident to the perceptions of those who recommend rival health resorts, is certainly not appreciable to the senses of an invalid, nor is it even cognizable to science, inasmuch as the hygrometer notes 72 degrees as the average amount of humidity in Funchal, and the best medical authorities give from 70 to 80 degrees of relative humidity as that which is most agreeable to human beings. As regards rain, there fall on an average but 29 inches in the year; and even this does not represent the full freedom from rainy weather enjoyed by Madeira, for when rain falls in the island, it falls quickly and heavily, and while in Torquay—our very best English winter climate— about the same annual amount of rain descends, they have in Madeira but 88 days of rain in the whole year, while the people of Torquay have to endure no fewer than 155.

This is all the foundation possessed by the three indictments commonly preferred against Madeira. On the other hand, no European climate has so mild and equable a winter, is so free from chilling winds,

sudden and excessive cold and dryness; in no
European station are the nights so warm, the noonday
sun so little scorching. No European town is so free
as Funchal from endemic or epidemic diseases—those
diseases, that is, which range from ague and marsh
fever to scarlet fever and typhus. At no European
station is vegetation of all kinds so luxuriant and so
lovely; in no other health resort is such varied
scenery to be enjoyed; and in no climate, probably
in the whole world, is it possible for an invalid to take
so much out-door exercise in the course of the year;
in none is dust on the roads so absolutely unknown;
and, what is perhaps of more importance than anything else, in none is locomotion, by means of ponies,
palanquins, and sleighs, so easy and so suitable to sick
persons.

These excellences in the Madeira climate have
recommended it, and continue to recommend it, as a
special resort for consumptive patients; but it is,
perhaps, quite as beneficial in a great variety of other
complaints, such as renal affections, asthma, bron-
chitis, gout, and certain forms of rheumatism, and,
above all, in convalescence from fevers. Madeira is
still resorted to annually by about three hundred
English visitors; and their number in future years
will probably suffer no diminution, though a variety
of circumstances have, to some extent, tended to
diminish the repute of Madeira as a desirable and
accessible health resort.

Among these, the stringency of the quarantine
laws, which are now relaxed, was at one time enough

to deter many intending visitors; moreover, for some years, the steam communication with England was irregular; and, added to all this, was the circumstance I have above spoken of, the adverse and not disinterested criticism of writers on some other European climates. To these several causes may be ascribed the non-increase in the number of English arrivals, but it is noteworthy that with foreigners of nearly every nationality, Madeira is in increasing esteem. Americans, Russians, Spaniards, and especially Germans, now resort to the island every year in increasing numbers.

That a comparatively large island like Madeira, not lowly and unobtrusive, like the coral-formed islets of southern seas, which barely lift their soil above the tides, but an island composed of a mountain range, with peaks as lofty as many not disdained by Alpine climbers—that such an island, visible for scores of miles on the surrounding seas, should for so many centuries have remained

'In the ocean's bosom unespied,'

is a fact sufficiently suggestive of the timorous navigation of the ancients, and the dearth of enterprise in the Middle Ages. When at last the Portuguese found it, the exploit had become magnified into absolute heroism by the very fact of so little having previously been achieved in the field of Western discovery. Men's ignorance and their fears had peopled these great unknown seas with supernatural terrors. The discoverers braved not only the dangers of an

untried navigation, but the perils of the unseen world,
—doubly terrible to men of their age and creed.
True, imagination had painted many delights to
lure them on, as well as horrors to daunt them. In
the vast expanse of this mysterious ocean were—

> ' Dire chimeras and enchanted isles.'

There was the fabulous Island of Bimini, with its
fountain of perpetual youth, in quest of which the
Spanish navigator, Juan Ponce De Leon sailed over
many a weary league of sea. There was the flying
island of St. Brandaran, where the last King of Gothic
Spain was fabled to have found a home, and which
was believed in and even searched for so late as the
eighteenth century; and there was the great
mysterious Island of Cipango, tenanted by the ghosts
of captive Christians, which Columbus himself did not
despair of finding. All these might reward the navigator who should tempt fortune on the ocean which
washes the western shores of Europe; but before
they could be reached, there was the terrible ' Sea of
Darkness' to be passed through, and this sea was
held to extend over the very spot where the Madeira
islands lie. Imagination had been busy in peopling
these unknown waters with

> ' Deformed monsters,
> Spring-headed hydras, sea-shouldering whales,
> Great whirlpools.'

If there was much, therefore, to impel a brave man
to a brave venture, there was more still to daunt
him.

The man who was bold enough to disregard these various terrors of the deep, was the Portuguese navigator, Da Camara, known to his comrades, and since to fame, as Zargo, the one-eyed or squint-eyed, and it was only by a kind of accident that Zargo, engaged on a voyage of discovery on the Western Coast, was carried by a tempest to Porto Santo. Leaving some of his men on this small and nearly barren island, Zargo betook himself to Lisbon with the news of his good fortune, and in the following year returned with two small vessels bearing colonists for the new discovered land.

On his return, Zargo learned from his men that certain supernatural phenomena had been observed on the western horizon. A singular darkness constantly dimmed the outlook towards the setting sun; strange noises from the same quarter seemed to suggest the existence, not far off, of some huge whirpool. The men began to fancy that at Porto Santo they were at the verge of the habitable world; beyond it, they imagined, was some abysmal vortex, hidden by a mysterious veil of cloud and mist. When Zargo announced his intention of sailing westward, it is reported that he was advised to abstain from rashly attempting to penetrate a mystery which the Almighty had not seen fit to reveal to his creatures. Disregarding these timorous counsels, the adventurer set sail, and in a few hours had discovered the lovely island of Madeira lying in these silent seas, in all the magnificent luxuriance of its virgin vegetation. No Portuguese mariner had, as yet, seen so fair a land.

or one so rich in the products of southern climes,
whose surface was so broken and diversified with hill
and dell, and enriched with such copious streams;
for the Azores and the Cape Verds were later discoveries, and Portuguese navigators only penetrated
to Cape Nun—the southernmost limit of the present
kingdom of Morocco—nearly twenty years afterwards.

The island was uninhabited and densely wooded.
Struck probably by its contrast with the treeless
slopes of Porto Santo and the barren shores of Africa,
they named it Madeira—the Isle of Woods. Landing
on its south eastern shore, they set up a cross; and
the place is still known as Santa Cruz—Holy Cross.
Passing westward, by the bold headland which our
sailors call the 'Brazen Head,' from its yellow colour,
they gave it the name, which it still bears on the
maps, of Cape Garajão, after the sea-birds of that
name which then tenanted the cliffs. Each point
and cove is still known by the name which the sailors
gave it on their first landing. Funchal and its bay
were so called from the fennel plant—*funcho*—which
grew on its shores. At one spot, some of the men
in wading a stream were carried off by the current,
and with difficulty rescued by their fellows, and the
river is known to this day as *Rio dos Soccorridos*, the
Stream of the Rescued Men. A black, isolated rock
seemed to them to stand up from the water like a
huge beetle, and is still called the Beetle Rock, *o
Gorgulho*. A little further they startled some seals,
which rushed by them into the sea—sea-wolves they
believed them to be—and they christened the site.

which now gives its name to a village, 'Camara de Lobos,' the Wolves' Lair.

Thus did the rocks and hills, which till then had perhaps heard no sound but of the wind, the wave or the torrent, the note of song bird or the scream of gull or kite, first get their baptism in human speech, and for the first time echo to human voices. Probably, but not certainly, for the first time, for, passing over the possible fact, to which I have alluded, of their ancient discovery, there is a persistent tradition that the first actual discoverer of Madeira was one Robert Machin, a native of Bristol, who, eloping with Anne Darfet, a young English lady of good family, fled by sea with his bride from her father's anger, intending to seek a refuge in some French harbour. The ship which conveyed them is related to have been caught in a storm and carried to Madeira, in the year 1346, where the lovers died. The crew, taking ship again, made for the mainland, and were captured and carried into slavery by the Moors. In Morocco they found a Christian fellow-captive, one Morales, to whom they told their story. This Morales was, long afterwards, delivered from captivity, and eventually found himself—so the tradition runs—in the service of the Portuguese navigator Zargo, to whom he of course imparted the strange history which had come to his knowledge.

This is the rather romantic story which has been repeated with every account of Madeira. There is nothing improbable in the fact of a ship being blown out of its course, and coming upon the Island of

Madeira, or that such a vessel should have contained a pair of English lovers ; the improbabilities are in the rest of the narration. Assuming the tradition to have remained in its original form for sixty or seventy years—which is of itself not likely—it is highly improbable that it should have reached the ears of Zargo in a credible shape, seeing that if that enterprising navigator had even suspected that so fair an island lay within three or four days' sail of Portugal, he would certainly straightway have made his way thither, whereas he was himself blown to the neighbouring Porto Santo by a tempest. Moreover, even had the account come to him as the vaguest tradition, he would have satisfied himself of its truth as soon as he had reached Port Santo, which lies actually within sight of Madeira on a clear day ; yet he did nothing of the kind, but as I have related, sailed homewards and postponed the actual discovery for a whole year, when it was all but in his grasp. The whole story has the flavour of a myth ; and as, in some sort, depriving a brave man of the credit of a brave deed, I reject it utterly.[1]

[1] It is a fact which is singularly illustrative of the almost abject ignorance and even incuriosity of the most learned and scientific men of the century, in regard to foreign travel and geographical discoveries, that fifty years after the discovery of Madeira, an Italian poet, the friend of the ablest contemporary men of science, seems to have been quite ignorant that the Straits of Gibraltar had ever been passed.

It is often quoted as evidence of the philosophical foresight of Pulci, that he makes one of his characters in the famous 'Morgante Maggiore' seem actually to presage the discovery of the New World. 'The ocean,' says the poet, 'is level through its whole extent, although, like the earth, it has the form of a globe.

The island of Madeira is volcanic in its formation; sea-cliffs and rocks, inland peaks and precipices, the lofty mountains over 6000 feet in height and the smallest pebble in the brooks, have all the same igneous origin; and all bear traces of having been cast forth, incandescent and liquid, from the great subaqueous furnace, and of having cooled and solidified in the spot where the upheaving force had thrown them. An idea of the natural configuration of the surface of the island may best be given by the illustration said to have been employed by Columbus when asked for a description of Jamaica. Crumpling up a piece of paper in his hands, he laid it upon a table as some representation of the variations of that island's surface of the sharp hill ridges, of the sudden declivities, of the gullies and narrow valleys, and the innumerable and indescribable inequalities of the land. Such as Jamaica is, such is Madeira, and such are most islands of similar volcanic origin.

This irregular contortion of the land might seem to possess all the elements of the picturesque, but it is only at first sight that its strangeness is attractive.

Mankind in former ages were much more ignorant than now. Hercules would blush at this day, at having fixed his columns where he did. Vessels will soon pass far beyond them, and may perhaps reach an unknown hemisphere.'

If we consider that Prince Henry, the Navigator, had long before despatched his exploring squadrons far south and far west of the Pillars of Hercules, and made the last of his great geographical discoveries twenty or thirty years before Pulci wrote, the poet's ignorance of past maritime achievements will seem far more wonderful than his fortuitous anticipation of the exploits of Columbus.

There is quite wanting in the bare volcanic rocks of Madeira that which constitutes true artistic picturesqueness; that is, the alternation of a manifested law or order, with interruptions of it. In the outbursts of lava torrents there is law indeed, but it is not apparent to most observers of it any more than in the forms of the huge clinkers that are shot out from an iron furnace. It is all seemingly accidental; and is, indeed, as anomalous and as hideous, æsthetically speaking, as the distorted limbs of a monster.

That this is so is shown by the fact that whenever these lava currents cease to be amorphous and begin to crystallize—that is, where they follow their natural law and take, for instance, the form of columnar basalt—they go to make up exquisitely lovely scenery, such, for example, as that of the Giant's Causeway in Ireland. Among the many hundred pictures and drawings from the master hand of Turner, I do not remember a single one where naked, amorphous, volcanic rock is represented; it is always either stratified or crystalline rocks which make the 'bones' of his works. But when these same Madeiran rocks are covered with the luxuriant vegetation which a volcanic soil produces, the barren ugliness disappears, the nakedness is clothed with rich and novel forms of plant-growth, so dense that we are only occasionally reminded that underneath there lies nothing better than a huge cinder-heap. The beauties of the island scenery are, therefore, but skin deep, so to say—they are on the surface and in the air, for there is a particular charm of aërial distance, and a singular richness and variety of colouring on the woods, the hill-sides and the shores of Madeira which I have seen nowhere else.

The nature and the number of the plants which clothe the surface of this small island, lying as it does nearly three hundred miles from the nearest point of Africa, and more than five hundred from the nearest European land ; and of the birds, beasts and insects which find shelter upon it—in other words, the Flora and Fauna of Madeira—have come to acquire a fresh interest when regarded from the point of view of recent developments in the science of Natural History. It is, therefore, not a little fortunate that a botanist and natural historian of established European reputation should have made Madeira his occasional residence for many years past. The ordinary foreign visitor to the island is little apt to interest himself in the more abstruse points involved in the partly European and partly African natural history of this semi-tropical island, upon which Mr. Lowe has written so much and so well.

When it is considered that Madeira is a very small island, and that the visitor is more or less confined to one corner of it, the wonder is that the many invalids who pass the winter there do not tire of what is virtually an imprisonment. Yet life in Madeira is by no means wearisome to the chance visitor or to the invalid. The situation of Funchal upon the sea, from which the town and the highlands behind it rise amphitheatrewise ; the view of the blue waters of the bay, always lively with boats and fishing-smacks; the daily arrival of great ocean-going steamers; the fine mountain scenery, with fresh vistas of jagged peaks and ravine chasms from every point of view, and varying hourly with every change of cloud and shadow; the charming seaside ride and drive, known as the Caminho Novo; the excellent English club and reading-room; and, above all, the hospitality of the English residents;—all these things help to make the visitor's time pass pleasantly.

A MADEIRA FISHERMAN.

CHAPTER X.

CUSTOMS OF THE PORTUGUESE PEOPLE.

THOUGHTFUL travellers in the Peninsula are generally
curious to find traces of the old Moorish culture in
the land, and this curiosity is no doubt partly due to
that *Orientalism* and sympathy with things Semitic,
which is latent in all of us of northern blood who have
read the *Arabian Nights* in our childhood, and have
dreamed of genii, and calenders, and enchanted
palaces. In the Peninsula, however, the interest and
the curiosity in things eastern come not alone from
any such false glamour of the fancy as this, which
vanishes (except in a few well-noted cases) in those
who come face to face with eastern life. Here, in
this south-western corner of Europe, we know we
are on the very footsteps of the vanished race who
first, in the night of the Dark Ages, woke all the
dormant arts of culture, who revived the long-dead
sciences ; among whom chivalry was born, humanity
was practised, the 'point of honour' made almost a
point of law, and the intercourse of man with man
softened and refined by fixed ceremonial usage. We
are here in the land through which mainly all this
passed to the rest of Europe, and among the very

people who were the first pupils of the cultured and
generous Saracens, who imbibed something of their
learning, their chivalry, and their civilization, and
overthrew them at last by the practice of some of
the very arts they had learnt from them. It is not
strange, then, that knowing this, strangers coming
to the Peninsula follow out with the deepest interest
the traces which so many hundred years have not
nearly effaced among southern Spaniards and among
Portuguese, and which traces are, in my observation,
far fresher in Portugal than in Spain.

It is interesting enough to observe how this culture and superiority of intellectual training and
accomplishment gave the Arabs (as we have recent
very good reason to know these qualities always
will give their possessors) military as well as social
and political ascendency, and how their lessons were
slowly imparted to the races they encountered; how
through the Saracens of the period of the Crusades,
not only the whole science of the attack and the
defence of strong places was taught to the more backward Europeans, but what was far more important,
the peaked saddle and firm stirrup-hold, the curb
and curb chain, the use of the lance, and the swift
evolutions of the Oriental horsemen became known to
the slow and unwieldy cavalry of the Peninsular kings
and princes. This invaluable knowledge had for
centuries settled the tenure of empire upon the
Saracens, and when it was imparted to the conquered
Goths, it helped mainly to turn the tide in their
favour.

It is not, however, upon these great causes of
the making or the marring of empires that I wish
now to dwell, but upon lessons taught in Saracen
times in the domain of domestic and social life—the
songs, the dances, the legends, the daily usages of the
people.   The Saracens had no doubt themselves much
to learn at first from the Romanized Goths and Semi-
Gothic tribes of the Peninsula; but when the tide of
conquest rolled back those of the Christians who
kept their independence to the fastnesses and back-
woods of the country, culture and civilization went
back too among them, while all the arts of peace advanced among the Saracens in a manner which is still
a marvel to the historian.   Those of the Christians
who remained in the country under Saracen dominion
became semi-Saracenized, and the existence of the
Moçarabes is proof enough how the Christians were
won by the superior culture of the conquering race.
In time came the long and final struggle for existence
between the two faiths and the two races—the
Peninsular Crusade which I have described in a previous chapter.   It was in the course of it that Christian and Infidel came into close contact, and an
incident of it was that the Saracens taught the uncouth Portuguese Cymons 'all the sweet civilities of
life.'

The graver historical student may not care to
consider whether, among other social customs, the
Serenade is a Saracen introduction into Europe.   I am
convinced that it is, and, in spite of its name, I believe

the guitar on which it is accompanied to be a modification of a Saracen instrument.[1] I defy any critic to
prove that any such nightly love-song as the true
Peninsular serenade, so accompanied, was ever
poured forth under the windows of any lady whatever, till the Saracens invaded Europe. The Greeks
knew of nothing of the sort, their domestic institutions were quite opposed to such proceedings ; so
indeed were, and still are, those of the Moslems themselves ; but the Moslems of Spain and Portugal were
never very strict observers of their own institutions.
The ancient Romans knew not of any night-sung
passion-song, nor, to the best of my belief, did any
barbarian nation. Again, the serenade has never
thriven in any land beyond those countries in which
the Arabs first taught it ; in Provence, in troubadour
times, it was a custom ; in Italy, in Spain, and in
Portugal it has never died out.

The serenade in these southern countries of course
has none of that foolish flavour of romance which we,
who frequent the opera and have heard the serenade
in Don Giovanni a dozen times, connect with it. It is
nothing more than a delicate compliment to the

---

[1] The older-fashioned lute is, I suspect, the origin of the guitar,
though the lute, in its latest form, was a more complicated instrument ; and the name guitar is no doubt a Romance word, and
was coined later than the instrument was first used in Europe.
I do not think it can be found mentioned before the *Roman de
la Rose*, and there it is called *guiterne*. If etymology could
quite be trusted, it was the Portuguese who first taught the
name and use of the Arabic lute to the rest of Europe, for they
only of European nations have preserved in *Alaude* its full Arabic
name, *Al ud*. Even in Spanish it is shortened to *laude*.

object of a man's affections, and means no more than
when an Englishman gives his future bride an engaged ring, a Frenchman a box of bonbons or a
bouquet, or than when a German sends his betrothed
a pound of knödels or a Strasburg sausage.

Not but that the serenade is a rare thing even in
Andalusia. The people there are not all young and
impulsive, or incautiously trustful of themselves to
the air of night. Even in Seville itself the guitar
tinkles chiefly to less romantic strains than those of
love.

The guitar is certainly, in our critical northern
eyes, an effeminate instrument, and a man who plays
upon it in an English drawing-room can no more
hope to preserve any appearance of manly dignity
than if he were piping upon a flageolet, or blowing
into that most ludicrous of all instruments, the flute.
That a man should be, as well as look, sentimentally
emotional under the painful circumstances of being
tied by a silk ribbon to such an instrument is,
however, clearly a matter of conventionality. In many
parts of Portugal, men play upon the guitar naturally
and as a matter of course : they strum as we Englishmen whistle. The peasants are universally given to
play upon this instrument, not often, however,
achieving more than a simple accompaniment to the
voice, of chords and arpeggios. In the towns the
artisans are often guitar players, and as they walk to
and from their work in twos and threes, they lighten
the journey with an accompanied chant or song.
My carpenter always brings his guitar with his tools

when he comes on a job. He is a fair performer, but my blacksmith, I think, has the lighter touch of the two on the instrument, and his tones are certainly fuller.

When the Portuguese workman or day-labourer has done his long day's work, he does not lean against a post and smoke a pipe—he does not favour any such 'contemplative man's recreation'—nor does he linger in the wine-shop; but, if it be a holiday or a Sunday, and in a rural district, he puts on a clean shirt, with a large gold or silver stud as a neck-fastening, and his newest hat, varying in shape according to locality, but always of black felt, and of the kind which we see in pictures of Spanish life. He throws over his shoulders a black cloth cloak, with a real gold or silver clasp. He takes his favourite ox-goad in his hand, as tall as himself, straight as an arrow, well rounded and polished, and bound with brass. He slings his guitar round his neck, and makes his way to the nearest fashionable threshing-floor — the peasant's drawing-room. Here are gathered old and young of both sexes, come together for gossip, song, and dance. If it is the time of the *Ceifa*—the reaping of the maize—or the vintage, or, above all, the *Decamisadas*—the husking of the ears of maize—and if corn or wine have yielded well, then are the peasants' hearts glad within them, and song and dance are more than ever joyous.

I cannot say that the dancing is particularly graceful. It is certainly chiefly, though not entirely,

Oriental in character, as dancing is over all the southern Peninsula; that is, it is slow and firm in movement, accentuated in time, and depends almost wholly upon the motions of the body and the arms. It has commonly been asserted that it was the Gipsies (who are far the best dancers in Spain or Portugal) who brought these dances with them from the East; but I am of opinion that this is a mistake, and that this wandering tribe of low-caste Indians, as we must now take them to be proved to be, never have, in spite of their apologists, remembered anything worth the memory, for the four hundred years they have been among us. They have forgotten, in this comparatively short period, their origin, the story of their own wanderings, their customs, their language and their religion. Why should they have remembered only their dances? Besides, I have seen Gipsies dance in England, in France, and in Tyrol: in none of these countries do they dance as they do in the Peninsula. We may conclude that they have everywhere adopted the national dances, and that in Spain and Portugal they dance not Indian but Moorish dances. They dance them better than the natives because, being by nature lazy and effeminate, their bodies are never stiffened by continuous labour, and perhaps also because they possess by race more of the artistic temperament. It is the same with that wonderful instrumental music of the Gipsies of Hungary, the Tsiganes. It is, according to Monsieur de Bertha, beyond all doubt, not of Gipsy, but of pure Hungarian origin. The Gipsies, coming to Portugal

long after the Moors had gone, evidently shaped into
an art what had been till then only a diversion of the
people. They are almost the only professional dancers
in the Peninsula, and all that the world at large
knows of Peninsular dancing, in the theatres of London
and Paris, came at first from the tinkers and beggars,
the bull-fighters and fortune-tellers of Andalusia,
who help, with members of other less respectable
trades, to make up the half-bred Gitano community
—a community composed chiefly of roughs and
idlers, swindlers and thieves.

Oriental dancing and the dancing of northern
peoples are as much opposed as two modes of doing
something of the same sort can well be. One is a
jig, the other a *bolero* ; one only the ebullition of
high spirits, the other, the expression of all the emotion
and poetry in the nature of the dancer. The Celts
and the northern Teutons have taught the world to
shuffle with their feet in time to lively music ; and
the impartial philosopher (if such a being exist)
who sees the Scotsman, the Irishman and the Englishman, the Dutchman, and, above all, the northern
German, dancing their various jigs, reels, and horn-
pipes, must always find it to be the cause of a struggle
for gravity to behold individuals of these nationalities,
rigid in body, grave in expression, and with no
life and movement in them but from the knees downward.

The Portuguese are neither an Oriental people
nor a purely northern, nor a purely southern nation,
but a race blending the character with the blood of

the North and of the South ; a nation educated in
its youth by Moors and Arabs. Their dances partake of their lineage and of their training. They
dance a jig, and are a little absurd—they dance a
bolero and are interesting.

In Portuguese dancing there is nothing cold and
conventional like the modern quadrille, or formal like
the minuet, or at all silly like the polka of the Hun-
garians, or in any way grotesque and offensive like
that which has almost become the national dance of
Frenchmen. The Portuguese are only, as I have
said, a little ridiculous, from our point of view,
when they stand in a circle, and dance something
between a jig and a reel.

Their *bolero* dances are simple, natural, and expressive—expressive of youthfulness and health, and
the exuberance of gaiety which goes with youthfulness and health, and the reaction coming from rest
after labour. That they are not always, or even often,
graceful I admit, for we (miserable fault-seeking
critics that we all are who write or read books) have
come to set up far too high a standard of graceful-
ness of motion, getting it in theatres and where there
are trained dancers, and these poor people are hard-
working peasants, their muscles cramped by labour,
their backs bowed with the carrying of burdens.
Hard field work and good dancing are quite incom-
patible things.

With the dance goes the song. Though there is
a kind of singing in parts of Portugal which has an
undoubted Roman origin,—the melancholy, long-

drawn, often unrhymed chaunting which is to be heard in the fields. and which often takes the form of a rude hexameter,—the singing at feasts and pleasure-gatherings is not generally of this kind.   Each district has songs peculiar to itself, as it has costumes and manners and legends more or less peculiar, so slow and difficult was locomotion till recent times, and so rare the traffic and exchange of ideas in Portugal in its long-enduring condition of roadlessness.   The national songs and airs of Portugal will stand comparison with those of any country, and have so much charm in their originality, their variety and their sweetness, that it is a marvel to me that they are not as well known as those of Spain and Italy.   How much the origin of such songs, and indeed of modern passion-verse generally in its lyric form, is derived from Arab sources, is now an old and, more or less, a settled question.   I need not dwell upon it.   Every good singer at a rural festival will have in his repertory several of such songs as these I have mentioned ; but if he is to become a performer of any local repute, he must be something more than a singer with a good ear and a memory.   He must be an *extempore* song-maker, and it is for this department of song, quite distinct from Italian improvisation, that I claim an undoubted Saracen origin.   The irregular quatrain in use by the Portuguese *improvisatore*, the curious unfamiliar accompaniment, monotonous but not unmelodious, the style of the sentiments, ranging from passionate emotion to a gay and rather downright humour, the frequent reference to natural

objects—so rare in the popular verse of other European
countries, so common in the poetry of Semitic races—
and above all the constant use of figurative speech
and a certain extravagance in imagery,—all this
points most unmistakably to the Oriental origin
of the Portuguese peasant songs.

Here is the lament of a girl-singer whose lover is
a sailor. It might be a translation from Persian or
Arabic. 'Evil be,' she sings, 'to the man who first
invented sea-going in ships, for he is the cause that
my eyes are rivers of tears : '—

> Mal haja quem inventou
> No mar andarem navios,
> Que esse foi o causador
> Dos meus olhos serem rios.

Here, again, is a quaint fancy that might occur to
an Oriental. 'If,' says a lover, 'I had but paper
made of gold I would buy a silver pen, I would polish
my style, and write you a letter : '—

> Se eu tivera papel de ouro
> Comprava penna de prata,
> Apurava os meus sentidos,
> Escrevia te uma carta.

It was the same singer who, apparently from
want of scholarship, gave up letter-writing, and,
extravagantly enough, *makes believe* that his spoken
declaration is really in letter form. The paper, he
tells his mistress, on which he writes is the palm of
his hand, his tears are his only ink, and his pen is
taken from his heart itself :—

O papel em que eu escrevo
Tiro-o da palma da mão,
A tinta sae-me dos olhos,
A penna do coração.

These quatrains and those which follow are not literature in any sense that should be criticized by rule and line. They have simply been taken down from the mouths of the peasant singers who were thinking of nothing less than of being reported. A thousand verses as good as or better than these are sung every summer night in Portugal.

The song is not always complimentary. 'When the cork-tree,' remarks a disdainful young lady, 'shall yield berries, and the bay-tree cork, then I may fall in love with you—if I can take the trouble:'—

Quando o sovreiro der baga
E o loureiro der cortiça,
Então te amarei, meu bem,
Se não me der a preguiça.

I have noticed that among the Portuguese peasant class, women hold a very independent position. They work very hard, they are active and cheerful, very helpful in any trouble, very genial and sympathetic, and yet full of quick answers and mother wit. They know well their value in the economy of life, and without any clamour for impossible rights, take their full share of all that is attainable in that way. Their suitors in love are very humble and persevering, but the women know well what is due to their dignity. Here is the petition of a lover who has too much failed in constancy to be well received. 'Let us,' he asks, ' be friends again as we used to be. People who care for each other always forgive, not one—or two—but three offences : '—

> Façamos, meu bem, as pazes
> Como foi da outra vez,
> Quem quer bem sempre perdoa
> Uma . . . . duas . . . . até tres.

And the girl answers, 'No, I will not be friends with you, as we used to be. Those who truly love commit neither one, nor two—far less three offences : '—

> Não quero fazer as pazes
> Como foi da outra vez,
> Quem quer bem nunca offende
> Nem uma . . . . quando mais tres.

The women assume a certain freedom in Portugal— as, for the matter of that, they often do elsewhere— and it is well for their lovers if they can always believe what is told them for their own good. 'I have,' says one very frank maiden, ' five lovers—three for the morning, two for the afternoon ; to all of these I tell falsehoods, to you alone I speak the truth : '—

> Eu tenho cinco namoros,
> Tres de manhã, **dois** de tarde
> A todos elles eu minto,
> Só a ti fallo **a** verdade.

An obviously plain girl recommends herself ingeniously : ' From the clefts on the mountain side grow out wild herbs and flowers. Hold fast to the herb as you climb up—it is strong ; leave the flower—it will break away : '—

Entre pedras e pedrinhas
Nascem raminhos de salsa :
Pega-te a feia que é firme,
Deixa a bonita que é falsa.

If it were not for the charges of inconstancy so frequently brought by the poets, love-songs would make duller reading even than they do. The peasant poets of Portugal have evidently as good reason as any others to inveigh against their mistresses' fickleness. In the following quatrain the disappointed lover attains in his bitterness almost to real epigram. Like most epigrams it is untranslatable :—

Os teus olhos, ó menina,
São gentios da Guiné,
Da Guiné por serem pretos,
Gentios por não terem fé.

The last example I will give has bitterness in it of a graver sort, and wit too of still higher alloy. 'For love of thee,' says the singer, 'I have lost Heaven ; for love of thee I have lost myself—now I find myself left alone without God, without love, without thee : '—

Por te amar perdi a Deus,
Por teu amor me perdi.
Agora vejo me só
Sem Deus, sem amor, sem ti.

It is in the centre and north of the country that I have chiefly heard this *extempore* singing and seen peasants dancing and singing at their *desgarradas á viola*—their village balls and concerts. It is not easy to give the reader an idea of the delight which these gatherings afford the people, of their gaiety, their quickness, and their ready appreciation of a jest, a local allusion, or the neat turning of a phrase.

The tinkle of the guitar in the night air, the *pizzicato* of the violin, have a marvellous attraction for them, as I have often seen, and these simple pleasures seem to be quite enough to redeem the monotony of their long laborious days. They ask nothing better of life than such distraction, and, in truth, rather shame a looker-on who may, perhaps, foolishly ambition some hardly attainable object, valueless or bitter when he reaches it. For the thorough-going Hedonist, who, with Mr. Pater, counts the thrills of pleasurable sensation in life as that which chiefly tells on the right side of man's account, the lines of a Portuguese peasant might seem to be cast upon not unpleasant times or places. He has, indeed, to work hard in a climate which is not altogether a perfect one. Hot suns and cold winds too often come together. The narrow strip of land which lies between the Spanish mountains and the Atlantic, and constitutes Portugal, is subject to fogs, and to rain which is almost tropical. It is an Atlantic climate, and our English winter sojourners in the South know little except of Mediterranean ones. There is a difference, and it is not altogether in favour of the climates of the Mediterranean shores. If the day climate of Algiers, Naples, or Messina, is better than that of Portugal, the evening, about sunset time, and the early morning, and above all, the air of night in this country, have a clearness and pleasantness which are not to be found elsewhere in Europe, and which are, no doubt, due to the modifying influence of the great ocean. The night air of summer is especially delightful—warm, soft, and genial. However hot and sultry the day may have been, amends are made at night. Once I was riding with a peasant guide, on a fearfully hot day, through the plain country of Estremadura. The afternoon sun glared into our faces as we rode westward, and the heat was as if a furnace door was being kept open above our heads. 'When night falls,' said my guide, breaking a long silence, 'I shall lie out in the fields to feel the air cool upon me and the dew.' The very prospect seemed to bring refreshment to him. He did as he said he would, and as do many Portuguese in the hot summer time, and the practice speaks well of the wholesomeness of the nights. So then, to sum up the good and bad in the Portuguese field labourer's lot—if he has a hot summer to toil through, he has no great severity of winter weather to endure ; if his summer day bring more than a common heat and burden, in the pleasant night he finds a constant respite and solace. Then again, there is abiding peace in the land. Hardly can the grandfathers in the hamlet remember the story of the time when men were pressed for civil war, and fields were ravaged, and rumours of war did, as they always do, more evil than even war itself; and it would take men of a generation further back still to tell the story of anything approaching the horrors of real warfare. 'Turtle-footed peace !' 'Peace with her wheaten crown !' and so forth. When one has had the horrors of war brought, as we all have had lately, so vividly before us, one is almost tempted to quote these old phrases of the poets, and to approve

their enthusiasm for Peace and Plenty. 'Ceres and
her sheaves!' 'Bacchus and his attendant train!' it
sounds stale and common-place, but one begins at
last to see the sense there was in what seemed the
sham classicalism of our schoolboy verses.   Anyhow,
Peace and her blessings are here for the benefit of
the Portuguese land-worker.   There is emigration to
Brazil too for him if population presses : wages also
are rising : so that altogether he is well off politically
and socially.   But what the Hedonist would count
his chief good fortune is that he is blessed with a
cheerfulness and a power of enjoying simple things,
which no philosophy that was ever invented can
bestow.

The celebrated and benevolent John Howard, the
prime mover in the reform of our then abominable
English prison system, and whose successors have,
in the opinion of some thoughtful persons, sometimes
carried the humane influence of the first reformer
into humanitarian excesses good neither for criminals
nor for honest men, clearly knew nothing of the
prisons and the prison system of Portugal.[1]   It is
not a good system at all points, or perhaps at many
points, but it has this of singular and of interesting

[1] It is curious that Howard left England on his first journey
to the Continent with the intention of visiting Portugal, a country
which he was fated not to see till quite late in life, for he was
captured on his way to Lisbon by a French privateer   He did
not see Portugal and its gaols till long after he had visited those
of nearly every European country, had made his published reports,
and had helped to bring about the great reforms of our English
prison system and discipline.

in it, that such as it is now it has been, with not many changes, for hundreds of years. The great charitable establishments of Portugal, which have taken the place of the lazar-houses of the Middle Ages,— models, like those of Spain, of good and liberal management, are more or less recent in their origin, and are either the work of priests, or of those strongly under priestly influence. The greatest of them, the Misericordia Hospital, which has branches throughout the kingdom, was founded in about 1510 by the pious King Emmanuel. With the prisons, however, the priests have never much meddled, beyond carrying the consolations of religion to the sick and dying. Such as the prison is to this day in Morocco or Tunis, such it is in Portugal, with only such differences as might be expected in the application of a system and principles between a retrograde and Moslem people, and a Christian, a humane and highly civilized one. As it was when Howard lived, so it is now with little change, and had he crossed the Pyrenees during his Continental travels, he would have found, I think, much food for reflection, and, not improbably, something to modify his own opinions.

There is something to be said against the prison system established in Portugal, but there is certainly a good deal to be said in its favour. I do not pretend to decide either way, but I could heartily wish that some of the more hardened of our habitual rogues in Great Britain could be committed to a Portuguese gaol for at least some portion of their terms. It would warm the loyalty of the influential class who spend a portion of their lives in gaol to learn, by the contrast that would be forced upon them, how well their comforts are looked after at home. The Portuguese are as humane, if not as humanitarian, a people as we are—more so even, for they have combined humanity with logic in abolishing capital punishment, holding it to be against their consciences to let an irrevocable punishment follow the sentence of a fallible tribunal. They substitute transportation to the coast of Africa for hanging, though, if he had his choice, it may be doubted if any rational murderer would not rather elect to be hanged at once than to be so banished. The Portuguese, like us, are wishful that the lot of victims of the criminal law should not be too hard a one, but they do not set about attaining their end as we do. They do not warm, and feed up, and carefully clothe, and separate, and classify as we do. There is, nevertheless, more of thought for many urgent wants of poor human nature in the Portuguese gaol management than in ours—more kindness and less comfort, more freedom and less system; and yet the kindness is, perhaps, a mistaken kindness too. The rogue and thief in every country has always something of the beggar about him, and in Portugal, even in prison, his liberty is not so abridged but that he still has liberty to beg: dangling his line and basket into the stream of the outer world, and fishing up bread and meat and copper coins from his dungeon windows.

There is often not a pane of glass in all a Portu-

guese prison, and every iron-grated window has its
four or five haggard faces pressed close to the crossed
bars—pale prison flowers turning to the light of day
and freedom. A wholesome example to evil-doers,
no doubt think those who manage these things; but
as all the main business of the convicts' lives can be
carried on through their grated windows, as they can
and do wrangle with their wives, court their sweet-
hearts, borrow of their friends, libel their enemies,
and beg of everyone—living in careless idleness, and
making life one long game of ' prison bars '—it may
be doubted whether the publicity is not rather a
familiarizer and diminisher than otherwise of the
terrors of imprisonment. To the convict anyhow the
weariness of confinement is lessened, and his lot can
certainly not appear a very hard one when he is
visibly idle and not the poorer, made a public show
and yet not disgraced. The feeling of the outer
world is with him rather than not. With them he is
not for very long the rascal who robbed their orchard
or their hen-roost, or the villain who murdered their
grandmother, but the simpleton who was guileless
enough to get caught. *Coitadinho!* a poor devil!
who will come out of the gates a sadder and a wiser
man, and be in future a more cautious criminal.

In consequence of all this, the criminal is not so
much held aloof from by the virtuous members of
society as the keen moralist might desire, of which a
striking proof came under my own observation ; for
happening once to find myself in the chief square of
a remote country town in company with a Portuguese

acquaintance of some social standing, we passed by
the gaol, at one of the ground-floor windows of which
was visible one particularly villanous countenance.

My companion advanced smilingly to the window,
gave a small coin to the owner of the scowling face,
inquired kindly after his health and that of his family,
and after a few more friendly and genial commonplaces, shook hands with the convict and rejoined
me.

'Pray, who is your friend?' I asked, as we walked
on, not without a certain amount of irony, provoked
by some lingering British prejudice in favour of a
sterner prison discipline.

'Oh! poor fellow,' said my acquaintance, ' he is a
man well known in these parts—a popular character ;
has a good deal of influence.'

'Wrongly imprisoned, no doubt,' I suggested ;
' or perhaps debt or some such trifle?'

'Well, no—in fact, he shot a man; some dispute
about land—a sudden thing—a quarrel—strong
words and hot blood : it was either his uncle or his
brother.'

'And is this all he gets for murdering his blood
relation?'

' Not at all—the murder was never quite brought
home to him. He is not here for that, but for steal-
ing ducks—a cat—a sheep ; I really don't remember
what. Perhaps he is innocent of any of these
animals—one can never tell ; but, knowing what one
does about the man, one really can't altogether pity
him.'

' One certainly cannot,' I answered.

If I recollect rightly, my friend was at about this time intending to do the Portuguese equivalent of ' standing for the county,' and some experiences of my own as to the condescension of English candidates towards English ruffians quite as great as this beetle-browed and hot-blooded person did something to assuage my insular prejudices.

If it was not for the fresh air they get, and the unceasing charity of the outer world, the lot of the inmates of Portuguese gaols would be exceedingly disagreeable, for the management is thrifty in the extreme as regards bed and board, and fire and lighting. So that British sailors of the occasionally disorderly and criminal class coming to Portuguese ports with their pleasant memories of the comforts and luxury, and even dignity, of prison life in England, who have incautiously found their way into Portuguese gaols, have been really quite glad to get out again.

CHAPTER XI.

CONCLUSION.

It is beginning to weigh a little on my conscience
that I may have caused some offence to the excellent
people who are the subject of the foregoing chapters.
Once before, I made free in print with what seemed
to me to be certain shortcomings in the Portuguese,
and I was taken to task pretty severely for doing
so. I had said that modern Portuguese poetry was,
in comparison with the nation's own great achievements in that line of past days, a dead thing. I might
have said as much of certain national literatures
nearer home, with as much truth and far less danger.

When my observations came under the Portuguese reviewer's lash, he was scornfully indignant :—
'What!' was the tenor of his remark, 'is this malig-
nant foreigner not aware that the great poet Costa,
the immortal Silva, Pinto,—that ornament of his
country '—(here followed a list of some score more of
contemporary immortals), 'still draw the breath of
life in Portugal?'

We English have ourselves so outgrown this sort
of sensitiveness, and mind so little what foreigners
say of us, that this bitterness and indignation came to

me with a certain freshness in it. A Portuguese writer who had stated his opinion that Milton and Shakespeare had no living representatives in modern England might perhaps feel as I did if an English weekly review answered his imputation by giving a list of the minor poets whom it massacres weekly, and a *catalogue raisonné* of the immortal Smiths, Browns and Jenkinsons of modern English song.

People who are thin-skinned about censure are not, unfortunately, correspondingly mollified by approbation, and hear the hint of a fault with an indignation that is none the less strong that such a hint is accompanied by a hundred compliments. Else I should be at my ease. If I have blamed, I have praised much oftener; but there is no pleading a *set off* in this kind of suit. It arrests all flow of soul in a writer to have to think of these things while he is writing, and, for my part, I do habitually not think of them. It never struck me till just now what a scrape I had probably got into; and now it is too late and no use to do anything but try and get out of it with the best grace possible.

If I have offended my Portuguese friends by plain speaking, I must make my justification for it in certain heterodox and unscientific opinions which I hold upon the races of mankind—a confession of which opinions nothing but the present emergency should draw from me. The reader shall perceive at once how it is my ethnology that shall excuse my plain speaking.

There are a certain number of plain men, of whom I am one, who refuse to entangle our under-

standings with prevailing dogmas on ethnology, and
are so little in the fashion that we commit ourselves
thoroughly to none of the many conflicting theories
on this subject to which the last twenty years have
given birth. I know enough of such theories to
know that not two of them fit into each other, and
that the advocates of each theory wrangle more and
more as they get further back into antiquity. Scepticism which would come very badly from an
ethnologist of any of the advanced schools is no
offence at all from me, who am an ethnologist (if I
deserve so learned a name) of no school at all.

I have listened to a great deal of profound and
complicated talk of Aryans and Caucasians and
Indo-Europeans, and of course as an unprejudiced
person I see that 'there is a good deal in it;' but to
be frank, an ethnology which teaches me that I am
first cousin to the 'mild Hindoo' finds me but a cold
believer. Better at once embrace the whole human
race and be that impossible being—a citizen of the
world. For my own part I am altogether wanting in
the tolerance necessary for this breadth of view, and
my sympathies have not latitude enough to make me
feel quite like a man and a brother towards Negroes,
and shock-headed Papuans, and skew-eyed Chinamen.
It is very narrow and uncharitable, but I hereby dis-
own all my poor and distant relations, and I utterly
disbelieve in the title of many who claim my cousin-
ship. I am an anthropological nonconformist, and am
not going to pin my faith to any new-fangled genea-
logical tree found for me, as heralds find coats of

arms for *parvenus*, by the last fashionable number of a learned Society.

Until things are made a good deal clearer to me, I refuse to trace my lineage direct to the Caucasus or the Himalayas. All that I can be quite sure of at present is, that I am a European: that is the world of which I constitute myself a citizen, and Europe is bounded for me by the nearest frontiers of Russia and of Turkey, for I will admit neither Turks nor Russians into my family party.

With these limitations, I find a sufficient family likeness to myself wherever I go in Europe, and Greeks and Italians, Dutchmen, Germans and Frenchmen, Spaniards and Portuguese, are all my friends and my kinsmen. Their ideas are my ideas, their logic is mine, I sympathize with their weaknesses, for I share them, and as often as not I agree in their prejudices. In what family do the members hesitate to point out a relation's foibles? Why should I then be shy of telling home truths to the Portuguese? I am of the family party myself, and have a family right to speak out my mind. If we were perfectly wise at home, it might be a point of generosity to hold one's tongue, but I know of no such cause for silence. I confess that I like the Portuguese all the better every time I discover the reflection among them of some fine old British prejudice, and my heart warms to them when I find that there are,—numbers for numbers,—almost as many fools in Portugal as in Great Britain. Every discovery like this is a new evidence of consanguinity.

Here then is my apology and sufficient excuse. Of course there is another side of the question for those who hold these old-fashioned views of the families of nations, and so far as Portugal is concerned it is, to speak quite seriously, a very pleasant side, and no Englishman can observe without a strong sympathy many qualities and aspirations in the Portuguese akin to his own; their loyalty to their king and their ancient liberties; the constant ardour of independence that has marked every page of their history; and their faith in good hard blows for the maintenance of their national existence against all comers. These things are recognized as desirable even if they are not always attained, wherever men of true European blood reside; and for my part, I am proud of, and claim kinship with, the nation where I find them :—

Ταύτης τοι γενεῆς τε καὶ αἵματος εὔχομαι εἶναι.

THE END.

LONDON : PRINTED BY
SPOTTISWOODE AND CO., NEW-STREET SQUARE
AND PARLIAMENT STREET